The Vanilla Killer

ALSO BY PETER BOLAND

THE CHARITY SHOP DETECTIVE
AGENCY MYSTERIES
Book 1: The Charity Shop Detective Agency
Book 2: The Beach Hut Murders
Book 3: Death At The Dog Show
Book 4: The Vanilla Killer

The Vanilla KILLER

PETER BOLAND

The Charity Shop Detective Agency Mysteries
Book 4

Joffe Books, London
www.joffebooks.com

First published in Great Britain in 2024

Cover art by Nick Castle

ISBN: 978-1-83526-912-1

PROLOGUE

Shifting a dead body is always so easy in movies. I've seen it a million times. Just grab it by the ankles and slide it out of sight, into a handy storeroom, behind a bush or rolled into a pre-dug hole. Easy. Let me tell you, that's all rubbish. Bodies are the most unwieldy things ever. It's like moving one of those blocks they used to build Stonehenge, except with arms and legs. I'm not even moving this particular body that far. From one side of an ice-cream van to the other. Doesn't help that the place is as cramped as . . . I don't know what. Even though Kevin here (he's the dead body I'm attempting to budge) is a slight little fellow — you know, one of those wiry types — he's so awkward to move. I'm sure I'm going to throw my back out. That's another thing that never happens in the movies. You never hear anyone say, "Yeah, I've got rid of the body, but I've slipped a disc and need to lie down for a bit." It doesn't help that he keeps flopping all over the place like a ragdoll filled with wet concrete. I know what you're thinking. What about rigor mortis? Well, clever clogs, I've got at least another hour or two before that kicks in.

I check his pulse to make sure he's well and truly departed. I've done this twice already — I really don't want him waking up later and pointing fingers just because I've been sloppy. I search for the thrum of blood in his wrist. Not a sausage. Soon he'll be as cold as the ice cream he sells — or sold, I should say.

1

Now for the hard part. Got to get him out of sight, which means hoisting him off the floor and stashing him inside the chest freezer at the back. Easier said than done. The top is high, much higher than a normal countertop, probably to maximise storage space. Flipping open the double lids, I receive a stale, sickly tang up both nostrils from some random frozen spillages of syrupy goo. It distracts me momentarily, but I discover that the gods are smiling on me (presumably Norse gods, as it's a freezer). The space is huge and, more importantly, empty — well, apart from a few boxes of lollies here and there. Easily big enough to accommodate Kevin's little frame. Just got to figure out a way of getting him up and over that high edge, then hopefully gravity will take care of the rest.

Professional high jumpers pop into my head and that odd technique they have of turning their backs to the bar. It's named after someone or other, the guy who invented it. What's his name? He died recently. Doesn't matter. Thing is, their head and shoulders go over first, then everything else seems to magically follow behind. So that's what Kevin's going to do. With my help, of course.

I grab him under the armpits and pull him into a sitting position, his back against the side of the freezer. No mean feat in itself. I take a breather, then ready myself for the hardest part. Using the same method as before, I hoist him up so he's sort of hugging my chest. It's hard to get any leverage, there's so little room in here, but I manage it. Then I push him backwards. His body jackknifes, arching at the waist. His head and shoulders clear the edge of the freezer, sending his hips thrusting upwards, as if he's executing the most awkward slow-motion leap possible, but in he goes, the momentum of his top half pulling the bottom half in. Only his feet and ankles stick out now, so I give them a quick shove and help them on their way. Within a second or two, his whole body has disappeared inside.

Then it hits me. I remember what that high jump technique is called. It's the Fosbury flop. I chuckle to myself. It sounds just like an ice lolly.

CHAPTER 1

Two months later

"I am partial to this Goldilocks weather." Partial Sue stood in the shop's open doorway, eyes closed, chin raised, her svelte body luxuriating in the warmth of the afternoon sun.

"Goldilocks weather?" Fiona was attempting to sort through a jumble of shoes, reuniting lefts and rights so they could be sold in the shop. Not all of them had partners, leading Fiona to wonder if, at that precise moment, someone else was sitting in another charity shop, performing the exact same task with a similar box containing the odd shoes she was missing. "Let me guess — not too hot, not too cold."

"But just right." Daisy sprayed too much Pledge on the countertop. "Oh, I do like that description."

"I thought you would." Partial Sue's eyes stayed closed as she bathed in the rich sunlight.

"That nice science man on the TV is always talking about Goldilocks," said Daisy.

"Who, Brian Cox?" Partial Sue asked.

Fiona stopped what she was doing. "Didn't Brian Cox play Hannibal Lecter?"

3

"You're thinking of the other Brian Cox," Partial Sue answered without shifting her position. "The Scottish actor, and it was Anthony Hopkins who played Hannibal Lecter."

"Yes, I know," Fiona replied. "But not a lot of people know that Brian Cox, the actor, not the scientist, played an earlier version of Hannibal back in the eighties."

Daisy put down her spray and googled it. "The film was called *Manhunter*. Mmm, I don't like the sound of that." Her tastes were more genteel than her two colleagues, who had an insatiable appetite for grim crime drama.

"That's the one," Fiona said.

"Really?" Partial Sue opened one eye in her direction. "You know, I never knew that. I shall have to watch it now."

Fiona smiled. "But coming back to Brian Cox, the scientist, not the actor. Why was he talking about Goldilocks?"

Daisy resumed her spray-polish assault on the countertop. "I heard him on a podcast. Apparently, our planet is in a thing called the Goldilocks Zone. Just the right temperature so we can have garden fetes and picnics. But if it was any hotter, we'd all burn to a crisp. A little colder and it would be like living in a freezer."

"That's a cheery thought," Fiona remarked.

"David Attenborough," Partial Sue said.

"Was David Attenborough on the podcast?" Fiona asked.

"I don't think so," Daisy said.

"No. You said living in a freezer. David Attenborough did that TV show, *Life in the Freezer*."

This was standard banter for the ladies of the Dogs Need Nice Homes charity shop. Conversations would start at Point A, wildly meander like a drunk on a child's bicycle, and arrive at a distant and unexpected Point B, stopping briefly at tenuous cultural references along the way. But Partial Sue was right about the Goldilocks' analogy. For once, summer had decided to behave itself, landing squarely on the solstice. Nothing but seamless skies of cornflower blue since the twenty-first of June, the sun shining like a freshly minted

4

gold coin. However, its potent heat had been tempered by an agreeable easterly wind gently caressing the south coast, making life and the temperature very pleasant indeed, especially at night, as none of them had been forced to switch to a thin duvet yet.

"I think I shall purchase a portion of fish and chips from that really good chippie in Tuckton," Partial Sue muttered.

"The Fryer Tuckton?" Daisy questioned.

Daisy and Fiona exchanged worried glances, wondering if Partial Sue was feeling okay. Had all that sun got to her? Normally, she would sniff and snort at the idea of buying any sort of takeaway food, not when she could 'make it for half the price at home'.

"Gonna drown them in salt and vinegar, take them up the top of Hengistbury Head, and munch away while I enjoy the view. Who's with me? I'm paying. My treat."

Fiona nearly dropped the shoe in her hand, while a spontaneous, unbidden squirt from Daisy's can of Pledge fired into thin air. Whatever was the matter with her? Partial Sue never offered to pay for anything. Maybe all that vitamin D soaking into her skin had put her in a positive and generous mood. Would wonders never cease?

Partial Sue quickly clarified her offer. "They do an early-bird deal. I'd never pay full price, and I've got a buy-one-get-one-free leaflet, so I can only pay for one of you."

Fiona relaxed. Nothing was wrong with their friend. "Count me in, and I don't mind paying for my own. Simon Le Bon would love a walk up to the headland with the promise of a few stray chips."

At the sound of a walk in the offing, Simon Le Bon, her dishevelled terrier (so-called because his hair reminded her of the eighties New Romantic) tumbled out of his bed and did a happy dance around Fiona's feet with that unrestrained excitement only dogs possess.

Partial Sue had had enough sunshine and came inside the shop. "What about you, Daisy? Fish and chips on me, up on the headland?" Technically, they weren't on her but on the chip shop, but the thought was there.

"I'd love that," Daisy replied. "But I'm cooking for me and Bella tonight."

Ever since her daughter had returned home after leaving Mark — her arse of a husband — Daisy had been the happiest person in Southbourne. Every day she'd come into work with an indelible smile on her face and cheerful tales on her lips of a mother and daughter reunited. She'd tell them about their non-stop talks into the early hours, until their throats grew hoarse. They had a lot of catching up to do when you considered the pair had not uttered a word to each other for quite some time.

They'd fallen out when Daisy, who normally minded her own business, had felt compelled to warn Bella about her impending marriage. She didn't want her daughter to marry Mark, the main reason being that he reminded her of Bella's father — also a complete arse. Truth be told, she didn't want Bella to make the same mistakes as she had. Didn't want her to endure years of unhappy marriage only for it to end in a messy divorce. She'd tried to warn her. But Bella hadn't listened, and had resented her mum's unwelcome interference, resulting in her treading the same miserable, thorn-ridden path.

Eventually, Daisy was proved right. Not that she cared about that. Like most parents she just wanted her daughter to be happy. After Bella had split from Mark, she'd returned home amid tears and apologies on both sides. But that soon passed, replaced by the sheer joy of mother and daughter reconciled. Daisy had wished for nothing else in the world and it had come true. Bella had now been blissfully living under Daisy's roof for over a year, but more recently Fiona had detected a few frayed edges.

"How's it going?" Partial Sue asked.

"Oh, fine." Daisy was never one to burden anyone with her worries.

"How's it really going?" Partial Sue asked.

6

Daisy stopped her polishing, and Daisy never ceased cleaning for anything, except maybe to swap her spent tin of Pledge with a fresh one, quicker than John Wick reloading a handgun. "Well, you know I love Bella to bits, and having her back home has been a dream come true. We do everything together, like we did when she was young, going around the shops — I've spoiled her rotten by the way — cooking and baking together, watching the soaps, going to the pictures, being silly and making each other laugh — we can both be daft as brushes. Honestly, it's been heaven. I feel like I've been given a second chance at motherhood and she's having a second childhood, apart from me being in my sixties and she's nearly thirty. But you know what I mean. I'm doing it properly this time."

Partial Sue smiled sympathetically. "Daisy, you did it properly the first time."

"That's nice of you to say. I guess what I'm really doing is making up for all that time we were apart, when we weren't speaking to each other. I'm not going to squander my second chance. Going to make the most of every second."

"Sounds like you already are, so what's the problem?" Fiona asked.

Tears gathered in the corners of Daisy's eyes. She blotted them with the heel of her hand to stop them from escaping. "It's wearing a bit thin." She immediately shook her head, as if disagreeing with herself. "I shouldn't be saying these things about my own daughter."

Fiona and Partial Sue joined her at the counter, throwing their arms around their gentle friend, attempting to comfort her as the tears fell.

When they'd subsided, Daisy continued, her voice small and fragile. "It was fabulous at first, as I said. But now she mopes around the house, always on her phone or watching Netflix. She never wants to go anywhere unless I drag her out. Even when the weather's like this. I just wish she'd do something. Anything."

"Thing is, she's getting over a divorce," Fiona said. "Quite a painful one. That's got to be hard. Probably why she's so down in the mouth."

"And she's not a little girl anymore," Partial Sue added. "She's a grown adult with a mind of her own. Does whatever she wants or doesn't, judging by what you just said."

Daisy gave a brief smile. "Well, at least she promised to go out and look for a job today. Not that she needs the money — her divorce settlement came through — and I've said she can stay under my roof rent free for as long as she wants. But I thought she could do with having a reason to get up in the morning."

"That sounds like a good idea," Fiona said. "What sort of work is she looking for?"

Daisy sighed. "That's the other thing worrying me. Bella's a bit like me. Head in the clouds. She wants to do something creative. Which is fine. I want her to pursue her dreams, but there's not much call for it round here. I feel she's setting herself up for disappointment. Going to come home empty-handed."

"Don't worry, Dais," Partial Sue reassured her. "I'm sure everything will turn out fine. She might surprise you yet."

In the distance, the tinny chimes of 'Greensleeves' drifted through the open door. Not the best recording in the world, it sounded like a copy of a copy of a copy — delightfully distorted, but growing louder with every second. Partial Sue jittered excitedly. "That sounds like an ice-cream van heading this way. I am partial to a ninety-nine and a bit of 'Greensleeves'."

Fiona also adored the spontaneous appearance of an ice-cream van. Nothing said summer like soft ice cream and the strained chords of Henry VIII's romantic ditty, although it was highly unlikely that the portly wife-murdering monarch had penned the pretty medieval love song. However, one thing was sure. No one from Tudor times, not even Henry himself, could have predicted that centuries later, 'Greensleeves' would herald the approach of frozen desserts.

"I think we could all do with something sweet and cold," Fiona suggested.

"Oh, that would be lovely," Daisy replied. "Let's hope it stops nearby."

Partial Sue led the way. "Maybe we could flag it down."

The three ladies trooped outside, just as the ice-cream van halted beside them, its tyres scuffing against the kerb. It was a bright-red transit covered in garish, clashing graphics, advertising all manner of lollies and ice creams along its flank.

"That's handy," said Partial Sue.

There was a reason the van had chosen the charity shop to pitch up, 'Greensleeves' still blaring. Leaning out of the driver's window was the unmistakable shape of Daisy's daughter. Just like her mother, Bella had a sweet-natured round face surrounded by bubbling brown curls, although they hadn't turned grey like Daisy's, which were about to become a lot greyer.

"Hey, Mum!" Bella called out. "Guess what? I've bought an ice-cream van!"

CHAPTER 2

A bundle of smiles and hair, Bella sprang from the van's cab, fizzing with energy while 'Greensleeves' continued clanging away into the warm air. In her T-shirt and baggy denim dungarees, she looked young for her age, resembling one of those overenthusiastic children's TV presenters. "Isn't she a beauty? What do you think, Mum?"

Fiona strained to hear Daisy's response over the chimes.

Bella reached in through the open window and shut the music off. "I said, she's a beauty, isn't she? What do you think, Mum?"

Daisy hid her disappointment. "Oh, well, yes, it's lovely. Bit of a surprise. I thought you were going to get a job."

"This is my job. I sell ice creams now."

Her mother surveyed the side of the vehicle from a safe distance through a pair of worried eyes. "Who did you buy it from?"

"Not who, Mum, where. I was going door to door, asking in shops if they needed any help. I got a bit lost round the back of Boscombe when I came across this big warehouse with a load of cars and people crowding around them. I thought it was some sort of daytime rave, but it was a car auction. I'd never been to one before. These cars started rolling by and people were bidding on them and a chap was talking too fast into a microphone. Then this ice-cream van goes past, and no one bid on it, so I got it for five grand! Only five grand! Can you believe it? Got myself a bargain!"

Fiona examined the side of the vehicle but stopped short of kicking the tyres. Dented and scratched, repaired here and there with dollops of filler, from what she could see, the van had seen plenty of action. A little shabby but still serviceable.

"Has it got an MOT?" Partial Sue asked.

Fiona knew where she was going with this. Ever money-conscious, Partial Sue was interrogating the finer details of Bella's purchase to make sure she hadn't bought a lemon — or, more appropriately, a lemon sorbet.

"Oh, yes. I'm not that daft, Auntie Sue. I wouldn't buy anything without an MOT." Bella smiled proudly at her purchasing prowess.

"And what's the mileage?" Partial Sue asked.

Bella's expression dropped. She gazed down at the pavement and mumbled something incomprehensible.

"Pardon?"

Bella mumbled again.

Daisy stepped forward. "How many miles has it done?"

"Two eighty-five," Bella said in a small voice.

"Thousand?" Daisy asked.

Bella nodded.

Daisy groaned.

"Mum, it's fine. That's probably why it was so cheap."

"Yes, I know, sweetheart, but that means bits of it will start falling off soon."

Bella put an arm around her mum and pulled her tight. "Mum, you worry too much."

Bella was right about that. At this moment, Fiona could imagine that Daisy's insides were a knotted mess of anxiety and confusion, writhing in a bag of disappointment.

Fiona decided to distract her from the van's biblical mileage. "What about equipment? Has it got a freezer and everything?"

"Oh yes, Auntie Fiona." Although she had only met Daisy's daughter a year ago, Fiona was touched that Bella affectionately referred to her as 'Auntie', as if she'd known her since she was a little girl. Bella had an endearing innocence, and she could see why Daisy worried about her. Sweetness and naivety could easily be perceived as gullibility, which was probably why her mother was afraid that someone had sold her a dilapidated old ice-cream van only fit for the scrap heap.

Bella broke away from her mum's side and stood by the van's large window, which was smothered in a bright, enticing menu of lollies and ice-cream flavours from a company called Somerford Ice Creams. She slid it open, leaned in and pointed out its various features. "It's got a fridge for drinks, a slushy machine and a great big freezer at the back and, best of all, a Carpigiani machine."

"Carpigiani machine?" Fiona asked.

"Yes, come and have a look."

They leaned through the open window while Bella gestured to a large stainless-steel box mounted on the far countertop, which had a big lever and a nozzle below like a beer pump.

"It's what makes the soft ice cream for the ninety-nines."

"Oh, I didn't realise they were called Carpigiani machines," Fiona said.

Bella smiled. "Neither did I, until today."

"Does it work?" Partial Sue asked.

Bella's mouth formed into an O. "Well, er, I didn't ask."

Daisy shook her head. "Oh, Bella, you should always check before you buy."

Bella's face reddened. "I'm sure it'll be fine."

"You're too trusting, Bella."

Though Daisy was right, the same could also be said about Daisy herself. Mother and daughter were too nice for their own good.

Fiona could see Bella's joyful enthusiasm dwindling at her mother's disapproval. Time to inject some positivity. "I'm sure it works just fine and, if it doesn't, Gail over the road at The Cats Alliance is a dab hand at fixing everything."

"That's right, and she does it for free." In Partial Sue's world, that was the best benefit. "She fixed my digital box just in time so I could watch the season finale of *Who Do You Think You Are?* If she can do that, I'm sure she can fix a . . . what's it called again?"

"Carpigiani machine," Bella replied quietly.

"You'll be selling ninety-nines in no time," Fiona said.

Bella's mouth curled back into a smile.

Ears burning, the Wicker Man appeared from the shop next door. "Did someone mention ninety-nines?"

Bella's mood brightened. "Hi, Uncle Trevor. Look what I bought."

Also known as Trevor, the Wicker Man sold — surprise, surprise — old-school wicker furniture. He didn't sell that much, to be fair, leading the ladies to have more than a sneaking suspicion that his shop was a front for something nefarious that they had yet to uncover. He did, however, have more than a passing penchant for speaking like an overacting amateur performing Shakespeare. "Is this fine contraption yours? How delightful. What say you rustle me up a swift soft serve?"

"I'd love to," Bella replied, "but I've only just bought it. I don't have any stock. That was the next thing on my to-do list."

"We have to make sure the thingamajig works first." Daisy bit her lip.

Bella ignored her mum.

"Well, have at it, Bella," the Wicker Man enthused. "Selling frozen confections is a most noble art if ever there was one. Spreading sweet joy to the neighbourhood. I have a feeling you shall become the cream of Southbourne." He winked.

Everyone nodded in agreement at his dairy pun, although Daisy's nod was performed with a clenched jaw.

Fiona could understand Daisy's reservations. Selling ice creams wasn't necessarily what you'd wish for your daughter.

It was unconventional, not like working in an office or a shop, but then Bella wasn't conventional. Bordering on Bohemian, being tied down wouldn't suit her free spirit — something that had been on the wane recently, according to Daisy. The poor girl had become downhearted and housebound after her divorce, robbing her of her get-up-and-go. Anything that rekindled that sense of adventure and got her out in the world had to be a good thing. Hopefully, given time, Daisy would see it this way and be happy that her daughter was having another stab at life — or, rather, a scoop. Okay, it wasn't the life her mother had imagined, but it was better than the one she had now, glued to her phone or bingeing boxsets. The more Fiona thought about it, the more this suited Bella — roaming the area peddling ice creams — as long as the sun stayed out and cloudy skies didn't put the kibosh on her fledgling business.

Speaking of overcast skies, Fiona shuddered as though a shadow had passed over her soul. She was suddenly aware of an evil presence. A malignant spirit hovering nearby. She turned to see a sinister silhouette turning the air frigid.

Sophie Haverford, manager of The Cats Alliance across the road, was standing with folded arms and a grin of whitened teeth you could see from space. "Well, isn't this a nice little gathering?" She swished forward supernaturally, almost as if her feet weren't touching the ground.

"Greetings, Sophie." The Wicker Man always deferred to Sophie's status as the unelected Queen of Southbourne. He was the only one of them who did.

Fiona summoned a sprig of conviviality from somewhere. "Hello, Sophie."

Sophie inspected the van, pacing along its length. "Well, well, well. What do we have here?" Dressed in a wide-brimmed trilby hat and matching white oversized linen trouser suit, she resembled the love child of a cricket commentator and a 1920s mafia boss.

"It's an ice-cream van," Bella replied. "My ice-cream van."

14

Sophie smirked. "Oh, this belongs to you, does it? Of course it does. I couldn't help noticing the distorted cartoon character badly painted on the front. You see a lot of low-rent illustration on ice-cream vans, don't you? I wonder if it's the same artist who does them all. Although that awful rendition of a muscle-bound savage on the front looks like it's been painted with someone's foot — and then there's that dreadful pun. And don't get me started on the copyright issues."

Fiona's breath hitched in her throat at Sophie's last remarks, sending a frozen index finger tracing down her spine — and it was nothing to do with Sophie's rather inappropriate choice of words.

Judging by Partial Sue's paling complexion, it appeared she too had had the same awful thought. Everyone rounded the front of the vehicle to inspect the bonnet which was dominated by a large, tanned, bare-chested illustration of Arnold Schwarzenegger. Sophie was right about one thing — the Hollywood star appeared a little askew, drooping to one side as if he were a waxwork left out in the sun too long. Adding to the bizarre sight were his hands — instead of holding aloft a sword, they gripped a giant ice cream, accompanied by the words *Cone and the Barbarian*.

Staring at the artwork and suppressing a gasp, Fiona's fears were confirmed. There could be no mistake. She knew this infamous van, had seen it before, and though it appeared bright, joyful and punny on the outside, something terrible had happened within.

The Wicker Man had also made the sinister connection. "Hey, isn't that—"

Before he could utter another word, Fiona managed a surreptitious nudge of his foot. "Yes, the bodybuilder Arnold Schwarzenegger."

The Wicker Man grunted, confused and not particularly happy at being cut off.

"Anyway—" Sophie fixed Bella with a poisonous stare — "I'm not here to discuss poorly conceived imagery. I want to ensure that you're not going to sell ice creams opposite my shop."

"Oh, no, I just pulled up to—"

Sophie didn't give Bella time to finish. "Good. Because I do not want grubby children accompanied by parents in singlets or pyjamas and slippers shuffling across the road, bringing down the tone just so they can buy low-quality ice cream."

"Bella can sell ice creams where she likes," Daisy snapped, surprising everyone with her abrupt tone. Sophie stared at her, slightly wrongfooted by her uncustomary outburst.

"It's okay, Mum. Don't worry, Sophie. I won't be selling around—"

Sophie regained her composure and cut Bella off again. "Good. That's all." She swished past them and slid back to her shop, almost leaving a silvery trail behind her.

Partial Sue congratulated Daisy. "Well done for putting Sophie in her place."

"I'm trying to be more assertive. Been reading up about it online."

"Well, it's definitely working. She didn't know what hit her," Fiona said.

Then the Wicker Man spoiled it all. "But she does have a point. Parents buying ice creams in their slippers is never very comely."

Daisy stuck up for her daughter again. "Bella can sell ice creams wherever she pleases and to whomever she pleases, whether they're in pyjamas, onesies, playsuits or birthday suits."

Bella blushed. "Well, maybe not the last one. But thanks, Mum."

"That's right," said Fiona, hoping to appear positive, although she felt anything but. "Don't let that Serena Waterford from over the road put you off."

Partial Sue snorted.

Bella thanked them, hugging them one at a time, even the Wicker Man, who didn't really deserve a hug after siding with Sophie, but he got one anyway. "Right, I'm off to stock up on ice cream and see if my Carpigiani machine works." She kissed her mum and climbed into the cab, a big, hopeful smile on her face. On starting, the van belched a cloud of diesel out of the back, while the cheap, low-quality speaker cranked out 'Greensleeves' once more.

Fiona watched the van rattle up the road, another distorted image of Arnie on the tailgate, this time as the Terminator, with a head a little too large for his body, and a speech bubble that read: *"Slow down if you want children to live."*

Fiona recognised the notorious van, as would many around Southbourne, just like the Wicker Man had — although Sophie hadn't, probably because of her short attention span for anything that didn't involve her. Daisy and Bella were also oblivious to its recent history, but for completely different reasons. The pair had been so wrapped up in themselves that the story hadn't lodged itself into their long-term memory banks. However, it was chilling (a word the press had somewhat overused) to the local community.

Back in April, just a couple of months earlier, the previous owner of Bella's ice-cream van had been found dead inside, wedged into its freezer. Murdered by someone who had become known as the Vanilla Killer.

CHAPTER 3

Fiona didn't like nicknames for murderers or serial killers. They either glamourised or trivialised the terrible things these monsters did. It made them seem beguiling and mysterious somehow, bold and daring evil geniuses. To Fiona, they were none of those things. They were simply nasty, vile and dangerous individuals who caused unnecessary suffering and misery and needed to be stopped — at all costs. The last thing that they should have bequeathed upon them was a natty-sounding nickname. Jack the Ripper, Night Stalker, Son of Sam — the list was as colourful as it was long, thanks to the media enjoying the circus, as if they were pantomime villains.

The Vanilla Killer didn't quite work as a moniker, she thought. It was catchy, but not one to be proud of. It made the murderer sound like a bland, beige-wearing dullard who ironed their underwear and queued outside the local post office twenty minutes before it opened. Admittedly, the Vanilla Killer wasn't a serial killer. Yet. They'd only killed once, but that still made them dangerous. They were still out there.

Fiona's foot fidgeted under the table. It had been doing that all morning, ever since she'd reminded herself of the story on a local news website. Kevin Masterson had been supposedly killed by a rival ice-cream seller, his frozen body dumped in his own freezer as a warning to others — that was the official angle. A grainy image accompanied the article. Not a professional shot, it had been taken from a distance by a member of the public from behind the police tape. The newspaper had had to enlarge it, hence its fuzziness. However, it was clear enough to make out the blurry shape of a not particularly well-painted Arnie on the bonnet, grasping a giant cone. There was a similar shot taken from the other direction, equally fuzzy but distinctive enough to make out the Terminator on the tailgate, warning drivers to be careful.

The same images that adorned Bella's van.

"Daisy has to know," Partial Sue said. "I'd want to know if it were the other way around."

All morning, the two of them had been debating whether to tell her or not. The discussion had become so heated that they'd neglected their normal tea-making ritual. A very serious state of affairs indeed. And the cake hadn't even made it out of Partial Sue's bag for life.

Fiona shook her head. "You saw the look on Daisy's face when Bella rolled up in that ice-cream van. She's already anxious. If we tell her the previous owner was found dead inside the freezer . . . Well, I dread to think how she'll react."

"What was his name again?" Partial Sue asked.

"Kevin Masterson."

Partial Sue got to her feet and paced up and down. Simon Le Bon followed her, possibly because he thought this was a sign they were about to go for a walk.

Partial Sue stopped abruptly. Simon Le Bon's nose shunted into the back of her leg, making him sneeze. "Maybe you're right. Maybe we shouldn't tell her. She'd be a nervous wreck if she knew that her beloved daughter had just bought a mobile murder scene. Probably why it was so cheap."

Fiona went quiet.

"What's wrong?" asked Partial Sue.

Fiona shifted in her seat. "I think we've just switched points of view. Now I'm thinking that you're right. Daisy should know. If something happened to Bella and we didn't tell her about this, we'd never forgive ourselves."

"That's true. Should we tell her?"

"I think it's the right thing to do."

Just then, Daisy burst in through the door, wheezing and nearly catching her maxi dress on a basket of wool and sending it flying. "Sorry I'm late. Me and Bella stayed up to watch this period drama set in Saxon times. She kept having to stop it and explain who everyone was. There were too many Ethels in it."

"Ethels?" the other two asked.

"Oh, yes. There were loads of them. There was an Ethel Red, Ethel Fled and Ethel and Stan."

"Oh," Fiona said. "You mean Aethelred, Aethelflaed and Athelstan."

"First proper king of England," Partial Sue chimed in.

"I thought that was the one who burned the cakes." Daisy collapsed into a seat. "No matter. Aethel or Ethel, *tomayto* or *tomahto*, we had to watch a boxset last night to wind down after we got Bella's ice-cream van ready . . ." Daisy suddenly became distracted by the table, or what appeared to be missing from it. "Oh, you haven't made tea yet. Everything all right?"

Fiona and Partial Sue exchanged worried glances.

"Yeah, fine," Fiona said.

Daisy may have been a gentle soul, but she wasn't stupid. "What's wrong?"

"Nothing's wrong," Partial Sue said — a little too eagerly.

"Well, I can see you haven't made any tea, so something must be up."

Tea was the lifeblood of Dogs Need Nice Homes. *"Cut us open and we bleed tea,"* Fiona would often declare, although Daisy never liked her saying it, the graphic imagery not sitting well with her genteel sensibilities. Partial Sue didn't like her saying it either, although for entirely different reasons. It would be a waste of good tea. But no day ever started without the large, chipped brown teapot brewing away in the centre of the table.

"Er, we were actually wondering how Bella was getting on with her ice-cream van," Fiona replied. It wasn't a lie exactly, but it wasn't the truth either.

The question distracted Daisy from the absence of tea. "Oh, yes. We gave it a deep clean and it's such a relief. Everything works and she's fully stocked up on ice cream. She's got all the flavours, even bubble gum, would you believe. And she's bought dairy-free and vegan — I've never tried a vegan ice cream before, and you know what? I couldn't tell the difference. Isn't that amazing? Although I didn't dare ask how much she spent."

"And what about the carpi-what's-its-face? The soft ice-cream machine?" Partial Sue asked.

"You know, I can never remember that name either. I call it the car pigeon machine. Yeah, that all works. She watched lots of how-to videos on YouTube. Did you know the ice cream comes in cartons and you pour it in the top like UHT milk?"

"Yes, I'd heard that."

"We had a ninety-nine to test it out." Daisy blushed. "Then another to celebrate, then another while we watched the Ethels on the telly. A bit naughty but they're so delicious."

They all giggled.

"So how do you feel about Bella's new career?" Fiona asked.

Daisy swallowed. "Much better, thank you. I guess it was a shock at first, you know? Not what I was expecting. But now the dust has settled, I quite like the idea. And she's so enthusiastic. It's nice to see her happy and so full of beans."

Fiona flicked a questioning glance in Partial Sue's direction. It was met by a very subtle but very definite shake of the head. No need for any telepathy to decipher what she was trying to communicate — this was not the right time to inform Daisy or Bella about the van's murderous past, and Fiona agreed. Not when things appeared to be going so well.

"So, she's all set for her first day then?" Partial Sue asked.

"Oh, yes. There's a couple of things she needs to get this morning, but after that it's full steam ahead. I can't see anything holding her back."

A stab of guilt skewered Fiona's conscience. She felt conflicted, and she bet Partial Sue did too. Had they done the right thing, letting Bella plunge into the world of ice-cream retail, ignorant of the van's past?

Perhaps it was best that she remained in the dark. Yes, what you don't know can't hurt you. At least that's what she tried to convince herself, but that didn't stop her fretting, and her tinnitus had been screeching all morning.

Hours went by like this, Fiona having little debates inside her head, the arguments flying back and forth to the shrill of her inner ear. She desperately wanted to talk to Partial Sue for some reassurance, but they couldn't with Daisy present. Daisy, on the other hand, bustled around the shop, humming sweetly to herself with optimistic energy, cleaning, tidying and serving, a smile never absent from her face.

Then it happened. Around eleven thirty, Daisy's phone pinged. "Oh, come and have a look, everyone."

They gathered around. Bella had uploaded an image to Instagram. The selfie showed Bella leaning out of the serving window, handing a rather top-heavy ice cream to a happy customer. The caption underneath read: *First one of the day!*

"That's wonderful!" Fiona gushed, happy for Bella, but also relieved that her fears hadn't come true — not yet anyway.

Daisy enlarged the shot with her fingers. "Looks like a blueberry ice cream."

Partial Sue took a more economic approach. "Looks like she's giving her profits away. I've never seen such a big scoop. The cone can hardly take the heft."

"It's her first customer," Fiona replied. "Got to make it a big one."

"Well, she needs to start downsizing," Partial Sue replied. "Otherwise she'll be eating into her profits, or other people will."

The minutes that followed were punctuated by pings on Daisy's phone, alerting her of further shots on Instagram, testifying to the multiflavoured success of Bella's first day. Ice cream after ice cream was passed into eager customers' hands. The generosity of Bella's dollops didn't decrease, much to Partial Sue's annoyance.

Fiona felt her shoulders relax. She didn't care whether Bella was handing out ice creams by the bucketload or thimbleful. She was selling them, regardless of the van's past, and that was all that mattered.

So it was with a great deal of surprise and confusion when a red-faced Bella burst through the door just before closing time. Fiona couldn't tell whether she was about to cry or blow her top.

Daisy rushed to her daughter's side. "Darling, what's wrong?"

Bella thrust a scribbled piece of paper into her mother's hands. "Someone left this on my windscreen. I can't believe it!"

Daisy held the note out in front of her. Fiona and Partial Sue gathered round.

The note read:

Go away. Your ice-cream van is not welcome here.

CHAPTER 4

They each took it in turns to examine the note, shock and outrage plastered across their collective faces. There wasn't much Fiona could deduce from it, other than exactly what it was — a hastily scribbled abusive message left on Bella's windscreen — although Partial Sue gave it a go, weighing it in her hands and drawing on her encyclopaedic knowledge of stationery. "Half an A4. Torn in half by hand. Eighty GSM, I'd say." She sniffed the writing. "Sharpie marker, definitely. We should send this to our friends DI Fincher and DS Thomas. Their lab guys could probably get a print off it — once they've discounted ours, of course."

Fiona sent her a cease-and-desist look. She meant well, but right now Bella needed comfort and reassurance, not an aggressive strategy to target the author of the note. That could come later. As for roping the police into this, she doubted they'd even register an interest.

They led Bella over to the table and sat down with her. Daisy leaned in to give her daughter a cuddle. "Don't let it upset you, love."

"I'm not upset. I'm just angry." Bella sniffed. "And disappointed. I only sold a few ice creams."

"What?" Daisy asked.

"But we saw the shots you posted on Instagram," Partial Sue remarked.

"Yep, they were the only ones all day. Everyone else steered clear."

Fiona shuddered. If the van had been recognised as the one where the Vanilla Killer had struck, it was no wonder most people had given it a wide berth, and perhaps why it had ended up with a note left on it. The sight of it back on the streets had probably terrified the life out of people, and the last thing anyone would want to do was buy an ice cream from a freezer that had once stored a dead body.

"Er, we thought you stopped posting because you couldn't keep up with the demand," Daisy said.

Bella sighed, shaking her head. "No, I stopped posting because I wasn't selling anything. Then to really make my day, I got that horrible note. It's a disaster."

Daisy did her best to comfort her daughter. "Don't worry, love. It's just your first day, and pay no notice to the note. Some people aren't happy unless they're being unkind. Probably some uptight person who doesn't like 'Greensleeves' and ice cream."

Partial Sue wouldn't suffer this fool lightly. "What idiot doesn't like 'Greensleeves' and ice cream? That's like saying you don't like puppies or Christmas."

"Maybe they're dairy intolerant," Fiona suggested.

"But I had dairy-free and vegan," Bella replied.

"Let me make you a cup of tea." Daisy got to her feet and headed into the storeroom. Partial Sue spun the shop's sign around to 'Closed', locking the door so they wouldn't be disturbed. After the kettle had boiled, Daisy returned with the chipped brown teapot — a magic object that could work wonders on a bad day. She poured them each a cup.

"So where was your pitch?" Fiona asked.

"By the riverside at Wick village. Really nice spot." Bella took her first sip of tea. "Oh, that's better. Thank you."

Tea always made things better.

"When did the note appear?" Daisy asked.

"I was just about to finish for the day, but I really needed to pee. So I locked up my van and quickly nipped to the public toilets. When I got back that note was tucked under the wiper. I have no idea who put it there."

"I have," said Partial Sue.

Everyone turned and stared at her expectantly, especially Fiona, who thought she was about to reveal the grisly story of the van's previous occupant. But Sue took a different tack, a more generalised one. "Ice-cream van owners are notoriously territorial. They each have their designated patch and their pitches. If you parked up on someone else's, well, that's breaking ice-cream-van etiquette."

Bella's face drained of colour. "Really?"

"Oh, yes. Ice-cream rivalry can get quite nasty. I read about it in the news. I think that note might've been a warning shot from another ice-cream seller."

"You can't be serious," Bella replied.

Daisy's lip quivered. "How nasty can it get?"

"Well." Partial Sue inhaled deeply through her teeth, like a builder about to give an inflated quote for a job. "The Glasgow Ice-Cream Wars were waged between two rival mafias who ran all the ice-cream vans."

Daisy clamped a hand over her mouth to stop herself from gasping.

Fiona decided to rein the discussion back to less traumatising territory. "Okay, let's remember this is Wick we're talking about. More famous for its peace and quiet, its ducks and riverside cottages. I bet it was a curtain twitcher who lives there. Got the same attitude as Sophie Haverford towards ice-cream vans. And it was more of a polite notice than a declaration of war."

Partial Sue disagreed. "It didn't say 'polite notice', and, even if it did, people who write 'polite notice' at the top of a note think it gives them carte blanche to be mean and rude."

With Partial Sue's cavalier approach to parking, Fiona felt she'd probably had her fair share of 'polite' notices left on her windscreen.

"I think it sounds threatening," Daisy said.

Fiona frowned. "But what counts as threatening in Wick is more of a wag of a finger or a severe tut."

Bella gave a nervous giggle. "Oh my gosh. This is ridiculous. Never in a million years would I have believed there'd be people offended by an ice-cream van in their neighbourhood."

Partial Sue stood up, bristling with righteous indignation. "You know what? I think we should knock on every door in that village and tell them to mind their own business."

Bella shook her head defiantly. "No need for that, Auntie Sue, but thank you. I'm not going to be intimidated by some uptight snob, whether they're a rival ice-cream seller or some neighbourhood-watcher standing behind their net curtains. I'm going back tomorrow. Show them I'm not scared."

Daisy didn't like the sound of this one bit. "Oh, Bella. Are you sure that's a good idea? I'll be worried about you."

"Mum, it's fine. You don't have to worry. These people are cowards. I mean, if they're too scared to confront me, then there's absolutely nothing to worry about. What's the worst they can do?"

There was a lot worse they could do. There was a lot worse they had done to Kevin Masterson. *The* worst thing that could be done to a person. Fiona glanced at Partial Sue. She gave a solemn but almost imperceptible nod. They couldn't hold back any longer. It would be irresponsible. They had to tell her the whole story.

Fiona spoke quietly and slowly. "There is one other thing you should know."

Bella regarded her. "What's that, Auntie Fiona?"

She wanted to put it as delicately as possible, both for Bella and her mother's sake. "I don't know about the note, but I think I know the reason why your sales were slow. That van you bought has a bit of a history."

27

"What? It's not stolen, is it?"

Fiona shook her head. "No, it's not stolen, but it has been involved in a crime. A very serious one. I think people may have recognised it."

Daisy trembled. "I don't like the sound of this."

Fiona wanted to reassure them both that it was fine and really nothing to worry about. One of those things that didn't merit a second thought. A trivial matter. But it wouldn't have been the truth. There was no sugar-coating Fiona could apply, or sprinkles, as if it were a soft ice cream from Bella's Carpigiani machine.

"Something went on in that van," Fiona began, before realising her words could be unintentionally misconstrued as seedy, as if the van had been used for some amorous after-hours hijinks. If only that were the case. She would take the blushing, mild embarrassment of that over a murder any day.

Daisy didn't pick up on the innuendo. "Is it haunted?"

"In a way, yes," Partial Sue replied.

Bella became excited. "Oh, cool. My ice-cream van has a ghost."

"I don't know about a ghost." Fiona swallowed hard. "But it does involve a dead body."

CHAPTER 5

Bella's face contorted into an unpleasant expression. "Wait, what? Someone died in my van?"

Fiona nodded. "Bit worse. Someone was murdered."

"Murdered? Are you sure?"

Shocked by the gruesome revelation, Daisy gripped the edge of the table, steadying herself.

"He was the previous owner," Fiona replied.

"His name was Kevin Masterson." Partial Sue pulled up the news story on her phone and handed it to Bella and Daisy.

Eyes rapidly scanning back and forth, mother and daughter speed-read the article.

Bella's eyes ceased flicking when they alighted on the images of the bright-red vehicle. She stared, unblinking. "That's my van. No wonder nobody was buying from me."

Daisy snapped out of her trance-like state and looked up from the phone screen. "You have to get rid of it, Bella. You have to sell it."

"I've only just bought it, Mum. I'm not selling it."

"But it says the police think he was killed by a rival ice-cream seller. Found frozen in his own ice-cream van. In the freezer!"

Bella's face turned pallid at the thought of a deceased person occupying the space where her strawberry splits and choc ices currently resided. She swallowed down any nausea and jutted out her chin defiantly. "We scrubbed and disinfected that freezer and everything else to within an inch of its life. It'll be fine."

Daisy's fears weren't allayed. "But you just got a nasty note on your windscreen. What if you're next?"

"Yes, but it also says the van was found in Mudeford and they think that was his patch. I'll just stay away from Mudeford."

"But there's a killer on the loose, murdering ice-cream sellers. You're an ice-cream seller."

"To be fair, Dais, he's not a serial killer," Partial Sue replied. "He's only killed one ice-cream seller."

"That's one too many." Daisy tensed up. Even her curls appeared to tighten before their eyes.

"That came out wrong." Partial Sue shook her head. "I didn't mean to make light of his death. What I meant was, the Vanilla Killer—"

"The Vanilla Killer? He has a name? Oh my gosh." Daisy was in full panic mode, wobbling on her chair.

"Yes," said Fiona. "But that's just the news jazzing things up. You know what they're like. It's a one-off incident, probably the result of an ongoing dispute about pitches."

"Yeah, and no other ice-cream sellers have been killed since then." Bella's face suddenly dropped. "Have they?"

"No, not that we know of," Fiona said.

"Not yet!" Daisy shrieked, sounding like a wounded animal. "I don't want you going out in that van, Bella. It's too dangerous."

Fiona knew Daisy well enough to realise that her uncharacteristic outburst didn't originate from a place of disapproval or anger, but from her instinct to protect Bella. A maternal urge that burned hotter than the core of the sun. Nevertheless, Bella interpreted it as an attempt to control her.

"You can't stop me, Mum. I'm not a little girl anymore."

Daisy sagged in the middle, her short-lived rage depleted. "Yes, I know, love. Sorry, I didn't mean to tell you what to do. It's your life, I know that. But I worry. I don't want anything bad to happen to you."

Bella's expression softened. She reached a comforting hand across to her mother. "I know you do, Mum. I'm sorry too. I don't want to give you nightmares. It's just . . . this is the first thing I've done since splitting from Mark that's made me feel like my old self. Like I'm finally moving on. I really enjoy it — well, minus the nasty note. I know I've only done it once and I haven't sold that many ice creams, but being out on sunny days in beautiful places doesn't feel like work. And seeing the smile on a kid's face when you hand them an ice cream . . . Well, there's nothing better."

"That must be nice," Daisy said quietly.

Partial Sue leaped to her feet. "I have an idea. Why don't one of us come with you each day? Take it in turns. Bit of security."

Bella smiled warmly. "That's very kind of you Auntie Sue, but I need to do this myself, and I wouldn't want to drag you away from the shop."

"Oh, don't worry about that," Partial Sue replied. "We're always finding excuses to drag ourselves away."

"I've got a better idea," Bella said. "Look, I won't ever pitch up in Wick again, and I'll stay well away from Mudeford. Find other pitches. Virgin ice-cream territory. How does that sound?"

"But how will you know that they're not already taken?" Daisy asked.

"I'll leave the second I get any rude notes or spot any disgruntled ice-cream sellers."

"Promise you'll leave before they become, er, gruntled," Daisy said.

"Deal. It's settled then." Bella got to her feet.

"But what about people recognising the van?" Partial Sue asked. "They'll know it had a dead body in the freezer. That's definitely going to affect sales." As ever, she was more concerned about the economic consequences.

Still coming to terms with the historically ghoulish content of her freezer, Bella was not going to be put off, even though she looked a little green around the gills. "I'll cover up the graphics with something. Don't know what, but I'll make it unrecognisable. Then I'll scout out some new pitches online. I'll see you at home, Mum, and don't worry."

She planted a kiss on Daisy's head, said goodbye and left the shop.

"You're still worried, aren't you?" Partial Sue asked.

Face racked with anxiety, Daisy slowly nodded.

"Thing is," Fiona said, "you don't need to lose any sleep over this. I think it's pretty clear this Kevin Masterson had an ongoing dispute with a rival that escalated."

Hope finally surfaced on Daisy's face, until Partial Sue dashed it against some rocks and ran it aground. "Unless it was one of those heat-of-the-moment things. Got into an argument. One thing led to another—"

Fiona cut her off before she could do any more damage. "But that's not going to happen with Bella. She's smart. Said she's going to get the hell out of Dodge before it comes to that. Isn't she, Sue?" Fiona's last words were through semi-gritted teeth, accompanied by a glare in Partial Sue's direction.

"Oh, yes, of course. Definitely won't come to that."

"And once she's changed the look of the van," Fiona added, "she'll be selling ice creams like nobody's business."

Judging by how much her hands shook, Daisy didn't appear comforted by this, the fear radiating off her like depleted uranium.

The shop went quiet, apart from the clock set into the panelled back wall, dependably clunking the day away.

"There is one way to make sure Bella is totally safe," Fiona said suddenly.

Daisy and Sue regarded her, their faces wide and inquisitive.

Fiona smiled at her friends. "We catch the Vanilla Killer."

CHAPTER 6

First things first — they inspected the scene of the crime. Bella had agreed to swing past the shop early that morning to let Fiona and Partial Sue have a nosy for clues inside the van. It was spotless, a pristine palace of hygiene. With Daisy's exacting standards of cleanliness, it had undergone the deepest of deep cleans. Fiona had no doubt that any germs or contaminates — which may have survived its brief sojourn as a dead-body cold storage — would have been eradicated with extreme prejudice. However, so too would any clues. Daisy and Bella assured them they had found nothing, and there were no marks of any significance, apart from a few wear-and-tear scuffs built up over the years. Certainly no signs of a struggle, and no indication that anything sinister had occurred within the confines of its tomblike freezer.

After parting ways with Bella, Fiona suggested they investigate the location where the note had appeared on the windscreen. Not exactly a crime scene, Wick village was probably nothing more than a site of outstanding rudeness. However, they needed to question its residents to establish if indeed one of them had left the note. Whether it had simply been a case of a busybody with too much time on their hands and too little tolerance — or if it had been a rival ice-cream seller and, God forbid, the Vanilla Killer.

It was more likely to be the former, but they had to keep an open mind and follow procedure. Although, to be honest, the ladies had no procedure of which to speak. Making it up as they went along was more their style.

They assembled on what Fiona considered to be Wick's fairly unique village green because of its triangular shape. She was a big fan of the humble village green. Up and down the country, these lawn-covered national treasures were a joyful sight, and she'd sought out all manner of them in her time. Small ones, square ones, rectangular ones, odd ones, ones big enough to play cricket on. She'd even had a picnic on a round one, but this was the only three-sided village green she'd encountered and although it was barely big enough to play 'down on one knee', it hadn't stopped some spoilsport from putting up a sign that read: *No ball games*. At least it hadn't been nailed to the green's one and only tree — an arthritic oak that bent in the middle.

They gathered beneath its branches, thankful for the shade, as the absence of the cooling easterly wind today had sent the temperature soaring. She'd wished she'd left Simon Le Bon at home to spare him the heat, but he would have given her the cold shoulder when she got back. He was enjoying this impromptu outing, his nose quivering away at all the smells around the base of the oak. At least she'd remembered to bring his portable dog bowl.

"Where should we begin? Or should we split up?" Daisy couldn't wait to get started. An angry momma bear in Scholls, she clutched the note tightly in her hand, ready to shove it in the face of unsuspecting residents.

"We stick together. Go house to house," Fiona announced.

"Cottage to cottage, more like," Partial Sue corrected. She was right. Apart from the large dwelling opposite, which appeared to be a manor house, Wick was mostly populated by two varieties of rural cottage — tall, dark and handsome red-brick Victorian, or squat and white-washed with ancient slate roofs. Both could easily adorn the lid of a souvenir biscuit tin. With its surrounding water meadows and riverside, Wick was achingly pretty and quintessentially English, apart from a few odd buildings that had showed up in the seventies to spoil things. But there was something unsettling about the place that Fiona couldn't quite put her finger on. It had an eerie quality that she could only describe as feeling as if she were being watched.

"Which road should we start with?" Partial Sue asked. A spiderweb of narrow lanes fanned out around them.

"We should start by the river," Daisy said. "That's where Bella pitched up. Then work our way back."

"Good idea," Fiona said.

After calling at the first dozen houses, a pattern emerged. Contrary to what they'd expected, the people of Wick seemed a rather happy breed, not the shrewish busybodies they were expecting. Almost every resident who'd opened their door offered up warm smiles and a plethora of pleasantries — until the mention of Bella's ice-cream van. Then they became withdrawn and timid, their complexions pallid. After a few rushed answers to the ladies' questions, their doors had begun to close, not out of rudeness but fear. Word had got around yesterday that the Murder Van, as the residents had collectively called it, was in their village — the one whose freezer had once entombed its owner. Its presence hadn't spurred the penning of an annoyed note, as far as Fiona could tell, but had made them stay indoors with the curtains closed, hoping it would go away. Not easy when the day had been so perfect for going out. Judging by the worry in their eyes, Fiona couldn't imagine any of them plucking up the courage to venture out of their homes and risk approaching the Murder Van to slip a note under its wiper.

After an hour, the ladies had nearly exhausted all the homes in Wick, apart from the large manor house and a small newish-looking 1970s bungalow — well, it was newish compared to the buildings around it.

"Let's try the bungalow first," Partial Sue suggested. "Leave the big one until last."

They rang the bell and waited. The door opened to reveal a short, bare-torsoed octogenarian, glossy with sweat and not enjoying the heat one bit, even at this hour of the morning. Dressed only in a vast pair of khaki shorts, he resembled an extra from the film *Ice Cold in Alex*. Mopping his brow with a handkerchief, he told them his name was Fred, but unlike everyone else they'd encountered, he appeared to be oblivious to the presence of Bella's van yesterday, and most put out. "Darn it, I wish I'd seen it. Will your daughter be back, and if so, when? I'll make myself a bit more presentable. Treat myself to an ice lolly."

"Unfortunately, she won't be back." Daisy showed him the note. "Someone put this on her windscreen."

He fished out a pair of bifocals from one of his capacious pockets in the side of his shorts. As he slotted them onto his sunburnt nose, Fiona noticed he had black semi-circles of dirt under his nails.

He held the note out in front of him. "What rotter wrote this? It's no wonder we never get any ice-cream vans down here."

"Really? None at all?" Fiona asked.

"Nope. They never come here. I think they forget about us. Unless it's these nasty notes keeping them away."

"Why do they forget about you?"

He handed the note back to Daisy. "Our village doesn't lead anywhere, see. Every road is a dead end, stopping at the water meadows or the river. You can't go any further, 'cept around the village green and back out the way you came."

In her mind, Fiona clicked her fingers. That was it. The underlying unease of the place was nothing sinister, merely a lack of through traffic — an inbuilt inertness due to it being one big cul-de-sac, albeit a very pretty one.

"Do you know anyone who could've written this note?" Daisy asked.

"No one I can think of. Everyone's very nice around here. But you could try the tearooms."

"Tearooms! Wick has tearooms?" Partial Sue jolted at this new revelation. "Why didn't we know about this?"

It was as much of a shock to Fiona and, no doubt, Daisy too. All three of them were self-confessed addicts of God's finest beverage, and knew every tea-serving establishment within a twenty-mile radius. Fiona had them marked on a virtual map in her head, just in case they got caught short and needed a swift cuppa. All establishments had been vetted and vigorously tried and tested to assess their suitability, although they hadn't drawn up any formal rating system yet — but give it time. The presence of tearooms in Wick gave Fiona what could only be described as a disturbance in the Force. Something was amiss. How had these tearooms slipped through what was a very fine and sophisticated net?

As if reading her mind, Daisy said, "Perhaps it's like that Brigadoon and only appears now and then."

"Oh, no. It only opened about a month ago." Fred pointed, and the ladies gazed in the direction of his finger which was aimed at the handsome manor house opposite the green.

"It's in there?" Partial Sue asked. "But there are no signs outside."

Fred gave her a gappy smile. "Well, let's just say Alan, the owner, likes to keep it a secret."

Fiona couldn't understand what kind of business owner went out of his way to hide his trade, to be so discreet that he'd neglected to put up even the most modest sign. How were the public supposed to know about it? Telepathy? Unless that was the point. It was an exclusive establishment and the likes of them weren't supposed to know.

Fred glanced left and right. "He's a bit picky about who he lets in. Snooty, you could say. I don't want to tell tales, but I'd say if anyone put that note on your daughter's windscreen, it would be him. Although you didn't hear it from me." He tapped his red nose.

CHAPTER 7

Partial Sue's limbs took on a life of their own, uncontrollably propelling her across the village green — like the scarecrow from *The Wizard of Oz* — such was her excitement. Though she saw herself as rather more heroic. "I feel like Howard Carter about to uncover the tomb of Tutankhamun, or Tea-tankhamun."

Fiona had to admit that the thrill of a new tearoom — a secret one, no less — also caused her pulse to thrum. What would they find behind its heavyset walls and imposing stone-mullioned windows? The handsome exterior boded well. She'd wager the interior was equally as impressive. Perhaps this place would become their new tea establishment of choice. She reminded herself that they were here to investigate, not indulge, although a quick cuppa wouldn't hurt anyone, and they could pose a few questions to the staff while the tea was poured.

The three of them took shelter from the sun in the cool stone porch. Fiona glanced around for any signs of branding, or clues that this was a place of hospitality. She feared that Fred had been having them on, and they were in fact standing in the entrance to someone's house. The only indication to the contrary was the thick dark timber door in front of them.

Adorned with wrought-iron latticework and vast matching hinges, it appeared to have been there since the civil war, but more importantly, it was open. Not so much that it appeared inviting, but just enough to tell her they weren't barred from entering. Partial Sue, eager to explore, pushed the hefty wooden construction open a little further and stepped inside, followed by Fiona and Daisy.

They found themselves in a churchlike vestibule, high ceilinged with bare wooden timbers and more bare stonework. The air had that ancient, musty tang, as if it hadn't been changed for centuries. Another wooden door confronted them on the other side, similar to the one they'd just come through but minus the ironwork. They were about to venture forward when a deep voice startled them.

"May I help you?"

They hadn't noticed a tall gentleman standing behind them, half-concealed by the wooden door. Dressed in a waiter's uniform — a starched white shirt, bow tie and pressed black trousers — he was as rigid as a mannequin.

"Oh, er, yes," stuttered Fiona. "Is this a tearoom?"

"That depends." He was acting like some strange gatekeeper. Fiona wondered whether they'd have to answer three riddles before they could proceed further.

"Depends on what?" asked Partial Sue, already losing patience. "Either it is, or it isn't."

He smirked. "Whether you have a reservation or not."

"No, we don't," Fiona said.

The tall waiter stood silently for several awkward seconds, not speaking. The ladies stared back at him, awaiting his response, but none came.

"Er, could we have a cup of tea, do you think?" Daisy asked. "I'm parched."

He suddenly came back to life. "I shall have to check with Alan," he replied wearily. "Do you have any children with you?"

Absurdly, the ladies looked about themselves, checking to make sure any stray youngsters hadn't snuck in and latched onto them. Satisfied they were child free, Fiona wondered why he'd asked such a question. She gave him an inquisitive stare.

"We do not allow children in here," he proclaimed proudly. He glanced down at Simon Le Bon by Fiona's feet. "But we do allow dogs. Well-behaved ones."

Daisy scowled. "Why do you allow dogs and not children?"

He smiled at her condescendingly, as if she were being utterly naive. "Tea drinking should not be spoiled by whining or fuss."

Fiona felt as if she'd stumbled into a bizarre Roald Dahl story where the antagonist hates children. Thing is, dogs were just as capable of whining and making a fuss as kids, perhaps more so. The waiter bustled off through the door opposite, and they were treated to their first glimpse of the hallowed tearoom. It was an impressive space, more of a hall than a room, dominated by a soaring hammer-beam roof, with dark hardwood floors which wouldn't be allowed these days. The tables were arranged with mathematical precision, each one swathed in a pristine white tablecloth with a chair tucked neatly at each side. At one table, a young female waitress — similarly dressed to the man they'd just encountered — ironed a tablecloth in situ, a cloud of steam rising up around her reddening face. A short, stout man, presumably Alan — with a flawless parting and wearing a navy-blue suit — monitored her work. Arms crossed, he followed her every stroke with a perfectionist's scrutiny.

The waiter approached him, whispering in his ear. Alan immediately broke away from supervising the pressing of the tablecloths and headed towards the ladies, deferentially followed by the waiter. He cleared his throat before speaking. "I understand you wish to have tea."

Fiona wondered why such a simple request had caused such consternation. She tried to remain civil. "If it's not too much trouble."

He grunted to himself. "We have sittings at ten a.m., eleven a.m., twelve p.m., one p.m., two p.m., three p.m. and four p.m., closing at five p.m. sharp."

"Oh, you have sittings?" Fiona had heard of posh restaurants having sittings, but never a tearoom.

Alan's face was cold. "That's what I believe I said."

"Your tearooms are very grand," Daisy said. "We never knew they were here, and we love a good tearoom, don't we?"

Partial Sue nodded. "Tea is our religion. You could say we're tea-ologians." She chuckled at her own wordplay.

Alan raised one eyebrow, as if this were the most tedious, or tea-dious ordeal he'd ever encountered.

"We didn't see any signs outside," Fiona said.

"We're like Rolls-Royce," the waiter sneered. "We don't need to advertise."

Partial Sue shared her knowledge of local history. "Interesting you should say that. Did you know that Charles Rolls died just a few hundred yards from here when his plane crashed?"

Alan didn't respond, his eyebrow remaining aloft.

"So can we have a cup of tea?" Fiona asked.

Alan examined his watch. "Unfortunately you are between sittings."

"Surely you could squeeze us in," Partial Sue said. "You don't look busy." A vast overstatement — the place was empty.

"We operate on a strict reservation basis," Alan replied.

"How do we make a reservation?" Partial Sue asked.

"All bookings are arranged through the Tea Connoisseurs Association website."

Daisy got on her phone. "Okay, I'm on it. What's your tearoom called?"

"Alan's Place."

All three ladies looked at him, slightly baffled. The name seemed incongruous with its heightened levels of pomposity, more suited to a burger van at a car boot sale. Partial Sue suppressed a snigger.

"Can't seem to find it," Daisy muttered.

Partial Sue failed to hide her disbelief. "Is it really called Alan's Place?"

Alan glared at her. "What's wrong with Alan's Place?"

"Nothing at all." Fiona surmised that they were quickly outstaying their welcome, judging by how obstructive Alan and his waiter — or, rather, henchman — were. It was clear they didn't want them there, sullying their high-end tea palace. The ladies probably weren't going to make it any further than the vestibule, but they still had questions that needed answering.

Fiona decided to take a more circuitous route to gauge whether they had anything against ice-cream vans. Although, to be fair, that would be a given. "Tell me, do you serve ice cream?"

"No, we do not," Alan answered emphatically. "We serve tea and the finest cake known to humanity. And nothing else. Ice cream is for children's birthday parties and people with no dignity."

"We have our own pastry chef," boasted the waiter. "Flown in from Dubai."

"What, every day?" Daisy asked innocently.

"Don't be stupid," Alan snapped. "We headhunted him a year ago and relocated him here."

Fiona flinched at his outburst against Daisy, as did Partial Sue. Nothing got their backs up more than someone insulting their kind-hearted comrade.

Daisy flushed with embarrassment and shrank back slightly, her head bowed, until she spotted something clutched in Alan's fist. "What's that in your hand?"

Alan revealed a marker pen. But not just any old marker pen. It was a Sharpie.

"Alan leaves Post-it notes for us," the waiter piped up. "To keep us on our toes."

"Does he now?" Fiona fixed Alan with what she hoped was an acidic stare. "So whenever something isn't to your liking, you leave a note. May we see one?"

"No, you may not."

Daisy's gentle persona was supplanted by a controlled rage, boosted by her new-found assertiveness. She shook with anger and took a step closer to Alan, glaring at him. "My daughter parked her ice-cream van near here yesterday. And this was left on her windscreen." She pulled the note from her pocket and held it up in front of him. "Did you write it?"

"Of course I didn't. Why would you think that?"

Partial Sue pointed to the note. "Because it was written with a Sharpie, like the one you have in your hand. I'm what you might call an expert witness when it comes to stationery."

Alan nervously smoothed down his parting, which was already immaculate. "I think it's time you left. There's nothing for you here."

"I think we have everything we need." Fiona smiled. "You've admitted you don't like ice cream. Therefore it's pretty safe to assume you don't like ice-cream vans, and you're fond of writing a note or two, which, judging by your rudeness, aren't going to be very nice, just like the one in Daisy's hand."

"I don't know what you're talking about," Alan replied. "I didn't write that. I had no idea there was an ice-cream van here yesterday."

"Nearly everyone in the village knew," Partial Sue pointed out. "How could you not know?"

"I'm too busy here," Alan replied. "I haven't got time to chase ice-cream vans."

Daisy took another step closer and stared at him, unflinching. "I'm sorry, but I don't believe you. Please don't leave any more horrible notes on my daughter's van."

"Are you threatening me?"

Daisy shook her head. "I'm asking you, politely. Because that's what decent human beings do. They speak face to face. They don't write cowardly notes when someone's back is turned, because that's, well, cowardly."

"Lily-livered," Partial Sue said.

"Spineless," Fiona added.

Alan's face flushed. His neck appeared to shrink into his torso. He looked away, no longer able to meet Daisy's accusing gaze.

The ladies turned and left Alan's Place, satisfied beyond all reasonable doubt that they had discovered the bitter, uptight author of the note. But was he the Vanilla Killer?

CHAPTER 8

Fiona was glad to be back in the warm, charmingly dishevelled surroundings of the shop, serenaded by the gentle tinkling of tea pouring into mismatched cups, and nobody caring that they were mismatched or that the teapot was chipped and the table wobbled. That's the way tea should be enjoyed — carefree and relaxed, where you feel at ease. Not in an uptight, elbows-off-the-table kind of place where you have to mind your Ps and Qs. She'd take the affable shabbiness of Dogs Need Nice Homes over that nonsense any day of the week.

Partial Sue snapped a digestive in half and dunked it in her tea, something that would undoubtedly be frowned upon at Alan's Place. She popped it in her mouth and swallowed it in one. The other half she used to jab the air to make her point. "So, we're all in agreement then. Pompous Alan—" they'd already assigned him a nickname — "has to be the one who left the note."

Daisy scowled at the mention of the man's name. "It's definitely him."

Fiona agreed, but not entirely. "Well, all evidence so far points that way, but I don't think we can say with one hundred per cent certainty that he did it."

44

Daisy frowned.

Partial Sue pointed at Fiona with her half a biscuit. "Oh, come on, Fiona. It has to be him." She plunged it into her tea and gobbled it down.

"Who else could it be?" Daisy asked. "No one else was bothered about Bella's ice-cream van being there except him."

Fiona realised she was backtracking a little, but she didn't want to be swayed by the emotions of the encounter, which had run high. "He said he didn't like ice cream. I added the bit about him not liking ice-cream vans. I'll admit, he is the most likely candidate, but firstly, he writes on Post-it notes, not torn pieces of A4. He's too fussy for that. And secondly, we never got to compare his handwriting with the note. That would've really helped."

Partial Sue huffed. "We don't need to see his handwriting, and he could've just grabbed a piece of paper because he didn't have a Post-it note on him. I mean, it's so obvious he did it."

Daisy nodded. "I agree, but what I want to know is, do we think he's nasty enough to be the Vanilla Killer?"

The question silenced Fiona, as well as Partial Sue who normally had something to say about everything. Writing nasty notes was one thing — killing someone would put him in a completely different league.

Fiona sighed. "I can't see it myself. I mean, yes, he's awful and stuck up, but my gut is telling me that *if* he did write that note, and it's a bit of an *if*, then it's a case of on-the-spot snobbery. Just like we witnessed yesterday with her over the road, telling Bella not to sell ice creams opposite her shop."

"Maybe you're right," Partial Sue said. "Much as I disliked the fellow, it'd be quite a leap for him to be the Vanilla Killer. I mean, why would he kill an ice-cream seller in Mudeford? It's nowhere near Wick."

Daisy wasn't about to let Alan go as a murder suspect. "Unless Alan lives in Mudeford, and got annoyed with Kevin Masterson for selling ice creams around his neighbourhood."

"That's a possibility," Fiona replied.

Daisy had her phone out and began sifting through various social media sites until she tracked Alan down. "Got him!" Her elation was short-lived. "Oh, he's got his home location down as Ringwood. But he could be lying."

Partial Sue peered at Daisy's phone and pointed at the screen. "Yeah, but that would be tricky when lots of his friends live in Ringwood too."

Daisy felt deflated. She was desperate for Alan to be the Vanilla Killer. All the evidence pointed at him being an out-and-out snob, and probably a whingeing note writer, but not a murderer. Not yet, anyway.

"I don't think he's our man," Fiona said. "Unless we find evidence to the contrary. But I think we should also explore other possibilities, apart from rival ice-cream sellers or snobby curtain twitchers. Kevin Masterson might have been murdered by a jealous lover, or had a falling out with a friend."

Daisy sighed. "Okay, fine." She didn't sound fine.

Partial Sue tried to cheer her up. "Hey, I wonder if Sophie and Alan know each other. The pair of them could start the Southbourne Snobs Society."

Fiona laughed. "Yes, they could have marches down Southbourne Grove, so they can look down their noses at everyone they pass."

"We could start a counter organisation," Partial Sue suggested. "The Kind Commoners of Southbourne — everyone welcome, as long as they're nice."

The two of them giggled, but Daisy didn't join in. Her eyes remained solemn, her mouth stuck in a harsh straight line. Fiona knew she didn't feel like indulging in any jollity at this time. Though she'd reluctantly accepted that Alan might not be the murderer, she had come face to face with the man who'd possibly upset her daughter, and it still smarted. She probably didn't feel satisfied with the very polite telling off she'd given him. Not used to confrontation, Daisy's hackles were still up, adrenalin high.

"Are you okay, Daisy?" Fiona asked.

She answered without hesitation. "There was something fishy about Alan's Place."

"Which part?" Partial Sue replied. "There was quite a lot of fishiness to choose from."

"How does it make any money?" Daisy asked. "The place was empty."

"Supply and demand," Partial Sue explained. "Probably appeals to a very small and select clientele who pay a fortune to drink fascist tea."

"Unless it's like the Wicker Man next door, and we think it's a front for something else," Fiona suggested.

"Shouldn't we look into that?" Daisy asked.

The conversation was interrupted by the distinctive tones of 'Greensleeves' clanging down the road.

Daisy's mood immediately improved. "That sounds like Bella."

They abandoned their tea and headed to the front door. Outside, Bella shut off the chimes as she parked but left her engine running. Fiona was heartened to see a big smile lighting up Bella's face as she climbed out of the cab.

"Come and look at this." Bella led them round to the front of the van and threw her arms wide. "Ta-dah!"

The ice-cream van had had a makeover. Gone were the distorted graphics of *Cone and the Barbarian*, having been covered up by something fresher, friendlier and fishier — a large, slick illustration of a happy purple-haired mermaid perched on a rock and joyfully swishing her tail, a top-heavy ninety-nine in her hand. Across the top of the van, above the windscreen, it read, *Mermaid Ice Creams*.

"What do you think?" Bella asked.

Daisy gushed. "Oh, it's wonderful, I love it."

"The van's completely unrecognisable," Fiona added. "What made you choose a mermaid?"

"I like mermaids."

"Fair enough."

47

Bella gestured to the brightly coloured graphic. "But, practically, it needed to be that shape. Her tail covers up the barbarian's giant cone."

"I am partial to a mermaid," Partial Sue said. "They're my favourite mythical creature."

Daisy joined in. "I do love mermaids, but I'd have to say a unicorn's my favourite."

"I could never see the appeal of unicorns," Partial Sue replied. "It's just a pony with a spike."

Fiona waded in. "Well, by that argument, a mermaid's just a person with a tail."

Partial Sue pushed back. "Yes, but they can breathe under water. Imagine that."

"Unicorns can fly," Daisy countered.

"I think that's Pegasus," Fiona pointed out.

Partial Sue got excited. "Now, I am partial to a flying horse. Although I'd prefer a flying shire horse if I had the choice." She was also partial to shire horses, and had the horse brasses at home to prove it.

But Daisy wasn't done yet. "Unicorns can do magic."

Fiona noticed Bella becoming a tad irritable as her revamped van was overshadowed by a debate as to who had the best fantasy creature. So she moved the conversation on. "Have you had the rear done as well?"

Bella brightened. "Yes, come and see."

They trooped around to the tailgate, where the Terminator had been concealed by the same purple-haired mermaid holding up a sign as if she were a lollipop lady, which read, *Sea you don't hurt a child.*

"Do you like my sea-based pun?" Bella asked. "I came up with it myself."

The ladies nodded.

"We love a good pun," Fiona said. "But how did you get these done so quickly? I thought it would've taken ages for someone to paint over."

Bella smiled. "It's not a painting. It's a vinyl. Just a big sticker, really. Place in Poole did it. All done with a computer. They stuck it on for me too."

Taking a closer look, Partial Sue tested the edge with her fingernail. "Well, I never. It's a giant sticker."

A deep, sonorous voice interrupted them. The Wicker Man emerged from his shop, no doubt on the scrounge for free ice cream. "Ah, mermaids. Delightful creatures. Sirens of the sea, their melodious ditties irresistible to seafarers down the ages, wrecking their vessels and sending them to watery graves."

Partial Sue grimaced. "Oh, that's put me right off them now."

"Apologies," he replied. "I shall remedy forthwith by way of an improvised joke. Why did the mermaid become a lollipop lady? Because she was good at dealing with tailbacks."

Everyone groaned.

"That's terrible, Uncle Trevor." Bella grimaced.

"Indeed, it is." He grinned, then rubbed his hands. "Now, on to more pressing matters. Is that Koi Carp thingamajig working?"

"Carpigiani machine."

"That's the feller."

"Probably easier if we just call it a soft ice-cream machine," Fiona said.

"It's working," Bella replied. "Would you like one?"

"I thought you'd never ask. Can I have a flake in it?"

"Of course."

"Please may I have one too?" Partial Sue asked, suddenly sounding like a nine-year-old.

Bella regarded the assembled folk. "Ninety-nines all round?"

Fiona didn't feel comfortable with her giving away all her profits. "We'll pay for them, Bella."

"We will?" Partial Sue and the Wicker Man replied together. Neither were fond of parting with their cash if they could help it.

"Bella, you can't give your ice creams away for free," Daisy said.

"No, it's fine, Mum. I insist. A round of complimentary ninety-nines coming up."

"Delay that order," a pompous voice announced. Sophie had appeared beside them, materialising like a demonic force that a foolish teenager had unwittingly summoned from a dusty old book found in an attic. Standing beside her for moral support was Gail, her mousy, long-suffering assistant — a technical wizard whose economy with words meant she never offered up more than one or two syllables at a time. The ladies counted her as a friend and had often attempted to lure her away from Sophie, but never with any success. Her overbearing boss had a sadistic hold over the poor woman.

Sophie planted both hands on her slender hips. "I thought I said no selling ice creams outside my shop."

"I'm not selling them," Bella replied. "I'm giving them away. Would you like one?"

Gail licked her lips. "'S'right."

Sophie answered for the both of them. "No, we would not. I do not touch ice cream or ice lollies."

This wasn't true. Fiona had seen her suck down a whole ice lolly once when she'd been in a state of severe stress and sleep deprivation.

"Ice cream is for people with simple tastes," Sophie continued. "Freezing cold and messy, they're essentially desserts you have to hold in your hand."

"Do you know someone called Alan? Runs a tearoom?" asked Partial Sue. "You sound just like him."

Sophie cackled. "Do I look like the sort of person who knows someone called Alan?" Then her face suddenly became serious, as she realised there was someone out there with a business whom she didn't know. As a social influencer and unelected Queen of Southbourne, no one escaped Sophie's network, for the simple reason that everyone deserved to know how wonderful she was. Right now, her brain probably couldn't fathom how Alan had slipped through the net and, more importantly, was managing to survive without the immeasurable benefit of her acquaintance. "Wait, who's this Alan?"

"He runs a tearoom in Wick."

Sophie scoffed. "There's no tearoom in Wick. If there was, I would know about it."

"There is," Daisy replied. "It's new. Well, new-ish. Called Alan's Place, because the nasty man who runs it is Alan, although we call him Pompous Alan." Daisy turned to her daughter. "We think he wrote the note."

"But we're not a hundred per cent sure," Fiona corrected.

Partial Sue frowned. "Well, as near as damn it."

Just moments ago, Bella had fizzed with pride, overjoyed that her newly rebranded ice-cream van was a hit. Now her enthusiasm dwindled and her face dulled. Then her eyes sparked with indignant anger. "Sorry, who is this guy?"

"He runs a strict tearoom," Fiona answered.

Partial Sue's features became pinched. "You could say he's a tyrant when it comes to tea — a tea-rant."

Bella neither reacted nor spoke as she got back into her van.

"Where are you going?" Daisy asked.

"To give this Alan a piece of my mind." Bella slammed the door, a little harder than absolutely necessary.

"Don't worry, your mum already did that," Partial Sue informed her.

Bella halted in her tracks. Giving people a piece of her mind was not normally in her mum's nature. She gazed at her through the open cab window. "What did you say to him?"

"I told him he was a coward for putting that note on your windscreen, and not to do it again."

"You should have seen his face," Partial Sue added. "He was terrified."

Bella got out of her van and hugged Daisy. "Thanks, Mum. For sticking up for me."

"You're welcome, love."

Fiona smiled. "I don't think he'll be putting any more notes on your windscreen."

"Or anyone else's, for that matter," Partial Sue said.

Sophie shattered the feel-good moment. "Well, this is all very lovely. A bit of mother–daughter bonding over denying someone their right to freedom of speech."

"Oh, shut up, Sophie," Partial Sue snapped. "There's a difference between freedom of speech and being plain rude."

Sophie snarled her lips. "How dare you cancel me!"

"How can you be cancelled if you're still talking?" Fiona asked.

The Wicker Man had had enough and began edging backwards. When the going was good, he turned tail and dashed into the safety of his shop.

Bella had also had enough. "No one's cancelling you. Someone put a rude note on my windscreen and my mum told him off, because she's got my back."

"'S'right." Gail made sure they all knew she sided with them, and not her hideous boss.

Sophie sent her a disapproving stare. Defiantly, Gail glared back at her, stopping short of poking out her tongue.

Bella thanked them for taking the time to find the culprit, kissed her mum on the cheek and got back into her van. "Now, if you'll excuse me, I have new pitches to find and ice creams to sell."

"Where are you heading?" Partial Sue asked.

"Don't know. I'm going to follow my nose."

"Watch out for other ice-cream sellers," Daisy said.

"I will." Bella waved out of the van's window and pulled away. The ladies waved back, while Partial Sue grumbled under her breath about not getting her free ninety-nine.

Sophie turned her nose up at the three of them. "Well, I might just have to reach out to Alan, make sure you haven't traumatised the poor man simply for expressing his opinion. It would appear he and I are cut from the same cloth."

"And what cloth would that be?" Partial Sue asked. "Asbestos?"

Sophie chose to ignore the jibe. "Come on, Gail."

Gail flashed the ladies a sympathetic smile and followed her mistress back to their shop.

"What now?" asked Partial Sue.

Daisy inhaled deeply. "The killer is still out there, and so is my Bella. I think we need to go back to where this horrible business all started."

CHAPTER 9

Jed Garret was an easy man to find. He made no bones about who he was or where he lived, mostly because of what he did. The owner of Flowers For A Fiver (where customers could go online and send a bunch of flowers anywhere in the UK for a fiver) never missed a promotional opportunity. He came from the school of thought that all publicity was good publicity. In all his interviews in which he explained how he'd found a dead body in an ice-cream van outside his house, he'd shamelessly worn a T-shirt emblazoned with the web address of his company.

The ladies had read articles on several different news sites. The story never varied. However, that didn't make it reliable. The fact they were called 'news stories' was a bit of a giveaway. Like fictional stories, they had editors, and editors liked to manipulate, embellish, cut, slice and sometimes torture a story until it surrendered and confessed to something that never actually happened, all to appease those who worshipped the god of sensation. How much more sensational could a dead body in an ice-cream van be? A foolish question to ask. Shocking could always be made . . . well, more shocking. Cranking up the fear and outrage was what sold stories, got them clicked, shared and talked about. The ladies would have to unpick fact from what was sideshow reporting, which meant hearing the tale firsthand from the source. It would also help to get a sense of where the murder happened. In this case, the well-to-do parish of Mudeford.

Not to be confused with Mudeford Spit on the other side of Christchurch Harbour (home to the most expensive beach huts in the world, but that's literally another story), Mudeford village had grown out of a tiny fishing hamlet, which had expanded over the centuries to become a sought-after area to live. It boasted two waterfronts, one facing the English Channel, the other skirting the pretty fringes of Christchurch Harbour. Jed Garret lived on Avon Drive, so-called because if you drove to the end, you'd find yourself at Avon Beach, a sweet, old-fashioned stretch of sand lined with beach shops, pine trees and its fair share of fifties' concrete sea defences. However, its soft, luscious yellow sand curved its way around Christchurch Bay, past the fairytale Highcliffe Castle, all the way to Barton-On-Sea, several miles away.

The quaint seaside neighbourhood was populated by a pick and mix of arts-and-crafts homes and more modern beach house developments. Both styles of houses were bordered by high fences and box hedges to dissuade any gawping. It was posh, sedate and calm — unlike Jed Garret, who currently sat opposite them with the raw, restless energy of a man who had things to do and people to Zoom. A 24/7, always-on mentality. Definitely a people-person, he'd invited them in without the slightest hesitation when they'd showed up on his doorstep enquiring about the events of the twenty-seventh of April.

The ladies were sitting in a large and playful lounge that had so much furniture it could have doubled as a posh youth club for youngsters who ate houmous and summered in Burgundy. An eclectic mix of elegant leather Chesterfields nudged up against sleek Scandi designs. A couple of sphere-shaped chairs dangled from the ceiling, secured by hefty chains. Fiona was surprised to find that there was no flat-screen telly the size of a solar panel, but then she guessed this was the type of house that probably had its own cinema room.

Jed raked his slender fingers through his floppy chestnut hair. Although he had a babyish round face, a few flecks of grey made their presence known around his temples. Fiona would put him in his late thirties. A millennial. One of the first generations to grow up with the internet, as normal to him as radio and library cards were to them. He was an archetypal dot-com entrepreneur, and had clearly been enjoying the rewards of the digital revolution for some time.

"I love your business, by the way." Naturally, Daisy had staked claim to one of the hanging chairs, and was making the most of it, gently swinging back and forth.

Jed beamed. "Oh, thank you."

"I always use Flowers For A Fiver."

Fiona agreed, but Partial Sue remained silent. She wasn't the type to send flowers or birthday cards, unlike Daisy, who went to the other extreme. Fiona was still trying to get the glitter out of her carpet from her last birthday.

Jed seized the opportunity to give them a potted history of his business. "It's been a great success. Better than I could have ever imagined. It's weird, but you've probably heard this story before, how I came up with the name."

They all shook their heads.

He appeared mildly offended that they didn't know his origin story, perhaps believing, like a lot of entrepreneurs who thought their business was the centre of the universe, that it should be common knowledge and taught in schools. "Oh, well, with online businesses, it's all about the domain name. You've got to have a good one, something memorable. That's the key. Trouble is, all the best ones had gone. So I kept brainstorming, riffing random names and phrases. I had no idea what business I wanted to start. Just knew it needed a catchy name. Then Flowers For A Fiver popped into my head. I didn't know anything about the flower business, but the name sounded cool. So I did a domain search, and it was available, so I immediately registered it. That's how I came to dominate the flower delivery business. It was kind of accidental."

Partial Sue shook her head in disbelief. "Well, I never."

Jed Garret continued to run through the timeline of his company, the highs and the lows — though according to him there weren't any lows, just varying degrees of business highs. Fiona smiled throughout, although she really wanted to wince. His rat-a-tat delivery appeared to have no end, no full stops for taking a breath and no natural breaks for her to divert the conversation back towards the real reason they were there.

Partial Sue, being blunter than Fiona and Daisy put together, spotted the tiniest gap in his verbal motoring, and cut in. "So you're a busy man. We better not take up any more of your time."

Jed frowned momentarily. Being the big boss, perhaps he wasn't used to being interrupted. He smiled. "Not at all. I'm always busy. Busy, busy, busy. I love it, though. But running an online business, I very rarely get to chat to people in the flesh. I mean, I talk online, but it's not the same. I was just saying this the other day to a programmer . . ."

They were losing him again. He'd cajoled the conversation back round to his business. Another never-ending monologue.

Daisy, who had a more emotional stake in finding the killer, cut him off with an abruptness that took them all by surprise. "Where were you on the twenty-seventh of April?"

He was knocked off balance for a second. "Well, I was right here. I found the body."

Daisy blushed. "Oh, yes. Of course you did."

Fiona continued. "I mean, we've seen all the news stories, but we wouldn't mind hearing it firsthand, if that's all right."

Jed settled into his seat, preparing himself for the verbal journey ahead. "So, it was early Sunday morning. I'd been looking forward to the weekend. I'm divorced and it was my turn to have the kids. I picked them up from school on Friday and brought them back here. Me and my ex-wife don't get on, you see. We're not one of those couples that stay friends after they've split up. When we were together, she said I was married to my work and never had any time for them, which I guess is true. Guilty as charged. So whenever I have my kids, I want to prove her wrong. I want them to think of me as the fun one, and their mum as the dull one who makes them do boring stuff. I know that sounds bitter and childish, but she badmouths me during the week, even though I'm paying for her luxury lifestyle. If you think this house is nice you should see the one she got in the settlement. So, whenever I have the kids, I always make sure my diary's clear so I can spoil them — cinema, bowling, water park, letting them stay up late. You name it, we do it. It's a chance for me to score points against her. That's what our relationship has boiled down to. However, she was the one who started it . . ."

Fiona sensed the conversation drifting out of its lane, veering off into a lay-by, the kind where people dump their rubbish by the verge and sometimes relieve themselves. "So what happened on Sunday the twenty-seventh of April?"

"Oh, yes. That morning—"

"Can you remember what time?" Partial Sue asked.

"Not exactly. I'd say before eight o'clock. The kids were awake and pestering me. They're all like, 'Dad! Dad! There's an ice-cream van outside! Can we have ice cream for breakfast? Please! Please!' Now I'd never normally agree to them eating ice cream as their first meal of the day, but I thought, 'Yeah, why not? That will really annoy my ex-wife.' So I agreed. I was still a bit bleary-eyed, and I didn't even think about what an ice-cream van was doing here at eight o'clock in the morning or whether it would even be open. I peeked out of the window, and, sure enough, there it was, so I threw on some clothes and we went outside to have a look."

"Was it open?" Daisy asked.

"It didn't look open. I peered in through the side window to see if anyone was home, but it was difficult to see in, all covered in pictures of ice lollies and different flavours. So I went around the front to look through the windscreen. It was empty. I thought maybe the owner had popped out to use the loos by the beach, so I told my kids we'd have to wait until they came back. By now, they couldn't contain themselves and I was regretting what I'd promised and worried they'd wake up the neighbours. I tried the van's door handle, thinking that it would be locked and that would be the end of it, but it was open. I thought maybe I could nip inside, grab a couple of lollies and leave the money on the side. So that's what I did."

"How did it look?" asked Partial Sue. "Any signs of a struggle? Broken cones everywhere? Was the engine left running?"

Jed shook his head. "Engine was off and it was fairly tidy. Same outside the van. No signs of a struggle, as you put it. I had a poke around, spotted the freezer at the back. It was a big one, high-sided. I lifted up the lid and nearly had a heart attack."

"You found Kevin Masterson's dead body," Daisy said.

Jed nodded and swallowed hard. "That's right. His eyes were closed, as if he was sleeping and he was kind of curled up into a ball, like a cat. I didn't really know what to do, so I said, 'Excuse me? Excuse me? Are you okay?' When I got no response, I leaned in and prodded him. Felt for a pulse. That's when I noticed his skin was cold."

"Then what happened?" Fiona asked.

"I panicked, I'm afraid. My kids were getting impatient and had climbed into the van after me. I slammed the lid down and shooed them outside and back into the house. I told them the ice-cream van was empty and we could get some later from one of the kiosks on the beach if they were good. They were disappointed, but they did what they were told. We went back inside, and they got themselves some cereal and watched TV. I went into a different room and called the police. They turned up and taped off the street. A bit later, Forensics arrived and began setting up a tent around the van, but not before a small crowd had gathered at the end of the road and started snapping pictures on their phones. I gave a statement to DI Fincher and DS Thomas. Then later, the press interviewed me. I know what people think, that I was shamelessly wearing a T-shirt to promote my business, but that's just what I threw on when the kids woke me up. My slobbing-out clothes. I never got a chance to change. You don't really think about what you're wearing when you've just discovered a dead body outside your house."

"How are your children?" Daisy asked.

"Oh, they're fine. I didn't tell George and Emily about what had happened. I just told them someone had lost their ice-cream van and the police were trying to find the owner. They were more interested in when they were getting their ice cream than they were about the police being outside."

"And do you think it's a case of a rival ice-cream seller bumping off the competition?" Fiona asked.

Jed sighed heavily, then nodded. "It seems the most likely explanation. Whoever killed Kevin Masterson didn't secretly bury him out in the forest. They left his body where they knew it would be found, knowing it would make the headlines. As a warning to others. Stay off my patch."

This had been the official line in all the news outlets, the presumed MO of the killer. Except whoever's patch this was had proved elusive. The mysterious ice-cream rival had never been identified or arrested.

"So, the million-dollar question. Who's your usual ice-cream seller?" Fiona asked.

Jed sighed and shrugged. "Gosh, I don't know. I'm sure we have one, but I have no idea who he or she is. Before this happened, I never really took any notice. You could try asking the neighbours."

"That's a good idea," Fiona said.

The ladies thanked him for his time and spent the rest of the afternoon knocking on doors in Avon Drive and some of the neighbouring roads, posing two questions. First, they asked if anyone had seen anything suspicious on the morning of the murder. It quickly became apparent that nobody had. At that time, the attention of every homeowner certainly hadn't been on the road outside. Most people had been in their PJs, either having a lie-in or reading the paper while waiting for their tea or coffee to brew and their toast to pop up, enjoying the Sunday morning bliss of not having to get their weary bodies ready for anything.

The second question they asked prompted an equally vague response, unless you counted a great deal of umming and ahing. No one had any idea who their local ice-cream seller was or what they looked like. However, unlike the residents of Wick, the homeowners of Mudeford were convinced that they did actually have one, and went as far as to say that they had seen an ice-cream van around the area on rare occasions. A small number had even bought an ice cream from it, but no one could recall anything about the van or who'd been inside it. They couldn't say whether it was Kevin Masterson or his rival, or when this had occurred. To be fair, although ice-cream vans were garish and noisy — and although Fiona had purchased her fair share of cones — if pressed, she doubted she could recall what any of the sellers had looked like. It wasn't the sort of information that lodged in one's long-term memory, probably because whenever an ice-cream van was encountered, all attention was on the glorious dollop of dairy loveliness about to be placed in your hand, not the person placing it there. Local ice-cream sellers weren't like postal workers or milkmen — when the country had them. They weren't a familiar daily fixture, because their appearance was sporadic by nature, governed by the clemency of the weather. Not enough regular contact to forge a personal, recognisable relationship.

Daisy flopped onto a bench and fanned herself with her sun hat. The searing late afternoon had turned into an equally hot early evening. "All this talk of ice creams is making me want one. Where's an ice-cream van when you need one?"

Fiona poured water into the portable bowl for Simon Le Bon, who lapped at it greedily. "What say we call it a day and head down to the beach for a ninety-nine and a paddle?"

"Now you're talking. Followed by fish and chips," Partial Sue suggested. "I didn't get my fish and chips the other night and it's still bothering me."

Daisy made a face. "But that's the wrong way round. You can't have ice cream then fish and chips."

Fiona was reminded of the John Shuttleworth song, 'I Can't Go Back to Savoury Now', brilliantly outlining the dilemma.

"Doesn't bother me." Partial Sue shrugged. "I can eat pudding any time. You've just been brainwashed by current meal conventions."

Daisy shuddered at the mere suggestion of having her sweet first. "Well, I can't do it. I either have to have fish and chips first and then ice cream, or ice cream first then a gap until I have something savoury. I can't do it straight after. It's just not right."

Partial Sue was keen to know the finer details of this arrangement. "How big a gap are we talking?"

"At least an hour."

"An hour! I can't wait that long."

"Let's just head down there and see how we feel." Fiona knew the smell of chips often overwhelmed one's desire for anything else.

They reached a band of pine trees on a bank above the beach. Thankful for the shade, they surveyed the coastline left and right, with its pretty golden sands and placid, shallow waters.

"Well, one thing's clear to me." Partial Sue continued scanning the beach. "We need to find out whose patch this is. Process of elimination. We question other ice-cream sellers in the area. One of them's bound to have Mudeford as their patch. Or know who works it. They'll be our top suspect."

"I have one of my stupid questions." Daisy had a tendency to think all her questions were of dubious intelligence when, in reality, they were often highly insightful. "Why would Mudeford have two rival ice-cream sellers in the first place? Why fight over a patch that's already awash with ice-cream kiosks?"

Not one but two ice-cream kiosks were clearly visible and equidistant from where they stood, a third was located towards Highcliffe Castle, and Fiona knew there was a fourth out of sight, by the side of the car park, and another beyond that on the quayside near the fisherman's cottages. Yes, why indeed would anyone with an ice-cream van fight over a place already overflowing with ice cream?

CHAPTER 10

The clouds had gathered, grey and non-descript, throwing a thick, stifling blanket over the land. A muggy and uncomfortable start to the day, not helped by a sudden and uncustomary surge in donations. A constant stream of people stopped by to drop off boxes piled high with an eclectic mix of unwanted items. The shop became a heaving and hectic hot mess as people huffed and puffed, waiting to bequeath their goods, impatient to get out of there and on with the rest of their day. However, the process of receiving charitable donations couldn't be rushed, and was not unlike searching bags at airport security. Fiona had never asked if anyone had packed their donations themselves. However, their contents needed to be checked — even with the best will in the world, people would often smuggle in items the shop couldn't sell or were masquerading as something else. Just the other day, Fiona had served a lady who'd decided to buy a copy of *Dirty Dancing* for her daughter. A lovely gift idea until, on closer inspection, Fiona found that the DVD case contained the second season of *Brush Strokes*. This outlined the pitfalls of not checking items thoroughly.

The queue for accepting donations worsened when actual customers began to drift in, wanting to buy things. The ladies found themselves having to break off one queue to serve another. This was the hazard of working in a charity shop — having to deal with donations coming in and going out at the same time. Daisy called this 'having trouble at both ends'.

Finally, they were blessed with a lull. The tea came out just as Fiona finished serving the last customer — hopefully — for at least the next ten minutes. She sighed as she flopped into a chair next to Daisy.

"Where did they all come from?" asked Partial Sue. "We were rushed off our feet."

Daisy placed cups in front of her colleagues. "I blame the weather."

Partial Sue stared at her, puzzled. "What's the weather got to do with it?"

"Well, we've had a run of sunny weather. People make the most of it. Then today, they look outside, see the clouds and decide it's a getting-things-done day, chance to cross things off their to-do lists, one of which would be taking donations to the charity shop that had probably been sitting in the hallway by the door for goodness knows how long."

Daisy's logic was impeccable. Fiona hoped she had more of that kind of thinking where the Vanilla Killer was concerned. "Any overnight thoughts on our little outing yesterday?"

Daisy clung to the conclusion she'd come to last night before they'd left to go home. "I still can't understand why two ice-cream sellers would be fighting over a patch that already has so many ice-cream kiosks. It's like selling coals to penguins."

Neither Fiona nor Partial Sue had the energy to correct her.

"You're right," Partial Sue said, "it doesn't make sense. It must be the least profitable patch in the area."

Fiona had to admit the logic didn't add up, but she had more confusion to add to the conundrum. "There's something else bothering me that I couldn't get out of my mind last night. In such a quiet area, how come no one heard anything on the morning of the murder?"

Partial Sue frowned. "The homeowners told us they were either asleep, making their breakfast, or reading newspapers."

Fiona nodded. "Yes, I get that no one saw anything. But they would have heard something. Think about it. Two ice-cream sellers having a territorial dispute in the street. They must've had a hell of an argument if it led to one of them being murdered. Would've caused a right old ruckus. But, from what we gathered, nobody heard a thing. No raised voices in the street, no accusations flying about, and certainly no heat-of-the-moment scuffles that got out of hand."

Daisy supplied one explanation. "Maybe they have very good double glazing. I've heard posh houses have acoustic glass now, and those houses are dead posh."

Partial Sue had an alternative theory. "Or Kevin Masterson wasn't killed in Avon Drive. Perhaps he wasn't killed in Mudeford at all. Maybe the murderer bumped him off else-where. Did the horrible deed out of sight, down a quiet lane or somewhere similar."

Fiona liked the sound of this theory. "Where there'd be no chance of any accidental witnesses. That would certainly be a lot easier. Then Kevin Masterson's body is dumped in the freezer of his own ice-cream van and driven to Avon Close. Killer leaves it there."

"Wouldn't the engine need to be left running, to keep the body cold?" Daisy asked. "I know Bella has to keep hers going to keep the freezer on."

"Jed said the engine wasn't on," Fiona replied. "So that ice-cream van definitely wasn't there to pitch up and sell. But the freezer probably kept running on the battery and, even if it didn't, they can keep things cold for hours after they're off. Otherwise we'd have to throw food out every time there was a power cut or you had an electrician in."

"Plus, if the murderer wanted to slip away undetected, they wouldn't want to draw attention to themselves by leaving a diesel engine running," Partial Sue said. "It was no accident the Vanilla Killer chose that particular road. All those high box hedges and six-foot fences, plenty of camouflage for an escaping murderer, blocking the view of any doorbell cams or CCTV, or a homeowner who happened to glance out of their window."

Daisy still wasn't buying it. "Then why risk going to all that trouble? Transporting his body from wherever it was, driving it all the way to Mudeford and parking it in Avon Drive? Why not just leave it in that secluded place, that quiet lane or wherever it was?"

"I think we already know the answer." Partial Sue wagged her finger. "Stay off my patch or else."

Fiona and Partial Sue allowed themselves an exchange of satisfied grins, until Daisy spoiled it all. "But doesn't that put us back to square one? Why would anyone defend a patch that's already awash with ice-cream kiosks? And if that patch does belong to a certain ice-cream seller, why haven't they been arrested? I know the neighbours had no idea who their local ice-cream seller was, but surely the police should have found out by now."

Doubt, heavy like a sodden duvet left out in the rain, dampened Fiona's brief enthusiasm. She had to face facts. "Daisy, you're right. The police will have already identified and interviewed whoever had this patch."

"Unless they don't know either," Partial Sue muttered. "Like I said before, ice-cream sellers might be protecting their own. Bound by some unwritten code of silence. Or they're all in on it. Maybe Kevin Masterson had been stepping on their toes, and they all agreed to take him out, which is why no one's revealed whose patch it is."

Fiona mused on this. "That's a good theory. They've closed ranks. Kept schtum. If that's the case, we need to talk to these other ice-cream sellers in the area. See if they're covering for one of their own, or if they were all in on it."

Partial Sue cranked up the melodrama. "What if it's an ice-cream mafia!"

Daisy's lower lip trembled. "I don't like the sound of that. I hope they don't come after Bella."

Partial Sue attempted to reassure her. "Don't worry, Dais. An ice-cream mafia wouldn't leave a note on her window. It would have been a horse's head."

Both Daisy's lips now trembled and her left eye began to twitch. Fiona glared at Partial Sue for her insensitivity and attempted to calm Daisy's nerves. "That was just a movie. Besides, we're pretty convinced it was Alan who left the note on Bella's van, and, if it wasn't, then as Sue quite graphically pointed out, it's not the mafia's style to leave grumpy notes on people's windscreens."

Daisy didn't appear comforted by this in the slightest, so Fiona resorted to distracting her with an alternative angle. "Don't forget our other line of inquiry. Kevin fell out with someone. What if the Vanilla Killer was a friend or lover who made it look like a rival ice-cream seller did it to cover their tracks?"

"That's a good idea," Partial Sue said. "It would certainly explain why no rival ice-cream sellers have been arrested."

"Daisy, do you think you could track down anyone who knew Kevin?" Fiona asked.

Daisy's phone was out in a flash, thumbs a blur as she scoured the web. Gradually her expression relaxed as the digital distraction drained the worry from her face. After half an hour of searching, she became puzzled, eyebrows meeting abruptly, as if they'd had a head-on collision. They relaxed momentarily, then went back to bashing themselves together. This pattern kept repeating itself in what could only be described as ever-increasing degrees of befuddlement.

"Everything okay?" Fiona asked.

Daisy didn't look up from her screen. "That's odd."

"What is?" Partial Sue asked.

"So, Kevin Masterson's not on any social media sites. Doesn't seem to have any friends online, not that I can find. And nothing on LinkedIn."

"Social media's not everyone's cup of tea," Fiona said.

"Unless someone's deleted them all," Partial Sue added. "What about ice-cream sellers in the area? There's bound to be plenty of them."

Daisy returned to her phone, head bowed, thumbs beavering away. Half an hour later, she came up for air. "I've found all of them."

"That's a good thing, isn't it?" Partial Sue asked.

"But there are only three."

"Three!" Fiona exclaimed. "Surely there must be more than that."

"I've tried searching lots of ways," Daisy said, "and using different sites, but the same three only ever come up — the Ice Queen, Sergeant Bilcone and the Icely Brothers."

"That can't be right." Fiona decided to do her own search, as did Partial Sue. Though it took them longer, they came to the same conclusion. "You're right. There's only three. How can that be possible?"

Partial Sue sucked in air through her teeth. "Could still be an ice-cream mafia."

"Three's hardly enough for an ice-cream mafia," Fiona said. "Bit hard to intimidate someone with those kinds of numbers. But this might be a clue to something else. What if there's only three ice-cream sellers because that's the maximum the area can sustain? Any more than that and it doesn't work. Profit-wise it becomes untenable. Maybe Kevin Masterson comes along, doesn't know the etiquette, treads on a few toes, eats into their profits and these three take him out."

"But isn't that the same theory we've had all along?" Daisy asked. "Except it's three rival ice-cream sellers rather than one."

Fiona took a sip of her tea and thought on this. "Yes, but it puts a slightly different spin on things, because it would mean Kevin Masterson hadn't been doing this long. He was a newbie, which would add more weight to the theory that this is about taking out the competition."

"How would we find out if he was a newbie?" Daisy asked.

"I know." Partial Sue went back on her phone. "I can find out on one of those vehicle-check websites. You can find out all sorts of things about a car before you buy it. Make sure it's not stolen or been written off, and the number of owners it's had — not their names, just the dates when the vehicle changed hands. Do you have Bella's registration?"

Daisy swiped through the photos she'd taken of her daughter's van with its new mermaid graphics. She stopped when she found one clearly showing the number plate and called it out. A few seconds later Partial Sue baulked in her seat. "Oh, my. The person who had the van before Bella took ownership of it on the twenty-first of March this year — that must be Kevin Masterson. He'd only had it a month before he got murdered."

The theory of the three taking out the new guy suddenly became very real and very likely. Fiona pictured the trio of established ice-cream sellers joining forces, uniting to see off the new whipper-snapping interloper.

The revelation was short-lived as Bella burst through the door, hot and bothered, and ready to do some murdering of her own.

Daisy was on her feet, rushing to meet her halfway. "Bella, what's wrong?"

"I need kitchen roll, soapy water and a scrubbing brush. Fast."

Daisy, who had every conceivable kind of cleaning implement and solution stockpiled in the storeroom, enquired as to the exact nature of the hygienic emergency. "Have you had an ice-cream spillage? Slushy dribblage? Sprinkles explosion?"

Bella's face darkened. "Nope. Someone's egged my windscreen."

CHAPTER 11

They closed the shop briefly and set to work, helping Bella clean off the smeared egg and splinters of shell that clung to the glass in a sticky, smelly mess. Most of it was easy to remove, but some of it had dried on and needed a scouring pad and plenty of elbow grease. Before long, their combined efforts had the van's windscreen pristine and shiny. However, the same couldn't be said for Bella's mood, which remained as foul as the egg they'd just cleared away. So they took her inside the shop, sat her down and soothed her with tea.

Daisy's hands shook as she placed a steaming cup in front of her daughter. "There you go, love."

Fiona could tell she was attempting to put a brave face on things for Bella's sake, while inside she'd bet that Daisy was a maelstrom of panic. Her words, up until now, had been measured and calm, keeping a lid on things. Suddenly, Daisy couldn't contain them any longer, and fired off questions with the urgency of a Bren gun. "What happened? Where did this happen? Did you park down at Wick again? Was it another ice-cream seller? Why didn't you leave when you saw them? Did anyone else see them? Was it that chap Alan?"

"Mum, slow down. I don't know what this Alan bloke looks like, and I wasn't anywhere near Wick. I wasn't even selling ice creams."

"Tell us who did this and we'll pay them a visit." Partial Sue punched her fist in her palm.

Fiona interjected, before Partial Sue worked herself up into a lather. "Hold on a second. You weren't selling ice creams?"

Bella shook her head. "No, it was too overcast, so I drove into Bournemouth to have a mooch around. I left the van in a car park and, when I came back, well, you saw the state it was in. Could barely drive it with all that muck on the windscreen."

"Had any of the other cars been egged?" Fiona asked.

"No, just mine."

Daisy reached a shaky, reassuring hand across to her daughter. "Don't worry, love. We'll find out who's doing this."

"Can't really blame this on Alan," Partial Sue said. "Pelting a van with eggs doesn't seem his style, unless he used quail's eggs."

"We need to know if it was him or not." Fiona snatched up her phone. "Bella, when did this happen?"

"Well, I was only parked there for an hour. Then it took me half an hour to get here."

Fiona called Alan's Place, withholding her caller ID, and put it on speakerphone. "Oh, hello. My name is Jocasta Wells. I work for *Tatler* magazine. I was wondering if Alan was free. We're doing an article on high-end tearooms."

Fiona found that a surefire way to catch the attention of anyone on the phone was to pretend to be from a magazine, one that was tailored to the aspirations of the person she was calling.

"*Tatler* magazine?" The girl at the other end gulped. "Er, he can't come to the phone right now."

Fiona really wanted to add, *"Is that because he's out egging vans?"* But she restrained herself. "Really? He can't come to the phone for a chat with *Tatler*?"

"He's on the train to London at the moment, going to view potential new business properties. But if you give me your name and number, I can pass on the message. He wants me to text him every twenty minutes to give him an update."

Yeah, I bet he does, thought Fiona. "Okay, great. My number is . . ." Fiona hung up. "Okay, definitely not Alan, unless she's lying about where he is."

"So who's doing this?" Bella asked. "Someone who really doesn't want me selling ice creams, that's for sure."

"Unless it's just mindless vandals on this occasion," Daisy said.

Fiona shook her head. "I don't think so. Bella's van was singled out. This was someone wanting to send a message."

"Like an ice-cream mafia," Partial Sue said.

Bella became alarmed. "What ice-cream mafia?"

Fiona gave her colleague a flinty look for creating more distress when it really wasn't called for. "She's being melodramatic. We think there are three other ice-cream sellers who may or may not — we don't know yet — have joined forces to see off any newcomers."

"And who are these three?" Bella's fists clenched.

"The Ice Queen, Sergeant Bilcone and the Icely Brothers," Daisy said.

Bella may have been a lot like Daisy, going about life in a gentle but shambling way, but unlike her mother, she possessed a naturally stubborn, defiant streak. Her eyes glinted with steel. "So they think they can intimidate me with stupid notes and a few broken eggs, do they?"

Fiona attempted to buffer her justified anger. "We don't know if that's the case yet. We need to be circumspect."

"What were their names again?" Bella demanded. "I'm going to pay them a visit." She spat her words out strongly and vengefully, but her hands betrayed her. She wrung them tightly in her lap, as if they were having a wrestling match with each other. Fiona didn't doubt her resolve, but she could tell it was tempered by fear. A fear that was completely justified, but one that Bella wanted to face, nonetheless. "I can fight my own battles."

Daisy smiled sympathetically. "We know you can, love. That's not what Fiona's saying. Actually, what is it you're saying?"

Fiona continued. "It's not about fighting battles. Not at the moment, anyway. We don't know enough about these people. Let's take the softly, softly approach. We'll talk to them. Get a measure of who we're dealing with and see what they have to say."

Bella sighed and slumped in her chair. "Okay, thanks Auntie Fiona. That sounds like the smart thing to do. But, in the meantime, it's not going to put me off. I'm going to carry on selling."

Daisy flinched with worry. "Oh no, Bella. That's not a good idea. Why not take a break, lie low for a bit?"

"Lying low is what criminals do," Partial Sue said. "Bella hasn't done anything wrong."

"Exactly," Bella replied. "This is my job and no one's going to stop me." She got up to leave. "Thank you for the tea. Now I have work to do. Sun's coming out later and people will be wanting ice cream."

Daisy stood up with her, attempting to change her mind. "Oh, please, won't you reconsider? I'll worry about you."

"Mum, there's nothing to worry about. These people are too frightened to confront me. They do things when my back's turned. They're cowards."

"That's true," said Partial Sue. "Cowards."

Bella hugged her worried mum. "I'll be fine. I promise."

CHAPTER 12

They decided to pay Sergeant Bilcone a visit first, as he only lived a few minutes away in Iford, a pretty little suburb of Christchurch. Dominated by a handsome fifteenth-century stone bridge, its sturdy wide arches strode across a sluggish stretch of the River Stour.

As Bella had predicted, the monochrome sky had slunk away, leaving a warm and pleasant sunny evening.

Sergeant Bilcone's canary-yellow ice-cream van stood on a rough patch of concrete in front of a bungalow where its front garden should have been. Grass and flower beds had been brutally replaced by low-maintenance hardstanding. Not shabby by any means, but not doing anything to enhance the look of the property either.

Caricatures of Sergeant Bilko — lifted straight from the opening titles of the '50's TV sitcom — adorned the top front corners of the van, except these ones clutched ice-cream cones in one hand and saluted with the other. The van's bonnet was up and greasy tools were strewn on the ground. A fan belt still in its packaging rested on the top of an open toolbox. The person who Fiona assumed had been about to replace it was also resting in a deckchair next to it, eyes tightly shut. The effort had perhaps become too much for him and he'd taken a break, which had turned into a snooze.

Dressed only in a pair of greasy red shorts, a vest and hiking boots, he was sunning his not inconsiderable girth, and bore absolutely no resemblance to Sergeant Bilko. Thick white hair fell about his shoulders, and his face was upholstered by a thick beard, whose bristles shot out in every direction as if they were attempting to escape. Snoring deeply, he looked like Father Christmas on vacation.

The ladies stood on the pavement outside, wondering what to do, while Simon Le Bon strained on his lead to get a closer look.

Daisy whispered, "Is it rude to wake him up?"

"I wouldn't worry about that," Partial Sue whispered back. "This might be one of the people responsible for egging Bella's van."

"Well, we don't know that—"

Before Fiona could finish, Daisy took her new assertiveness for another spin. "Excuse me! Where were you on the twenty-seventh of April?"

The man started, doing that waking-up thing as if he'd just fallen from a tree. "Uh-wh—" He raised his head, eyes opening briefly, then returning to their closed position. He snorted, then sank back to sleep, like a giant slumberous submarine.

"Quick, he's going under again." Partial Sue dashed onto his property, followed by Fiona and Daisy, prodding him verbally to prevent him diving any deeper. "Hello, hello, hello!"

Two brown eyes slowly opened, squinting at first against the sunlight, then opening fully. He regarded the three women standing in front of him curiously, and dozily smacked his lips a few times. "Sorry, I'm not a believer. I like birthdays and Christmas too much, so I won't require a copy of the *Watchtower* today."

"We're not Jehovah's witnesses," Fiona said.

He sat up. "Oh, you're not?"

"No, we're detectives. We'd like to ask you some questions about Kevin Masterson."

Still a tad bewildered from being woken up, he glanced down at his feet, as if the answer might be there. "Kevin Masterson. Kevin Masterson."

Simon Le Bon distracted him, wagging his tail and wanting to make friends. The man responded by giving him a very welcome — judging by the blissful look on Simon's face — rub behind the ears.

Fiona reminded him of the reason they were there. "He was murdered by the Vanilla Killer."

"Oh, yes. I remember. Terrible, that was."

"Sorry, can I ask your name?" Fiona said. "I'm assuming it's not Sergeant Bilcone."

"No," he smiled. "My name's actually Tom."

"Are you a big *Sgt. Bilko* fan?" asked Partial Sue.

"That was the chap who owned the van before me. I mean, I don't mind it, but I kept the name. I think it's a good one."

He got to his feet and extended a greasy hand, then withdrew it when he realised how grimy it was. Instinctively, Daisy whipped out a wet wipe and handed it to him, which he put to good use, turning it filthy black in seconds. He stuffed the spent wipe in his pocket. "Right, what can I do for you?"

"Kevin Masterson, we're investigating his murder."

"Oh, yes. That's right. Murder." He made light of it, his hands waving in a gesture of faux innocence. "It wasn't me, I swear."

Fiona nor the others saw the funny side of this.

"Sorry," he said.

Daisy spoke plainly. "Where were you on the twenty-seventh of April?"

Tom shook his head, and kept repeating himself. "Twenty-seventh of April. Twenty-seventh of April. Oh, yes. That was the day of the murder. I remember. Police interviewed me. I was up bright and early, pressure-washing my van at the garage. Got down there at seven in the morning. Have to be early on a Sunday. World and his wife want to clean their cars. Plus, it takes ages to wash it."

"Were you scared by his murder?" Fiona said. "Worried for your own safety?"

"Shocked is more the word. But not scared. Should I be?" Tom asked innocently.

"Well, he was a fellow ice-cream seller," Daisy said. "Weren't you worried you'd be next?"

"Not really. I mean, if a fisherman gets murdered do all fishermen suddenly become frightened for their lives? Who's to say he wasn't murdered for some other reason?"

Fiona looked at the others. He made a good point. One they would have to keep an open mind about. Although she couldn't help thinking that a killer who'd gone to the trouble of squeezing Kevin Masterson into a freezer was trying to send a message.

"Can we ask about patches?" Fiona asked.

He joked again. "Nicotine patches?"

"Ice-cream sellers' patches."

"Oh, yes, I have my patches — Springbourne, Littledown, Fairmile and my own neighbourhood here in Iford. We're very respectful of one another's patches in ice-cream circles. We have a strict code — no Venn diagrams." He grinned.

"Venn diagrams?" Daisy asked.

"No overlapping on other people's areas. Big no-no."

"So everyone knows their place," Partial Sue said.

"Absolutely."

"So which was Kevin Masterson's patch or patches?" Fiona asked.

"I have no idea. Like I said, I didn't know him. Never heard of him until I saw the story in the news."

There was a strong possibility he was telling the truth. Kevin Masterson had taken possession of his van at the end of March. Winter had been coming to an end, but summer was still a long way off — not exactly prime ice-cream-selling weather. It was unlikely their paths would have crossed before Kevin met his end.

"Which ice-cream seller has Mudeford as their patch?" Daisy asked.

Tom brightened. "Ah, now that I can help you with. It's no one's. We call it Switzerland, because it's neutral. No point selling there because there are too many ice-cream kiosks. Waste of time."

Fiona and Partial Sue sent Daisy a small congratulatory sideways glance. Her theory had been spot on.

Tom continued. "I mean, people have tried selling there, me included. You might make a few bob now and again, but nothing like the other patches where there aren't ice-cream kiosks to compete with."

"So he wasn't killed as a warning — stay out of Mudeford or else?" Fiona asked.

"Well, there'd be no point."

"What if he'd been on another ice-cream seller's patch, somewhere else, and they'd got annoyed? Killed him and then dumped his body there, as a warning to others."

Tom winced. "Sounds a bit extreme to me."

"What if a few ice-cream sellers joined forces to get rid of the newbie?" Partial Sue eyed him intensely to see how he reacted.

Tom ruffled his thick beard with his equally thick fingers, then slowly shook his head. "I can't see it myself. Maybe in the past, before my time, when things were more competitive, but not nowadays."

"How so?" Fiona asked.

"Well, there's not many of us. We're a dying breed. Did you know, in the fifties, there used to be twenty thousand ice-cream vans in the country? Now there are less than five thousand. We get smaller in number each year. It's not other ice-cream sellers that're the problem. Every corner shop sells ice cream, even the petrol stations. It's mostly rising costs that are the enemy. Price of fuel and stock."

"Who supplies you with ice cream?" Fiona asked.

"Somerford. Unless you want to sell cheap muck. We all use them because they haven't hiked up their prices like everyone else. Can't say the same for fuel. Every time it goes up, our profits go down. Gets harder and harder to make ends meet, so we all have to supplement our income in other ways."

"Like what?" Daisy asked.

"Take a guess." He chuckled heartily and gestured to his face, specifically his beard.

"Playing Father Christmas," Daisy said.

"Correct!" He shouted as if he were a game-show host.

"Really?" Daisy gushed affectionately. "I bet you make a great Father Christmas."

Tom gave a bow. "Why, thank you. Suits me just fine. Not because of how I look, but because it gives me work when it's cold and no one's buying ice cream. I'm in high demand during the festive season, I can tell you, especially being an RBS."

"Royal Bank of Scotland?" Partial Sue asked.

"Real-beard Santa." He proudly tugged his bristles. "Not one of these fakers who wear a clip-on. Can't beat the real thing. Means I can charge more."

"So where do you perform?" Fiona didn't know if that was the correct term for someone who impersonated Santa.

"Used to be department stores, but they've all gone. It's mostly garden centres now, but I do a stint around the New Forest pubs at lunchtime Christmas Eve and Christmas Day. That's my favourite. Nice little earner too."

Daisy gushed. "Oh, that sounds lovely."

"How do you get from pub to pub? By car? Doesn't that spoil the spectacle?" Partial Sue was keen for more details.

"Oh, no." He smiled. "I ride on a horse and cart with presents in the back for the kids. It's only Mars selection packs, but they love it."

Partial Sue's eyes lit up brighter than a pair of headlights. "What sort of horse?"

"Obviously, it'd be better if it were a couple of reindeer, but no one has any tame ones around here, so we use a heavy horse. A shire." Tom had said the magic word.

"A shire horse." Partial Sue beamed. "Oh, I'd like to see that. I am partial to a shire horse myself."

Tom threw his arms wide and bellowed louder than Brian Blessed. "Then the three of you should come along this Christmas! It'll be wonderful to see you!" His tone changed to become more cautionary. "But you'll need to hurry. Those New Forest pubs get booked up quickly."

Daisy and Partial Sue needed no further encouragement and had their phones out, desperate to make a booking in one of the pubs where Tom made his festive rounds. Fiona joined in, but with more than a degree of cynicism, conscious that Tom had sidetracked them with his jolly Santa act. But also because talk of Christmas in the middle of summer made Fiona's skin crawl, especially when she'd just applied sun cream to said skin. It just wasn't right. She adored Christmas as much as her colleagues, loved talking about it and planning for it, but as a rule, never before the clocks had gone back.

"May I recommend The Oak," Tom said. "Just outside Lyndhurst. That's the most Christmassy of all the New Forest pubs."

"Oh, yes!" Partial Sue jittered excitedly. "That's a lovely pub."

Daisy had their website up on her phone. "They've still got tables available for Christmas Eve and Christmas Day. How lucky."

"That's because it's only July," Fiona muttered.

"Shall I book it?" Daisy asked.

"Do it, Dais." Partial Sue rubbed her hands gleefully.

"Why not," Fiona said through gritted teeth.

Daisy hit the booking button. "Done!"

Tom moved closer, speaking conspiratorially. "And between you and me, I often have a few selection packs left over, which might find their way into the hands of three very charming ladies." He winked.

Daisy and Partial Sue giggled excitedly at the prospect of Christmas dinner, meeting Santa and free festive chocolate. Fiona returned the conversation to more serious matters. "Coming back to the dwindling numbers of ice-cream sellers, is that why we could only find three of you online?"

Tom thought for a moment and frowned. "I'd say so. There's plenty of room out there for everyone. So, if you're looking for the murderer, I don't think it's going to be an annoyed ice-cream seller. There's not enough money in it, hence why we all have second jobs."

Daisy winced, probably wondering if it was worth Bella pursuing a career selling ice creams if she would have to supplement it with something else.

"What about people leaving notes on your van?" Fiona asked.

"Oh, I've had plenty of them, and people giving me the verbals. Don't like my chimes or me leaving my engine ticking over. Stuff those killjoys! But I wouldn't say it led to murder. I just move somewhere else until I find somewhere more welcoming. You know, you should talk to Claire, Jacob and Benjamin." He began thumbing his phone.

"Who are they?" asked Fiona.

"My fellow ice-cream sellers. Claire is the Ice Queen and Jacob and Benjamin are the Icely Brothers."

"Oh, that's where we were heading next," Partial Sue said.

"I'll just text them to say you're on your way."

"No need to do that." Fiona didn't want them being tipped off that three lady detectives were coming to question them, giving them time to prepare and get any stories straight — if they needed to.

"Oops, sorry." Tom smiled apologetically. "Message has gone." His phoned pinged with a response almost immediately. He examined it. "Oh, that's a spot of luck. Claire's working just around the corner. About to finish up. You can catch her if you're quick."

"I thought this was your patch," Fiona said.

"It is, but she's not selling ice creams. She's supplementing her income."

"Doing what?"

"If I told you, it would spoil the surprise."

CHAPTER 13

Fiona grumbled as they made the short walk to catch Claire the Ice Queen, doing whatever it was she was doing. Tom had taken great pleasure in refusing to tell them, which had only heightened their curiosity.

"He's hiding something, I can tell," Fiona grumbled.

"I really liked him," Daisy smiled.

"Me too," Partial Sue added.

Fiona didn't like how quickly Tom had bewitched her two colleagues, turning them misty-eyed with the promise of Christmas dinners in the forest, shire horses and Mars selection packs. Were they that easily swayed? Or was Fiona being far too cynical?

"He had an alibi for the time of the murder," Daisy pointed out.

"Well, strictly speaking," Partial Sue said, "we don't exactly know when Kevin Masterson was murdered, only when his body was discovered. But the police were satisfied with Tom's alibi. What makes you think he's hiding something?"

"Wasn't it obvious?" Fiona asked.

Her question was met with a pair of blank stares.

Fiona sighed. "Didn't you notice how quick he was to tip-off his fellow ice-cream sellers that we were on our way? He's robbed us of our element of surprise."

Daisy bit her lip self-consciously.

Partial Sue's mouth dropped open. "Oh, jeez. I didn't even notice."

Daisy piped up, eager to defend their lack of vigilance. "But, if he was hiding something, he didn't seem that flustered or bothered about being questioned."

"Yes, but if he's a Santa impersonator, he's going to be a good actor," Fiona said.

Partial Sue snorted derisively. "I'm not sure playing Santa counts as acting."

"True, but I still think he's hiding something. I don't like it when people are too nice. Makes me even more suspicious of them."

"Well, let's see what this Claire is like," Partial Sue said. "Maybe she'll shed some light on things."

They walked in silence, apart from the chuntering of Simon Le Bon, who was attempting to stretch his lead to its limits, urging them forward, beckoned on by new smells. As they rounded the corner, they came across an ice-cream van halfway down the road. Pale blue with a repeating icicle pattern around the top, it was parked outside a bungalow with balloons tied to its fence posts.

"That'll be the Ice Queen's van," Partial Sue said.

"Where's that music coming from?" Daisy asked.

The first few bars of a pleasing yet melancholic tune drifted over the warm air towards them. Played on piano, it was eerily familiar, yet tantalisingly just out of reach of Fiona's recognition. "I'm sure I've heard it before."

A sweet female voice began singing live, accompanying the lonely piano chords.

"I know what that is," Daisy said. "That's 'Let It Go' from *Frozen*. I love *Frozen*."

"Who doesn't?" Partial Sue asked.

Their pace quickened towards the source of the music originating from the balloon-festooned bungalow. They slowed as the front garden came into view. A five-year-old's birthday party celebration was in full swing, judging by the inflatable number fives tethered to garden furniture. A young woman dressed as Elsa, with white-blonde hair and a shimmering aqua-blue satin gown, was belting out the tune to a backing track from a small portable speaker. A gaggle of enrapt five-year-olds, also dressed as Elsa, bounced, twirled and swished in front of her with abandon. They knew every word and were singing their little hearts out.

Fiona couldn't help being moved by the sheer undiluted joy on their faces. "That must be Claire the Ice Queen."

"She's good, isn't she?" Daisy gushed. "She's not even using a microphone."

Claire seemed to be enjoying herself as much as her audience, singing with the virtuosity and conviction of a seasoned West End performer.

Daisy and Partial Sue wanted to cross over the road, desperate to get closer, but Fiona held them back. She already felt uncomfortable about gawping at a children's birthday party. Moving nearer would certainly not be appropriate. However, she felt slightly better when a couple of other passers-by stopped to listen. A few neighbours also came out to hear Claire's stunning performance, then several more until she had quite an audience.

Fiona found herself humming along to the irresistible tune, as did Partial Sue. Daisy, however, not content with merely humming, sang along and, of course, like the little girls in the garden, knew each and every word. The music escalated to a breathtaking high. Claire's voice soared, gaining in strength and volume. As she reached the crescendo, she thrust out both arms. Silvery streamers fired from her hands, like shards of ice. The little girls squealed with delight, magic occurring before their eyes, whipping them up into even more of a frenzy.

When the song had finished, the ladies clapped, joined by everyone who'd stopped to listen. The little girls thronged around Claire as if she were the real animated Elsa brought to life. Staying in character, she heartily praised each one of them for their marvellous singing, then unfastened the streamers from her wrists and gave them to one child, who Fiona presumed was the birthday girl. She immediately ran around the garden with them above her head, chased by the others, all squealing with delight. Her parents then announced it was time to blow out the candles on the cake. The maelstrom of tiny Elsas quickly diverted inside, giving Claire a chance to pack up her things and carry them over to her ice-cream van.

The ladies hurried across the road to catch her before she left. On closer inspection, Claire's hair was real, not a wig as Fiona had first suspected. Perhaps, like Tom's Santa gig, a real white-haired Elsa could charge more than a bewigged one.

Daisy was first to congratulate her. "That was amazing. It sounded just like the film."

Claire smiled self-consciously but wouldn't catch her eye. "Oh, thank you." Still panting from her exertions, her voice sounded husky. "It's usually better, but I've got a bit of a sore throat."

"Really?" asked Partial Sue. "We'd never have guessed."

"Those little girls are never going to forget that," Fiona said. "You've given them a great memory. You should be on stage."

"That's very kind of you." Claire kept her gaze low, concentrating on loading the portable speaker into the cab. She was a lot less sure of herself out of character. "I don't think I'd be good enough for that."

"Of course you would," Daisy said.

Claire dismissed this with an uncertain smile. "Five-year-olds are a lot easier to please than a theatre full of adults."

"Nonsense. You'd be a hit, I'm sure," Partial Sue said.

Fiona decided to broach the subject of the Vanilla Killer. "I believe Tom or Sergeant Bilcone, as he's known, texted you about us."

If Claire had been awkward before, she now appeared as if she desperately wanted to be somewhere else. She swallowed hard. "Er, yes. I got his message just before I started singing."

"Do you mind if we ask you some questions?"

Claire nodded her head, but her eyes didn't look as if they agreed.

"Can I ask where you were on the morning of the twenty-seventh of April?" Daisy asked.

"Erm, I was at my mum's all weekend."

"Is she local?" asked Fiona.

Claire shook her head. "She lives in Southampton."

"Did you know Kevin Masterson?" Fiona asked.

She shook her head.

"Do you know which was his patch?"

She shook her head.

"Which are your regular patches?"

"Burton, Purewell and Highcliffe," she answered in a small voice.

"Have you ever had any altercations with any other ice-cream sellers?"

She shook her head.

"Anyone said anything nasty to you?" Fiona asked.

"Left any rude notes on your van?" Daisy added.

Claire shook her head.

"Is there an ice-cream mafia around here?" Partial Sue asked.

Claire shook her head again.

Fiona, Daisy and Partial Sue fired more questions at her, including the same ones they'd asked Tom. Each one was met with a shake of the head or monosyllabic answer. No matter what angle they took, or how they phrased or rephrased the question, the Ice Queen, despite the song she'd just sung, wasn't letting anything go.

CHAPTER 14

Partial Sue hunched over the wheel, grumbling as they sat in thick, wearisome traffic — rush hour, combined with people eager to get outside and enjoy the fine evening after the dull, monochromatic start. Fiona hated forcing them to sit in grid-locked traffic, but she wanted to strike while the iron was hot and question the Icely Brothers sooner rather than later.

"How far is it?" Daisy asked.

"They're in West Parley." Partial Sue moaned. "Going to take for ever. We have to go past the airport. Road's always chocka at this time."

Fiona chose not to bite, instead opting to use the time to focus on the people they'd just questioned. "You know, it strikes me that Tom and Claire are very similar."

"Really?" Partial Sue asked. "They're like chalk and cheese. Tom's jolly and affable, and Claire's the opposite."

"Yes, I get that, but I think they were both hiding something, covering it up. Claire was more obvious about it. Tom was overdoing it with his cheerfulness."

"But we don't know these people," Daisy said. "Maybe that's just how they are. Tom had an alibi and so did Claire. She was in Southampton."

Fiona muttered cynically. "We'd need to question her mum, and even if she did back up her story, Southampton's not that far away. Early Sunday morning you could get down here in three-quarters of an hour. Plenty of time to commit murder. But at the very least, I think Claire was definitely frightened of something. Tom too."

"Claire, maybe," Daisy said. "But Tom seemed so jolly."

"Fear manifests itself in different ways," Fiona said. "Someone shy like Claire may clam up completely, while extroverts like Tom cover it up with banter. Become more verbose."

"Okay," Partial Sue said. "So do you think they murdered Kevin Masterson?"

"Not sure. I haven't got any evidence. It's just a hunch. But something's going on with the pair of them."

Partial Sue ground the gearstick back down into first, forcing the car to lurch forward. "Well, I suppose it's a good job we're paying the Icely Brothers a visit next. If they start acting sheepish, we'll know something's definitely up."

The car nudged its way along the never-ending road, curling around Bournemouth Airport. Daisy gazed out of the window at the modest-sized passenger planes parked beside the terminal. "I love going past the airport. Always reminds me of holidays."

"Me too," Fiona said. "You know, they've started doing flights to Venice."

Daisy's eyes glistened. "Have they? I'd love to go. So romantic."

"Oh, it's amazing. Most beautiful city on earth," Fiona said.

"Maybe we could solve a murder mystery there," Daisy cooed. "Like Hercule Parrot."

"You mean Hercule Poirot." Fiona became enrapt by the idea. "But yes, imagine following clues down labyrinthine streets, drifting lazily along canals and wandering into grand medieval piazzas."

The dreamy image was shattered by Partial Sue. "Chance would be a fine thing. I've heard you can't move for tourists. Bit like being in this traffic jam."

Eventually the cars thinned out and the ladies found themselves in the cul-de-sac that the Icely Brothers, Benjamin and Jacob, called home. Their van was parked out on the road and was unlike any ice-cream van they'd encountered before. No ubiquitous transit van for these guys. This was a classic American Dodge, going by the badge on the bonnet. It reminded Fiona of the A-Team van, except rather than black with a sharp red strip along the side, this was a more mellow affair, painted in brown tones with graduating beige horizontal stripes, giving it a distinctly seventies feel. Completing the theme, the iconic 'Summer Breeze' by the Isley Brothers (where their play-on-words name undoubtedly originated) blared out of the vehicle.

After the ladies had parked up, they headed around the back of the van and found its two rear doors wide open. Like Bella's, the large freezer dominated the back space up to waist height, except in this instance it doubled as a DJ booth with record decks resting on top. Two hefty built-in speakers were mounted on either side, blasting the soul classic into the balmy air, the perfect accompaniment for the weather.

Jacob, or perhaps it was Benjamin, stood over the decks, headphones on, concentrating on cuing up the next record. Lost in the music, he didn't notice the three ladies and one small dog standing in front the van's open doors.

"The music's loud, isn't it?" Daisy remarked.

Partial Sue cupped a hand to her ear. "Sorry?"

"She said it's quite loud." Fiona had to mouth her words, as she had no chance of competing with the volume, which could've drowned out even Claire's rousing voice. Though she adored the sublime song, she couldn't help wondering what the neighbours felt about this acoustic assault.

Another chap appeared from out of a nearby house, dressed in baggy combat shorts and an equally baggy vest, cradling a stack of vinyl LPs in his arms. He gave the ladies a warm, friendly smile, then produced an ear-splitting whistle to his partner on the decks, who glanced up and immediately killed the music. "You must be the detectives Tom texted us about. I'm Benjamin." His voice was rich and Caribbean. He put the LPs down and offered them each a fist bump.

Jacob climbed out of the van and joined him. "Sorry about that. I was miles away." Softly spoken, he had a very slight Indian lilt. "We've got a gig tonight. It's our little sideline. I was just warming up the decks."

"That's okay." Fiona introduced herself and her colleagues. "We were hoping to ask you some questions about Keven Masterson's death. We've just spoken to Claire the Ice Queen."

"We heard her singing," Daisy said.

"Oh, man. That girl's got one helluva voice on her," Benjamin said.

"We've been trying to get her to lay down a track with us," Jacob added. "She never wants to know. Girl's got no confidence."

"And yet so talented," Daisy said.

"I know, right?" Benjamin replied. "Such a waste. Anyways, you want to know about Kevin Masterson's murder."

The ladies nodded simultaneously.

Benjamin shrugged. "Sorry, ladies. We have no idea. Been through it with that police detective, the one whose wages goes on her threads. She has got some fine clothes."

"DI Fincher?" Fiona asked.

Benjamin nodded. "Can't say the same about her gym-bunny partner. Although he has got a good set of guns on him."

Daisy's eyes narrowed. "I didn't think they were allowed to carry guns."

"Guns are slang for biceps," Partial Sue said.

"Oh." Daisy thought for a moment. "Is that because guns are also called firearms, and your biceps are on your arms?"

Benjamin's perma-smile dropped at this revelation. "You know, I've never thought of it like that."

"Where were you on the twenty-seventh of April?" This time Daisy asked rather than demanded, although her face hadn't lost any of its seriousness.

"Like we told the police," Jacob replied, "we were in London. At a music festival, all weekend.

"Were you DJing?" Partial Sue asked.

"Yep, at the Camden Soul Man festival." Benjamin pulled out his phone and found the website. He showed it to the three ladies. It still advertised this year's lineup with the Icely Brothers appearing in the afternoon, both on Saturday and Sunday. "We've been doing it for the past five years, slowly creeping up the billing."

Fiona steered the conversation back to Kevin Masterson. "How did you feel, knowing that another ice-cream seller had died?"

"Well, nothing, really," Jacob said. "I know that sounds harsh, but we didn't know him."

Benjamin nodded in agreement.

"Do you have any idea who could have done this?" Fiona asked.

"Like Jacob said, we didn't know him," Benjamin replied. "Much less who would've had it in for him."

"You think someone had it in for him?" Partial Sue asked.

Jacob nodded. "I suppose. I mean, why else would he have been killed?"

"Could it have been another ice-cream seller or sellers?" Partial Sue asked. "I know there are only three of you around here."

Benjamin stared at them. "Wait, Tom and Claire didn't tell you?"

"Tell us what?"

Benjamin shook his head dismissively. "Those two are too nice for their own good. Worried about trashing other people."

Jacob smiled cheekily. "Whereas we don't care about that."

"Care about what?" Fiona asked.

Benjamin made a fist to press home his point. "We are totally legit."

Fiona thought this was more slang, meaning they were good at what they did. "Er, yes. I'm sure you are. Er, totally legit."

93

"Nah, you don't get it," Jacob said.

Benjamin folded his arms. "We're legit, as in we pay our dues. Officially registered as street traders with the local council. So are Tom and Claire. We're all licensed to sell ice cream. The real deal."

"Didn't you think it was weird that there are only three ice-cream vans in this area?" Jacob asked.

"Yeah, we did a bit," Partial Sue said.

"Bet you thought there would be more ice-cream vans than that."

Fiona nodded. "We did."

"Well, there are," Benjamin explained. "Plenty more, except they're unlicensed. Doing it on the sly. That's why you can't find them online. They keep it on the down-low. Hide their vans in garages and only take them out when the weather's hot, to make a bit of tax-free cash."

"Do you know who they are?"

"No, but I definitely wouldn't buy an ice cream from them. They don't follow hygiene rules. Have freezers that are on the blink, and don't keep the stock cold enough. Well dodgy."

"I don't like the sound of them." Daisy trembled, clearly worried for the safety of her daughter.

"Was Kevin Masterson registered?" Fiona asked.

"I have no idea, but that would be a good place to start. You could look it up on the local council website. I think Environmental Health lists all legitimate traders."

Before he'd finished speaking, Daisy had her phone out, delving into council records.

"Do they annoy you, these unlicensed ice-cream sellers?" Fiona asked.

Benjamin scowled. "We pay for the right to sell our ice creams, and they don't. We tell them straight to their face if we ever come across them. But I know where you're going with this. We wouldn't get violent and kill someone just because they didn't have a licence. That's a bit extreme. Not

94

sure anyone would do that. However, like I said to those two coppers at the time, if I was looking for Kevin Masterson's killer, that's where I'd start."

"Do you know where we can find these unlicensed ice-cream sellers?" asked Fiona.

"No, they're unpredictable. They pop up when the weather's good, in nice places, then disappear just as fast."

Daisy peered up from her screen, her research complete. "Kevin Masterson was a registered street trader."

Fiona didn't know how this helped, whether it was a good thing or a bad thing, but they needed to find out.

CHAPTER 15

The following morning, all they could talk about was Kevin Masterson's legitimacy and what it meant for the murder case. Did it point the finger at ice-cream sellers who possessed a licence, or the ones who didn't? The debate had been raging for hours.

Fiona made the case for the latter. "Dodgy ice-cream sellers aren't going to be bothered about Kevin Masterson selling ice creams. If they're not bothered about getting a street-trader's licence, why would they bother about him?"

"You've answered your own question," Partial Sue said. "Because they're dodgy. They don't play by the rules."

"But what reason would they have to get rid of him?"

"Because he was muscling in. More competition."

"But the number of ice-cream sellers has dropped," Daisy said. "Plenty of room for everyone. That's what Tom said."

Partial Sue waved her mug around to make her point, nearly sloshing tea everywhere. "Yes, plenty of room for registered ice-cream sellers. There are only three of them, but not these dodgy ones. Who knows how many there are? Could be hundreds. Registered or unregistered, they're not going to be happy about another ice-cream seller coming on the scene, taking a slice of an ever-decreasing cake."

Daisy tittered. "I suppose it would be a baked Alaska."

Fiona was surprised at how chipper she was, considering all this talk of ice-cream sellers taking out newbies — which would put Bella squarely in the firing line.

Partial Sue ignored the cakey joke and continued. "It could be either side who took his life. Or all of them working together. Mafias are made up of legitimate businesses as well as shady ones."

Fiona had a different spin on things. "But didn't you think it was odd, how quickly Jacob and Benjamin were to take the focus off themselves and point the finger at these unlicensed sellers? Implying that the murderer was one of them."

"Well, I wouldn't go that far," Partial Sue frowned. "They just said that's where we should start looking. Plus, like Tom and Claire, they all had solid alibis. They were at a music festival."

Fiona scoffed. "The murder was committed early Sunday morning. They weren't on until the afternoon. Plenty of time for one or both of them to nip down here, kill Kevin Masterson, then nip back again. Same with Claire. And as for Tom, he was at a garage, cleaning his van. We don't know the time of Kevin Masterson's death. Who's to say he didn't kill him before that, leave his body in Mudeford, then clean his van in front of the garage's CCTV, cementing his whereabouts? Maybe he wanted to clean his van to get rid of the evidence because he'd had a body in it. And I thought someone with all those tools and who does their own van repairs would at least have his own pressure washer."

"Whether he owns a pressure washer or not," Partial Sue replied, "it wouldn't get rid of DNA. I don't pretend to know how this works or fits together, but we need to track down these back-street ice-cream sellers and question them. Just to be sure."

"So how do we find them?" Fiona asked.

"I don't know. They don't want to be found, which puts us at a distinct disadvantage. Do you have any ideas, Daisy?"

"I don't think it's them," Daisy said.

Fiona stared at her. "What, you think it's Claire, Tom and the Icely Brothers?"

"I don't think it's them either."

Fiona gulped, not hiding her surprise. With an emotional stake in this investigation, namely Bella's safety, she'd assumed Daisy would want these illegitimate sellers tracked down as a priority. "Then who do you think did this?"

"I don't know. But Kevin Masterson was new to all this. Hadn't even had his van for a month. He got it at the end of March, when it was still cold weather. I can understand a feud with another ice-cream seller in the middle of summer, when the stakes are high, but not at that time of the year, when no one's buying ice creams. Well, I know I wasn't. I was in a winter coat and drinking hot chocolate, and I'm guessing everyone else was too. There'd be no chance of ice-cream pitch rivalry because no other vans would be out on the road."

Partial Sue had a counterargument for this. "Maybe they'd got wind of him another way. Saw his name pop up on the council's approved list, decided to snuff him out before he got going."

"That's very possible," Fiona said, "but then that would point the finger at legitimate sellers — Tom, Claire and the Icely Brothers."

"Why just them?" Partial Sue asked. "Why wouldn't it point the finger at unregistered ice-cream sellers?"

"Because if they have a cavalier approach to selling ice creams, would they really be monitoring council websites, and be bothered about a new licensed seller appearing on the scene?"

Partial Sue shrugged. "Unless it's as simple as getting rid of the extra competition."

And with that the argument had come full circle again. The roundabout of theories spun several more times until Fiona decided she'd had enough. "Okay, this isn't getting us anywhere. But I do agree we need to question these unlicensed sellers, and I think there's only one way to do that. We have to scout for them. Wait until the weekend, trawl the beauty spots, the nice places people go when it's hot. Dodgy ice-cream sellers are bound to be there too."

Partial Sue frowned. "That could take ages."

"I can't think of any other way."

Daisy grinned contently. "Well, it'll be a nice treat. Gives us an excuse to buy plenty of ice creams."

"Now there's a silver lining to an investigation if ever I've heard one," Fiona said.

CHAPTER 16

Sunday didn't disappoint. With bright, blinding sunshine, the cooling easterly had returned to create another Goldilocks day. Not too hot, not too cold, but just right for a jolly in the New Forest with its shifting landscapes of copper heathland, wild-pony-strewn meadows and ancient woodlands. The narrow forest roads thronged with cars, loaded up and ready for picnics under mighty oaks or beside gentle streams, or perhaps a lingering lunchtime in the garden of a thatched pub. However, Partial Sue's car was probably the only one on these meandering B roads with the more sober intention of tracking down ice-cream vans without the correct documentation.

Fiona had prepared an itinerary, an essential document for the day's activities. The forest was peppered with gravelly car parks — prime spots for illegitimate ice-cream vans to ply their trade to weary walkers. A plan of action was essential if they were to hit each one and avoid driving around aimlessly.

Fiona stared out of the window at the glorious panoply of trees scrolling past. "How far to Rufus Stone?"

"Only a couple more minutes," Partial Sue replied.

Rufus Stone was the first stop on the itinerary. Located in the far northeast corner of the forest, it made sense to start there and work their way back. It was also a big draw for visitors, which would logically make it the most likely place for an illegitimate ice-cream van to set up shop. This was due to its dark history — William the Conqueror's son, nicknamed Rufus, the then king of England, died there in a hunting accident. Or had he been murdered? No one was quite sure. Well, apart from Partial Sue. "He was bumped off. No doubt about it."

"How do you know that?" Daisy asked. The ladies couldn't help getting into a murder-mystery debate, especially a cold case involving a monarch from the Middle Ages.

"Because I've looked at the facts. Big hunting party goes out for the day. Rufus and Sir Walter Tyrrell get separated from the main group. Tyrrell fires an arrow at a deer, but it misses and bounces off a tree, killing King Rufus. An arrow bouncing off a tree? I ask you! That's the worst excuse since 'the dog ate my homework'. Last time I checked, arrows have pointy bits that're very good at sticking in trees, they don't bounce off them. Maybe I could believe it if it weren't for the fact that Tyrrell was one of the best archers in the country. He'd obviously been picked to be the assassin. Once Rufus breathed his last, Tyrrell was never seen again. Oh, apart from stopping to have his horse reshod with the horseshoes pointing backwards to throw off any pursuers. I also submit to the jury that everyone hated Rufus, nobles and peasants alike, which is why his body lay dead on the forest floor, unclaimed for days. He was so unpopular that they did away with him. Case closed."

"I have to admit, that's compelling evidence," Fiona said.

Daisy disagreed. "I don't know. Maybe Tyrrell got scared because he thought no one would believe him."

"Also true," Fiona said.

Partial Sue had a rebuttal — of course she did. "Yet Rufus's brother Henry was crowned almost immediately after the burial as King Henry the First. That's a conspiracy, I tell you."

"Yeah, but you know what kings were like back then," Fiona said. "Probably making a grab for power, seizing the opportunity."

Daisy veered off the subject. "Didn't Tyrrell used to be the name of John Lewis's own-brand products? I wonder if that's where they got the name from."

Partial Sue snorted. "What, they named their brand after a murderous king-slayer?"

"I think Tyrrells were a subsidiary of John Lewis," Fiona said.

"I do like their crisps," Daisy said. "Especially the vegetable ones."

"I think that's a different brand," Fiona pointed out.

"Aren't all crisps vegetable?" Partial Sue asked. "I've never come across meat crisps. Although, thinly sliced, fried meat in a bag would make a great snack food."

"These ones are made of beetroot and parsnips," Daisy explained. "As opposed to potato. Mmm, I could eat some right now."

Their little medieval murder-mystery debate, which had somehow taken an improbable segue into artisan crisps, had to wait. As they approached Rufus Stone, their attention was diverted from the black iron-clad monument marking the fateful spot, to the gravel-strewn car park beyond. At the entrance, tucked in beside the verge, a man was selling ice creams from a bright-pink van. And doing a hearty trade, judging by the queue snaking away from its serving window and onto the grass.

"Bingo," Fiona cried.

Partial Sue gasped. "An unlicensed ice-cream seller in the wild!"

"Let's hope so," Daisy said.

Partial Sue nearly slid the car sideways into the car park, its tyres crunching deliciously on the gravel as she searched for a space. They were lucky to find one. This was prime picnic real estate — a site of historical interest in a pretty clearing of lush green grass trimmed short by local wild ponies and framed with thick deciduous trees. Many parties had already staked their claim — picnic blankets spread out, indulging in sandwiches — even though lunchtime was at least an hour away. Others had left their hot cars and hooked straight onto the end of the queue for ice cream, seeking a cooling hand-held dessert before heading over to examine the modestly sized memorial to King Rufus.

As they exited the car, Fiona identified a very British dilemma. "We need to talk to that ice-cream seller, but do we barge in and start asking him questions? Or should we queue like everyone else?"

"Join the queue," Daisy said.

"Barge in," Partial Sue replied.

Daisy looked worried. "They'll get the hump if we do that. I'd get the hump if someone did that to me."

Partial Sue huffed. "But it will take ages if we queue."

"We need information from this chap," Fiona said. "We don't want to spook him by causing a scene. I think we queue."

Partial Sue conceded. "I suppose you're right. Queue-jumping in this country is worse than . . . well, actually, it *is* the worst thing you can do."

"Can we still buy ice creams from him? That's still part of the plan, isn't it?" The desperation was evident in Daisy's voice.

Fiona reassured her. "Oh, absolutely."

They crunched across the gravel and joined the line of people waiting patiently. At least it gave them the chance to examine the unauthorised ice-cream van. Fiona had been expecting a rundown, dilapidated vehicle, freckled with rust and riddled with germs, but the bright-pink vehicle was clean and well-kept. The usual stickers adorned the side, advertising its wares, supplied by the ubiquitous Somerford Ice Creams, but apart from that it was devoid of character. There were no punny names or badly reproduced cartoon and film charac-ters. The only embellishment Fiona observed was a no-non-sense 'Ice Creams' written above the windscreen in a Helvetica font. As they edged closer, Fiona got a good look at the man working inside. Possibly in his late twenties or early thirties, he had loose, velvety black curls that fell about his bearded face, reminding her of a young Cat Stevens. Handing out ice creams with a quiet, well-drilled efficiency, he appeared to be working alone.

"What are you going to have?" Fiona snapped off a few surreptitious shots with her phone.

Daisy licked her lips. "I can't get enough of the bubble-gum flavour Bella sells. I hope this chap stocks it."

Fiona liked the sound of this. "Oh, I might try that. Sue, are you game for trying something new?"

Partial Sue remained stoic. "Nope, vanilla all the way for me."

"Don't you want to try something different?" Daisy asked.

"No, I don't want to be disappointed. There's nothing worse than being saddled with an ice cream you don't like. So I play it safe. Vanilla is reliable, steadfast. Never lets you down."

"Isn't that a bit boring, just having vanilla all the time?" Fiona asked.

"Nope. Vanilla's hardworking. The Swiss Army knife of flavours. Goes with apple pie, apple crumble, banana split, mince pies, brownies, sticky toffee pudding . . ."

While Partial Sue appeared intent on listing every conceivable dessert combination, Fiona wondered if she should buy Simon Le Bon some doggie ice cream to cool him down. She glanced down to check he wasn't too hot and saw his ears suddenly prick up, as if summoned by a dog whistle.

"Can anyone hear chimes?" Partial Sue asked.

At the periphery of her hearing, Fiona could make out the odd tinkling note. "Yes, I think I can."

"Me too," Daisy said. "Sounds like another ice-cream van coming this way."

The chimes were getting louder. The three of them looked up and down the road but couldn't see anything. Fiona couldn't help noticing that the man in the ice-cream van had heard it too. His body language changed. Tensing up, he worked faster now, hacking away at the scooped ice cream, as if his life depended on it. Every time he handed a cone to a customer, he would scan the road for the approaching vehicle, worry in his eyes.

"That sounds like 'Summer Breeze'."

Daisy was right. The iconic soul classic had somehow been transformed — or, some might say, bludgeoned — into ice-cream chimes, and sounded strangely sinister. A second later, the Icely Brothers' van came into view, screeching around the corner. It skidded to a halt in front of the other ice-cream van, throwing up a cloud of dust, and the queuing people leaped back for their own safety, the ladies included.

The bearded man slammed his serving window shut and jumped into the driving seat. Jamming the engine into gear, which had already been running to power his freezer, he took off just as quickly as Benjamin and Jacob had arrived, but not before they'd jumped out and given him an earful.

"This is our pitch!" Benjamin growled.

"Never come back, you hear!" Jacob slapped the back of the van as it sped away.

CHAPTER 17

There didn't seem much point in the ladies standing there now that the ice-cream seller they wanted to question had fled, scared off by the Icely Brothers' aggression. The orderly queue began to scatter. People had come out for a relaxing day in the forest, a bit of tranquillity among the trees, not to see an ugly altercation between ice-cream sellers. Although it was extremely one-sided, truth be told.

Watching potential customers disperse, the Icely Brothers' attitude quickly changed, shifting back to the smiley, laidback personas Fiona remembered, although she now wondered if that was all a front.

Benjamin attempted to win back the crowd. "Sorry about that, ladies and gentlemen, but the ice-cream van you were about to buy from was dodgy."

"Unlicensed," Jacob added. "We're totally legit. Paid up and signed up, so you can buy with confidence. We'll be ready to serve you in just a second."

Their attempts were unsuccessful. Everyone had lost their appetites and continued to scuttle away. The only ones who remained were the ladies. The Icely Brothers' smiles faltered for a second when they caught sight of them.

"Hey, what are you three doing here?" Benjamin asked.

"You know what." Partial Sue didn't mince her words. "We were about to question that unlicensed ice-cream seller until you scared him off."

"He's the first one we've been able to track down since we last spoke to you," Fiona said.

Jacob dismissed their concerns with a wave of his hand. "Oh, don't worry. I'm sure you'll find plenty more."

"Not from what we've heard," Daisy replied. "They don't hang around for long, as you've just demonstrated."

Benjamin attempted to appease them. "Don't feel sorry for him. Those guys are trouble, give us legit sellers a bad name. But listen, no hard feelings. How about we rustle you up three ice creams, on the house? Now, what would you like?"

Normally this would be music to Partial Sue's ears, but those ears were practically smoking. "No thank you. But you can answer why you were so aggressive with him."

"Yes, you caused quite a scene," Fiona said. "Was that really necessary? What happened to all this 'there's plenty of room for everyone' business?"

"We never said that," Jacob said.

Benjamin's smile dropped. "But we did tell you that if we come across anyone unlicensed, we'd tell them straight to their face."

"Yes, but you scared a lot of people," Daisy said.

"Oh, don't worry about that. They'll be back," Jacob replied.

"That's not the point," Fiona remarked.

"Well, sorry you had to see that," Jacob said. "Now, if you'll excuse us."

The pair of them turned and climbed back into the van, flipping open its serving window, ready for business — which showed no signs of happening any time soon.

Defeated, the ladies traipsed back to the car.

"They didn't seem to be bothered about what just happened," Partial Sue grumbled.

"No," Daisy said. "I distinctly remember Benjamin saying they'd never get violent with an unlicensed ice-cream seller, but then Jacob slapped that poor chap's van as he drove away."

"I really would like to speak to him, get his side of the story," Partial Sue said. "But I suppose that's not going to happen now."

"What about putting his registration into one of those vehicle websites?" Daisy asked.

Partial Sue shook her head. "They only tell you when the vehicle's changed hands, not the identity of the owner."

Fiona brightened, trying to be positive. "We carry on as we planned. Go to the next car park and the next until we find another unlicensed ice-cream seller. There can't just be one out in the forest today."

Unfortunately, that was the case. They visited one car park after another, sticking to Fiona's strict itinerary. Illegitimate ice-cream sellers, or any ice-cream sellers for that matter, were conspicuous by their absence. Daisy had a theory that perhaps the Icely Brothers had been to each one that morning, scaring them off, until Partial Sue did some quick maths — taking into account the number of car parks and the average time it'd take to drive between each one — and worked out they would've had to start at around five in the morning to achieve such a monumental task.

Wearily, Partial Sue pulled out of the last car park on the list after another disappointment. She yawned. "What now?"

It was nearly teatime, and their stomachs were grumbling.

"I think we call it a day," Fiona said.

Relief spread around the car as they headed back home in silence, although it was tempered by a deep sense of failure. Their mission had amounted to precisely nothing. They had managed to speak to zero illegitimate ice-cream sellers. No new information to analyse and no further along in the case.

CHAPTER 18

The disappointment of yesterday spilled into Monday, hanging over the shop like a cooking smell you can't get rid of. The three of them harrumphed around the shop, not doing much apart from trying to avoid one another's gaze.

There would usually be plenty to distract them on the first day of a new week. After the shop had closed on Saturday afternoon, people would dump their donations outside the front door, despite the signs politely asking them not to. Normally, they'd spend the morning moaning about people not following the rules, as they sorted through a mess of overflowing boxes and bin liners which had been left on the pavement. Then they would be inundated by a second wave of donations, brought in by people who had actually bothered to follow the rules. It was always their busiest day because the weekend was always a good opportunity for a clean out. But today, after another fine weekend, donations were non-existent, presumably because people would rather be outside than stuck in dusty lofts or cupboards under the stairs, getting sticky with sweat having a clear-out. All of which left the ladies with an annoying amount of spare time to dwell on their lack of progress.

Something caught Partial Sue's attention outside. "I don't believe it. Well, actually I do."

Fiona and Daisy twisted their heads in the direction of their colleague's gaze.

Across the road, outside The Cats Alliance, Sophie was welcoming Alan — the priggish owner of Alan's Place – with open arms, smothering him with foo-foo kisses.

"What's he doing there?" Fiona asked.

"Maybe he wants to buy something second hand for his tearoom," Daisy said.

"Him? Not a chance," Partial Sue snorted. "Maybe it's as we feared. The pair of them are forming the Southbourne Snobs Society as we speak."

Fiona shuddered. "Oh, God forbid."

The doorbell jangled, making all three ladies jump, snapping them out of their incredulous state at the sight across the road. Jed Garret appeared at the door. He had two very well-behaved and very smartly dressed children with him, a boy and a girl, aged around seven or eight. He must have noticed the stunned looks on the ladies' faces. "Have I come at a bad time?"

Fiona couldn't really divulge the source of their discomfort — that their arch nemesis and their least favourite person in this investigation were, at this minute, possibly forging a vile union of pomposity of the most grandiose proportions. She quickly dismissed the question. "Gosh, no. Please come in."

Dressed only in a T-shirt, shorts and flip-flops, the owner of Flowers For A Fiver stepped inside, followed by the two similarly dressed children. "This is my son and daughter, George and Emily."

The two children approached Fiona and took turns politely shaking her hand. "Very pleased to meet you," they both uttered, then swiftly moved on to Daisy and Partial Sue, greeting them as if they were at a formal dinner. Simon Le Bon tumbled out of his basket and performed his own welcome, wagging his tail and entwining himself around their little bare legs as they chuckled with delight.

"I thought it was time they learned about charity," Jed said, "and how important it is to give back, so today they're spending their pocket money here."

"Oh, how lovely," Daisy said.

"Have a browse, kids." Jed pointed them towards the racks and shelves. The two children scuttled around the shop, carefully examining the weird and wonderful objects on display, as if it were a school project and they'd be asked questions afterwards.

Jed drew closer, shrinking slightly as he spoke quietly, making sure his children were out of earshot. "There's another reason I'm here." He held up a Post-it note tacked to the end of his finger. A phone number was scribbled in blue ballpoint. "This is the home number for Trisha Masterson, Kevin Masterson's mum. Poor lady. As you can understand, she's desperate for information and the police are being tight-lipped. I hope you don't mind, but I mentioned that you were doing your own investigation. She wanted to meet you. Said she'd answer any of your questions if it would help find the killer. But I thought I'd better ask you first."

Fiona plucked the note from his finger. "We'd be very happy to meet her. Thank you. This will be extremely useful."

He straightened up, relieved. "Oh, good. I wasn't sure how these things worked. If there was some protocol that needed to be followed. I'm guessing procedure is important in investigations. Just like in business . . ."

Fiona sensed another entrepreneurial TED Talk coming on and cut him off. "Please, anything you have, feel free to come to us."

"I certainly will." Jed glanced over at his two children who were delving deep into boxes and sifting through items. He turned back to the three ladies. "How's the investigation going?"

This was always a tricky question to answer — how much to reveal about an ongoing case. Enlightening a member of the public about what they'd discovered was never a good idea.

Lucky for them there was nothing much to report, apart from yesterday's humiliating debacle in the New Forest.

"Oh, er, fine." Fiona didn't sound convincing in the slightest.

"Daddy?" George suddenly appeared, holding a boxset above his head. "Please may I have these Narnia books?"

"Oh, what a good choice," Daisy said.

"And please may I have this book on astronomy?" Emily held up a hardback nearly the same size as her.

"Of course," Jed replied.

"Thank you, Daddy," they chorused.

"Just one moment." Unable to resist upselling, Fiona made a beeline for the storeroom and returned with a recent donation — a telescope on a tripod that she hadn't priced up yet. "Well, if you're reading about the stars, why not gaze at them as well?"

Both children gasped.

"Oh, please, Daddy. Please," George pleaded. "May we have a telescope as well? We could have a competition to see who can spot all eight planets in the solar system."

"Of course, it used to be nine," Emily said eruditely, "but Pluto was recently reclassified as a dwarf planet. We learned that from Brian Cox."

Daisy grinned. "We like Brian Cox."

When Jed had mentioned he had kids, and that he spoiled them, Fiona had imagined some demanding and mouthy brats who got whatever they wanted, whenever they wanted it. But these two charming little children were not what she had expected at all. If she didn't know better, she'd say George and Emily had been plucked straight out of a 1960s Ladybird Book.

Jed gave them a wide, warm smile. "Why not? That sounds like a lot of fun."

"Yeh!" George and Emily pogoed up and down, faces full of glee. They suddenly calmed, remembering their manners.

"Excuse me," Emily asked. "May we try out the telescope?"

Fiona handed it to the pair of them. "Be my guest. See what you can see."

They scurried off with their wholesome new educational toy, setting it by the window, shifting it around and playing with the angles to find the best position.

The joyful sight was short-lived by the arrival of an evil presence from across the road — or Sophie, as she was better known. Alan hovered behind her, further sullying the atmosphere.

"Greetings one and all," Sophie announced. Her expression dropped as her eyes alighted on George and Emily. Sophie never had children in her own shop. To discourage them, she always rejected any donations of toys or games, on the basis that they'd been touched by small hands that hadn't been washed properly and could be carrying all manner of diseases. "Oh, you have children in here." She said it as if she'd spotted damp on the walls or mould on the skirting board.

Jed took umbrage. "What's wrong with that?"

"Oh, they're yours, are they?" Sophie eyed up Jed's casual attire, no doubt forming a catalogue of derisive first impressions in her head. She grimaced. "I try not to mix with children. I find them to be sticky and unpredictable."

"That's why I don't allow them in my tearooms," Alan piped up.

Fiona was about to tell him she didn't allow rude people in her shop, or ones who had possibly left nasty notes on ice-cream vans.

But Jed snapped, getting there before her. "I can assure you my children are neither sticky nor unpredictable."

Sophie smirked. "Of course not, darling. They look very clean . . . well, from where I'm standing. I'm merely stating an opinion, which is my God-given right."

"The other good thing about opinions is that you can keep them to yourself," Daisy said.

"Yes, good point." Fiona lowered her voice. "Which I'll kindly ask you to do, especially since there are two very

nice children present, otherwise you'll both have to leave."
Fortunately, George and Emily were too engrossed in their
telescope to notice they were being talked about.

"I think we'll go," Jed announced. "How much do I owe
you for the books and telescope, Fiona?"

"Oh wait, please," Sophie said. "I'm sure you'll all want
to hear what I have to say. It'll be the talk of Southbourne,
and you can boast that you heard it here first."

"I doubt it," Jed muttered.

Sophie ignored his comment and beamed as if she were
about to accept an Oscar. "I've come to tell you that I shall
be investing in Alan's chain of premium tearooms. There'll
be an Alan's Place in every major town. The name will be
synonymous with class and quality." She grabbed him by the
shoulders and thrust him forward like a pushy mum, then
gave them both a round of applause. She was the only one
in the room who did. Daisy looked as if she wanted to throw
something at them. Jed failed to suppress a snort.

Alan scowled. "What's so funny?"

"Oh, nothing."

"No, come on, what is it? This is a big business venture.
An elite tea-drinking experience. I'm sure we'd all love to hear
your expert opinion."

Jed sighed. "Well, it's just that business names are important, and I just think 'Alan's Place' doesn't sound very premium to me."

Alan glowered at Jed. "Excuse me? I've put my name to
the business, as a guarantee of quality. You can do a lot with
the name Alan."

Daisy giggled. "Like a special event on the fourteenth of
February called Alantine's Day." One side of the room giggled
with her.

Undeterred by the mocking, Alan persevered. "It's a well-
known technique. Just like Jamie Oliver with Jamie's Italian."

"Didn't that go bust?" Jed asked.

"That's not the point," Alan snapped. "Anyway, what would you know about it?" He clearly had no idea who Jed was or what he did.

"Oh, nothing."

"Yes, you do, Daddy." Emily didn't take her gaze from the eyepiece of the telescope. Everyone had assumed the children hadn't been listening, but they'd been absorbing every word.

"You always tell us how long it took to come up with the name of your business." George's head was stuck in the first chapter of *The Lion, the Witch and the Wardrobe*.

Alan scoffed. "And what's the name of this business?"

"Flowers For A Fiver."

It was fortunate that Alan's jaw was fixed to his face, otherwise it would have hit the hardwearing and well-vacuumed carpet of Dogs Need Nice Homes. "Not the giant online flower business?"

"The very same."

At the mention of success, Sophie's demeanour changed. She became a gooey saccharine-sweet blancmange, sliding in front of Alan and blocking his view of the dot-com entrepreneur. "Well, isn't that a coincidence? Flowers For A Fiver is one of my favourite websites. I have it bookmarked. Use it all the time. I adore sending flowers as much as . . . as . . ." She struggled to find a worthy enough simile.

Daisy had a suggestion. "As much as you dislike children?"

Sophie snorted. "Oh, please. I never said I disliked children. I adore them."

Emily's honesty was brutal, accurate and unforgiving. "You said children were sticky and unpredictable."

"And then you made a face like you were going to be sick," George added.

Sophie attempted to wriggle out of it. "Well, yes. I suppose I adore them as long as their hands have been probably sanitised, and they haven't been drinking buckets of cheap orange squash."

Smelling the pungent reek of opportunity, Alan pushed past Sophie to make his business pitch to Jed. "There's still investment potential for Alan's Place if you'd like to jump on board. We have some amazing locations lined up. You see, we only open tearooms in places with historical merit — Grade II listed buildings. That's our USP." He held his hands up dramatically, as if spreading his vision. "It's Starbucks meets *Downton Abbey*. But obviously with tea, not coffee."

Fiona wondered if this was why Alan's Place lacked any proper signage, because listed building regulations wouldn't allow it.

Sophie reclaimed her rightful place, barging in front of Alan. "Oh, you should see his place in Wick. Most impressive. A Gothic mansion, no less."

Partial Sue sneered. "That's if he'll let you in."

Sophie ignored her. "And the toilets have both handwash and hand cream dispensers."

"I don't like those," Daisy said. "I always pick the wrong one and end up washing my hands with moisturiser."

Alan popped his head around Sophie's shoulder. "It's an amazing investment opportunity. Going to be big."

Jed shook his head. "No, I'm good thanks. Already got enough on my plate."

Alan slipped a business card from his pocket and handed it to Jed. "In case you change your mind." He then turned his attention to the ladies of the charity shop. "How about you three?"

Sophie's giggle was forced and cruel. "Them? They haven't got any money."

"How do you know?" Fiona asked.

"Well, your collective attire says it all." Sophie tittered. "You're supposed to be selling charity clothes. Not wearing them."

"I suppose it might not be a good idea," Alan said. "We want investors who align with our three brand values: smart, elite and discerning."

"Oh," said Partial Sue. "I thought your brand values were the three P's: pompous, pretentious and priggish."

"Last time we were there you couldn't get rid of us fast enough," Fiona reminded him.

Jed pulled out his slab of a phone. "You know, on second thoughts, I am going to part with some cash."

Alan gulped hard. "You are?"

"Yes."

"How much?"

"Five grand."

Alan hid disappointment well. As investments went, five thousand pounds would barely touch the sides, but it was not to be sniffed at. "That is most generous of you. You certainly won't regret it. This will be like getting in on Apple or Google, right at the start."

Jed shook his head. "Oh, no. I'm not investing in your business. I'm donating my five thousand to Dogs Need Nice Homes."

"What!" said Alan.

"What?" asked Sophie.

"What?" the ladies chorused.

Jed opened the banking app on his phone. "I'd like my money to go to something useful."

Alan became flustered as the opportunity slipped through his small hands. "But you won't see any return on that money. It's madness."

"No, I will. Lots of dogs will get a home. Dogs make people happy, whereas I get the feeling your tearooms are just going to make people more uptight."

"That's true," said Daisy.

Sophie abandoned Alan's sinking ship. "Well, I for one think that is a most noble gesture. Giving to charity is such a worthwhile and satisfying pursuit. I manage The Cats Alliance across the road, and I know that many, many poor and neglected cats will—"

Jed interrupted her. "Yeah, I like cats, too. Trouble is, I don't like you. So I will donate an equal amount to a cat charity — just not your one."

Sophie swayed. Had no comeback. There was no effective PR spin she could put on that brick wall of a statement.

Jed smiled. "Just expressing my opinion, of course."

CHAPTER 19

Trisha Masterson's hands shook as she placed teas in front
of Fiona and Partial Sue (Daisy had elected to stay behind,
as they didn't want to overwhelm the grief-stricken woman).
However, she seemed pleased to have visitors and had used her
best vintage bone china, matching cups and saucers decorated
with a tasteful floral pattern. The same could not be said for
the tea, which was the colour of brandy, strong enough to
make a builder wince.

"This is lovely china." Fiona hadn't yet taken a sip of the
harsh, bitter beverage.

"Thank you. It was my grandmother's." Trisha's voice
was strained and breathless, possibly from the mountain of
grief pressing down on the poor woman's shoulders. The stress
of not knowing who had killed her son, or why, must have
been unbearable.

Fiona glanced around the room, wondering where to
begin. The lounge of Trisha's bungalow hadn't changed since
the eighties. A chintzy ensemble of furniture and wallpaper, it
was slightly garish, apart from the chunky, grey, top-loading
relic of a video player that sat beneath the TV. A glass cabinet was pressed against the wall, stacked with more beautiful

china, presented like museum pieces. Judging by their pristine state, Fiona suspected they rarely left their glass confinement. Everything in the room gleamed with polish, there wasn't a speck of dirt anywhere, the fastidious cleaning perhaps fuelled by her sorrow, distracting her from the horror of losing her one and only son.

"You have quite the collection," Fiona said.

"Yes, mostly Mum's and my grandmother's, although a few bits are mine."

Several picture frames perched on top of the cabinet. Trisha on her wedding day with a red-faced husband, together with a selection of pictures of Kevin at various stages of his life, including the ubiquitous school photos, documenting the trial and error — mostly error — of youthful, gel-heavy hairstyles.

"Did Kevin have any brothers or sisters?" Fiona knew he didn't, but thought it would be a gentle way to steer the conversation towards the murder.

"No," said Trisha. "His dad passed away soon after he was born. I never remarried. I didn't want him growing up with a stepfather."

"What about friends? Girlfriends?" asked Partial Sue. "Any falling outs, disagreements?"

"He wasn't very close with anyone for that to happen. They never stuck around long enough."

"Oh. Why was that?" Fiona asked.

"Kevin could be a bit moody, I'm afraid to say, and it put people off. They'd assume he was angry with them. He wasn't. He would just get frustrated with himself or a situation. But, unfortunately, it drove anyone away before they could become anything more than acquaintances."

"How did that affect his life?" Partial Sue asked.

"He never held a job down for very long."

"Did he get fired a lot?" Fiona asked.

"No," Trisha replied. "That's the thing. He would leave before they had the chance. Get frustrated and walk out. Square peg, my Kevin was. A loner."

120

Their only alternative angle of inquiry — that the Vanilla Killer might have been someone he knew, a theory that had been overshadowed somewhat by rival ice-cream sellers — faded before it had a chance to be explored.

"Do you think that's why he bought the ice-cream van? So he could be his own boss?"

Trisha brightened. "Yes, absolutely. He was so pleased when he got it. I'd never seen him so happy. Full of the joys of spring, he was. It felt like his life was about to start."

"Can I ask how he paid for the van?" Fiona hoped there might be a lead here somewhere. A figure lurking in the shadows that he borrowed the money from, possibly a loan shark who had asked for it back, plus the extortionate interest.

"I lent him the money," Trisha said. "Something I've regretted ever since. If I hadn't done that he might still be here today." Her voice cracked on the last syllable.

Partial Sue attempted to comfort her. "You can't blame yourself, Trisha. You had no idea this would happen. You were doing what you thought was best for your son."

Fiona nodded. "This is someone else's fault. Not yours. And we'll try our hardest to find whoever did this."

"Thank you." Trisha sniffed.

"Where did Kevin buy the van?" Partial Sue asked.

"I think he got it off eBay. I was really proud of him for getting that van. Normally he'd have these big ambitions and grand ideas that would never happen. But this was different. He knew it would suit him and he really got stuck into it. Researched everything. Learned how to use the equipment and look after it properly. Got his street-trader's licence. Sorted out an ice-cream supplier."

"Was that Somerford?"

Trisha nodded. "He had everything all set up, ready for the summer."

"How many times did he actually go out selling?" Partial Sue asked.

"Oh, not many. Only a handful. Weather wasn't great back in March and April. But on some of the nice days he went out to have a few test runs and scout out locations. Sold a few dozen ice creams."

"Did he like it?"

"He loved it. Came back grinning from ear to ear."

Fiona took another sip of tea. "Did he ever encounter any other ice-cream sellers?"

Trisha shook her head. "No, none."

"And what about vandalism? Did anyone damage his van? Leave rude notes on it?"

Trisha shook her head again. "No, never. I would've certainly heard about it if they did."

"So, before that fateful day in April, how did he seem?"

"Well, he went through a few emotions. When he first got the van, he was elated. Positive, for once. Then about a couple of weeks before his murder, he became subdued, quiet. I just thought it was nerves, a bit of self-doubt. He became security conscious, fitted an alarm to the house and told me never to open the door unless I was expecting someone."

"Do you know why?" Fiona enquired.

"I asked him, but he would just say there are a lot of bad people out there. Then suddenly his paranoia disappeared. He became calmer. I'd almost say he was a little smug."

"Smug?"

Trisha nodded. "Yes, that was completely unlike him. You see, all his life he thought the world was against him. He was downtrodden. It made him bitter and cynical. But a few days before he died, he had a swagger about him."

"Do you have any idea why?" Fiona asked.

"No, it wasn't like him at all. But he did say he'd soon be able to pay me back every penny I'd lent him — with interest."

"Had he come into any money?"

"I recently had to close down his bank account — there was very little in it."

Partial Sue rubbed her chin. "So how would he be able to pay you back so quickly? Can you think of anything he might have been involved in?"

Trisha looked doubtful. "Well, that's just it. Kevin didn't want to be involved in anything. He'd finally figured out that he was better off alone. Got himself a job where he only had to answer to himself, and his interaction with people was minimal. He could serve customers and never see them again. Perfect for him."

No one said anything for a while. Minds digested the information, trying to make the pieces fit.

"Would you like to see his room?" Trisha asked.

"Oh, yes. That would be good." Fiona hadn't realised that he'd still lived at home. But like most people these days, flying the nest was a luxury few could afford.

Trisha must have read this in Fiona's face. "He told me he was going to get his own place after he paid me back."

If he could reimburse his mum and put down a deposit on a house, then Kevin must have been coming into a tidy sum of money. Short of winning the lottery, where would someone like Kevin get his hands on such a hefty lump sum?

She led them to a white-painted, wood-panelled door at the end of a narrow hall. There were no indications that the room belonged to Kevin, apart from Fiona noticing it was the only internal door that had a keyhole.

Trisha noticed Fiona eyeing up the lock. "He liked his privacy and had that fitted. I mean, he was an adult, so that was fine." She pushed open the door and beckoned them in. "Please feel free to rummage around, although the police have done a thorough search already."

"Did they find anything?"

Trisha shook her head.

"Did he have a computer?" Partial Sue asked.

"No," Trisha said. "Only a mobile phone, but the police took it."

"Did you clean his room?" Fiona asked.

She shook her head. "Kevin liked things just so. He kept everything spotless. But I do come in here to dust now and again."

The bedroom resembled the rest of the bungalow — neat and tidy. There was a single bed in one corner and an orangey pine wardrobe in the other, plus a matching chest of drawers below the window, and not much else. A few posters adorned the wall: one of Michael Caine in *Get Carter* holding a shotgun, and another of *Pulp Fiction* with Uma Thurman looking suitably vampish. Fiona would have made some connection with crime dramas, although that theory was dashed by a third poster showing a scowling Captain Mainwaring.

"He liked *Dad's Army*, I take it?" Fiona asked.

"He loved it." Trisha smiled. "It was his favourite TV show, even though it was before his time. He joked that Captain Mainwaring reminded him of himself." She giggled. "I used to call him it sometimes. That was the strange thing about Kevin — he had no problem with people making fun of him. He could take a joke." Her smile faded back to her default sadness. "I'll leave you to it."

Partial Sue and Fiona slowly circled the room, not touching anything, just observing and absorbing. First impressions gave nothing away, apart from a son who liked to be as tidy as his mum. Fiona began delving into the drawers and found neat stacks of clothing, folded precisely and squared away. His clothes were basic — just jeans, T-shirts and sweatshirts. She lifted each pile to check for anything hidden underneath, but nothing revealed itself. She knew this would be a fool's errand. The police would have bagged and tagged anything of investigative value, though it didn't hurt to look.

Partial Sue searched the wardrobe and also came up empty-handed. The pair of them switched places. Nothing but more clothes on hangers and a couple of pairs of trainers and some formal leather dress shoes in the bottom.

"There's nothing here," Partial Sue said. "What about under the bed?"

124

Fiona risked her knees and got down on all fours to poke her head underneath. She quickly retracted it. "There are magazines under here."

"Well, pull them out."

"You pull them out."

"I'm not pulling out magazines from under the bed of a thirty-something man who lived with his mum."

Fiona had a brain wave. She set the camara on her phone to flash mode. Without looking she shoved it under the bed and snapped off a few shots, then examined the screen and showed it to Partial Sue.

"The *Ice-Cream Seller*." Partial Sue relaxed. "It's a trade magazine."

"Looks like we made a gross assumption." Fiona reached under the bed and slid out the magazines, then got to her feet and spread them on the duvet. There were four copies in all, starting in January and ending in May. The last copy was still wrapped in cellophane and addressed to Kevin.

"What do you make of that?" asked Fiona.

"He must have subscribed to the *Ice-Cream Seller* while he was setting up his business. I'm guessing the May copy must have arrived just after his death. Probably why it's unopened."

"But where are the other copies?" Fiona asked. "June and July. Surely they would have kept sending them, unless Trisha threw them away or cancelled his subscription."

"Let's ask her," Partial Sue suggested.

The ladies went back into the lounge and found Kevin's mother gazing aimlessly at some vulgar TV show. Contestants were guessing which celebrity's face had been merged with another celebrity's face. It appeared to be sending her to sleep. She started when she saw them. "Everything okay? Did you find anything?"

Fiona held up the stack of magazines. "Kevin had a subscription to this trade magazine."

"Yes, that's right. He read them cover to cover. He wanted to be good at what he did. Said he wanted to keep up with the latest trends."

"The last one's unopened," Partial Sue said. "Did any later issues arrive?"

"Er, no, I don't think so."

"Did you cancel the subscription?"

Trisha shook her head. "No, it hadn't even crossed my mind. Unless he cancelled it."

"I wonder why he would do that when his business was poised to take off?" Fiona asked.

"Maybe he had everything he needed," Partial Sue replied. "Probably didn't need the magazine anymore."

"Not if he wanted to keep up with the latest trends," Fiona said.

"That's right," Trisha agreed. "Kevin wanted to keep his finger on the pulse."

"So why would he cancel his subscription?" Fiona asked.

Partial Sue shrugged. "Maybe he needed to save money. Especially if his bank balance was low."

"Possibly," Fiona said, "although he'd claimed he had the money to pay back the loan for the van and possibly move out. Keeping something as small as a subscription wouldn't have been a problem. So why cancel it?"

Though it seemed a trivial matter, she couldn't help thinking this was an indication of something bigger, especially as he'd cancelled right before he died. What did that imply? She didn't know, but it seemed too much of a coincidence.

CHAPTER 20

The next day, they brought Daisy up to speed with what they'd learned. She launched straight into her own theory. "If Kevin Masterson was a bit moody, maybe it was a simple case of road rage. Someone cut him up. He loses it and gets into a fight with another driver."

It was a plausible idea, but one that didn't stand up to scrutiny.

"Possibly," Fiona replied. "But from what his mum said, he'd get more annoyed with himself than other people. But let's just assume he did get into a fight with another driver who inadvertently killed him. Would that driver hang around and lift Kevin's body into his van, then hoist him into the freezer?"

Partial Sue agreed. "Road rage offenders are always in a rush, that's why they happen in the first place. The other driver would've panicked and drove off. Plus, they're noisy, aggressive affairs. The residents of Avon Close didn't hear a thing. No squealing brakes or screeching tyres. No car horns blasting."

Daisy's face was strained. She tried to make sense of it all while pouring tea at the same time. "Okay, I get that, but I still don't understand the way Kevin was acting before he died. First off, you said he was happy because he'd got his van. Then he got scared, then he became smug, then he was coming into some money, so he cancelled his magazine subscription, and then he was murdered."

"Well, when you put it like that, it does sound odd," Partial Sue said.

"Okay, we need to look for cause and effect," Fiona said. "First bit is obvious — he's happy because he's got his van, can be his own boss. But then after that he became scared. To me, it implies that someone threatened him."

"Another ice-cream seller?" Daisy asked.

"His mum didn't think so. Perhaps they demanded something off him, or they wanted him to do something he didn't want to, hence his behaviour."

Daisy scratched her head. "But how does the money come into this? And if he was smug before he died, that doesn't sound like the behaviour of someone being threatened."

Fiona thought for a moment, then clicked her fingers. "Maybe these people are offering to pay him to do something illegal. At first, he doesn't want to know, but then the amount of money they're dangling is far more than he'll ever make selling ice creams. He accepts and, once he's comfortable with the idea, he thinks of how much he'll earn, and that makes him smug. He can pay back his mum, cancel his subscription because he's not going to need it anymore, and move out."

"But if he cancelled his subscription, why would he keep his van?" asked Daisy.

"It would take a while to sell an ice-cream van, but it's more likely he needed it, as a front, if he was doing something against the law."

"Oh my gosh!" Daisy cried. "You don't think that will happen to Bella, do you? Someone's going to force her to do something criminal?"

"I don't think so," Partial Sue reassured her. "We asked Trisha Masterson if Kevin's van ever got vandalised. She said it hadn't. Also, he'd never got any rude notes left on it. These people must have approached Kevin at some point, but nobody's approached Bella for anything. However, there's one thing about your theory that doesn't add up, Fiona."

"What's that?"

"If Kevin Masterson agreed to do what these people wanted, why was he killed?"

"Maybe they had no further use for him," Fiona said. "They tied up a loose end, which would also mean they didn't have to pay him, hence why he never saw that money."

A sly grin formed on Partial Sue's face, one that made Fiona uncomfortable. "You know what would explain it. An ice-cream mafia. Like the Glasgow Ice Cream Wars. Two rival gangs fighting over turf, using ice-cream vans to sell stolen goods and drugs. Kevin Masterson joins one side, making money selling illegal stuff, but then gets killed by the other side. And to make an example of him, his body is dumped in Mudeford because it's neutral ground. Switzerland. Neither side has claim to it."

Fiona was worried Daisy would be quaking in her Scholls, terrified that Bella would get tangled up in something equally horrific. But Daisy's face appeared surprisingly calm. "I can't see it myself. Maybe in a big city like Glasgow, but here in Southbourne, Christchurch and Mudeford, surely we'd have heard about it. When were these Glasgow Ice Cream Wars?"

"Back in the mid-eighties," Partial Sue replied.

"Nearly forty years ago," Fiona added. "The streets of Glasgow were a battlefield back then. Ice-cream vans shooting at each other in the streets, houses set alight. Daisy's right, two rival factions fighting for supremacy on our quiet streets would stand out a mile."

"Maybe they've just got better at hiding it," Partial Sue said weakly.

A secret criminal organisation would certainly answer a lot of questions, especially Kevin Masterson's odd behaviour before he died, Fiona thought. But it would also be very difficult to keep something like that quiet in an area where hanging baskets going missing made the headlines and had neighbours informing on each other.

Just before five o'clock, Bella's van pulled up outside, chimes clanging away. Daisy was relieved to see a bright, positive smile on her daughter's face as she entered the shop.

Daisy hugged her. "How did it go today?"

"Spectacular," Bella said. "I sold a ton of ice cream."

Fiona congratulated her.

"That's great news," said Partial Sue.

Simon Le Bon emerged from his basket, not aware of why everyone was so elated, but happy to join in, nonetheless.

"I had a bit of a brainwave." Bella grinned. "I can't believe I didn't think of it earlier. I've been trying to sell ice creams in all the obvious places — a few beauty spots, a few urban areas. Nothing much to write home about. So I tried thinking outside the box, or the ice-cream tub, as it were." She smirked. "I thought, where would you be desperate to have an ice cream to cool off because you were so hot?"

"Inside a sauna," Daisy suggested. "Or a desert."

"Yes, that's good, Mum," Bella replied, "but I don't think either of those are realistically going to happen. However, I did think of hospitals."

"Oh, yes," said Partial Sue. "They're always really boiling, even in winter. In this weather they must be unbearable."

"That's right, so I parked outside one and had a constant queue of people coming out wanting an ice cream. Never been so busy."

"Oh, that's great news." Daisy gave her another hug.

"Thanks, Mum. I sold out of a lot of flavours."

"Did you sell out of vanilla?" asked Partial Sue.

"No, I always keep extra. It's the most popular flavour."

Partial Sue gave them all a knowing smile.

Bella had more good news to share. "But that's not all. After I left the hospital, I passed by a school just before home time."

"Oh, yes," said Daisy. "Classrooms were always so stuffy in the summer term."

"Yep, so I pulled in and waited for the kids to come out. When they did, it was like a frenzy of ice-cream-eating locusts.

They cleaned me out. It's the most money I've made in a single day!"

The happiness on Bella's face and the sheer relief on Daisy's, warmed Fiona's heart. Finally, some good luck had come Bella's way. Well, it had nothing to do with luck. Bella had used her smarts to play on the simple principles of supply and demand. Go where demand would be highest. "So, you've hit the jackpot. Schools and hospitals from now on."

"Yes, indeed." Bella beamed. "I mean, the schools will be breaking up soon for summer holidays, but I thought churches could also be good. Everyone coming out in their Sunday best would welcome an ice cream to cool them down after all that hellfire and brimstone."

"Although would you risk having ice cream if you were in your Sunday best?" Partial Sue, ever the cynic, could always be relied on to find a chink in anyone's plan. Bella ignored the question. Nothing was going to bring her down today, but that was all about to change.

A small middle-aged man in a grey suit with an ID badge slung round his neck and a clipboard under one arm stepped into the shop. Poker-faced and with thinning blond hair, he didn't smile or look angry, just neutral. Fiona knew he was trouble because he wasn't there to shop or donate. He had the look of someone with a serious job to do. Plus, Simon Le Bon didn't greet him, a surefire indication of his malevolence. As he approached the gathering of ladies, their collective happiness drained more with every step.

Fiona examined his ID badge. His name was Craig Hill, local council, regulatory department.

"That your van outside?" he asked.

Bella nodded.

"You're in violation of several government regulations concerning the selling of ice creams from a van. You must desist from trading immediately and must not return to trading until two years from today. If you do not desist from selling, you will face an immediate fine of one thousand pounds."

Bella swore.

CHAPTER 21

With her gaze transfixed on the bland-looking man from the council, Bella held her tongue. Fiona watched her examining his face, as if trying to interpret his expression or perhaps get some sort of response from him, but it was immovable like a statue's. Suddenly, Bella burst out laughing. Not happy laughter, but the distraught, manic kind. The kind that's painful to witness. "Well, that's just great, isn't it! I'm so stupid. I should have guessed it was too good to be true. Just when I thought I was having a good day, the only good day since buying that van, and this happens! As if the vandalism and the smashed eggs and the rude notes weren't enough! It just keeps getting worse."

"I'm sorry. I'm just doing my job," Craig replied.

"What's Bella actually done wrong?" Daisy asked.

Craig thumbed through the sheets on his clipboard, then cleared his throat. "To start with, *Chimes cannot be played more than once every two hours in any one stretch of the highway. Chimes cannot be louder than eighty decibels . . .*"

"How do you know her chimes were louder than eighty decibels?" Partial Sue asked.

Craig pulled back the edge of his suit jacket, as if he were a special agent revealing a concealed weapon. But instead of a

132

firearm, a device with a digital readout and a microphone was clipped to his belt. He continued, "*Chimes must not last more than twelve seconds. Chimes can be played only once on the approach to a selling point and only once while stationary. There must be an interval of at least two minutes between the chimes being played. Chimes cannot be played within fifty metres of a hospital or a school during school hours.* Oh, and just in case you were thinking about it, *Chimes cannot be played within fifty metres of a church or place of worship on a Sunday.*"

"Okay, well, I'm sure Bella's very sorry for playing her chimes inappropriately," Fiona said, "but I do think it's a little harsh to give her a two-year ban."

Craig gave Fiona the stink-eye, slightly annoyed that his flow had been interrupted. "I haven't finished yet. I was working up to the bigger issues, the main one being that she doesn't have a street-trader's licence."

Bella slapped her forehead. "That's what I meant to do. I was going to get one, I swear."

"I did remind you about it the other day," Daisy said.

"Yes, I know, I know." Bella grabbed two fistfuls of her curly hair as if she wanted to yank them from her head. "This has been a complete disaster. Why the hell did I think I could do this?"

"It's okay, love." Daisy attempted to comfort her. "You just overlooked something."

"Yeah, the something that comes with a two-year ban. Why couldn't I have overlooked something unimportant like filling up the slushie machine or buying napkins?"

"Is there any way we can get around this?" Daisy asked.

"Do you mean a bribe?" Craig appeared shocked, the first emotion to trouble his bland face.

"Gosh, no." Partial Sue flinched at the idea of parting with any cash. "What if the next thing Bella does is apply for her street-trader's licence, the second she leaves this shop."

Daisy nodded profusely.

Bella clasped her hands together, pleadingly. "I'll apply right now. The second I get home, I swear."

Craig thought for a moment, chewing the inside of his cheek. "I'm not allowed to do that. These licences are there to protect the public, to stop rogue traders who don't follow hygiene guidelines and sell subpar products."

Daisy begged. "Please. Bella's not a rogue trader, and you can inspect her van. It's spotless. I help her clean it. I'm a cleaning enthusiast." Just like Craig earlier — pulling back the flap of his suit to reveal his decibel metre — Daisy pulled out the contents of her deep pockets to reveal her arsenal. Disinfectant wipes and various dusters were extracted for his inspection, plus a small bottle containing an unsavoury dark-brown liquid with a spray applicator. She noticed Craig eyeing it curiously. "It's window cleaner, my own recipe — cider vinegar with a dash of washing-up liquid. Works like a dream, apart from it looking like I'm dropping off a sample at the hospital."

"And Bella sells only quality ice cream," Fiona added. "From Somerford."

"That's right." Bella pulled a receipt from her back pocket, supporting the claim.

Craig examined it but showed no signs of caving. "There's also the matter of Environmental Health."

"Environmental Health?" Bella asked. What new level of hell was this?

"You're also supposed to register with Environmental Health. It's my duty to report this to my colleagues in that department."

Bella's head flopped, admitting defeat, the weight of it all too much for her to bear.

"However—" Craig's tone shifted slightly — "I can see you're genuinely sorry for your actions, or lack of them, so I will accept your proposal."

Bella's head snapped back to its upright position. "What proposal?"

"The one you made earlier. If you apply right now for your street-trader's licence, without delay, I'll hold off putting you in our system. But I'll be monitoring your compliance. If I don't see your application in the next twenty-four hours, then my actions will resume their natural course. A street-trader's licence application can be made online, so you have no excuse not to do it immediately."

Bella grabbed his hand and shook it vigorously, much to his discomfort. "Thank you! Thank you! I will go and do that right now." She kissed her mum on the cheek, but stopped short of giving Craig a peck too, then rushed back out to her van.

Craig regarded the ladies. "Well, I'll be on my way."

"Thank you," Daisy said. "That was very decent of you."

"Don't thank me yet. Your daughter still has to upload her application and get it approved."

"I'm sure she will," Daisy said.

Craig gave a half-hearted smile and was about to leave when Fiona held him back. "Er, can I ask you about ice-cream sellers who don't have a licence?"

His eyes became alert, shoulders hunched. "If you know of any other illegal ice-cream sellers, it's your duty to tell me as law-abiding citizens."

"No, I was wondering how you track them down?"

Craig relaxed, but only a little. "Sheer luck, I'm afraid. Like today, I spotted Bella selling by the roadside. Checked the registration of her van — I can see who owns it in an instant — then I cross-referenced that to see if she was licensed and, well, the rest you know. But I will say this. They're a sneaky bunch. Slippery. All I know is this — they don't stay in one place for too long, so they don't get caught."

Partial Sue seized the opportunity to test her pet theory. "Have you ever heard of an ice-cream mafia around here?"

This time Craig's smile was genuine. "That's going back a bit." He chuckled. "I don't think they exist anymore. I think they went the same way as milk floats and the man who used to collect the football pools. And, even when they did exist, it certainly wasn't around here. I would know about it if they did."

For once Partial Sue remained silent at the word of an expert.

CHAPTER 22

The Wicker Man wandered into the shop the next day, and for once he didn't appear to be on the scrounge for anything edible, which was usually his only reason for popping in.

But just in case he was hiding it very well, Partial Sue set him straight. "If it's cake you're after, there isn't any."

Due to their less than positive state of mind caused by a lack of progress — not helped by visitations from uptight council workers — it didn't seem appropriate to be indulging in anything sweet and spongey.

"How about a cup of tea?" Daisy offered.

The Wicker Man shook his head. He didn't seem his usual flamboyant self. Perhaps the negative mood was catching. "No, thank you. Truth be told, I'm here for a dutiful task — to impart you with news of a baleful nature."

Fiona really wasn't in the mood for his Shakespearian shenanigans. "What is it, Trevor?"

"I had a customer in just now. Imparted a tasty morsel of information."

Fiona didn't know which was more surprising — that he had information or that he had a customer. He never seemed to sell anything. "What did he buy?"

"A nice coffee table. But he resides near the airport. Said he was awoken by the right old ruckus of fire engines last night. An ice-cream van had become an inferno of Dantean proportions."

Fiona clarified his convoluted account. "What, it was on fire?"

He nodded.

Fiona wobbled slightly. "It has to be the Icely Brothers' van. That's where they live."

"Was anyone inside it?" asked Daisy.

"I haven't the foggiest."

Daisy got on her phone and scanned the website of the local paper for mentions of the story. Burnt-out cars never made the headlines unless bodies were found inside them, or if it was a spate of arson. "Nothing. Do you think it was started deliberately?"

"We have to find out," Fiona replied.

Partial Sue's eyes widened. "I wonder if it was that bearded chap in the forest who did it. The unlicensed ice-cream seller they scared away. A reprisal."

"Let's not jump to conclusions until we know the facts," Fiona warned.

They thanked the Wicker Man, closed up the shop and immediately drove out to the airport to check on the state of the Icely Brothers' van, if indeed it was the same one. Fiona couldn't imagine there'd be another ice-cream van in that vicinity, unless it was one they didn't know about.

The van was parked in exactly the same spot as the first time they'd met the Icely Brothers, except the brown-and-beige Dodge van was a blackened mess, like something out of a post-apocalyptic movie.

Daisy gasped. "Oh, my gosh. What a terrible sight."

Partial Sue parked up at a safe distance. They climbed out and approached cautiously, unsure whether the remains of the vehicle were still smouldering and perhaps dangerous. There wasn't really much to see. As they circled the destruction, they discovered that everything had either burned, charred or melted.

"I hope this doesn't happen to Bella," Daisy worried.

"I don't think so," Partial Sue reassured her. "Like I said before, I think this is a revenge attack by that chap in the forest for getting kicked off his pitch."

Daisy wasn't so sure. "I don't know. That's a bit extreme, isn't it? He didn't look like the type to set fire to someone's property."

"But then, who does?" Partial Sue said.

"The fire could've been caused by an engine fault or something electrical," Fiona pointed out. "We should check with Benjamin and Jacob before we jump to any conclusions." Fiona led the way up to the front of their house and rang the doorbell. There was no reply. She tried again and again but nobody was in. She pulled out her phone and called the number on their website. It went straight to voicemail. She left a message asking them to call her.

Daisy began to panic. "Oh my gosh. You don't think they died in the fire, do you?"

"Not if it happened in the middle of the night," Partial Sue replied. "Who'd be in an ice-cream van at that time?"

"We should ask the neighbours," Fiona said. "See if anyone saw anything."

One by one they knocked on every door in the cul-de-sac, hoping someone could shed light on what had happened. Their questions were met by disappointing shakes of the head. All they could ascertain was that everyone had been asleep until they were woken up at roughly two thirty in the morning by flashing lights and firefighters.

Fiona pulled out her phone and called her window cleaner, Martin, who was also a part-time firefighter. He answered first time. "Hello, Fiona. How are you?"

After exchanging pleasantries, Fiona put the call on speakerphone. "I was wondering if you were on duty last night. It's about the burnt-out ice-cream van near the airport. Do you know if anyone was inside it?"

"I was on duty last night," Martin said. "And no, no one was inside. We responded to a call a shade after two fifteen in

138

the morning. No one was hurt, and thankfully it didn't spread to any other vehicles or property."

"How did it start?"

"From what I could tell, the driver's window was smashed. Then a can of petrol was poured on the seat, and some on the bonnet. Would've gone up in seconds."

"So it was deliberate."

"Oh, definitely."

"We're trying to reach the owners, Jacob and Benjamin," Fiona said. "Were they around last night or did they stay somewhere else?"

"No, we didn't speak to them. Didn't see them. None of the neighbours we spoke to knew where they were either."

Fiona thanked Martin for his time. He promised to fill her in if any other information came to light.

"What do you make of that?" Fiona asked.

"Maybe they've gone away," Partial Sue suggested. "To do a gig."

"But they left their ice-cream van here," Daisy replied.

"It could be an indoor gig, and they just took their records up there, on the train."

Daisy got on her phone and began searching. "Can't find any soul events featuring the Icely Brothers going on last night in London, or anywhere else, for that matter."

"Mmm," Partial Sue murmured. "It doesn't have to be a gig. It could have been someone's birthday. Or maybe they've just gone away for the night. There could be any number of reasons they weren't here."

Fiona knew there was probably a rational explanation for their absence. Whatever it was, the Icely Brothers would have a nasty shock when they returned home.

"We should at least tell DI Fincher," Partial Sue said.

"The police will already know about this." Fiona kicked through some charred debris with her foot. "DI Fincher's not going to be interested in a burnt-out van."

Partial Sue jittered, desperate to get her point across. "But she will if she knows it was involved in an altercation with another ice-cream van. The bearded chap who did it could be the same one who killed Kevin Masterson."

Fiona didn't want to start pointing fingers at people without evidence, but if there was the slightest chance he was involved, it would be irresponsible not to inform the police. She called DI Fincher. It went straight to voicemail, so she left a message, outlining what they'd witnessed in the forest yesterday.

After putting her phone away, Fiona noticed a lump of glass that had escaped the full force of the fire. She reached down and picked it up. Beneath a thick layer of soot, she could make out the blackened shapes of a once-colourful logo. She swiped the mess away with her thumb to reveal the ubiquitous woodcut emblem of Somerford Ice Creams, albeit a little cracked and distorted. Something occurred to her in that moment. Something so obvious that she was baffled how she hadn't seen it before. "Everyone around here uses Somerford Ice Cream. They're the one thing that links all the ice-cream sellers together, licensed and unlicensed. They're the lowest common denominator."

"I wouldn't say they were common," Daisy was quick to point out. "It's premium ice cream."

"Yes, but they are the lowest," Partial Sue replied. "Everyone uses them because they haven't put their prices up."

"Exactly," Fiona said. "Prices have skyrocketed. Food, petrol, insurance, phone bills, bank charges. How can they keep their prices down when everyone else is putting theirs up?"

Partial Sue's eyes twinkled as if she'd been handed a winning lottery ticket. "Unless it's a front. A legitimate business subsidised by a shady one. An ice-cream mafia, using ice-cream vans to push their illegal wares."

Fiona had never been a big fan of Partial Sue's pet theory. It was too brash and vulgar for such a genteel area, but perhaps that's why no one suspected it. Implausibility was great camouflage, and the idea made a lot of sense. Maybe the Vanilla Killer was not a person but an organisation, and now it was time to yank back the curtain.

CHAPTER 23

Fiona's naivety annoyed her. She'd been duped by the branding of Somerford Ice Creams — a cow grazing next to a tumbledown cottage with hills and a village church in the distance. It had graced the side of every ice-cream van she'd encountered so far. She wasn't so naive that she imagined the real-life version to be an exact replica of this rural idyll. But, every time she saw it, her mind conjured up tasteful barn conversions, clad in that rather fetching black wood, arranged around a central courtyard, tucked away up a woodland lane, maybe shared with a farm shop and an organic wine merchant. A place where diligent ice-cream makers went about their craft, serenaded by cows in the fields outside, the very same ones who supplied the milk for their honest trade.

The reality was a very jarring experience indeed. Partial Sue flung the car sideways, off the vast roundabout clogged up with rush-hour traffic. She'd already missed the exit once and didn't want to miss it again. At least the place was actually located in Somerford, just not the rural part. This was all takeaways, hand car washes and DIY warehouses. Perhaps this boded well, befitting a shady organisation masquerading as a purveyor of fine ice creams.

The car swerved into an industrial estate, a maze of identical units, row after row of them, numbered in a way that didn't make sense. They were looking for Unit D4, which they logically thought would come after units A, B and C, but when they reached the end of C, the sequence jumped to H.

Partial Sue's numerically analytical brain didn't like this one bit. "What are they playing at? What's happened to D, E, F and G?"

"We're in an industrial estate," Fiona said. "The rules of the outside world don't apply."

"So how do we find it?"

"I have a way that always works," said Daisy. "You just keep driving round and round until you stumble across it."

Fiona really wanted to employ a different method, one that had an efficient process to it, but for the life of her she couldn't think of anything.

"Try down there?" She suggested a little offshoot that curled away from the main drag, one of many they'd passed.

No such luck, so they tried another and another. On their fifth attempt, Daisy blurted out, "There it is!"

The unmistakable logo of Somerford Ice Creams appeared, bolted above a scuffed-up roller door big enough to fit a juggernaut. The ice-cream maker was sandwiched between a national chain of windscreen repair shops on one side, its skip piled high with shattered glass, and a plumber's merchants on the other, which stated in no uncertain terms that it supplied to trade only.

"This doesn't feel very premium," Daisy said. "Every time I have one of Bella's ice creams, I'm going to picture this place now."

"Aren't you worried Bella could be buying from the mafia?"

Daisy shrugged. "I still can't see it myself."

Partial Sue parked up and they headed through the door marked 'reception'. The interior had gone a long way to make amends for the state of the outside. The floor was covered in artificial grass, not the cheap kind that lined butcher's windows, but the type that could be mistaken for the real thing, as long as you squinted and didn't take your shoes off. A selection of old-fashioned metal milk urns occupied one corner, while a countryside mural of green fields and cows wrapped itself around all four walls. Three upright glass-fronted freezers hummed away in another corner, stacked to the brim with a rainbow of lollies and small ice-cream tubs.

"Do you think they're free?" Fiona asked.

"Never take from the mafia," Partial Sue hissed. "You'll be in their debt. Or worse."

Fiona wondered if Sue had seen one too many Martin Scorsese movies.

Daisy neutralised the melodrama. "I think Bella said you can try before you buy. But only if you're buying in big quantities."

Fiona turned her attention to an unmanned reception desk, made of mismatched reclaimed wood to further enhance the rustic feel of the place. An old-style brass desk bell sat on the counter, just begging to be pinged.

"Ooh, can I ring it?" Daisy asked.

Fiona nodded. "Why not?"

Daisy didn't hold back and slapped the top of it. The ringing in Fiona's ears was louder than the worst dose of her tinnitus.

A door with a keypad opened and a tall, slender man with well-groomed silver hair ducked his head under the frame. As he emerged, Fiona hoped she'd witness the magical art of ice cream making behind him, but all she glimpsed was a second door, firmly closed with another keypad.

Wearing a lemon-yellow polo shirt with the company logo embroidered on the left breast, he slotted himself at the desk.

"How can I help?" He was well-spoken.

"We were wondering if we could talk with the owner, or perhaps the manager," Fiona said.

"That would be me," he replied. "Our receptionist has left to take her daughter to ballet, so I'm on desk duty. I think it's important for the owner of a company to do all the jobs his staff does. Keeps me grounded, and it's good for staff morale." He didn't smile, telegraphing that he wanted to make a serious point.

His magnanimous approach wrongfooted Fiona. It wasn't what she'd expected from a potential mafia boss. Unless he'd just returned from a management training course and was regurgitating a line straight from a PowerPoint presentation. "Er, yes. That's very good of you. We're investigating the death of Kevin Masterson and would like to ask you some questions."

He raised his right eyebrow. "Do you have any ID?"

"We're not the police," Daisy informed him, "but we do want to catch Kevin's killer."

"Have you ever heard of any rivalries between ice-cream sellers?" Fiona asked.

"Sure. In the past, ice-cream sellers had a reputation for getting aggressive over pitches, but that was long before our time."

"When did you start your business?" Fiona asked.

"About six years ago, and I can tell you, in my experience, ice-cream sellers aren't in competition with one another. There just isn't enough of them, not when there's a convenience store on every corner selling takeaway ice cream. It's not a stable industry to be in. Everyone relies on a good summer to tide them over the lean winter months. A bad July and August can wipe them out. But ice-cream vans have it the hardest. Their number gets fewer and fewer each year. If anything, I'd say there was a camaraderie between sellers. A kind of Blitz spirit, that they're all in this together."

"So are you a sympathetic shoulder?" Fiona asked. "Do they confide in you?"

He shook his head. "Not really. They're usually in and out to pick up their stock. They don't hang around for much of a chat. But generally, they do strike me as a downtrodden bunch. Like they've accepted their fate — that it's a dying trade. I can honestly say I hate seeing it. Ice-cream vans are part of our heritage. It'd be a terrible loss if they disappeared from our streets. I try to help them out as much as I can."

If he was a mafia boss, then he had a very convincing cover story worked out. But she wasn't buying the idea of the benevolent business owner, trying to help out the little guy. Not in an age where everyone's profit margins were being squeezed.

"Do you remember selling to Kevin Masterson?" Fiona asked.

"I don't, I'm afraid. He definitely bought from us, because he set up an account, but our records show he only stocked up with us the one time, and then, unfortunately, he was murdered."

"Do you have any ideas about who could have done that?"

The owner shrugged and shook his head. "I don't, I'm afraid."

"Tell me about your illegitimate customers," said Partial Sue.

His eyebrows, which up to that point had both been arched, either in surprise or sympathy, suddenly angled steeply, like a couple of angry Stukas. "It's not against the law to sell ice cream to someone without a trading licence. In the same way it's not illegal to sell petrol to someone who doesn't have road tax." As he became conscious of his outburst, his features relaxed a little, as did his tone. "Thing is, I'd rather they sell our products to the public than some cheap muck from the cash and carry."

Partial Sue wanted to interrogate this further. "But surely if things were so tight, ice-cream sellers, whether legitimate or illegitimate, would buy the cheap muck to save money, rather than sell premium ice cream like yours. Yet they all buy from you, without exception. Don't you find that odd?"

The owner wasn't rattled by this, and maintained his serious business stance. "Not really. People's tastes have changed, or, should I say, they've become more demanding. We all used to drink instant coffee. Now people want proper coffee. Doesn't matter where it's from. It's the same with ice cream."

Now the million-dollar question. "So how do you manage to keep your prices so low when everyone else has put theirs up?" Fiona asked.

He smiled. Not the reaction she was hoping for. "Nice try, but I can't go revealing our trade secrets to anyone. Otherwise our competitors would start doing the same."

"Could we have a look at your operation?" Partial Sue asked. "A quick tour."

Daisy's eyes lit up. "Oh, yes. I'd love to see how ice cream's made. Is it like *Charlie and the Chocolate Factory*? Hey, that could be a sequel — *Charlie and the Ice-Cream Factory*."

"*Charlie and the Great Glass Elevator* is the sequel," Partial Sue said.

"Oh, yes, of course it is. Silly me," Daisy replied.

"So, how about that tour then?" Fiona was eager to see what was going on behind those key-padded doors, but for completely different reasons.

"I'm sorry, I can't," he said. "We don't do tours, I'm afraid. Now, if you'll excuse me, I really have to get back to work. But I do hope you find the killer." He gave them a half-hearted sympathetic smile, got to his feet, marched to the back and punched in the code. The door slammed abruptly behind him.

The ladies regrouped outside to sift through their findings.

"What did you make of that?" Daisy asked.

Partial Sue grumbled. "I'm not buying all this 'I'm keeping my prices low out of the goodness of my heart' rubbish. How can he sell his ice cream so cheap? He can't be making any money. It doesn't add up. And he didn't like it when we wanted to look around his factory. He's definitely hiding something."

Fiona interrupted her rant. "To be fair, most businesses wouldn't let three strangers who've turned up on their doorstep have a nose around behind the scenes."

Partial Sue shook her head. "That's not why I think he's hiding something. It was the airlock."

Both Fiona and Daisy stared at her, bewildered. "Airlock?" they chorused.

"The door he came through," she explained, "or doors, I should say. Two of them, both with keypad entry and a small space in between. It's a security feature called an airlock. I can't be a hundred per cent certain in this instance, but usually you can only open the second door once the first one has been shut and locked behind you. Did you notice how quickly it slammed?"

Fiona and Daisy both nodded.

Partial Sue continued. "Basically, anyone unauthorised who manages to slip through the first door will get penned in that space between, without any hope of getting any further. They're used in places that need the highest security, like prisons and where large sums of cash or gold are kept."

"So why would an ice-cream manufacturer need so much security?"

Partial Sue smiled. "Because there's something dodgy going on that they don't want anyone to see."

CHAPTER 24

Partial Sue stopped short of stamping her foot and making the shop's displays wobble. "We have to call DI Fincher! Tip her off about Somerford Ice Creams."

Fiona sighed and shook her head for the umpteenth time. "I don't think we've got enough evidence. All we have are some double doors."

"Airlock doors," Partial Sue corrected. "There's a big difference. That's a high-security feature in a place that makes ice cream, come on."

Fiona swallowed. "Okay, airlock doors and cheaply priced ice cream."

"That sounds like more than enough as a front for an ice-cream mafia. They're hiding something. A drug lab or a tonne of stolen goods, or both."

The ping-pong debate had been raging on all morning, until Daisy broke the deadlock. "Why don't you get a second opinion?"

"What do you mean, a second opinion?" Partial Sue asked.

Daisy had been quietly scrolling through her phone while the two of them had been going at it. She flipped it around so the pair of them could see a website on the screen. "They're not the only local ice-cream maker in the area."

Partial Sue read out the name of a website and shrugged. "Lyndhurst Ice Creamery."

Fiona had a more enthusiastic response. "That's not a bad idea. Any business worth its salt will keep a close eye on their competitors and what they're doing. Especially their pricing. It'd be good to pick their brains and make sure we're not making two plus two equal five."

Partial Sue grudgingly acknowledged a good plan. "Fair enough."

Fiona dug out her own phone. "I'm going to call them."

"Are you going to say you're investigating Kevin Masterson's murder?" Daisy asked.

Fiona shook her head. "Might put them off. I think I'll play the journalist card. See how it goes." She dialled the number, placed the phone flat on the table and put it on speaker.

It rang twice and then a cheerful voice said, "Hello, Lyndhurst Ice Creamery."

"Oh, hello there." Fiona attempted to match her chirpiness. "I'm doing interviews for an article about the challenges facing regional businesses and was wondering if I could ask your managing director a few questions."

The receptionist's tone dropped to a more pessimistic one. "Oh, no. She wouldn't have time for that. She's far too busy."

Fiona had prepared a strategy for dealing with a possible brush-off. "Oh, okay then. It's funny but a lot of ice-cream parlours and businesses I've asked have also said no."

"Well, that's because it's our busiest time of the year. What with all the good weather."

Fiona went in for the kill with a bit of corporate one-up-manship. "Yes, the only one who's agreed to speak to us is Somerford Ice Creams. It's a pity. They'll be the only one mentioned in the article. I would've liked another for balance."

The receptionist hesitated. "Er, one moment please. Let me see if she can spare a few moments."

Fiona winked at the others, hoping her little ruse would tempt the MD into taking the bait.

A quick-talking woman came on the phone. "This is Stella Maclin, managing director. I can give you two minutes."

"Thank you for your time," said Fiona. "We've recently spoken to Somerford Ice Creams regarding the challenges facing local businesses, specifically rising costs and having to increase prices. They've managed to keep theirs low. We were wondering how you're managing as a company?"

Stella Maclin released a tense breath. "Well, if I'm honest, I don't know how they're doing it. The cost of everything is going up — ingredients, labour, transport, just keeping the lights on. We've cut our operation back to the bone without sacrificing quality. I still can't figure out how Somerford can sell their ice cream so cheaply and make a profit. I could understand it if it was cheap rubbish, but it's premium quality. Obviously not as good as ours." She gave a nervous laugh. "I still think our ice cream is better than theirs. But that said, I can't see how it adds up."

"Has it always been like this?" Fiona asked.

"We're a family business. Been making ice cream for over thirty years. We dominated the local market until they came along. They undercut us from day one. We began losing customers. Ice-cream vans were the first to go. They went overnight. Luckily, they only made up a small portion of our profit. But then restaurants, hotels and ice-cream parlours followed. I have to fight tooth and nail to keep the customers we've still got, but we can never match Somerford on price. I've racked my brains, but I still don't know how they make it so cheaply. I'm sure they must be up to something."

"You don't think they're selling drugs, do you?" Fiona half-joked.

Stella Maclin laughed. "That would explain a lot! No, I don't know what their secret is. Probably skimping on an ingredient here and there, whereas I can assure you our product is one hundred per cent premium. We have and will never cut corners! But, if you find out, please let me know. Listen, I'd better go. I have a list of invoices as long as my arm I need to pay."

Fiona thanked her and hung up.

Partial Sue jumped straight in. "I don't need to hear any more evidence. Unfeasibly low prices, over-the-top security and every ice-cream seller around here on their books. I smell something illegal."

"What do you think, Daisy?"

"Something fishy is going on, definitely."

Fiona agreed. She called DI Fincher, who, uncharacteristically, answered first time. "I hope this is important, Fiona."

"It is," Fiona replied. "I have a lead for you in the Kevin Masterson case. A big one."

CHAPTER 25

The following day, nails were bitten down to the quick as the ladies waited on word from DI Fincher. Fiona was itching to call the detective, desperate to hear how it had gone down with the infamous yet invisible ice-cream mafia, and whether they'd been dragged kicking, screaming and squinting into the light for all to see.

Allowing herself a little indulgent fantasy, she pictured the owner of Somerford Ice Creams and his minions, hand-cuffed and being frogmarched out of their industrial unit and into the back of waiting police vans, followed by lines of officers ferrying labelled boxes of evidence (which may or may not have included tubs of ice creams) into the boots of waiting patrol cars. DI Fincher and DS Thomas would be coolly look-ing on, perhaps the young female detective allowing herself a wry smile as she luxuriated in the bust of the decade. It'd probably make the national news. The pair of them would announce the arrests in front of a packed press conference, shutters clicking and pens scratching. Maybe the young DI would make an ice-cream-related pun about this being a big scoop for the assembled reporters.

Fiona was getting carried away. What was she thinking? DI Fincher wouldn't make puns about something so serious.

Actually, she doubted the young detective made puns full stop, even when she was off duty. But there might be a chance the Charity Shop Detective Agency would get a mention — anonymously, of course. The assembled press would hear how three diligent ladies, whom the police had come to rely on for their unique insight into the criminal mind, had given them a valuable tip-off. Fiona shook her head, annoyed with herself. She was becoming puffed up and proud, and knew only too well what came after that.

She took a little comfort from Partial Sue, who'd been thinking along similar lines. "I'd love to be there. Watching it all go down. Place surrounded by police cars."

"We could go and have a look," said Daisy. "Nothing stopping us."

Fiona shook her head. "I don't think that would be a good idea. DI Fincher wouldn't want us getting in the way of a raid."

"No, I suppose not," Partial Sue said. "I'm sure she'll let us know in her own good time."

DI Fincher's own good time turned out to be a shade before five thirty, as the ladies were preparing to close up and go home for the evening. Fiona knew something wasn't right the second DI Fincher walked in with DS Thomas. He looked his normal tatty self, his expression poker-faced as always, but the young DI had a fierce, bothersome heat radiating off her that appeared to warp the air around her.

She got straight down to it. "Well, I've used up all my favours with the magistrate's court, pushing through an urgent search warrant, under section 23 of the Drugs Act, and all for nothing."

Fiona's heart plummeted. "You didn't find anything?"

"Oh, yes. We found something. Ice cream. Lots of it. A complete and utter waste of time, not to mention we'll be the butt of everyone's jokes at the station. It wouldn't surprise me if our desks are covered in sprinkles and strawberry syrup when we get back."

"There weren't any drugs?" Partial Sue asked.

"Nope." Her reply was stern and economic.

The humiliating experience silenced the ladies, their collective heads hanging heavy.

Partial Sue dared to raise hers above the parapet. "Okay, but how did they explain their cheap prices?"

DI Fincher glared at her. "Well, we're going to be tied up for ages with their accounts, thanks to you, which I doubt will reveal anything, but the short answer is, you didn't look into the owner's previous business, did you?"

The ladies exchanged blank glances.

"No," Fiona replied.

"Well, if you had, you'd know he used to own a company that specialised in streamlining. That's going into other firms and showing them how to save money."

Fiona didn't dare ask the detective why she hadn't carried out this background check herself before they stormed the premises, clutching a search warrant.

DI Fincher continued her angry rant. "The only thing Somerford Ice Creams is guilty of is being very good at working smartly." DI Fincher shook her head in disgust. "This is my own stupid fault. I knew this was a mistake. We ruled out the idea of ice-cream mafias from the start because we didn't find any traces of drugs in Kevin Masterson's van when we first searched it."

Partial Sue wouldn't be deterred. "What about their airlock doors? Bit over the top for a place that makes ice cream."

DI Fincher was ready to go into meltdown, so DS Thomas stepped in. "Owner says he has a secret recipe for ice cream that was his Italian grandmother's. He's paranoid. Keeps it locked in a safe. Doesn't want anyone catching accidental glimpses of their secret ingredients or methods. Hence the airlock."

DI Fincher still hadn't finished their dressing-down. "Now, if you hadn't already guessed, I'm none too pleased with being sent on a fool's errand, especially when it's cost me so much in time, effort and boots on the ground. Next time, leave the detective work to us professionals. This was incompetent, ladies."

The young detective turned on her heel and stormed out of the shop, followed by her nonchalant DS who, at least, did not feel the need to slam the door.

CHAPTER 26

Fiona found herself shuffling around the shop vacantly. She'd head off to a corner, intent on doing something, then forget what that something was when she got there. Partial Sue was sitting, puffing out her cheeks, while Daisy gazed into space, mindlessly munching on her favourite snack which she called a prawn cocktail cocktail, which was a packet of prawn cocktail crisps into which she'd decanted another flavour, in this case smoky bacon. Yesterday's disappointing police raid on Somerford Ice Creams had robbed them of any fervour for solving the case, forming a humid atmosphere of negative apathy, not helped by the knowledge that they were in DI Fincher's bad books. She wasn't pleased with them at the best of times, but now Fiona could imagine the young DI seething at her desk at the mere thought of them, unintentionally snapping pencils in her fist.

Their spell of feeling sorry for themselves didn't last very long. Bella burst through the door, angry tears raking her face. "That's it! I've had enough! I'm fed up with that bloody ice-cream van!"

This was starting to become a bit of a habit.

Daisy was by her daughter's side in no time. "Oh my gosh, Bella. What's the matter now?"

"My tyres have been slashed! I'm selling it. First thing tomorrow, it's going on Autotrader!"

Daisy gently guided Bella to the table and poured her a cup of tea. She wrapped her hands around it, not drinking it, just clutching the vessel — a warm, ceramic comforter. In between sobs and gulps for air, and the odd bout of rage, she attempted to explain what had happened. "It's my own fault. I can't believe how stupid I've been."

"Why? What did you do?" her mother asked.

"I pitched up by the river again at Wick."

"Where you got the rude note?"

Bella nodded as more tears fell from her face.

"Oh, Bella, why did you do that?"

Bella gave a sad smile. "Well, I was in a really good mood this morning. My trader's licence came through online so I wanted to go back to Wick and show them they hadn't won, that I wasn't scared."

Partial Sue clenched her fists. "I bet it was that smarmy Pompous Alan, from Alan's Place."

Bella shook her head. "That was my first thought too. But the place had been closed up all morning. Nobody there."

"So where were you when it happened?" Fiona asked.

"Same as before. I'd only been open for an hour. Really needed a wee. I waited for a lull, locked up the van, then nipped along the river to the toilets. When I got back, all four tyres were slashed."

"So where's your van now?" Daisy asked.

"Still down there. I had to leave it locked up with the engine running so the ice creams wouldn't melt. Then I walked here."

"You should've called," Partial Sue said. "I'd have picked you up."

"Thanks, Auntie Sue, but I didn't want to bother you, and I thought the walk might calm me down, but it hasn't." Fresh tears streaked down either side of her face. The sadness was short-lived. She jutted out her chin and narrowed her eyes. "I'm fed up with it all. I'm selling that van, soon as it's fixed."

"I'll pay for the new tyres." Daisy pulled out her phone and began searching for mobile tyre fitters.

"No, Mum, it's okay. It's my mess. I need to fix it."

"It's not your mess," Fiona said. "You're not responsible. The person who slashed your tyres is, and I would just like to say—"

Bella interrupted her. "Please don't try and talk me out of it, Auntie Fiona. I don't want to do this anymore."

"I wasn't going to, especially when I tell you that yours wasn't the only van to be damaged in the last few days."

Bella stared at her with wet, unblinking eyes.

Fiona continued. "Some guys we know, the Icely Brothers, had their van set alight in the early hours of Monday morning. I think it's getting dangerous out there, so I whole-heartedly support you stopping."

"I sense a 'but' coming," said Bella.

Fiona gave her a sympathetic smile. "You're very perceptive. There's also an opportunity here to catch the person who's been doing this, and possibly the person who killed Kevin Masterson."

"I don't like the sound of this," said Daisy. "Is Bella going to be in danger?"

"Not if we do it right."

Partial Sue shuffled her seat forward, eager to hear more. "What's the plan?"

Fiona turned to Bella. "Once the van's fixed, and you've had a chance to recover from the shock — give it a few days, take as long as you want — I propose you go back down to the same spot and sell ice creams, then nip off to the loo, just like you did today."

"But won't the same thing happen again?" asked Daisy.

"That's exactly what I'm counting on. However, this time, we'll be there, out of sight, watching."

"A stakeout!" Partial Sue exclaimed.

"Yes."

A smile finally appeared on Bella's face. "We catch them in the act."

Fiona nodded.

Bella nodded back. "I'm in."

CHAPTER 27

Bella hadn't needed any time at all to recover herself. After hearing Fiona's plan, her distress had transformed into a righteous energy, an implacable rage that had to be satisfied immediately. She'd wanted to put Fiona's plan straight into action so she could catch the scumbag who'd been sabotaging her fledgeling business.

Fiona could understand her impulsiveness, and the powerful need for closure, but persuaded her it would be wise to wait. The chances of the perpetrator still being in the area were slim, and, even if they were still in the vicinity, it might be pushing their luck to expect them to risk attacking her van a second time that day. Plus, there might be an outside chance that they would sense it was a trap.

Bella took Fiona's advice. Once the tyres had been replaced, she picked up her ice-cream van and drove home. She agreed to wait twenty-four hours. The next day, however, Operation Van-detta, as Partial Sue had punnily named it, was a go.

It meant closing the shop again. This time for the whole day, which was sure to elicit complaints from customers, but it had to be done. This would take all of them to pull it off — plus they'd need two cars.

At around ten thirty, Partial Sue took up position along the road, just outside the village. With only one way in and out of Wick, the perpetrator would have to pass her, whether they came in by car or along the footpath beside the river. However, there was another route out of Wick, on the other side of the village, which could be accessed by foot. A kissing gate set in a dense hedgerow led to the river meadows, a choke point of the prettiest kind. To cover this exit, Fiona nabbed the nearest parking space to the gate. From there, she and Daisy could see everyone who came through it and had an uninterrupted view along the riverside to Bella's van, parked further down.

"Do you think she'll be okay?" Daisy asked.

"She'll be fine," Fiona said. "This person is a coward, sneaking up on her van when she's not around. And we're here keeping an eye on her."

Simon Le Bon sniffed, as if to remind them that he was also here, or perhaps because he wanted a snack. Daisy had already broken the seal on her vast stack of provisions, nervously eating her way through them, starting with a packet of cheese straws whose days were numbered, judging by the fierce rate at which she was tucking into them. She broke off the end of one and tossed it to Simon, but he missed and it disappeared down the gap between Fiona's seat and the centre console.

"Sorry," Daisy said.

"That's okay."

Undeterred, Simon Le Bon forced his furry little muzzle down the chasm, upending his bum for all to see. This was not how Fiona imagined most stakeouts went.

Daisy's phone pinged. "It's Sue."

"Has she spotted something?" Fiona asked.

"No, she's asking if we have."

"We've only been here half an hour."

The time dragged on, boredom being their only companion throughout a very long and uneventful day. The Goldilocks weather, though just right for luring people to the riverside for an agreeable stroll, also warmed the car up, caressing them into

160

a light snooze. The only thing that kept their eyes popping open were the constant pings from Partial Sue, like a bored child asking if anything was happening. At least Bella was having a good day. The fine weather prompted a healthy trade. However, today she wasn't here to sell ice creams. She was here to dangle a carrot, and tempt a miscreant into attacking her van. So, roughly every hour, whenever it coincided with a lull in business, she would lock up the van and head to the toilets to provide the perfect opportunity for the vandal to strike. Having performed this pantomime at least five times so far, she'd returned on each occasion to find her vehicle still intact.

The day dissolved into early evening, a beautiful one at that. Bella was still managing to sell ice creams, but as the sun dipped and dusk descended, customers became fewer and far between.

Fiona's phone pinged. This time it was a message from Bella.

What should I do? It's getting really quiet.

Fiona thought about calling it a day. Everyone was tired and dozy through lack of stimulation, but something stopped her. She remembered that stakeouts were a game of persistence, sticking it out until something happened. But maybe they could force the hand of fate. Up the stakes of the stakeout and give the perpetrator a target they couldn't resist.

Fiona replied.

I have an idea. Lock up the van and leave it here overnight. That'll make it more attractive for our vandal. We'll stay here keeping guard.

If I switch off the engine the freezer will eventually run out of power, and everything will start melting.

Oh, I forgot about that.

It'll be fine. There's not much stock left. Just be a
few puddles to clear up tomorrow.

Great! You go home and get some rest.

Nope. I'm staying. I want to catch this creep.

Good for you!

As the last light of the day evaporated into the darkness, Bella killed the engine and shut up shop, leaving her van alone and vulnerable. She hurried along the riverside and, when she was sure no one was looking, quickly darted into the backseat of Fiona's car. Her mum immediately thrust a Tupperware box of sandwiches under her nose. "Have something to eat, love."

"Oh, great. I'm famished." Bella squinted, trying to identify what was what.

Daisy pointed them out. "That's cheddar and pickle. There's BLT — that's Sue's favourite, but I forgot she'd be in another car. That's prawn cocktail, my favourite. That's brie and cranberry — Fiona's favourite. Egg and cress . . . oh, and tomato and mozzarella."

"Jeez, Mum. How many sandwiches did you make?"

"Well, I only used a couple of loaves of Best of Both."

"Do you mind if I have one of your cranberry and bries, Auntie Fiona?"

"Of course not, be my guest."

Bella took two large bites and groaned. "Oh, that's better. All I've had today is a ninety-nine, a slushie and a packet of crisps. Do you think this is going to work, Auntie Fiona?"

"I have no idea, but I think an unattended ice-cream van at night might be too much of a gift horse for our perp to ignore."

Bella continued grazing, Daisy joining her, eating their way through the Tupperware box. Despite their rate of consumption, they still only managed to empty half of it. After all that carbohydrate and protein, plus the warm night air and the darkness enshrouding the car, both Daisy and Bella slid into deep sleeps, as did Simon Le Bon now the food had been put away. Fiona stayed alert by exchanging texts with Partial Sue, who never had any problem staying awake, although her texts were mostly to complain about how she'd run out of food ten minutes ago. Not that long for most people, but with her metabolism it would be the equivalent of four hours without sustenance. Fiona didn't have the heart to tell her there was nearly a full complement of BLTs and other assorted sandwich flavours residing in a gargantuan Tupperware box in her footwell.

As the night wore on, quiet and uneventful, the texts from her colleague gradually subsided until they ceased completely. With no more stimulation, fatigue also came for Fiona, gravity tugging at her weary eyelids. She nodded forward a few times, almost diving headfirst into slumber and just managing to pull herself back from the precipice. But, like an addictive drug, sleep's beguiling siren call came again and again, and she could no longer resist. It pulled her down into its dark, delicious depths.

At around two thirty in the morning, a ping woke her.

Groggily, she found her phone and glanced at the screen. A text message from Partial Sue.

Look lively. Ice-cream van heading your way.

CHAPTER 28

A pair of sinister headlights raked the darkened road ahead. Fiona shrunk down in her seat, out of sight, Simon Le Bon still snoozing soundly on her lap. She didn't need to worry about Daisy or Bella, as mother and daughter had been slowly slipping further and further down their seats since falling asleep.

The engine noise increased as the ice-cream van came closer, but then suddenly changed tone. Fiona chanced a peek over the top of the dashboard. It had passed Bella's van and was now executing a three-point turn. It was too dark to make out any distinguishing features or a number plate. Completing its hurried manoeuvre, the van drove away.

Fiona's phone pinged. A message from Partial Sue.

What's happening?

Fiona thumbed a rapid reply.

Nothing. Van heading away.

I see it. It's gone. False alarm.

Wait. Could be a recce.

Fiona waited. Her two companions were still sound asleep. Still oblivious. This would be a good opportunity to wake them, just in case the van decided to reappear. As she shifted herself back to an upright position, Simon Le Bon suddenly woke with a start. He panicked and leaped off Fiona's lap and onto Daisy's. She screeched loudly, waking up Bella in the back.

"Wh-what! What's happening?" Bella slurred.

Simon Le Bon got on his hind legs and licked Daisy's face. "Oh, hello, little one. I must have dozed off."

"You both did," Fiona said.

"What time is it?" Bella asked.

"Two thirty."

"Two thirty! We've been asleep for hours."

"Don't worry about that now," Fiona said. "We've had a visitation."

"A fizzletation?" Daisy mumbled.

"An ice-cream van just came down here."

This sobered up Bella quicker than a shot of intravenous caffeine. "Has my van been damaged?"

"No," Fiona replied. "They turned around and drove back out."

"So it was a false alarm. But we still need . . . to be on our guard . . . I suppose . . ." Daisy's voice trailed off as she slid back into sleep.

"We're waiting to see if it comes back, so I wouldn't get too comfortable, Daisy."

Daisy jerked upright, pretending she was wide awake. "Yes, Daisy Lambkin here." She answered as if the teacher had called the register.

Fiona's phone pinged. "It's Sue. She says the van's on its way back. We need to get low, so we're not spotted."

Like a trio of synchronised swimmers, they sunk down into their seats. A second later the drone of an engine reached their ears, growing louder by the second, then it levelled off, not ceasing but not coming any closer either. Just ticking over.

"What's happening?" asked Bella.

Fiona was about to risk poking her head up above the dashboard again, but Daisy had a better idea. She fished out her phone, set it to camera mode and held it like a digital periscope. They all peered up at the screen. In the gloom, they could see the van had stopped next to Bella's with the engine running, but the lights off. A hooded figure slid out of the driver's side, a man from what they could tell, but that was all they could discern. He momentarily reached back into the cab to retrieve something.

"What's he doing?" Daisy asked.

"Nothing good," said Fiona. "Are you recording this?"

"You bet," Daisy replied.

The figure reemerged with one shoulder slumped. His body language appeared uncomfortable, his movements stuttered and unsure. He shuffled around to the front of Bella's van and faced the bonnet. He hesitated, statue like, almost as if he were contemplating what he was about to do. He remained that way for several seconds, not stirring. Then, glancing left and right, he slowly raised his right arm, like a bowler about to pitch a ball. His intention became clear when they glimpsed what was in his hand: a large brick.

Before he had a chance to send it crashing through the windscreen, Bella leaped out of the car and shouted, "Oi! Stop that!"

She ran towards him, Daisy following her, still recording. Fiona reached across and switched on the car headlights, spotlighting him in the act. The vandal froze as if the light held him in a forcefield.

Fiona exited the car, joining the chase. The vandal dropped the brick and dashed back to his van. After a grinding of gears, the van reversed, then lurched forward, back out the way it had come.

Fiona texted Partial Sue a single word.

Block.

Partial Sue sent back a thumbs up.

They'd planned ahead for this scenario, it being the most likely outcome. If he tried to make a getaway, Partial Sue would throw her car across the narrowest part of the road, blocking his exit. She'd then get a safe distance away, just in case the driver became desperate and attempted to ram it movie-style. They all knew this would be dangerous but couldn't think of any other way to cut off his escape. Partial Sue had immediately volunteered her car, mostly for economic reasons rather than heroic ones. After its last MOT, she'd been informed that a great deal would need replacing soon, adding up to more than the car was worth. So it would be no great loss if it was written off by a rogue ice-cream van. Always thinking with her purse, she could claim on insurance and buy something else.

The only problem with this part of the plan was that it was happening out of sight, on the other side of the village, where the road narrowed to a single lane.

Fiona didn't need to worry or wonder any further. She got another ping.

He's heading back your way.

From down the road, she heard the strained vocals of an engine abruptly reversing, far too quickly. The ice-cream van reappeared, or rather, its rear end did. Careering all over the road, it sped past Bella and Daisy, who continued filming. Just before it reached Fiona, the van screeched to a halt — perhaps the driver realised he had nowhere to go, unless it was through the dead end formed by the dense hedgerow behind her. Good luck with that, thought Fiona. Sherman tanks had had trouble penetrating hedgerows in World War Two. She doubted an ice-cream van would make it through. The driver must have come to the same conclusion. The van held its position, the driver possibly contemplating how he'd become trapped in Wick of all places.

Bella ran towards the van shouting and swearing — mostly swearing. "Why do you keep attacking my van? Hey, I'm talking to you."

Daisy brought up the rear, her phone raised.

Suddenly, the driver's door flew open, startling everyone. Killing the engine and cutting his losses, the hooded man abandoned his vehicle and made a sprint for it. Bella tried to chase him, despite her mother's protestations. He dashed across a wide expanse of grass and trees, heading for the houses beyond. Sprinting down the drive of the nearest one, he sprang onto its recycling bin then vaulted onto the garage, disappearing into the back garden. Bella attempted to follow, but her sandals weren't the best choice for scaling single-storey buildings. She rejoined the others.

Partial Sue appeared, hurrying down the road, breathless. "What happened?"

Bella was panting. "We lost him. He's probably escaping across people's back gardens as we speak."

"Did anyone get a good look at him?" Daisy asked.

"No," Fiona said. "But I know who he is." She gestured to his ice-cream van. The ladies turned to examine the abandoned vehicle. Daisy threw some light on it with her phone torch. It was pink with 'Ice Creams' written above the windscreen in no-nonsense Helvetica.

Daisy gasped, recognising it first. "It's the one from Rufus Stone! The chap the Icely Brothers chased away."

"I knew it would be him!" Partial Sue blurted.

"Who?" Bella asked.

"We don't know his identity," Fiona explained. "He's an unlicensed seller we saw in the forest, but he was scared away by a couple of guys from another ice-cream van — the one that got torched."

"By him!" Partial Sue proclaimed. "It was so obvious he'd be the culprit. Well, we've got his van now."

In his panic to flee, he'd left the door wide open.

"How does that help?" Daisy asked.

"We can search it. Find out who he is." Partial Sue flicked on the torch of her phone.

Bella did likewise. "I'll help you."

Fiona watched the pair of them climb on board and heard them rummage around inside. It didn't take long. Shaking their heads, they emerged empty-handed.

"Nothing," said Bella. "He hasn't left his keys in it either."

"Wait here." Partial Sue scuttled back down the road, out of the village. A minute later she pulled up in her car and retrieved something from the boot — a large, flat, cumbersome metal contraption looped with heavy duty chains and a meaty padlock.

Bella recognised it first. "A wheel clamp?"

"You keep a wheel clamp in your car?" Fiona asked.

"Yeah," Partial Sue replied. "You never know when you might need it. Like now. We clamp his van. Then it's our turn to write a rude note on *his* windscreen. Tell him, if he wants it back, he can come and have a little chat with us at the charity shop."

"But he's left it parked really badly," Daisy said.

"All the more reason for him to come and see us," Partial Sue replied.

Bella smiled devilishly. "Can I write the note?"

CHAPTER 29

They'd all come in early the next day, Bella included, eagerly anticipating the arrival of the vandal ice-cream seller. Everyone sat tensely around the table, eyes transfixed on the door. Fiona had furnished them all with a cup of tea and a piece of cake, but no one had touched theirs. Perhaps their minds were too busy, their imaginations on fast forward, concocting little scenarios about how this might play out. Or maybe it wouldn't play out at all. After seeing him off in the early hours of the morning their spirits had been high, brimming with bravado and adrenalin. Positive that they had him over a barrel and he'd have to come to them with his tail between his legs. But now, in the cold light of day, that seemed like wishful thinking.

Cynically, Partial Sue turned on her own plan. "He's not going to show. He's been a coward up until now. He's not going to suddenly change his ways and face the music."

"But what about his van?" Daisy said. "He can't just abandon it."

"People abandon cars all the time," Fiona said. "I think Sue's right. We need to be realistic. Would an illegitimate ice-cream seller who's been skulking around causing havoc suddenly come and face us?"

170

"Probably not," Daisy said. "Especially if he also killed Kevin Masterson."

Fiona glanced up at the door, as she had been doing all morning, except this time she noticed the open sign was round the wrong way. She got up and flipped it the right way. As she turned back to the ladies at the table, their faces turned pale. Partial Sue's mouth fell open. At first, Fiona thought it was fear, but quickly realised it was astonishment.

"What?" asked Fiona.

"He's behind you." Daisy's response seemed more suited to a pantomime, but was wholly appropriate.

Fiona turned. On the other side of the door stood the villain they'd been expecting. Dressed in black, his hood up, the young ice-cream-selling Cat Stevens lookalike from the forest held his hands up in surrender. "Can we talk?" His voice was soft but filled with desperation, his eyes wide with fear.

She held the door open for him. He stepped in immediately and didn't stop until he was deep inside the shop. Only then did he pull his hood down, setting his tousled brown hair free.

Bella scowled. "You've got a nerve coming here."

"Er, we did ask him," Partial Sue pointed out.

"I really need my van back. As soon as possible," he said.

"Not going to happen." Bella rose from her seat and approached him, fire in her eyes. "You've got some explaining to do, so talk."

He wouldn't meet her stare. "Please, I really need my van back. It's not what you think."

Bella folded her arms. "And what do I think it is? What possible reason could you have for attacking my van and causing me all this misery, unless you really hate me?"

"I swear, I don't hate you. Quite the opposite. I was trying to protect you."

Bella scoffed. "What, by writing rude notes, egging my van and slashing my tyres?"

"Don't forget, he was going to put a brick through your windscreen," Partial Sue added. "We've got it all on film, sunshine."

The man didn't answer. Just bowed his head in silent shame.

Fiona drew closer to him. "What's your name?"

He looked up at her and swallowed. "Vernon. Vernon Coles."

"Let me see some ID," she demanded.

"Why do you need to see ID?"

Fiona glared at him.

Vernon didn't argue and slid his driving licence out of his wallet. Fiona examined it. He was who he said he was. She made a mental note of his address and handed it back to him. Now she had confirmation of his identity, there was an important question Fiona needed answering before Bella unleashed her full wrath on him. "Did you kill Kevin Masterson?"

The question blindsided him. "What? No, course I didn't. I'm not a murderer."

"You see, we have a bit of a problem believing that," Fiona said. "Due to your recent antisocial behaviour."

"That's an understatement," Bella sneered.

Daisy, who had been sitting quietly up until now, suddenly exploded. "Why have you been so horrible to my daughter? What has she ever done to you? She's a kind, gentle person and you're a nasty, nasty man! Excuse my French. You should be ashamed of yourself."

Out of all the things that had been said since entering the shop, this seemed to injure him the most. Humbled, he stared at the carpet, eyes almost tearful.

"Well?" Fiona asked.

He wouldn't speak, but kept staring at a spot on the floor.

Fiona changed tack. "Did you attack the Icely Brothers' van?"

His head flicked up and his expression changed to one of surprise. "No. What happened to it?"

"It was burnt to a husk. Did you do that?"

"No, I swear I don't have a problem with the Icely Brothers."

"Really?" Fiona asked, with more than a hint of scepticism. "Well, they had a problem with you. Kicked you off your pitch in the forest last Sunday. We were there. Saw the whole thing. Then you retaliated. Torched their van in the early hours of Monday morning. Make a habit of that, do you? Attacking other people's ice-cream vans?"

Vernon scratched at his beard nervously. "I didn't do that, I swear."

"Then who did?"

Vernon clamped his mouth shut, as if the answer might accidently escape. He stared cautiously at the door. "Please, I really need my van back. I have things to do."

"You can have your van back as soon as we get some answers." Bella snapped.

Partial Sue made sure the financial element in all this hadn't been forgotten. "And you need to reimburse Bella for all the expensive repairs you caused and all the stress."

Vernon paced up and down like a caged animal. "I'll pay for the repairs, whatever the cost. I swear." He started shaking his head. "But I can't tell you anything."

Fiona decided to up the ante. "It's either tell us or we call our friend DI Fincher and let the police deal with it."

"And we show them the video," Daisy added.

This halted him. His agitation ceased. He stared at them both with pleading eyes. "No, don't do that. I'll tell you, but it's going to put me in a lot of trouble."

"Aw," said Bella. "What a shame. That's what happens when you do bad things."

He cleared his throat and straightened up into a more dignified posture — he'd accepted his fate. "I didn't torch the Icely Brothers' van. I have no idea how that happened. Have you spoken to them?"

"No, we couldn't get hold of them," Fiona said.

"That makes sense."

Fiona exchanged confused looks with the other ladies, then turned back to Vernon. "What makes sense?"

"Desperate times call for desperate measures," Vernon said cryptically. "I doubt what happened in the forest on Sunday was personal. They needed someone to create a motive for burning their van and I just happened to be there. Of course, I'm not happy that they used me, but I can understand it. I've been thinking of similar ways to get out."

"You're not making any sense," Partial Sue said. "Get out of what?"

Vernon became silent again, his face downcast. He took a deep breath. "Their obligation."

"What obligation?" Bella asked.

"The one I was trying to save you from." He looked at Bella sadly.

"I don't understand," she replied.

Vernon gestured to the table. "May I sit down?"

Fiona nodded and took a seat, as did Bella.

"Do you think I could have a cup of tea?" he asked.

Fiona shunted the teapot in front of him. "It might be a bit cold."

"Oh, that's okay. Warm and wet as they say." He gave a weak, quivering smile as he poured himself a cup, taking a sip with trembling hands. "It's probably best if I start at the beginning." He sighed defeatedly. "I used to work in an office but it really didn't suit me. I don't like the nine to five. Don't like being tied down, so I saved up some money and bought an ice-cream van."

"When was this?" asked Partial Sue.

"Six years ago," he replied. "I loved it. The freedom, the flexibility. I could work when I wanted and where I wanted. I was really happy. Then something happened. A few months later, I got photographs of my family in the post. My mum and dad coming out of their house. My sister leaving her house to take her little boy to school. My younger brother on his way to college. The shots were taken from a distance, probably using one of those big lenses, like the paparazzi use."

"Did they say who they were from?" asked Fiona.

He shook his head. "No. No explanation, nothing. I was terrified."

"Did you go to the police?" asked Partial Sue.

"I was about to when this guy turns up on my doorstep. Another ice-cream seller."

"Who was it?" Bella asked.

"A guy called Tom. Although you probably know him better as Sergeant Bilcone. Said I had a job to do or else it would turn out very bad for my family."

A collective gasp came from around the table. Fiona felt her stomach plunge. She had always thought Tom was hiding something with his jollity, but never in a million years did she think Sergeant Bilcone was blackmailing one of his own. How could the real-beard Santa be behind all this?

CHAPTER 30

The ladies spoke over one another, frantic for answers, firing questions like verbal Gatling guns.

"Did he kill Kevin Masterson?"

"Why did he pick on you?"

"Did he force you to vandalise my van?"

"What did he stand to gain?"

Vernon held up his hand for ceasefire. "Please, it's not what you think. Sergeant Bilcone, sorry, I mean Tom, was as distraught as I was. He was just the messenger. He's as much a victim as me."

"How so?"

"He'd also received photos of his family. All ice-cream sellers around here have. Whether they're licensed or unlicensed, they all get recruited to sell drugs from their vans. If they don't, then something nasty will happen to them or their family."

"An ice-cream mafia! I knew it!" Partial Sue exclaimed. "Sorry, please continue."

"Do you know who they are?" Fiona asked.

"No, never seen them. It's all completely anonymous. All done with a dead drop. Whether it's messages, collecting the drugs or dropping off the money. You have to do what they say or else something happens to your loved ones."

"Do you think they killed Kevin Masterson?" Fiona asked.

"Absolutely."

"He hadn't had his van for long," Fiona said.

"Yes, that's right. My personal theory is they tried to recruit him, but he refused and they made an example of him for the rest of us. They usually wait a month or two after someone's bought an ice-cream van, to let you settle into it, find your feet and get comfortable, then you get the threatening photographs in the post." He turned to Bella. "That's why I've been attacking your van. I've been trying to put you off, so you'd give up, get rid of your van before they came for you."

Bella's face turned white.

Vernon continued. "I'm really sorry that I couldn't tell you. It's too dangerous. I'm taking a big risk just talking to you now. But, even if I'd said something, you probably wouldn't have believed me, or thought I was making it all up. You looked so happy selling ice creams when I first saw you in Wick. I thought, I can't let something horrible happen to such a nice person. Knew I had to do something. I'm sorry it was such a horrible way to do it, but I couldn't think of anything else. So I started with the note and then . . . Well, you know the rest."

The anger subsided from Bella's face. "I had no idea. So you *were* trying to protect me."

He nodded.

"I'm sorry for the things I said about you," Bella apologised.

"Me too," Daisy said. "You're not a nasty man. You're a very nice man, although I don't approve of your ways. But Bella's still in terrible danger from these people."

"Yes," Vernon said. "There's still a bit of time before you get the photos in the post. You need to get rid of your van as soon as possible."

"But then the next person who buys it will suffer the same fate," Bella said.

"Not if you sell it in another part of the country," Vernon replied. "Far away from here, or you do what the Icely Brothers did — torch it."

"Would I have to disappear? I'm not sure I could do that."

"No," Vernon said. "You have an advantage. Unlike the Icely Brothers, you haven't been recruited yet. You've got at least a couple more weeks before that happens."

"You could take it to a scrapyard," Fiona suggested. "You won't get much for it, but it will take the van out of the game — completely."

Always money-conscious, Partial Sue piped up. "Make sure you take out the soft ice-cream machine and the slushie machine first. You can always sell them separately on eBay."

"Your safety is more important than money," said Daisy. "You should scrap it. Be done with it."

Bella thought for a moment. "Let me try selling it up country, but if I can't get a buyer straight away, I'll just scrap it."

"And nobody has any idea who's behind all this?" Fiona asked.

Vernon shook his head.

"Has anyone staked out this dead drop?" Partial Sue said "To see who's leaving the drugs and picking up the money?"

Vernon became agitated. "We're all too terrified that something will happen to our families. We keep our heads down. Please don't tell me that's what you're planning to do. If they get wind that someone's been watching them, you could be putting my family in danger, and everyone else's. Please promise me you won't do that."

Fiona allayed his fears. "Okay, we promise. But is the dead drop always in the same place?"

"No, they change it every now and again. Which reminds me, I really need my keys back. If I haven't left cash or made a pickup, I'll be in trouble."

"Of course," Fiona said.

Partial Sue handed him a key. "That's for the wheel clamp. Just leave it on the grass and I'll pick it up later."

Bella got up and gripped his hand reassuringly. "Don't worry, Vernon. Everything will be all right. My mum and her friends will find out who's doing this and put them behind bars. You'll see."

"We've done it before," Partial Sue enthused. "Several times."

Vernon attempted a smile, but it came out as more of a grimace, as if he didn't believe that was possible. "Please, don't let anyone know that I've been here or talked to you. Otherwise, my family will be in danger. And I'd drop your investigation. Leave it alone, or you could end up like Kevin Masterson." He flipped up his hood, put his head down and hurried out of the shop.

The ladies stared at one another, the shock not budging from their expressions. Their nocturnal efforts had paid dividends, thrusting the investigation forward enough to give them all whiplash. Digesting this new and profound information would take a while, and Fiona could already feel her brain buzzing with possibility.

CHAPTER 31

Bella did the smart thing and left immediately to take her van off the road, hiding it from view in Daisy's garage. She'd only ever drive it one more time, either to sell to someone who lived a safe distance from this awful ice-cream mafia, or to take it to the local scrapyard. Before she left, Fiona had detected conflict in her face. Tinged with sadness, the bittersweet decision had been forced on her, and, deep down, Fiona suspected that Bella really didn't want to get rid of the van. It suited her personality, her quirky and bohemian lifestyle, and had brought a fleeting happiness into her life. But, more importantly, it symbolised a new independence. Divorced from her husband, it represented freedom and a fresh start. But from day one it had also been the bane of her life, sucking out the hope and scraping away what little self-confidence she had. The continual attacks on her van had taken their toll, and although Vernon had honourable and compassionate reasons for doing them, she must have felt violated and under siege. But that was nothing compared to what could have happened if he hadn't intervened. Her new fledgling life could have been enslaved by these anonymous drug dealers. He'd saved her from the awful fate of being held to ransom by the fear they might do something terrible if she didn't comply.

Despite Vernon's warning to drop the investigation for their own safety, Fiona was determined to catch the people responsible. They had to be stopped before anyone else fell victim, but also to release all the innocent ice-cream sellers already in their vile clutches. First the ladies had to figure out how to do this without endangering their lives and the lives of their loved ones. This had led to a stalemate around the table. Pondering the delicate, volatile situation, they found themselves continually hamstrung. Suggestions would erupt only to be quickly derailed by worry that it would lead to mafia reprisals. People could get hurt if they weren't careful.

"You know what's weird about this?" asked Partial Sue. "The police must know they're dealing with an ice-cream mafia selling drugs. Kevin Masterson's van would have been analysed. Forensics would have found traces of drugs."

"But remember what DI Fincher told us?" Fiona asked. "She said there were no traces of drugs in his van. And according to Vernon's theory, Kevin Masterson probably hadn't started selling for the mafia yet. They tried to recruit him, and he'd refused. There wouldn't have been any drugs in his van to discover."

"That's true," Partial Sue replied.

"But that also doesn't make sense," Daisy said.

Everyone looked at her, puzzled.

Daisy continued. "From what we've been told, this ice-cream mafia gets people to do their bidding by threatening their families. If Kevin refused, surely they would've done something to his mum, until he did what they wanted."

"She never mentioned being threatened," Partial Sue said.

Fiona nodded. "No, they went straight to killing her son. They don't seem to be following their own logic."

"Unless there was some other reason they killed him," Daisy suggested.

Partial Sue snapped her fingers. "Maybe he did start selling for them and began keeping some of the money for himself, until he had enough to pay his mum back. In mafia circles, skimming off the top is definite grounds for execution."

"But if that were the case, there'd be traces of drugs in his van," Fiona pointed out. "The police would've detected them, suspected an ice-cream mafia and hauled in every ice-cream van from here to Rufus Stone to check them for drugs, but we know that hasn't happened."

"Well, I have something else that's puzzling me about Bella's van, which has only just occurred to me," Daisy said.

"What's that?" Partial Sue asked.

"Why is it out in the world?"

Fiona wondered if this was some deep metaphysical question about the nature of reality and why we're all here. "How do you mean?"

"Well, isn't the van evidence? Shouldn't it be locked away in a police cupboard or in a labelled bag? I mean, it would have to be a big cupboard and a big bag."

This hadn't even crossed Fiona's mind before now. She had no idea how long evidence was kept for, especially if it had four wheels, but in an ongoing murder case, it did seem odd that it had been released back into the wild, as it were.

"Maybe the police got everything they needed from it," Partial Sue said. "Which is why it was auctioned off."

Fiona shook her head. "Daisy's right. It's evidence in a murder investigation. It should be under lock and key. I'm going to call DI Fincher."

Daisy suddenly became worried. "Is that wise? We're not very popular at the moment."

"I realise that," Fiona replied, "but we need to make her aware of this situation. Even if we're making a nuisance of ourselves."

"Hey!" Partial Sue became excited. "We can tell her what we've learned about Vernon and the ice-cream mafia. Get her to talk to the other ice-cream sellers?"

Fiona frowned. "She doesn't believe it's an ice-cream mafia, especially not after our tip-off. And the ice-cream sellers will never confide in the police. They're all too scared."

"What about Vernon?" Partial Sue replied hopefully. "He could tell her what he told us."

Fiona shook her head. "There's no way he'd do that."

"He's too frightened," Daisy added. "It'd put his family in danger."

Partial Sue screwed up her nose.

Fiona called the DI. It went straight to voicemail, so she left a message.

One hour later, DI Fincher slipped into the shop, almost as if she hoped no one would notice her. The ladies had never seen her without DS Thomas by her side or bereft of confidence. She appeared decidedly sheepish, her eyes never making contact with any of the ladies.

"On behalf of Dorset Police, I must apologise for a gross clerical error." The DI appeared to be aiming this statement in Daisy's direction. "The ice-cream van currently in your daughter's possession should not have gone to auction. There was a clerical mix-up. Human error. A builder's van with an almost identical registration should have been sold off."

"You should be apologising to Bella, not me," Daisy said coolly.

"A separate team from the station will contact her to secure the van's safe return. She will be reimbursed for the full amount she paid. But I thought I would come here and apologise in person."

Consternation wracked Daisy's face. Fiona felt sure she wanted to offload how much grief the van had caused her and her daughter, which could have been avoided if the police had kept it under lock and key. But then the ladies wouldn't have met — or rather encountered — Vernon, and now have the possibility of catching the Vanilla Killer, who was almost certainly a member of the local ice-cream mafia. Speaking of which, she looked across to Partial Sue, whom she knew would be itching to impart this information to the young DI.

Even in her current, humiliated state, the detective would not be receptive to the idea after what had happened with

Somerford Ice Creams. Not until they had conclusive proof. Fiona caught Partial Sue's eye and surreptitiously shook her head. Sue glared back at her.

"I hope this is acceptable," DI Fincher said quietly.

Daisy exercised a great deal of restraint. "Apology accepted."

Partial Sue wasn't about to let her get off that lightly. "Last time you were here, you called us incompetent. I'd say losing evidence is incompetent, especially when it's got four wheels, weighs a couple of tonnes and plays 'Greensleeves'—"

Fiona cut her off before she went too far or divulged any information about Vernon and the ransomed ice-cream sellers. "Well, all's well that ends well. It was nice of you to drop by, DI Fincher."

The detective didn't hang around and made a swift exit. Partial Sue did not look pleased at all.

CHAPTER 32

Days had passed and still no consensus could be reached on how to move forward with the precious information that had dropped into their collective laps. At times it felt as if the three of them were clutching a Ming vase, precariously shuffling along a never-ending corridor strewn with mouse traps, and they'd all neglected to bring their slippers.

"You know, the simplest way to catch this mafia would be with another stakeout. Monitor the dead drop. That's the weak link in their system. I mean, if there's a way to do it without being detected."

Fiona sighed. "Well, that's the problem in this case. Normally stakeouts are fine, but if money and drugs are involved, you can bet the dead drop is being monitored. If they see anything out of the ordinary, like a trio of ladies sitting in a car nearby, we could end up being the next victims. It's clear these people have no problem murdering anyone who gets in their way."

"We could set up cameras again," Partial Sue suggested.

"Same problem. If we attempt to set up a camera and we get noticed, then they'll come after us. Let's think about this laterally first. See if we can come up with another way of figuring out who's behind this. One that doesn't involve putting us or anyone else in danger. But, before that, I need more tea."

"I'll make it." Daisy gathered up the vast brown teapot in both hands and disappeared into the storeroom.

Partial Sue lowered her voice to a whisper. "Do you think Daisy's okay? She's had quite a stressful time."

Fiona leaned in. "You know, after everything that's happened, I think she's relieved that Bella's finally got rid of that van."

"That's true. She doesn't have to worry anymore. Well, apart from Bella getting her money back."

"She still hasn't been reimbursed?"

Partial Sue shook her head.

Daisy returned a few minutes later with the steaming brown teapot. She placed it in the middle of the table to let it brew, then poured them each a cup. The ladies went quiet, minds intensely cogitating, the silence only interrupted by little slurps here and there, but no suggestions or ideas came forth on how to identify the ice-cream mafia. Hours passed like this with nothing to show for it, apart from bellies full of tea and having to break off every now and then to serve a customer, or pop to the loo.

No matter how hard they tried, the deadlock wouldn't budge. Like a stubborn stain, it refused to shift, despite several washes on the hottest setting and using life hacks learned online.

"What if we tell DI Fincher about the dead drop?" Partial Sue suggested once again. "Leave Vernon's name out of it. Undercover police could monitor it."

Daisy glared at her. "We made a promise to Vernon. Said we wouldn't mention anything. It'd put too many lives at risk, his in particular. And I doubt he'd reveal where it is."

"DI Fincher could offer to put him and his family in police protection," Partial Sue said.

Fiona shook her head. "Firstly, she wouldn't believe us. She's convinced the ice-cream mafia is a fantasy, and, secondly,

186

we're all out of favours where she's concerned. And, thirdly, I don't want to jeopardise anyone's safety."

Partial Sue clicked her fingers, another idea popping into her head. "What if we show DI Fincher the blackmail photos Vernon got of his family? I bet that would convince her."

"I can't imagine he'd agree to that either," Daisy said.

Partial Sue fidgeted with frustration. "Then nothing's going to change. This will keep happening again and again. A constant cycle of ice-cream sellers and their families being held to ransom. Bella got lucky. She got out before it was too late. Can you imagine what would've happened if she hadn't?"

Daisy's eyes dulled with sadness at the terrible thought. "You're right. We have to do something."

"I can't see any other way," Partial Sue said. "We have to persuade Vernon to tell us where this dead drop is. That's the only link to the ice-cream mafia."

Fiona sighed and reluctantly nodded in agreement. "I think you're right. I can't see any other way forward. We'll have the opportunity to ask him. Here he comes now with Bella."

Daisy leaned forward, conspiratorially. "Oh, I forgot to tell you, those two have become quite good friends."

Partial Sue's eyebrows rose so high they almost disappeared into her hairline. "Well, I never. Who'd have thought it? Good friends with the chap who vandalised her ice-cream van."

"Yes, once you get past that, he's a very nice, polite young man, although I have to remember he did all that for a good cause."

"That sounds like he was doing it for charity." Partial Sue chuckled. "Maybe sponsored vandalism will overtake sponsored walks as the favourite money raiser. By the way, has he paid her back for all the damage?"

"He offered," Daisy said, "but she wouldn't hear of it."

Talking of money, Bella pushed open the door, flashing a cheque and a smile, cautiously followed by Vernon, his hood up and his head constantly twisting over his shoulder, surveying the street outside. Once safely ensconced within the protective walls of the shop, he lowered his hood but remained ever vigilant.

"Is that the cheque from the police?" Partial Sue asked.

"Certainly is." Bella waved it in front of the ladies triumphantly. "Full amount. I'm just off to pay it into the bank."

"You'll be lucky." Partial Sue snorted. "Bank's not there anymore. They shut it ages ago. Got to use your phone now."

Bella screwed up her face. "Really? I hate doing that."

"You won't get any argument from me," Partial Sue said. "I prefer handing it to a real person."

"Do you want me to do it for you?" Daisy asked.

"Yes, please, Mum. I've got the app but, whenever I try to do cheques, my hand wobbles when I take a picture of it. I can never seem to get it in the guidelines. It's too fiddly."

"Me too," Partial Sue agreed. "They're not designed for people with shaky hands. Thankfully, your mum's hands are like the Rock of Gibraltar. By that, I mean super steady, not a giant lump of limestone."

Daisy didn't take offence. She took the cheque from Bella and proceeded to flatten it on the surface of the table, preparing to take a photo with the app on her daughter's phone. Bella and Partial Sue gathered around to watch the proceedings, but Fiona's eyes were drawn to Vernon. Positioning himself away from the window, in the darkest corner of the shop, he appeared conflicted and preoccupied, shifting uneasily.

"You okay, Vernon?" Fiona asked.

He smiled. "Yes, I'm fine. Thank you."

Clearly he wasn't. The chap had feelings for Bella, that was plain to see. Fiona could tell by the way he gazed longingly at her, but then his face would twist and grimace as his eyes darted towards the door, evaluating it for possible threats. This must have been a bittersweet moment for him. He'd stuck his neck out to save Bella and it had worked — in a clumsy, roundabout way. He'd spared her from an inevitable life of enslavement under the cosh of the ice-cream mafia. But who would save him?

Fiona didn't see any point in beating about the bush. "We have a proposition for you, Vernon."

Everyone at the table spun around, curious to hear what she had to say.

Fiona had to be careful how she phrased this. "There might be a way of catching the ice-cream mafia, but we'd need your help."

Daisy spoke softly. "You came to Bella's rescue, saving her from them. It's only right we do the same for you."

Vernon glanced nervously at the assembled faces. "I don't know what you have in mind, but I'm sure it's not a good idea."

Fiona hoped to assuage his fears. "Listen, we won't do anything you don't want us to."

Hope flickered briefly in his fearful eyes. "What is it you want to do?"

"The dead drop is the only connection to whoever's behind this," Partial Sue said. "It's the weak link. The chink in their armour."

"We need to monitor it somehow," Fiona added.

Vernon took a subconscious step back, not that there was any room to do this, and nearly collided with a display. "No, no way. It's too dangerous. If I'm implicated, my parents and my sister and my brother could get hurt."

"We know," Partial Sue said. "But what if we plan something together? Perhaps there's a way we could safeguard you and your family. Maybe you could all go away while we do this."

"They'd get suspicious. Would want to know why they have to leave town, and my sister has a little boy at school. She couldn't just take him out."

"Okay," Fiona said. "What if we think of another way? One that wouldn't put you or your family in danger."

"What do you have in mind?"

Fiona was stumped. "Nothing yet, but together I'm sure we could think of something."

Vernon flipped his hood up and began edging towards the door. "No, this is a bad idea. My whole family could end up getting killed."

Bella reached out and grasped his hand. "Vernon, at least see what they come up with, then decide. These ladies have done this before. Caught criminals the police have had no luck catching. They can do this."

"I don't doubt that." Vernon sighed. "But it's too dangerous."

"It will be dangerous," Fiona said. "We can't promise you otherwise. But we'll try our best to keep everyone as safe as possible."

"And the alternative is unthinkable," Partial Sue added. "Doing nothing means you'll be at the mercy of the ice-cream mafia for the rest of your life, with your family held hostage. They'll never be safe and neither will you."

Vernon studied the wall, then hung his head low with the weight of inevitability. "Okay. But I want my say and to veto anything I don't like."

"We wouldn't have it any other way," Fiona said. "Now come take a seat." They all pulled up a chair and sat at the table.

Vernon lowered his hood. "So how does this work?"

Daisy rose to her feet and gave him a reassuring smile. "First things first. We make tea."

CHAPTER 33

The table became a hotbed of ideas. Fiona listened as they came thick and fast. Some good, some bad and some average. Some were simple and others were more complicated than putting the CERN Hadron Collider back together wearing boxing gloves. But they all had one thing in common — none of them were feasible or particularly safe. Vernon sat in silence, shaking his head to each one. Yes, he was being over cautious, but, to be fair, he had good reason. The chances of pulling this off without endangering the lives of anyone in the room, or any family members being threatened by this group of gangsters, were non-existent.

"Why don't we just do a stakeout like we did down at the river?" Bella suggested. "We caught this one in the act." She nudged Vernon playfully.

He reacted with a weak smile. The poor lad didn't appear to be enjoying this very much.

"There's a strong possibility they'll have someone monitoring the dead drop," Fiona replied.

"That's right," Vernon said. "I've heard that from other ice-cream sellers, though I've never seen anyone."

"But what's the point of a dead drop if you have to keep an eye on it?" Bella asked. "Surely it's not a dead drop then."

"It's always been called a dead drop." Vernon shrugged. "But I guess it's just a drop."

Partial Sue, the spy expert, filled them in. "Dead drops are normally to avoid face-to-face meetings, so no one witnesses the exchange. Live drops, on the other hand, are when two operatives meet to exchange something of value. I suppose this is a mix of both. The mafia want to avoid contact with ice-cream sellers to protect their anonymity, but they also want to monitor the drop so they can collect the money once it's deposited, instead of having it sitting there unattended." She turned to Vernon. "I'm guessing you can make a drop whenever you want."

"That's right. They like us to keep it random. No set patterns. And once we've left the money or picked up the drugs, we have to leave immediately."

"And is the dead drop always in different places?" Partial Sue asked.

"Yes," Vernon answered. "They'll use a location for a few weeks and then move it somewhere else. Never the same place twice."

Partial Sue rubbed her hands excitedly. "If they need eyes on it all the time, they're bound to have someone sitting in a car twenty-four-seven. We stake out the person who's staking it out, as it were."

Vernon shifted uneasily in his seat. "The problem with all your ideas is that there's a chance you'll be noticed. They'll be suspicious of someone sitting in their car all day, looking for someone else sitting in a car."

"Depends," Partial Sue replied. "I mean, you didn't spot us staking out Bella's van down at the river."

Vernon flushed with embarrassment. "That was different. I wasn't expecting it, whereas these guys will be on high alert."

"Where is the current dead drop located?" Fiona asked. This was the million-dollar question, the one Vernon had been holding back on. His last line of security and the real test of whether he genuinely trusted these ladies. Once it had been revealed, then the safety catch was well and truly off.

Vernon hesitated. That was to be expected. After swallowing hard, he spoke slowly. "Redhill Park. There's a car park facing a large flat stretch of grass, with a main road on one side, and pine trees on the other. Very exposed. I've been instructed to pull up in the car park and make the drop at an ugly concrete litter bin nearby."

Fiona knew how hard that must have been for him, so she didn't make a big deal of it. "I know that park."

"How do you make the drop?" Partial Sue asked. "Is it put inside the bin?"

Vernon shook his head. "There's a crack in the side of it. The drugs are stuffed into a crisp packet wedged in the crack. Just looks like litter. I take it and, when I've sold all the drugs, I reverse the process. Put the money into the crisp packet and stuff it back into the crack."

"And how do you know when the dead drop has changed?" Fiona asked.

"They leave a message in the crisp packet."

Daisy gathered her thoughts. "Okay, so we sit in a car all day watching out for someone else sitting in a car all day. Assuming they don't spot us first. What then?"

"All we need is their car registration," Fiona replied. "Hand it to DI Fincher."

Partial Sue spotted a problem. "This person's probably just a lackey, a foot soldier. Sure, the police would get them for dealing, but we need to take down the big boss if this is going to end."

"Wouldn't this lackey give up the name of the boss in return for a deal?" Daisy asked.

Partial Sue's nose twitched. "Highly doubtful. They'd be too scared. Snitches get stitches, as they say."

"Worse than that," Vernon added. "They'd end up like Kevin Masterson."

His last words stumped everyone. Though harsh, Vernon was right. This was how these organisations worked, whether you were on the outside or the inside. Fear and intimidation kept everyone in line, ensuring their loyalty, buying their silence and keeping the boss safely ringfenced at the top.

"What if we follow them?" Bella suggested. "There has to be a shift change, a point where one lackey takes over from the other. Surely at that point they take the money to their boss."

Vernon didn't like the sound of that either. "Following them would be dangerous."

For once, Partial Sue agreed. "Not to mention tricky. There's an art to tailing a car without being detected. Realistically, none of us are experienced or skilled enough to pull that off." Her eyes suddenly glinted with possibility. "But there is a safer way to find out where they're going. We put a GPS on their car."

Vernon quivered with terror, his mouth twisting into an awkward shape. Fiona could sympathise. A minute ago, the talk had been of simply staking out the dead drop, which was dangerous enough, but now they were in the realms of stealth missions, sneaking up to a gangster's car and somehow attaching a tracking device to it. His head shook rapidly. "This is getting out of hand."

Fiona agreed. "That's a great idea, Sue. But one, how are we going to get close enough to do that without being spotted? And two, there's a strong possibility that this person hands the cash to the next person up the chain, and when they do, the trail will go cold."

Desperate to make her idea work, Partial Sue began having a little debate with herself. "What if we . . . No, that wouldn't work . . . How about we . . . No that wouldn't work, either . . ." Eventually she flopped back in her seat, defeated.

Silence consumed the shop as yet another idea had the kibosh dropped on it. No one spoke, and many arms were folded around the table, accompanied by a great deal of sighing.

Bella broke the deadlock first. "Okay, it seems to me that we need to think of the ideal scenario, then work backwards, figure out how to make it happen."

Partial Sue harrumphed. "The ideal scenario would be this lackey going straight to the boss, so we can see who's behind this all. Oh, and without any of us being seen. That's a big ask."

"It is, but at least it gives us something to work with," Bella said.

"If you want the lackey to go straight to the boss, it'd need to be something big and dramatic," Vernon said. "Big enough so it would merit more than just a phone call. That's assuming they've got a direct line to the top."

More silence. Minds ticking over like engines idling but not actually going anywhere. Daisy stood up. "I'm going to make tea. Who wants one?"

Nobody responded verbally, they were too deep in thought, but she did get unanimous nods.

Daisy lifted the empty teapot from the table and headed into the storeroom. A few minutes later she returned with the tea-laden pot. "What's a mafia frightened of?"

It sounded like the start of a joke found in a budget Christmas cracker. The question snapped everyone out of their contemplative state.

"Pardon?" Partial Sue replied.

"Well, I was just thinking in the storeroom. Everyone's frightened of this mafia, terrified, even the people who work for them, so I just thought, what if we turned the tables. Make them scared for a change. People do foolish things when they're scared. What made me think of it was bin day. I remember one time I woke up scared that I hadn't put the bin out. Went out at three in the morning to drag it onto the pavement."

"Well, that's not foolish," Partial Sue said. "That's sensible."

"Yes, but it wasn't bin day."

"Hey, that's not a bad idea." Fiona loved the way Daisy's mind worked. Only in her head could two things as disparate as bin day and the mafia become lassoed together, and sent tumbling down her neural pathways, knocking into things until they emerged from her mouth as a potentially great idea.

"How do we make a mafia scared?" Bella asked. "They're not scared of anything."

Partial Sue shook her head. "They're certainly not scared of the police."

"They must be scared of something," Fiona said.

Bella reached out for the teapot, then hesitated, her hand hovering inches from the handle, as if an invisible force was preventing her from grasping it. "What about another mafia? That's what usually happens in the movies."

Partial Sue clicked her fingers. "You're right! Another gang muscling in on their territory. A rival firm!"

"Good idea, Bella." Daisy smiled warmly at her daughter. "That would definitely give them the willies."

It must have been a good idea, because the teapot remained in the middle of the table, ignored, while the possibilities abounded. However, some practicalities had to be established first.

"But how and where are we going to get another mafia from?" Fiona asked. "It's hard enough finding this one."

"Yes," Vernon agreed. "And if we could find one, aren't we playing with fire, inviting another, more powerful mafia to take over?"

It was the best idea they'd had all day, a strong idea that would undoubtedly achieve what they wanted, but like a high-performance sports car in the hands of a teenager, it had the potential to accelerate out of control. The silence resumed, as everyone attempted to wrangle it into some sort of workable solution.

After a minute or two, Fiona spoke. "We don't need another mafia. Not a real one, anyway. We just need the current mafia to believe one exists. We pretend. Create the threat, but it's completely non-existent. Make believe. Just enough to scare this lackey to go crying to his boss."

They all exchanged glances, checking one another's reaction. Smiles spread around the table, a positive affirmation. Even Vernon cracked a fleeting grin.

Partial Sue drummed the edge of the table excitedly. "That's brilliant! That's how we get them!"

"I think that deserves a cup of tea." Daisy stood, lifted the pot and began pouring.

Celebrating the breakthrough, they raised their cups and took deep, well-deserved swigs. Gurning faces swiftly followed, accompanied by a bevy of bleurghs from everyone. The tea had gone stone cold.

CHAPTER 34

Now that one breakthrough had been made, others were quick to follow. The mental walls that had been holding them back began toppling, liberating their thoughts and allowing them to think more clearly.

Most notably, they realised a long-winded and risky stakeout to locate and identify the lackey guarding the dead drop really wasn't necessary. Normally, stakeouts were performed to catch someone in the act. The endless hours would be whiled away, waiting for the mark to show up and hopefully do something they weren't supposed to be doing. Vernon, a case in point. However, according to what he had told them, the lackey would already be there, monitoring the dead drop and conveniently not moving an inch for hours and hours. All they had to do was spot this person fixated on a bin and move on. Not that difficult unless he was hidden up a tree in the nearby park with a pair of binoculars and a flask. More likely he'd be ensconced in a vehicle somewhere.

The car park would be the obvious place. It had an uninterrupted view across the grass to the dead drop. However, it was too exposed. Someone intent on sitting in their car for hours on end would stick out like the proverbial sore thumb.

Vernon confirmed that, from recent pickups and drop-offs, he'd not seen anyone in their car gazing at a concrete litter bin. The only people he'd seen frequenting it were dog walkers.

Logically, the ideal position would need a clear line of sight across to the park but from somewhere a little less exposed. Fiona pulled up a Google map of the area on the shop's laptop and they all gathered around.

Fiona pointed at the screen. "That main road running adjacent to the park has three smaller roads turning off it at right angles. Anyone parked in the mouth of one of these roads, facing the park, would have the perfect observation post."

"That makes sense," Partial Sue agreed. "Our lackey's bound to be parked up in one of them."

"But how are we going to safely spot this person?" Daisy asked. "And how do we tell who's a gangster from someone innocently waiting to pick up a friend?"

"By the law of averages," Partial Sue said. "We each take it in turns to drive down all three of these roads, maybe a couple of hours apart. Nothing fancy. No stopping or slowing down, just behaving like normal motorists passing through, but we keep our eyes peeled for anyone sitting in their car. If we all see the same car and the same person sitting in it, say, over a six-hour period, law of averages says that's our lackey. Unless the friend they're waiting for is taking a hell of a long time to get ready."

For once, Vernon's face didn't contort into a mask of worry. "Sounds simple enough."

"May I use the laptop?" Bella asked.

"Of course." Fiona slid the laptop in front of her. "What are you looking for?"

"I just want to see what these side roads are like." Bella switched the map to Google Street View. One by one, she flicked along each of the three roads with their lines of sturdy red-brick baby-boomer houses. "Mmm," she muttered. "Nice roads with nice houses with nice people living in them

— people who'd take notice of a car with someone sitting in it, day after day and night after night."

"There are three roads to choose from," Vernon said. "Probably rotates position each day."

"But they still need to park near the entrance of each road," Bella said, "to get a view across the main road to the park. Whoever owns a house on the corner or next door is going to notice someone in a car who appears every three days, watching the park for hours on end."

"Bella's right," Daisy said. "People get funny about things like that."

"Patterns get noticed," Partial Sue agreed. "If someone appeared outside my house every three days, I'd think they were casing it for a burglary."

"Okay, good point," Fiona said. "What about on the main road, adjacent to the park? There aren't any houses on that side."

Bella scrolled her way back out onto the main road. "No, all double yellows. And he can't park on the other side either, because that's also double yellows, and more houses." Bella continued along the main road, until she came across a break in parking restrictions in the form of an incongruous lay-by. "That's odd, having a random lay-by in a suburban area." She jiggled with the view, observing it from different angles. "It's outside a very high fence and some gates. But I can't see a house."

"Maybe it's a very small bungalow," Partial Sue suggested.

Bella switched to Google Earth and zoomed in from above. It appeared to have a house on it, albeit a very tiny green one in comparison to the very large grey slated roofs around it. "What is that?"

They all leaned in for a closer look.

"It's not a house," Vernon said. "I think it's an electrical substation."

Bella went back to Street View and played around with the angles again. Frustratingly, the image kept leaping forward, but she just managed to settle on one that revealed a tiny triangle of yellow attached to the fence. "I think you're right.

200

I bet that's the edge of a warning sign not to enter, but Street View has cut most of it off. This has to be a substation, which would make the lay-by in front the ideal place to park up. No prying eyes and twitching curtains. I think this is where we'll find our lackey."

A series of positive smiles spread around the table as the logic slotted rather nicely into place.

"Okay then. We start our series of drive-bys to spot this lay-by lackey." Fiona's catchy alliterative name raised a few smirks.

Partial Sue pointed to the image on the laptop. "Remember, nothing fancy. Drive past once and that's it."

"What if the lay-by lackey is, er, not in the lay-by?" Vernon asked.

"We try the three side roads," Fiona replied. "If no one's parked up in a car, no U-turns to have another look or driving around in circles. This lackey might be somewhere we haven't thought of, but still keeping an eye on things. The last thing we want is to draw attention to ourselves. Come straight back. We regroup and have a think." Fiona nodded in the direction of Bella and Vernon. "I think it's best if you two stay out of this part and leave it to us three."

Vernon and Bella agreed.

"So who's going first?" asked Partial Sue.

"I will," Fiona said.

CHAPTER 35

After the shop had closed for the day, Fiona embarked on the first recce to detect the lay-by lackey, as he'd come to be known. Nipping home first to pick up her car, she dropped off Simon Le Bon, filling his bowl with dog food (she wouldn't have heard the last of it if she hadn't). She did briefly consider bringing him along, but he'd only start crying and whimpering if he sensed they were driving past a vast grassy park with no intention of stopping for a walk — a distraction she could do without on this important occasion.

At a shade past six thirty, Fiona pulled off the roundabout at Wimborne Road and headed south along Redhill Avenue. The road became immediately enclosed by thick, unkempt woodlands. Devoid of much traffic or pedestrians, it provoked feelings of isolation and vulnerability. Her nerves began to prickle beneath her skin and she instantly regretted leaving Simon Le Bon at home. Fiona's hands tightened around the steering wheel and her tinnitus played a shrill note in her ears. She had to marshal her emotions, reminding herself that this was just a recce — or a looky-loo, as Daisy had more playfully put it.

Knowing this did nothing to quell her rising fears. This could be the first proper brush any of them had had with the ice-cream mafia, albeit a lowly foot soldier. Paranoid thoughts danced in her head. What if he saw her and knew what she was up to? What if he suddenly leaped out and caused her to crash? Apart from the obvious, her cover would be blown. A lot was riding on this, but it all depended on stealth. The mafia couldn't know someone was on to them. Not just yet, anyway.

Fiona shrugged off these unhelpful thoughts and rationalised the situation. The lackey would have no idea who Fiona was or what she was up to. He'd barely register her. Just another motorist on their way to somewhere else. But what if no one was there at all? What if this was all a complete flight of fancy? Nothing more than a fabrication dreamed up by their overactive imaginations. That would be far worse than the former scenario. A lot was riding on someone being in that lay-by. In fact, everything was riding on it. They needed someone they could manipulate, who would lead them to the boss. It was their one and only strategy. There was nothing else.

Fiona had to put these thoughts out of her mind. Stick to the plan. Drive the car straight. Do not be distracted. It seemed to work. However, her anxiety still lingered and, subconsciously, she pushed the accelerator closer to the carpet, eager for this to have a conclusion, one way or another.

Her car satnav bleeped twice, as it always did when it detected a speed camera up ahead. She slowed the car down, along with her thoughts. Stick to the plan. Drive the car straight. Do not be distracted.

As the trees thinned out, suburbia resumed on her left while Redhill Park appeared on her right, wide and sprawling, a vast groundsheet of green. A few couples crisscrossed it with dogs chasing sticks, while a father ran alongside his small child on a wobbling bike, teaching them how to ride. It was the perfect place to learn — gently sloping with few obstacles to get in the way.

Up ahead, a speed camera came into view, perched on top of a grey pole, like a robotic vulture. She reduced her speed to under thirty, as she passed beneath it and kept it that way. The traffic became busier now as cars filtered in from the first of the three side roads on the left. This was good. Crawling traffic would be more favourable for getting a look at the lackey in the lay-by without being obvious — as long as he was actually there. Passing the second road, her heart rate increased, thumping against her chest. Not long now. Before she'd reached the third road, the lay-by appeared beyond, just as she'd seen it on Google Street View. A strange feature in an urban setting, in front of a gap in the houses, punctuated by the high fence guarding the substation behind it. Except in this real-life version, a car occupied the space. A grubby white Vauxhall Corsa. Her adrenalin spiked. And there was someone sitting in it. She got another hit of adrenalin.

The early evening light was generous enough to reveal a lone male in the driver's seat, but that was all she could tell from here.

The traffic slowed some more as she approached the Corsa. Edging forward, there were only a few car lengths between her and the mark. A second later, up ahead, a car pulled out of a driveway unexpectedly, forcing the traffic to brake and bunch up, then slow to a standstill. A godsend. There was only one car length between her and the Corsa now, giving Fiona the perfect opportunity to observe the occupant from a close but safe distance. She drummed her fingers on the wheel. In case they locked eyes, it would appear that Fiona was just another impatient motorist on her way home. She needn't have worried. The chap was engrossed in his phone and not particularly vigilant when it came to keeping an eye on the dead drop. Young, possibly in his early to mid-twenties, he had a skinhead haircut and was wearing a white T-shirt several sizes too big for him.

While the handbrake was on, she did something illegal but extremely necessary. She wasn't about to look this short-cropped gift horse in the mouth. Snatching her phone from her pocket, she swiped the screen to camara mode, quickly pointed it at him and his car, and held the shutter button down. It rattled off dozens of shots, as many as she dared. A second later, the phone was back in her pocket just as the lackey looked up, checking the scene in front of him. Fiona had timed it perfectly. She played the impatient motorist once more, sighing and drumming on the steering wheel. He bought it and was lured back to his phone screen. The traffic resumed its slow procession. Lowering the handbrake, she set off, careful to keep her eyes facing front and resisting the temptation to give him one last sideways glance.

The level of adrenalin pumping through her arteries was now off the charts. Not only had she spotted the lackey, but she had photographic evidence too. Her fear and anxiety morphed into overwhelming elation. She couldn't be too cocky and had to check her emotions once more. As Daisy had quite rightly pointed out, he could just be some random guy, sitting in his car, checking his phone.

When she'd put a good distance between her and the Corsa, she pulled over and studied the shots she'd taken. They weren't bad for a bit of hurried, impromptu photography. However, there wasn't much else to glean from them that she hadn't already seen with her own two eyes. Just a lad in a T-shirt with clippered hair, almost down to the skin. No matter, she had photographs of a possible member of the ice-cream mafia, and that was a breakthrough.

Selecting a couple of shots, she texted them to Partial Sue and Daisy, who immediately sent back replies full of congratulatory thumbs ups and other bright, positive emojis. Allowing herself a moment of small joy, Fiona sat back and took several, measured deep breaths to calm her flustered nerves before pointing the car back home.

Simon Le Bon welcomed her from the moment she opened the front door, tail wagging and lots of snuffling excitement. Seeing his happy face, combined with the relief of being back home, melted all the tension she'd been holding onto. It was delicious to be finally making progress, but she'd have to wait until Daisy and Partial Sue had successfully completed their surveillance runs before she could celebrate properly. However, for now, she'd take this as a win.

Famished by it all, she headed into the kitchen, Simon Le Bon's wet nose never far from her heels. Her exertions had left her without the mental capacity for making food, so she pulled a homemade frozen lasagne from the freezer and popped it in the oven. Her version of the dish included aubergine, chiefly because she liked the texture it added. She'd mentioned this culinary quirk in the shop once. Both ladies had turned their nose up at the notion. Partial Sue because it was sailing dangerously close to moussaka territory, and Daisy because aubergines were sometimes called eggplants, and she had an irrational fear of that particular combination of words.

After demolishing the lasagne, making sure she saved some bits of ground beef for Simon Le Bon, she slid into a doze right there on the sofa, until her phone pinged and woke her with a start. It was a text from Daisy, sent at exactly eight thirty.

I've spotted him. Young lad with a skinhead haircut
in a T-shirt that needs taking in. In a Vauxhall
Corsa. Needs a wash. The car I mean, not the lad.
Going to celebrate now with a fun-size Twix.

Fiona texted her, partly to congratulate her and partly to make sure she hadn't pulled over within visual range of the lackey to delve into her bag of chocolate. Daisy texted back to inform her that she hadn't and was now on her way to the Co-op to buy milk, bread and marmalade — she'd seen an advert for Paddington and it made her want toast and marmalade. Being so suggestible, Daisy was a marketing person's dream. Although, thinking about it, hot toast smeared with melted butter and smothered in marmalade would make a nice tangy dessert after her lasagne. Fiona got to her feet and headed into the kitchen, accompanied by Simon Le Bon.

Two hours later, her phone pinged again. This time a text from Partial Sue, its tone far more serious and direct.

Target acquired. Sighting confirmed. Positive ID. Male. Caucasian. Early to mid-twenties. White T-shirt. Grade 1 buzz cut. White Corsa. Plates match. Returning to base.

The law of averages had come good. One sighting could be interpreted as an accident. Two, a coincidence. But three had to be confirmation. There could be no doubt. The theory had been proven. The rumour and hearsay had been validated. The lay-by lackey was real. An ever-present guardian of the dead drop, when he wasn't on his phone to stave off the boredom, that is.

They now had a small tenuous link to the boss, but a link nonetheless. One they could manipulate and exploit. Tomorrow, all going to plan, they'd twist that link to their will, creating a knock-on effect that would go all the way to the top. Whoever was the head of this criminal organisation — currently basking in their anonymity, enjoying untouchable status — was about to have a very bad day.

CHAPTER 36

At the shop the next morning, Fiona and Partial Sue waited eagerly for the arrival of Daisy, who would be in possession of the lynchpin to the whole plan. Fiona sipped her tea at the table, while Partial Sue strutted up and down in front of the window, scanning the road outside, pausing now and again to glance at her watch. It was only half past ten. Simon Le Bon moaned from his basket, sensing their collective unease.

Partial Sue was fretting. "Where is she? I'm going to call her."

"No, don't," Fiona said. "You'll only panic her. Daisy will come in when she's good and ready."

"How long does it take to make a business card?"

"You know Daisy. She's a perfectionist. She'll want to do a good job. Make it look convincing."

That last sentence was crucial. Though a simple and unassuming object, the business card was destined to have a devastating effect. The plan was to leave it on the windscreen of the lackey's car, while he was distracted by something not entirely legal but highly necessary to get his attention. The card would convey a warning from a rival but fictitious ice-cream mafia, informing the incumbent that they were no longer top of the food chain. A new criminal gang was moving in, taking over their territory. An incursion. A classic gangster storyline and source of dramatic conflict. However, they'd got the idea of communicating this message on a business card from the note Vernon had left on Bella's windscreen, remembering the fear, confusion and anger it had caused. But it would take a lot more than a business card slotted under a windscreen wiper to provoke him into calling someone higher up the chain to get a message to the boss. For this, they'd need to make a point. A big, horrible one that couldn't be ignored.

This was where the plan became a little precarious, not to mention dangerous, verging on downright reckless. A lot had to fall into place for it to work, but the end result would see the lackey being summoned by the boss, with said business card in his shaky, fearful hands. They were banking that the boss would want to see this business card in the flesh and interrogate the lackey firsthand, to verify his story. This would hopefully eliminate the card being handed to a middleman, and result in the lackey taking it straight to the head of the mafia. What would happen next was anyone's guess. Perhaps anger and fury, probably involving said item being crushed and thrown across the room, or perhaps ground under a booted heel. It didn't matter how that rage was manifested. All that mattered was that the lackey took the business card directly to the big cheese.

Partial Sue jittered with excitement. "Here she comes. Here she comes."

Daisy bustled into the shop, red-cheeked and flustered. "I'm sorry I'm late. I'm still getting to grips with Photoshop."

"Have you got it?" Partial Sue bounced along beside her as Daisy navigated her way through the shop.

"Sue, let her have a cup of tea and get settled first," Fiona said.

"It's okay. Yes, I have it. Actually, I have a few different options to choose from." Daisy dumped her bag on a chair next to Fiona and pulled out a hardbacked A4 manilla envelope. She slid its contents onto the table, scattering a selection of business cards in various shades that were slightly oversized due to a superfluous clear plastic coating.

Partial Sue reacted first. "Er, you've laminated them."

"Yes, I bought a laminator machine, just in case it rains, and the card gets soggy."

"Oh, er, good idea." Fiona couldn't put her finger on what it was about laminated objects. Though practical and hardwearing, the addition of a transparent coating reminded her of late-night takeaways rather than ruthless mafias.

Partial Sue snatched up a card and examined the single graphic on one side. "What is that?"

"A skull, like we agreed," Daisy replied. "Skulls are scary."

"Yes, but it looks odd."

Fiona had to agree. The big eye sockets and long snout gave it an almost cartoonish appearance. "What sort of skull is that?"

"A rabbit," Daisy said. "I've put it on all of them."

Partial Sue's eyebrows peaked like a couple of mountain tops. She examined the other versions on the table. "A rabbit? I don't want to be judgy, but a rabbit skull doesn't say 'criminal underworld' to me. It says 'pet cemetery'."

"Yes, but I thought the whole point of this was to get attention. Human skulls have been done to death, excuse the pun. But a rabbit skull, now that's different. They're going to take notice of that."

There was a bizarre logic to Daisy's argument that made sense to Fiona in an irrational way. "I have to admit, it is rather sinister. I can't stop looking at it."

Partial Sue stared at the simple graphic, unblinking. "Yes, it's definitely sinister. Okay, I'm convinced." However, her faced dropped when she turned the card over. "Who or what is The Bridport Collective?"

Daisy became enthusiastic. "Ah, yes. I made up a name for our fictitious ice-cream mafia. Just as an option."

"Why Bridport?" Fiona asked.

"And why Collective?" Partial Sue added.

"I've never been to Bridport," Daisy answered. "I thought it sounded gangster. And Collective sounds big. Like a huge network."

Again, there was a strange, skewed logic to Daisy's thinking, but the end result didn't have the same unsettling effect as the peculiar rabbit skull, as Partial Sue was quick to point out. "The Bridport Collective sounds like a regional performance arts group."

"Yes," Fiona agreed. "I think it's more threatening if the card is anonymous."

Daisy didn't get precious. "Okay, right. Fair enough. No names." She cleared away the cards bearing the name of the short-lived Bridport Collective and slotted them back into the envelope. "Now, which colour do you want to choose?" She held up a bright-yellow version. "I like this one. Really says ice cream to me."

She was quickly outvoted by Fiona and Partial Sue, who wanted to stick with a classic black-and-white business card.

Daisy didn't put up much of a fight and slotted the rest of the cards back into the envelope, leaving only the monochrome version on the table.

As an ex-publisher, Fiona was keen to check the wording for any mistakes. "Shall we just give it a quick proofread together?" She held up the winning card so they could all examine the simple warning it carried.

We know who you are.
We know where you are.
We are taking over.
Leave now or we'll burn everything down.

"All looks good to me," Partial Sue said. "This mafia boss is going to get one hell of a shock reading that."

"You know, I think so too," Fiona added.

Daisy shivered. "Well, it certainly gives me the willies. But do we have to set fire to the litter bin?"

This was the one element to their plan that had created a moral dilemma for the ladies. As law-abiding citizens, who took it upon themselves to do no wrong and bring criminals to justice, vandalising public property really didn't sit well with them. But it had to be done.

Fiona sighed. "I can't see any other way. We need to convince this ice-cream mafia that we're a real threat. A business card left on a windscreen won't cut it. Words have to be backed up by actions, specifically aggressive ones, otherwise they won't take it seriously."

Daisy winced. "I know, but it's damaging public property and it's dangerous."

Partial Sue scoffed. "It's just a rubbish bin, an ugly one at that. I doubt anyone's going to miss it. And it's being used to pass on drugs and illicit cash."

"And the fire won't spread," Fiona said. "The bin's concrete. It'll be contained, and we'll be doing it in the middle of the night."

"But does it have to be a fire?" Daisy asked. "I'm uncomfortable that we're starting a fire."

"We also need this lackey to be distracted long enough so we can slip this card under his wiper," Fiona explained.

"And pop a GPS on his car, to find out where his boss lives," Partial Sue added.

This part of the plan relied on a big assumption — that the lackey would leave his car briefly, providing them with a small window to sneak up and furnish it with both items. Their timing would have to be impeccable, so they wouldn't be spotted. Therefore, they required a big, brash distraction that would force him out of his car, and only a fire would do this.

Truth be told, Fiona was as uncomfortable as Daisy at the thought of starting the blaze. They'd be committing arson. Her window cleaner, Martin, the part-time firefighter, would be extremely disappointed if he ever found out. However, this gave Fiona an idea that might appease both their consciences.

"Tell you what. After the card and the GPS is on the lackey's car, we call the fire service, just to be on the safe side."

Daisy thought for a moment. "Well, I'm still not happy about it, but okay."

"You okay with that, Sue?"

Partial Sue nodded, then became distracted. Something outside had caught her attention.

Bouncing its way up onto the kerb, a delivery van halted at a jaunty angle to a chorus of beeping horns as the driver hadn't bothered to indicate, which was considered a hanging offence to the well-heeled drivers of Southbourne Grove. Out jumped a uniformed delivery driver, a small brown box in one hand and a device in the other. Partial Sue met him at the door and squiggled a signature on the device's screen. She took the box from him and brought it back to the table, a gleeful expression on her face. Wasting no time, she tore off the top, plunged her hand into the packaging and plucked out a small black object.

"Is that the GPS?" Fiona asked.

"It is indeed." Partial Sue held up the cubelike device about the size of a small packet of Oxo.

"It's tiny," Fiona chirped.

"Neat, isn't it?" Partial Sue said.

"Are you sure it won't fall off the lackey's car?" Daisy asked.

"Well, the sales blurb said the magnet has seventy kilograms of pull. Let's try it." She marched over to one of the metal display units. As she brought the device closer, it flew out of her hand and clamped itself to the surface. She had a job prising it off. "Yeah, I'd say that works."

"And how long does the battery last?"

Partial Sue picked up the enclosed handbook and shuffled through the pages. "Six weeks. More than enough." She flicked on a few pages and flattened a double-page spread with the heel of her hand. "Right. I'm going to pair this with my phone so we can track this lackey wherever he goes."

Daisy raised her hand. "What if it's a different lackey in the lay-by?"

"Doesn't matter," Fiona replied. "Whoever's parked up in that lay-by still has to keep an eye on the dead drop."

Partial Sue finished her prepping. "My phone's now tracking the GPS. I think we're ready."

"Let's go over the plan one more time." Fiona attempted to sound confident, but she knew from experience that plans had a nasty habit of . . . well, not going to plan. And this one seemed particularly prone to going awry. She worried that they were relying on a great deal of luck rather than design, but it was the only plan they had.

CHAPTER 37

Phase one was simple. Ensure the bin went up like a bonfire on the fifth of November. They couldn't risk it being anything less. A damp squib would certainly not cut it. This had to send a message to the ice-cream mafia that they were being threatened, that a new and ruthless rival was in town and meant business. Thankfully, the weather had been consistently warm. Discarded rubbish inside the bin would be as dry as tinder and catch alight nicely. However, *nicely* wasn't the effect they were after. This had to be nasty. It needed to go up with a roar, rather than a whimper, which meant the contents of the bin would have to be primed. Guaranteed to go up with the single strike of a match — they'd only get one chance at this.

Fiona winced as she sat in her car, considering what they were about to do. The sun was dipping below the horizon, throwing ominous reds and oranges into the sky. Later tonight, they would break the law in a very antisocial manner. Fiona abhorred this sort of behaviour, despite the fact they would call the fire service immediately afterwards. But the more she thought about it, the more her tinnitus whined in protest.

Was there another way to grab the attention of a ruthless mafia that didn't involve setting fire to their dead drop? What about rear-ending the lackey's parked-up car? That would definitely get attention. And, in the confusion, it would be easy to slip a GPS onto his vehicle, as long as it was still drive-able. But then the lackey would be unlikely to go running to his boss just because he'd had a prang. And Fiona didn't want a dose of whiplash for the next few months.

No, they'd stick to the plan. At least it had a chance of working, and it was too late to change it now. Fiona would have to turn a blind eye to the law-breaking and remind herself that it was for the greater good: to bring a dangerous mafia down and prevent them from holding innocent ice-cream sellers to ransom. She thought of Vernon, Tom and Claire and all the other innocent people who were living and working in fear of this secret organisation. Tonight, if all went to plan, it wouldn't be a secret for much longer.

It had to be done.

Decisively, Fiona flung open her car door. She went around the back of the car and popped open the boot to retrieve her equipment. It was hardly what you'd call equipment — one large disposable coffee cup and lid, plus one large can of lighter fluid. However, it would get the job done. Carefully, she emptied the contents of the lighter fluid into the cup and secured the lid, then closed the boot and locked it. She'd leave the car where it was in the first side road, then head towards the park.

Having crossed the main road, she began strolling around the furthest edge of the park, bordered by pine trees. A few stragglers were leaving as twilight descended — someone loaded with carrier bags taking a shortcut from the nearby Co-op, another couple finishing their late-evening dog walk. The endearing sight of a happy canine, cavorting from place to place, made Fiona's heart yearn for Simon Le Bon. She dearly missed his comforting furry presence, but she simply couldn't have risked bringing him along. His gentle chuntering snuffles would have calmed her nerves, which were currently causing her eyes to flick about wildly and her heart to race.

Since entering the park, she'd become paranoid that the lackey in the lay-by knew what she was up to. She'd driven past him once before parking, and for some reason had got it into her head that he'd noticed her and was now tracking her every move. The logical part of her brain told her this was an impossibility for all sorts of reasons. Mostly practical. In the dim light, from this distance, even if he was staring right at her, she'd appear like a stick person from a Lowry painting. And just how would he know what she was up to? Unless he was telepathic or had premonitions. These perfectly rational arguments should've reassured her, but her tinnitus said otherwise, whistling in protest. Quickening her pace, without thinking, she lifted a shaky hand to take a nervous drink from her coffee cup. The pungent whiff of lighter fuel reminded her that this wasn't frothy coffee, and she stopped short of taking a vile mouthful.

She really wasn't thinking straight and needed to take a beat to regain her composure. Heart racing faster, she headed to a nearby bench and perched on its edge, feeling anything but relaxed. She had to calm down, otherwise she'd cock up this part of the plan. Though, to be fair, there wasn't really that much to cock up. Fiona became annoyed at this debilitating state of affairs. Why was she getting so worked up about such a simple task? Did she feel ashamed of what she was doing? Was it fear of mucking it up, or fear of the ice-cream mafia? Possibly a combination of all three. She pushed these corrosive thoughts from her head. All that was important was that she steadied her nerves enough to carry out this little task, which now seemed mountainous.

It made her think of an article she'd read about how long-distance cyclists tackled horrifically steep mountains. They'd do it by not looking up at the top. Instead, their eyes would be fixed on the tarmac a few metres ahead of them, so they weren't constantly reminded of the seemingly endless, gruelling climb to the summit. Adopting the same technique, she stared at the stretch of grass in front of her and nothing

217

else. All she had to do was cross it. She'd only think about the next stretch of grass once she'd crossed that one, and so on. This was enough to focus on for now. She adopted a more relaxed pose, allowing herself to lean against the back rest. Finally, her breathing slowed, and her tinnitus subsided. She found herself rising to her feet and resuming her journey. One step at a time, eyes firmly down.

She made good progress, not thinking about anything apart from what was immediately in front of her. Gaining more confidence, her strides lengthening, she allowed her gaze to wander and was rewarded by the comforting and unmistakable shape of Daisy, a fair distance away, cutting across the park at right angles to her. Though Daisy had made it plain that she had no desire to set the bin alight, she had agreed to help them prime it. In one hand she was carrying a large recycled brown paper bag, the kind used for takeaway food, and, in her other, a broadsheet newspaper. Both had been soaked in lighter fuel and allowed to dry.

They'd made the decision earlier not to make eye contact or acknowledge each other if their paths crossed. Eyes firmly forward, her dear friend didn't miss a step as she approached the bin and casually threw in both items. Daisy continued on her way, heading to the main road, where she crossed over and continued on down the second of the three side streets.

Now it was Fiona's turn. She glanced about her, a little paranoid that she was being followed. There was no one behind her in the descending darkness, and it appeared that she was the last person in the park. She pressed on.

A minute later she was about five steps from the bin, still holding her inflammable coffee cup, her grip much firmer now. She focused on one job at a time. Get a little closer. Shift her thumb up to below the rim of the lid. Prise it off, so it sat loosely on the top.

The streetlights were on along the main road, offering just enough light on the target. She'd arrive at the bin in a matter of seconds. *Don't trip up now* she told herself.

Three more steps and she'd be there. Two more. One more. Finally, as she passed the bin, Fiona tossed in the coffee cup, upending it as she did so. The lid slipped off without a hitch as the whole lot went in. Marching away without a break in her stride, she briefly heard the dribble of lighter fluid as it filtered down the contents of the bin. Inside her head, Fiona gave herself a high five and a fist bump.

CHAPTER 38

Fiona met Daisy back at Partial Sue's Fiat Uno, parked along the main road, several cars behind the lackey, who was holed up in his lay-by outside the electrical substation. They'd walked back the long way, looping around the houses to avoid passing him. From their current position, the three ladies could glimpse the edge of his car — just the driver's door and the wing mirror. Not enough to keep an eye on what he was up to, but that didn't matter. It was probably safer this way. If they couldn't see him, then he couldn't see them. But, crucially, they'd be able to see him well enough once he got out of his car which, all being well, would be fairly soon.

"It's quarter to eleven. I should go." Decked out in black, Partial Sue resembled a member of the SAS about to be dropped behind enemy lines, minus the boot polish smeared over her face. Although she'd been totally prepared to go for full-face camouflage, Fiona thought it might draw more attention, especially as she had to pass the Co-op to get into position.

"Wait until eleven," Fiona advised. "The council dims the streetlights at eleven. It'll give you extra cover when you approach the dead drop to set it alight."

Daisy still had reservations. "Are you sure it's not too late in the evening for this lackey to call his boss? Personally, I don't answer the phone after nine o'clock."

"He's a mafia boss," Partial Sue replied. "They stay up late. Probably playing poker in a smoky den full of guys called Paulie and Big Tony."

"This is Dorset, not New Jersey," Fiona said.

"Probably enjoying a biscuit and a cup of rooibos," Daisy suggested.

"Why rooibos?" Partial Sue asked.

"Because it doesn't have any caffeine in it. You can sleep better."

Partial Sue sniffed. "This mafia boss sounds a bit pedestrian to me."

"Have you got everything?" Fiona asked.

Partial Sue patted herself down, unzipped a pocket in her top and rattled two small boxes of matches. "All set. Got a lighter too, just in case."

"Remember," Daisy said, "don't set the bin alight if someone's next to it. We don't want anyone innocent getting hurt."

"Who'd be hanging around a bin at eleven at night?" Partial Sue replied. "Actually, who hangs around a bin at any time of the day?"

"Shall we go over it one more time?" Fiona's nerves were getting to her again. They'd been over it several times already.

But Partial Sue would repeat it anyway. "I take the long way around the houses. Enter the park from the far side, through the trees. Cut diagonally across the grass, towards the dead drop."

"Won't the lackey see you?" Daisy interrupted.

Partial Sue gestured to the park across the road. "It's pitch black over there. Apart from near the dead drop. The streetlights on the main road throw a bit of light on it, but not much. He might see me at the last second or two, but by then it'll be too late. I'll have tossed in the match, turned tail and be heading back into the darkness."

"What if he chases you?" Daisy asked.

"He won't be able to follow me in the dark, but I'll zigzag just in case."

"I doubt he'll chase you," Fiona said. "The dead drop will be on fire. The one thing he's been sent to guard. He'll be panicking."

"Are you both all set for when that happens?" Partial Sue asked.

Daisy pulled the rabbit-skull business card from her pocket. Fiona produced the GPS from hers.

"I think we're ready." Fiona's hand shook as she said this.

They all smiled nervously, wishing one another good luck.

Eleven o'clock arrived and, right on cue, the streetlights dimmed. Partial Sue exited the car and began walking up the road, slowly at first, but her speed increased with every step. She took the same path Daisy and Fiona had taken back to the car, except in reverse, so she wouldn't have to pass the lackey. Fiona twisted the rearview mirror so she could watch Partial Sue hastily making her way up the street, until she disappeared from sight. All they could do now was sit and wait.

It had only been a few minutes, but Fiona's heartbeat increased, thumping against her chest. She wondered where Partial Sue was now. Possibly heading down the backstreets on the outskirts of the park, but knowing her jittery pace, she might already be in the park itself. Unless something had gone wrong. Fearful thoughts bombarded her mind as her imagination ran away with her. She would have descended into a spiral of paranoia, except Daisy suddenly yelped, snapping her out of it.

"What is it?" Fiona hissed.

"I think the lackey's car door is opening."

Fiona blinked several times. Daisy was right. The edge of the driver's door was ajar. It opened fully and one long leg extended from out of the car, then the other. Under the muted glow of the streetlight, they got their first proper glimpse of the skin-headed lackey as he began to emerge. He was tall, almost having to unfold himself from the driver's seat. Easily six-foot-four. Fiona wondered how such a big frame fitted in such a small vehicle. Dressed in an oversized white T-shirt and equally baggy jeans, he stretched, as if he'd just got out of bed.

"What's he doing?" Daisy whined.

"I have no idea," Fiona replied. "But this isn't good."

He closed his car door and started to cross the road.

"Oh, no!" Daisy shrieked. "I think he's heading towards the dead drop."

Fiona grabbed her phone. She had to warn Partial Sue. She really wanted to call her but, not knowing her exact whereabouts, or if her phone was on silent, she was worried she'd give away her position to the lackey as their paths converged. If that happened, their plan would be scuppered, or worse, she'd put her in danger. Clumsily, she thumbed a rapid text. Just one word.

ABORT

They watched in horror as the lackey loped across the road, and then onto the grass, the dead drop directly ahead of him, a few metres away.

Fiona's eyes flicked from him to her phone screen, urging Partial Sue to reply with something, anything, preferably a thumbs up to confirm that her message had been received and understood. "I can't get hold of Sue."

"Let me try." Daisy whipped out her phone and punched in a message far quicker than Fiona ever could.

"Any reply?"

"Give it time," Daisy said.

Fiona shook in her seat. "We haven't got time. He's nearly there."

Daisy panicked. "Oh my gosh! He's going to catch her in the act."

Among her tumultuous thoughts, Fiona managed something rational. "No, she'll see him first, but he won't see her.

I'm sure of it. Remember, she's coming out of the darkness."
At least, that's what she hoped.

They watched in horror as the lackey appeared to be hovering around the dead drop for no apparent reason. She recalled Partial Sue's words about people not hanging around bins. Words which were possibly about to bite her in the behind.

"What's he doing?" Daisy asked.

The lackey was being cautious, checking to see if the coast was clear, trying to act as if everything was normal but not doing a particularly good job of it. With his gangster swagger, shoulders swinging, he circled the dead drop several times, then pulled something from his pocket. He appeared to discard it in the bin but leaned over a little too much for it to be natural. Whatever it was did not get thrown into the top of the bin, but shoved against its concrete side, lower down. He squidged it with his hand a couple of times just to make sure it was secure. The next second he was upright again.

Relief spread through Fiona's body as the lackey jogged back across the road, towards his car. "It's okay. I think he was just leaving another stash of drugs for someone to pick up. Remember what Vernon said? They're put in a crisp packet, and left in a crack in the side."

"I reckon you're right." Daisy was equally relieved. "But what's happened to Sue?"

That was a good question, and it was answered as they gazed through the windscreen, desperate for any sign of her. Suddenly, bright orange flames shot from the top of the bin, lighting up the park.

Sensing the glow behind him, the lackey spun around, nearly losing his footing at the sight of a column of fire, which had undoubtedly melted the crisp packet and all the drugs within. He stumbled back towards the park and onto the grass. His body jigged awkwardly like a string puppet controlled by an inebriated puppeteer. Not handling the crisis very well, he appeared to be a mess of confusion and panic.

"Now!" Fiona cried.

They exited the car, Fiona remembering to lock it with Partial Sue's keys, which she managed not to fumble. Swiftly, they marched along the pavement, side by side, never taking their eyes off the lackey, who currently had his back to them, transfixed as he was by the small inferno. Fiona wondered what was going through his head right now. But the timing couldn't have been more perfect. He'd certainly have to explain to his boss why a fresh supply of drugs had disintegrated into a molten mess, and possibly his career with it.

Reaching the lackey's car, Fiona crouched down, ignoring the strain on her knees, while Daisy kept an eye on him. Fiona stretched her arm under the chassis, holding the GPS in her hand. Its powerful magnets latched onto the metal with a satisfying clunk. She straightened up and in the next moment they switched. Fiona kept watch while Daisy leaned across the windscreen to slip the business card under the wiper. The pair of them continued on their way, as if nothing had happened, although Fiona's insides were overdosing on adrenalin, and it took all her willpower not to break into a dash.

Turning into the nearby side road, Fiona finally experienced a modicum of relief. However, curiosity got the better of her, and she couldn't resist one last glance over her shoulder. Still with his back to them, the lackey was edging away from the blaze with his phone to his ear. She couldn't hear what he was saying or who he was calling. Hopefully it would be his boss or at least a superior. Whichever it was, their evening was about to get a whole lot worse when the lackey returned to his car and discovered the business card on his windscreen.

Somehow, their rickety plan had worked — so far. Just one more part had to fall into place, and they'd have this ice-cream mafia in their clutches. But first, she needed to call the emergency services to report that some highly irresponsible individuals had set fire to a litter bin.

CHAPTER 39

Earlier that evening, they'd decided to leave Partial Sue's car where it was for the night, to avoid returning to the scene of the crime, as it were. Instead, the three of them arranged to regroup a safe distance away at Fiona's car where she had left it in the first side road.

Reunited and quite understandably elated, they gave one another awkward hugs inside the cramped vehicle. A momentous occasion celebrated inside a very small car. Fiona felt her nervous energy depleting, to be replaced by an almighty relief. It was partly due to successfully pulling off phase one of their plan, but mostly because Partial Sue had made it back in one piece and, crucially, had been unseen by the ice-cream mafia foot soldier.

"What happened?" Fiona asked. "We were so worried. We texted to warn you that the lackey was out of his car."

"Thank you," Partial Sue replied. "I felt my phone vibrate, but I didn't dare move."

"Where were you?" Daisy asked.

"Nearly at the dead drop. About ten paces away. I caught sight of him crossing the road and was terrified he'd seen me. So I stopped in my tracks and stood still, praying that the dark would hide me."

"Then what happened?" Fiona asked.

Partial Sue's response was brisk and breathless. "I saw him shoving something in the side of the bin. Guessed he was stashing drugs there. The second he'd finished and started walking back to his car, I made a dash for it. Pulling out my matches, I grabbed two at once. Lit them together. Threw them in from about a metre away — I didn't want to get too close in case it went up with a bang. Turned tail and ran. I kept looking back. At first, I thought I'd mucked it up, because nothing happened. Then *woosh*! It went up like a roman candle."

"Well done, Sue!" Daisy gave her knee an affectionate squeeze. "We're glad you made it back safely."

"Hear, hear," Fiona added.

"Did you stick the GPS and the business card on his car?" Partial Sue asked.

"Sure did," Daisy answered. "Slipped it under his wiper."

"And I stuck the GPS under his chassis," Fiona said.

"And he didn't see you?"

"Nope," Fiona replied. "It all went to plan. His attention was on the fire, not on us."

Partial Sue wasted no time pulling out her phone and tapping on the newly installed app. "Right, let's see if this lackey's been summoned by his master."

"Let's hope so." Daisy said. "But what if he doesn't tell him about the fire?"

"He'll have to say something," Fiona replied. "Explain why a stash of drugs has gone up in smoke. That was fortuitous for us. Once he gets back to his car, and gets over the shock of seeing the business card, if he's smart, he'll use it as an excuse. He can tell his boss this new mafia did it. Not his fault. Might even embellish the story a bit and say he was outnumbered, pushed up against a wall and threatened. Who knows?"

Partial Sue tapped on the app. They all leaned in, staring at the bright screen now dominated by a map of Redhill Park. A pulsing red dot appeared in the middle, not going anywhere.

"He's still there," said Daisy. "Why isn't he moving?"

Partial Sue, the mafia expert, supplied her theory. "Probably hasn't got direct access to the head honcho. Might take a while for his message to be passed up the chain of command, then back again."

"What if that's it?" Daisy asked. "The message gets passed on and he just stays put."

"I doubt it," Fiona replied. "I think the boss will want to see this business card and look him in the eye, make sure he's not making up some cock-and-bull story. Plus, he's parked near a burning bin. He won't want to hang around for very long."

Just as Fiona uttered her last words, sirens whined in the distance, signalling the approach of fire engines. A sound guaranteed to make a guilty conscience flee. But the pulsing red dot refused to budge.

"He must hear the sirens," Daisy said, "but he's still not moving."

The sirens became louder and louder.

"They're going to be here any second," Fiona remarked. "What's he waiting for?"

Finally, the dot began to move.

Fiona started up the car. "Will you navigate while I drive?"

"Ready when you are." Partial Sue settled into her new role with immediate aplomb. "Proceed when ready."

Daisy fretted. "Jeez! He's moving fast. You better step on it, or we'll lose him."

"Relax, Dais," Partial Sue reassured her. "We've got the GPS. We can follow at a leisurely pace."

"Oh, yeah. Silly me."

"Enemy is heading south towards the university. About one click away." Partial Sue had been handed the rare opportunity to talk like a field agent for Homeland Security and wasn't about to squander it.

"Right you are." Fiona shoved the car into first and pulled off an erratic three-point turn.

"Target now heading southwest into Talbot Woods."

They kept a safe and steady distance behind him and were barely troubled by any cars coming in the opposite direction. The roads were eerily quiet as they entered the desirable postcode of Talbot Woods. Its grand, widely spaced, red-brick Victorian mansions were the kind that Rightmove would describe as 'palatial' with 'plenty of period features'.

"I bet this is where the boss lives," Daisy proposed. "A posh house bought from ill-gotten gains."

"Where's he going now?" asked Fiona.

"Hang a left at the end of Glenferness Avenue. He's on Branksome Wood Road."

A few minutes later they turned off at a set of empty traffic lights into a leafy road that led directly into Bournemouth town centre.

"He's going to all the nice places," Daisy said. The road ran alongside a particularly splendid example of Victorian landscaping known as the Central Gardens, a procession of ornamental trees, exotic plants and grassy glades. It followed the meandering course of the Bourne Stream, extending all the way to the seafront.

"I could see myself in one of those." Daisy gazed out of the window at the balconied apartments up on a steep bank, overlooking this very pleasant sleeve of green, complete with tennis courts and café. It was all very agreeable, or would have been, if the local planners hadn't decided that all this beauty was far too much for one town and had decided to offset it with a concrete flyover and a couple of multistorey car parks.

Partial Sue had reservations about the area, tutting as they passed the tennis courts, closed up for the night but still drenched in floodlighting. "Why doesn't anyone switch those lights off? Goodness knows how much that's costing in electricity. There's been letters about it in the local paper and everything." Glancing back at her phone screen, she quickly dropped the angry taxpayer persona and reverted back to her FBI parlance. "Target now heading north into Braidley Road. My gut's telling me he's heading for Meyrick Park. ETA one minute."

"Oh, I love Meyrick Park," Daisy began, reminiscing. "That was where my dad taught me to ride a bike, and we would go conkering in autumn. Dozens of horse chestnut trees, there are."

Partial Sue was back to her old self momentarily. "I am partial to a game of conkers. I used to boil mine in vinegar."

Daisy didn't like the sound of this. "That's cheating. I had a niner once until someone smashed it. Then I found out he'd covered his in nail polish. There should be laws against that sort of thing."

Partial Sue plunged back into character. "Target has turned away from Meyrick Park and is now heading west on the bypass, towards Poole."

"Okay, no problem." Fiona turned into Braidley Road, the grand town hall marking the corner. "I'll take a right onto Richmond Hill, then I can get onto the town's bypass at the top."

"Delay that order. He's stopped. Turn around." Partial Sue's bureau-speak abruptly halted, confusion taking over. "I think this must be glitching. It says he's back at the tennis courts. Well, actually in them. But that can't be possible."

"I didn't see him," Daisy said.

"Me neither." Fiona wheeled the car around. "We were distracted by talk of conkers and floodlighting."

"He's still not moving," Partial Sue remarked. "Maybe that's where he's meeting his boss."

"What, at the tennis courts?" Daisy asked. "Why would he meet there?"

Fiona pulled the car over to the kerb.

"Well, it is a bit gangster," Partial Sue informed them. "It's beside a flyover. They always meet beneath flyovers in mafia movies."

"We need to be careful," Fiona warned. "If we've already passed him, we might get noticed if we drive past again, especially as the roads are so quiet."

Daisy didn't want to rush into anything either. "Let's give it a minute or two. He might start moving again. Or the GPS might glitch. Show him somewhere else."

Partial Sue fidgeted in her seat. "But what if he's meeting his boss right at this moment? We can't afford to miss this."

"Good point," Fiona agreed. "But I don't think we can risk driving round there a second time. We'll park here, head back to the GPS location on foot, into the Central Gardens. There's a path on the far side shrouded by trees and hedges. It'll give us plenty of cover so we can get close without being seen. If the meeting's taking place there, hopefully we can spot the boss's car, get its registration number and give it to Freya. I'm sure our friendly neighbourhood IT expert can get us the owner's name and address. Then we'll know who's behind this."

"Might not be the big boss," Daisy said. "Could just be middle management."

"Better than nothing." Fiona wrenched on the handbrake and killed the engine.

Partial Sue restarted her phone and opened the app. "Seems to be working fine now. Well, apart from saying his car is in the middle of a tennis court, but I know GPS sometimes only gives an approximate position. He's probably parked up beside the road. Let's go before he starts moving again."

The three ladies climbed out of the vehicle and scurried in the direction of the Central Gardens. After passing beside the monolithic war memorial, they located the narrow path on the other side of the stream, hurrying along it towards the tennis courts. Dense hedges and trees formed a dark tunnel around them. Despite the mild weather, the air was dank and loamy. All they had was Partial Sue's phone screen to light their way, as she constantly monitored the lackey's location.

"This is creepy," Daisy whispered. "I doubt I could do this without you two with me."

Up ahead, the bright lights of the tennis courts shone through the vegetation. Cautiously, they edged closer. Fiona put her finger to her lips for radio silence to commence. Step by careful step, they closed in on his location, stopping now and then to peer through the leaves and branches, but they glimpsed nothing apart from empty tennis courts. Chancing a closer look, the three ladies took up position behind a sprawling rhododendron which, according to Partial Sue's app, was directly opposite the lackey's position — dead centre of the last tennis court.

They observed the scene in absolute silence. Any second now they'd get a glimpse of the lackey, along with his shadowy ice-cream mafia boss, or at least a high-ranking member of the gang.

CHAPTER 40

Nothing stirred. No sound reached Fiona's ears. Not a raised word, nor a breath, not even a movement of air from a shaken fist. The only noise came from the babbling stream nearby, which sounded oddly sinister in their current predicament, as the ladies remained shielded behind a bush in the still hours of the night.

After several minutes, Partial Sue whispered, "Nobody's here."

"We don't know that for sure," Fiona whispered back.

"Look around. The place is empty." Partial Sue nodded in the direction of the vacant road beside the gardens. "I thought they might be doing that classic, 'the boss wants to see you', where the lackey is summoned into his limo to sit in the back for a dressing-down, but there's no cars here whatsoever. Not even the lackey's Corsa."

Fiona surveyed the road beside the gardens. Partial Sue was right. Bereft of any cars whatsoever, the facts refused to line up in Fiona's mind. The app on the phone clearly showed his car at the tennis courts — right inside them. She sighed. "This doesn't make sense."

Short of anything better to do, Partial Sue bashed the side of her phone, hoping it would suddenly produce the answer they wanted. "Maybe I shouldn't have bought the cheapest GPS from the spy catalogue."

Much as Fiona would've liked to blame the current lack of results on her colleague's tight-fistedness, or shoddy quality, the GPS had been working perfectly up until the point when they'd needed it most. Coincidence? Fiona didn't think so, and an odd prickling sensation rose up from the soles of her feet. Not quite a feeling of failure, but on its way to being one.

"What's that over there?" Daisy had been staring through the foliage this whole time. "On the tennis court, just in front of the net."

Stooping down, Fiona attempted to get a better look. Her gaze tracked along the base of the tightly wound netting until it alighted on something small and black. Her heart plummeted. She recognised its size and shape, and its location matched the exact position on Partial Sue's app. She didn't want to believe it, her brain refusing to let the words come out of her mouth.

Partial Sue had no such inhibitions. She swore. "I think we've been busted. That looks like the GPS."

There didn't seem much point in cowering behind the bush, not when the device that had allowed the stealthy pursuit of the lackey's car now lay in the middle of the tennis court, like discarded litter. Emerging from their hiding place, they crept up to the high chain-link fence surrounding the courts and pushed their disappointed faces against it. At this distance, there could be no doubt that the black, boxy object was indeed the GPS.

Quickly finding the entrance through the fence, Partial Sue gave it a good rattle, but it had been secured for the night with a sturdy padlock. She stepped aside, letting Daisy do what she did best. Out came her kit of slender picks, and after a few minutes of meticulous pushing and poking, the lock clicked open. Once inside, they hurried over to the device and formed a circle around it, staring in bewilderment at how it had come to be there, as if it were a meteorite that had dropped from the sky.

Picking up the GPS to examine it, Partial Sue rubbed it with her cuff. Apart from a few scratches, the device was in one piece. "Looks like he's tossed it out of the car while he was driving past."

Fiona evaluated the high enclosure surrounding them. "That's one hell of a throw from a moving car, to get it over the fence and in here."

"I reckon I could pull it off." Partial Sue smiled.

"Yes, but not everyone's got a right arm like yours." Fiona rubbed her chin, craning her neck up at the flyover towering above them. "I think he threw it from up there, as he drove by. Remember, one minute the GPS showed him on the bypass, the next it showed him down here. It wasn't glitching. It was working fine. We just couldn't make sense of it."

"But he must've stopped to remove the GPS at some point," Daisy said. "We didn't see him stop."

"More importantly, how did he know where it was?" Partial Sue stared at Daisy. "Are you sure he didn't see Fiona sticking it underneath his car?"

"Not a chance," Daisy replied. "I was watching him the whole time."

"So how did he know where to find it?" Partial Sue asked.

The strange sensation that had started in Fiona's feet reached her midriff, swiftly rising through her neck and into her head, like pins and needles all over her body. Her tinnitus joined in as well. She groaned. "You know what? I think we've underestimated this ice-cream mafia. Specifically, whoever was on the other end of the phone to the lackey. Whether it was the boss or this guy's superior, after their dead drop went up in flames, they probably got spooked and were being ultra cautious. Instructed the lackey to check his car before he drove off. That's the only explanation."

Daisy clicked her fingers. "There was that time when he stayed parked up at Redhill and we couldn't understand why. Fire was raging, sirens approaching, but he hung around. He must have been on his hands and knees with his phone torch, looking under his car."

"That makes sense." Partial Sue winced. "They're a lot smarter than we've given them credit for."

Fiona knew she was right. They hadn't expected them to be so clever or so cautious. But something else was niggling Fiona, and it wasn't just the pins and needles of disappointment tingling all over her body, or the tinnitus squealing in her ears. It felt as if a predator was stalking them, silent and unseen, circling them from a distance. Reaching out with her senses, the hairs on the back of her neck stood up. She could feel a presence, but had no idea what it was or where it was, just that it had them in its sights.

Fiona tried to rationalise this feeling of dread. Scrutinising her thoughts, she came to the conclusion that the explanation about the GPS landing in the tennis court made perfect sense, but it also made no sense at all. "Okay, so the lackey finds the device on his car at Redhill Park. Why didn't he just ditch it there and then, or toss it into someone's garden? He drives all the way across town with it and then throws it from that flyover up there, so it drops down here. Why here?"

Partial Sue shrugged. "Why anywhere? It's just a random place, far enough away from Redhill Park and the dead drop."

"Possibly, but it just seems unnecessary to hang on to it for so long and then get rid of it, especially if he knows someone's following him."

Partial Sue shrugged again, as did Daisy, probably believing Fiona was reading too much into it.

Screaming in her ears, Fiona's tinnitus begged to differ. She just needed to put it all together, gather some evidence for her random hunch. Slowly, she turned 360 degrees, examining her surroundings, hoping a clue would emerge.

Geographically, they were standing in a miniature river valley. The gardens and tennis courts occupied the flat valley floor; with apartment buildings and multistorey car parks on the steep banks either side, which formed an elongated amphitheatre. Not forgetting that vile concrete flyover tower-ing above them. Then there were the tennis courts themselves. If she disregarded the fencing and netting, it was basically a very large flat open space, very rare in the middle of a densely populated town. Then there were the lights. It was dazzling, like the place had its own miniature sun, whereas everything else around them was either dark or dimly lit. And thanks to the brouhaha in the newspaper, it had become common knowledge that this place always left its lights on.

She juggled with these elements, but they still wouldn't line up in her mind. Something was missing, something she hadn't considered. Fiona took stock of the facts one more time, which weren't that many. A natural valley, an open space in the middle of town, which also happened to be lit up at night. Fiona scratched her head, a deduction not forth-coming. There had to be some reason why the lackey had been instructed to drop the GPS down here in particular. It wasn't an accident, she was sure of it. There had to be something unique about this place. It had to be of strategic importance.

That word, 'strategic', though it had popped into her head unbidden, suddenly gave her a different angle on the sit-uation. How would a military person view this? For a start, all those high-rise buildings would be of high value. Lots of ele-vated positions, perfect for keeping an eye out for the enemy.

Those last few words made her heart freeze and her knees nearly buckle.

"Fiona, are you okay?" Daisy asked.

"We have to go." She darted towards the entrance of the tennis courts, but her colleagues were slow to follow. "Come on! Quick!"

"What's the rush?" Partial Sue was normally the one in a hurry.

"No time to explain." Fiona's breath caught in her throat, nearly choking her as the panic intensified. "We have to leave." She led them out of the tennis courts, back to the path, con-cealed by bushes and trees. They had to get back to the car, not that it would make much difference now. The damage had already been done. Getting to safety was the only option left. But where would they be safe from the omnipotent reach of the ice-cream mafia?

CHAPTER 41

Fiona's car was so stuffed full of bedding that she couldn't see out of the rear window. The parcel shelf had been removed to accommodate all the pillows, bed rolls and sleeping bags, but mostly Daisy's duvet (she didn't like sleeping bags because they only had one way in and out, which made her feel claustrophobic). So her maximum-tog duvet took up most of the boot, filling it like an exploded can of expanding foam.

Imploring them to forsake the comfort of their own beds, Fiona had sounded like the worst tinfoil-hat-wearing conspiracy theorist when she announced that they were no longer safe in their own homes. Daisy and Partial Sue had taken some persuading, screwing up their noses at the idea that they had unwittingly made themselves the next target of the ice-cream mafia. But they'd seen the panic in her eyes. Fiona had become more impassioned until, gradually, the logic lined up and they began to believe it too, leading them to the awful truth that they were now on the mafia's hit list.

This had led them to drive from house to house, stocking up on bedding and overnight essentials, which had included picking up Simon Le Bon and Bella. Luckily, Bella hadn't been asleep, and had been up worrying about how the ladies' surveillance mission had gone — clearly not well, seeing as she was now squashed in the back of a car in her dressing gown and slippers, with a toiletries bag and a change of clothes on her lap.

"I don't see why we couldn't have booked into a hotel," Daisy said.

"It's too expensive." Partial Sue's eyes keenly scanned ahead for any sort of threat, but, so far, the roads had been deserted.

"I don't care where we stay," Fiona replied, "but I thought the shop would be safer. It's very public, on a main road lined with CCTV. No one will be able to creep up on the place without being seen."

Bella yawned. "Are you sure this mafia is coming after us?"

"There's no other explanation." Fiona was ready to expand on her deduction once more. "There's only one reason we were lured to that particular spot in the middle of the night — so they could get a good look at us. Think about it. A brightly lit open space, surrounded by lots of tall structures. Plenty of places for them to observe us without being seen. Get a measure of who they're dealing with. They took our threat seriously. Very seriously, and now we're in danger."

"But you can't be sure of that," Bella said.

Fiona ground the gears clumsily as she shifted up. "There's only one reason they'd want to get a look at us, and it's not to see what we're wearing. We have to prepare for the worst-case scenario. They've been very smart, and we've been very stupid."

"We haven't been stupid," Partial Sue said. "We just underestimated them. I bet as soon as the lackey discovered the GPS on his car, they arranged for someone to be on top of one of the multistoreys to wait for us with a telephoto lens."

"But they would have seen we're not a mafia," Daisy said. "Just three retired ladies."

"Doesn't matter to them." Partial Sue didn't mince her words. "We've kicked the hornets' nest, like the girl with the dragon tattoo, and now they'll come after us."

The bottom of Daisy's lip trembled. "Yes, but they don't know who we are or where we live."

Partial Sue shook her head. "If they can find the names of every ice-cream seller and their families and take shots of them, they can find us too. It's just a matter of time."

"What are we going to do?" Daisy fretted.

Bella put a reassuring arm around her mother — not easy among all the bedding. "Don't worry, Mum. Everything will be okay."

Fiona also wanted to offer words of comfort to settle Daisy's nerves, and her own for that matter, but she knew that this wouldn't be okay. Far from it. "I'm so sorry, everyone. I've really made a mess of things. This plan was a terrible idea."

"Hey, stop that," Partial Sue chided. "It's no one's fault."

"If anyone should take the blame, it's me," Bella said. "I'm the one who had the idea of creating a rival mafia."

Partial Sue attempted to nullify their individual guilt. "Yes, but we all came up with the plan together. All agreed on it and knew what we were signing up for."

Fiona had a different opinion, but she kept silent. They hadn't signed up for this bit. Running scared from their homes in the middle of the night. She blamed herself for that. She should have seen this coming. Should've known that prodding the big mafia bear had consequences that would result in said bear tracking them down and seeking blood. Just as it had with poor Kevin Masterson. How had she been so blind, so naive? Possibly because she'd allowed herself to get caught up with the thrill of their daring plan. The belief that they could outwit the mob and come out of it smiling. She had to make this right somehow, but in her present state of inner turmoil, she had no clue how to achieve that, or if it were even possible.

It was the early hours of the morning when they arrived outside the shop, all clutching their bedding in their arms like a bunch of schoolgirls about to have a sleepover, but without the excited giggling and bags of junk food. The mood was sombre and downcast at the prospect of sleeping on the shop's floor for the foreseeable future, the threat of a mob hit hanging over them. The only one who appeared happy was Simon Le Bon, his tail wagging excitedly, wondering what new adventure this was.

Once inside, they each picked a spot on the carpet and laid out their bedding, attempting to make themselves as comfortable as possible among the jumble of clothing and stacks of household items. At least it felt friendly and familiar, like a second home to the ladies.

Being the lightest sleeper, and therefore the most likely to wake at the slightest sound of trouble, Partial Sue took up position near the door. She unrolled her sleeping bag with one flick of her slender wrist, then plonked a pillow at one end, arranging her temporary settlement without much care or attention. Job done, she stood upright, hands proudly on hips. "We should arm ourselves."

"That's a good idea," Fiona replied. "Everyone grab something and sleep with it."

Naturally, they gathered around the kitchen utensils section, perusing its wide selection of implements — both the sharp and blunt variety. Partial Sue went straight for a large machete-like carving knife. Fiona went for a comedy classic — a rolling pin — while Bella picked up a hefty meat tenderiser. Daisy, on the other hand, took her time, appraising and examining each utensil for its potential defensive capabilities. Bizarrely, she settled on a large metal camping spork.

"What are you going to do with that?" Partial Sue asked.

"I thought it would give me options." Demonstrating its versatility, Daisy held the spork in her hand, jabbing at the air. "I can stab with the fork." She flipped the hybrid implement around. "Or bash them with the spoon end."

"Fair enough."

"Does anyone want tea?" Bella asked.

"Yes, please." Fiona never normally drank any caffeine before bed, for obvious reasons, but these were exceptional circumstances. Besides, she was positive that sleep would elude her tonight, and she desperately needed the warmth of nature's finest liquid comforter clasped in her hands. And so, it seemed, did everyone else, all of them responding with a resounding and unanimous yes.

After the tea had been made, they all settled around the table in their pyjamas, sipping in silence. Acting as unofficial guard, Partial Sue craned her neck with increasing frequency, checking the window for any sign of midnight assassins. "Do you think they'll send one hitman or a whole bunch of them?"

Fiona shuddered at how the situation had come to this. "I don't know, but from now on, no one leaves the shop alone, and we stay on Southbourne Grove. No straying down the back streets or anywhere that doesn't have CCTV. Not until this all blows over." She cringed at her last choice of words, as if their situation would somehow improve like the weather, with Carol Kirkwood appearing, hands pushing the air to one side, her warm Scottish lilt providing reassurance. "*The high threat of murder that's been hanging over the shop will soon move away southeast, leaving a fine outlook for the Charity Shop Detective Agency.*"

As if reading Fiona's mind, Bella asked a question. "How long until it blows over?"

Fiona felt the pins and needles of fear intensifying. "I don't know."

Daisy put her cup down. "Why can't we just call the police? Surely they'll protect us."

"We haven't got any proof," Partial Sue said. "Apart from the lackey, and, as we said before, he'll be more frightened of his boss than the police. He'll keep schtum or just deny at all. It'd be our word against his, especially as I set the incriminating evidence alight."

"We've got Vernon," Daisy said.

"There's no way he'd go to the police," Bella replied.

They sipped their drinks with nervous slurps and wary eyes, all of them unsure about the future or whether they would even have one. Fiona desperately wanted to reassure them that everything would be all right. Wanted to present a course of action that would remedy their diabolical situation, which she felt responsible for putting them in, but she had nothing. No direction and certainly no reassurance to give. Damage limitation was all she could offer at the moment, in the form of the steadfast walls of the shop, their only trusted ally in all this. She prayed that it would be enough.

Quietly, they each took it in turns to use the loo and then brush their teeth at the sink in the storeroom. When their ablutions were complete, the ladies wished each other good-night, slipping beneath their bedding. Partial Sue checked the door was firmly locked several times, then switched off the lights, plunging the shop into darkness, apart from an eerie orange glow that seeped in through the front window, supplied by the dimmed streetlights outside.

Fiona had never felt so uncomfortable, both physically and mentally. Constantly shifting and corkscrewing in her sleeping bag, she attempted to find a suitable position, much to the annoyance of Simon Le Bon, who'd forsaken his bed to nuzzle against her. In the end, she gave up hope and lay flat on her back, staring at the ceiling, jealous that everyone else had succumbed to slumber, judging by their deep, rhythmical breathing.

At some point she must have dozed off because she found herself in the nonsensical world of a dream. A large dinosaur charged after her, not through some overgrown and humid prehistoric jungle, but down the disinfected corridors of her old school. As it gave chase, its large head knocked strip lights from their mountings in showers of sparks, and its shoulders scuffed against the walls, dislodging student projects that had been pinned up for display.

In classic dream narrative, her feet were as heavy as two cannonballs, and she couldn't get any purchase on the polished linoleum floor. The beast always seemed just inches from her, snapping at her head. Terrified for her life, she crashed through a fire door and found herself in the grim confines of the playground. She ran to the shelter of a wooden climbing frame, its cage-like structure providing protection against the terrible lizard. But as she cowered beneath its timber struts, the monster transformed into Big Bird from *Sesame Street*, and began pecking at the wood, a jabbing tattoo. If she hadn't been so horrified, Fiona would have laughed at the absurdity of it all.

The scene began to shift, and her vision blurred, as if a powerful undertow was dragging her down. Moments later, she surfaced somewhere else. Bewildered and drunk with sleep, her eyes opened, slowly adjusting to the morning light. Still slotted in her sleeping bag with Simon Le Bon snuggled by her side, Fiona discovered that she wasn't being chased by a dinosaur or Big Bird, but was on the floor in the shop, a rolling pin clutched loosely in her hand. However, the relentless pecking from the dream had followed her into the real world, incessant and ominous, but it wasn't coming from a giant puppet bird.

It was coming from the front door. Someone was trying to get in.

CHAPTER 42

Fiona's drowsiness melted away, replaced by a heart-thumping panic that the mafia were outside, attempting to break in. Gripping the rolling pin tightly in her fist, she lay flat and still, listening as the soft tapping came again and again. Had anyone else heard it?

She twisted her head slowly to survey the state of her colleagues. Oblivious to the potential intrusion, they barely stirred. So much for Partial Sue's guarding prowess, or Simon Le Bon's, especially as his canine ears had an evolutionary advantage over all of them. He slumbered blissfully by her side. Fiona was on her own.

Immobilised by fear, all she could do was listen. *Tap, tap, tap.* The noise repeated itself over and over. Gradually she realised the incessant sound was not an attempt to force the door open, but a gentle knocking. Would the mafia resort to such polite means of entry? Unlikely. Slowly, she craned her neck, risking a look at the front door.

A dark silhouetted figure, hood up, stood with one hand around their eyes, trying to peer in, while the other hand lightly rapped on the door. Fiona knew that silhouette. It was Vernon. She allowed herself to relax a little, but kept a tight hold of the rolling pin, just in case the mob had put him up to it and were standing out of sight, ready to barge in the moment she unlocked the door.

Fiona pushed her sleeping bag off, eliciting an indignant grunt from Simon Le Bon. Avoiding any slumbering bodies, she tiptoed her way to the front of the shop and opened the door.

Vernon quickly stepped inside, lowering his hood. "Sorry, I hope I didn't startle you."

Fiona's voice was croaky when she managed to speak. "Morning." She closed and locked the door behind him.

Vernon immediately noticed Fiona was in her pyjamas. The various bodies asleep on the floor now beginning to stir. "What's going on? Why are you all sleeping in here?"

Bella pushed herself up on her elbows and regarded him through half-lidded eyes. "Oh, hi, Vernon. What time is it?"

"Ten past eight," he replied.

Partial Sue and Daisy woke up simultaneously. Brains clearly not in gear, judging by their vacant stares, all they could manage by way of a greeting was a half-hearted wave.

"I was desperate to know what happened at the dead drop," Vernon said. "Bella wasn't answering her phone. I called round her house just now, but no one was in. I started worrying, so I came straight here. What happened?"

Fiona dreaded breaking the awful news to him. All along he'd warned them not to aggravate the ice-cream mafia because it would put everyone's lives at risk, and now here they were, cowering in a charity shop for protection. "Er, how about a nice cup of tea first?"

Vernon and the ladies gathered around the table, pyjama-clad and bleary-eyed, steaming cups of tea in front of them. Vernon bit the side of his lip nervously while he waited for answers that Fiona was reluctant to give. The others were silent too, although that was probably more to do with the shellshock of waking up on the floor of Dogs Need Nice Homes.

"So what happened?" Vernon asked.

Partial Sue suddenly sprung to life, sparing Fiona from having to break the bad news, her early-morning bluntness cutting to the chase. "It didn't go well, and we've put a target on our backs. Hence why we're all sleeping here."

Fiona wondered how he would react. Angry? Disappointed? Or with "*I told you so*"? All these reactions would be quite justified. The poor lad was worried about his family, and although he'd had nothing to do with the events of last night, it was highly probable that the mafia would come after him at some point, and the other ice-cream sellers, to find out if any of them had tipped off these meddling ladies.

Vernon stared at Fiona. "What went wrong?"

Fiona cleared her throat and began her detailed account of the night's events. He listened patiently and calmly, keeping his emotional cards close to his chest. When she'd finished, Fiona added a heartfelt apology. "I'm so sorry, Vernon. You warned us of the dangers, and we didn't listen."

Daisy and Partial Sue also apologised, but Vernon stayed silent, contemplative, not moving.

"Are you okay?" Bella asked.

Vernon looked up, his face unreadable. Fiona feared the worst, that the consequences of the failed mission had sent him over the edge into oblivion, or that he might explode in a white-hot rage at their reckless incompetence.

Unexpectedly, his eyes shone with satisfaction, as if a deep thirst had been sated. "You know what. I feel quite liberated."

"Liberated?" Fiona asked.

"Yes, liberated," he replied. "I've been living in fear of these bullies for years. A nervous wreck, if I'm honest. Built them up in my head as this all-powerful force that cannot be hurt or beaten. But last night you struck a blow. You frightened them. Before that, they probably thought they were untouchable. Then someone sets fire to their dead drop and leaves them a business card that says, 'We know who you are'. No wonder they wanted to get a look at you. They're scared of you."

Astonishment, wild and baffling, swirled around inside Fiona's head. She hadn't expected this reaction, and neither had anyone else, judging by the wide eyes and open mouths around the table.

With fire in his eyes, Vernon didn't seem to notice the shock on their faces. "This has made me realise something. I'm sick and tired of being intimidated by these people. I think it's their turn to be bullied for a change."

"Good for you," Partial Sue blurted out. "It's the only way to deal with a bully. That's what I did to Tracey Townsend. She kept picking on me at school until I punched her in the face."

"I agree," Fiona said. "I don't advocate punching anyone in the face, but I'll make an exception with this lot. But you know what's better than one person punching a bully in the face? Lots of people doing it all at once. Figuratively speaking, of course."

The whole table stared at her, puzzled at where Fiona was going with this, especially as she was never a fan of physical violence. But Vernon's words had sparked a moment of inspiration. She saw an opportunity here. A way to capitalise on the situation, shifting the balance of power in their favour.

She turned to Vernon. "I'm wondering, if you feel like this, there's probably a good chance the others will too."

"You mean all the other ice-cream sellers," Vernon said. "The ones I know are terrified, but they're also fed up with their lives. Sick of having this forced on them. I think it's time for a change."

Swept up with the bravado of his words, there were murmurs of assent and nods of agreement from around the table — all except Daisy. "Hold on, hold on. I don't want to be a Daisy Downer, but have we all forgotten what this mafia is like? What they can do to everyone and their families? These people are dangerous."

"Yes, that's true," Fiona said. "That hasn't changed. However, the situation has. Vernon's right. We've got them on the back foot, in more ways than you think. And it's only just occurred to me, they can't lay a finger on us yet, because there's something very important that they need."

"What's that?" Partial Sue asked.

"I'll come to that in a minute. What I want to propose will end their reign of fear for ever, but we have to act now. We only have a small window of opportunity."

"What are you proposing?" Bella asked.

Everyone leaned in, eager to hear what master plan Fiona was about to bestow on them — hopefully a courageous strategy to crush this infernal and murderous mafia once and for all.

However, Fiona's reply was a little underwhelming. "I want to create a WhatsApp group."

CHAPTER 43

Later that day, Claire, better known as the Ice Queen, arrived at the shop in a pretty cornflower-blue summer dress, her freshly conditioned platinum hair shimmering in the bright sunlight. Fiona quickly ushered her inside, keeping a wary eye on the street for any signs she'd been seen. Closing the door behind her, she led her to the table and offered her a seat.

Daisy smiled warmly. "Would you like a cup of tea?"

Claire declined with a nervous shake of the head. "Can I ask what this is about?" For someone with such a big singing voice, her spoken words wouldn't startle a mouse.

"Probably best if we wait for Tom," Fiona replied. "Then we can tell you both together."

Claire seemed content with this answer, although her hands, which lay in her lap, writhed around themselves nervously.

"Did you leave your ice-cream van at home, like we asked?" Partial Sue said.

Claire nodded.

The ladies attempted to make conversation, but their guest was reluctant to engage in any kind of small talk. Despite this, Daisy — being a huge fan of *Frozen*, and being in the presence of an Elsa lookalike — fired question after question at her.

"What's your favourite bit in the movie?"

"Who's your favourite character, apart from Elsa?"

"How many times have you seen the stage show?"

"Do you prefer it to the movie?"

Claire replied with monosyllabic answers, never making eye contact. The one-sided conversation continued for a good forty minutes, until Tom, the real-beard Santa, better known as the owner of the Sergeant Bilcone ice-cream van arrived. Fiona had staggered their arrival on purpose, just to be on the safe side.

By contrast, Tom burst through the shop door, dressed the same as the last time they'd seen him, in grubby shorts and vest, his white hair exploding in every direction. Rosy-cheeked with sweat dotting his brow, he gave them a happy, blustering greeting. "All right, ladies!"

"Thank you for coming, Tom," Fiona said. "Did you leave your ice-cream van at home?"

"I did, indeed." He sounded very pleased with himself. "Strode all the way from Iford, along the river, and I was very glad I did. I saw this flash of blue across the water, and I thought, 'That's a kingfisher'."

"Oh, how wonderful." Partial Sue was a bit of an amateur twitcher. "I am partial to a kingfisher or two."

"Not to eat, I hope," Tom guffawed.

"No, silly. Seeing them. Not eating them. What a lucky sight."

"I know. I'm friendly with a couple of local bird photographers — amateurs, mind — who've sat by the Stour all day, hoping to snap one and not seen a dicky bird. Pun intended." He guffawed again. "Would never have seen that if I'd taken the bus or walked along the road. Nature's marvellous, isn't it? Now, what's all this about?"

"Let's have tea first," Fiona said.

Tom rubbed his hands together. "Now you're talking!" He took a seat next to Claire, then proceeded to talk their ears off about the health benefits of tea. When he was half-way through a diatribe about how freshly picked tea didn't need any milk, his voice suddenly fell silent, and all the jollity left his face. The reason for this sudden mood change had appeared at the door. Vernon quickly stepped inside the shop and lowered his hood, followed by Bella.

"Hello." Vernon smiled.

Tom didn't reciprocate.

Fiona remembered that these two were acquainted. When the ladies had first questioned Tom, he had initially denied knowing any ice-cream sellers apart from Claire and the Icely Brothers. However, they had later learned that he'd been the one elected to break the bad news, passing on the bleak message to Vernon that he now had to do the ice-cream mafia's bidding, otherwise awful things would happen. Probably something Tom wasn't proud of or wanted anyone to know about.

Tom stared at Vernon, while Claire wouldn't tear her gaze away from the floor. Eventually Tom turned to Fiona, his face cold and expressionless. "What's going on here?"

Fiona chose her words carefully. "We've come across an opportunity. Something that could put an end to the misery of the ice-cream mafia, but we need your help."

"I don't know what you're talking about," Tom replied without hesitation.

"Me neither." Claire sounded sheepish. She wasn't a very good liar.

"Oh, come on, both of you," Vernon said. "There's no point denying it. You know what we're talking about. No need for the vow of silence. These ladies know all about the ice-cream mafia and how they're holding you and your families to ransom."

Tom and Claire refused to answer or respond.

"Okay, we'll take that as a yes," Partial Sue said. "Now the real question is, do you want to do something about it?"

Again, no response from either of them. Fiona had expected this and knew they weren't being awkward or stubborn — they were frightened, terrified that the mere mention of the ice-cream mafia would unleash untold horrors on them. Perhaps they might have a different reaction once they'd heard that the ladies had struck a blow against this mob. Perhaps it would embolden them, as it had with Vernon, and make them realise that they didn't have to live their lives in fear, that their captors were vulnerable. Fiona attempted to lay a positive foundation. "There's something you should know about the ice-cream mafia. Something that might change your outlook."

Both Tom and Claire regarded Fiona suspiciously, as though dreading what would come next.

"We've got them on the back foot," Partial Sue said.

Tom frowned. "What do you mean, 'got them on the back foot'?"

Fiona explained the events of the previous night — the fire, the GPS tracker and being led to the tennis courts. "There's an opportunity to put a stop to them, but we need to capitalise on our advantage."

Claire went pale. Fiona was worried that she might faint, but then she flinched as Tom suddenly blew his top.

"How on God's green earth is that an advantage! You haven't got them on the back foot, you've riled them up is what you've done. I can't believe this! We're all going to be for it now. How could you be so stupid? So reckless. They're going to make us all suffer." Tom's anger turned to fear. "My auntie's in a care home. They sent me pictures of her asleep in the day room. She's my only living relative. They could be there right now. About to do something nasty."

"They're going to kill us." Claire was shaking. "Like they did with Kevin Masterson. I'm going to end up dead in a freezer. Then they'll kill my family."

"No, they won't," Fiona said. "They'll come for me, Daisy and Sue first. They got a good look at us, and one thing we know about this mafia is that they're experts at finding people. It's just a matter of time."

"Yes, and then they'll kill you," Tom said.

"No, they can't do that," Fiona said. "Not yet, anyway. They need something from us."

"And what's that?" Tom asked.

"They're vulnerable at the moment," Fiona explained. "Their secret operation is no longer a secret. They've been compromised, which is why they're on the back foot. There are people out there who know about them — us. They've probably already figured out we're not a rival mafia, but they can't get rid of us until they find out how much we know and what we've done with that information, who else we might've told. They might even figure out that we're amateur sleuths and think we have a ton of thick files on them. Evidence of who they are."

"But you don't know who they are," Tom stated.

"They don't know that," Partial Sue replied. "First, they need to find out what we know. Which means they'll come here, demanding we tell them. Until then we have a window of opportunity. A small amount of time to prepare a trap. We're already the bait, so we might as well use it."

"So your plan is to flush them out." Tom shook his head. "I can't believe I'm hearing this. It's madness. Do you know who you're up against?"

"No," Vernon replied. "Nobody does. Their power is their anonymity. No one can get to them. It's a smart, efficient crime network. But it only works if that network is compliant. As long as we're obedient and in constant fear, they call the shots. However, if that network turns on them, they're in big trouble."

"No, out of the question." Tom stood up abruptly. "Come on, Claire. We need to get out of here before they do something else stupid."

Claire rose to her feet, her head bowed, following Tom towards the front door.

Partial Sue called out to them. "Then nothing's going to change. You'll be stuck like this for the rest of your life, in drug-pushing limbo."

"Unless you set fire to your van and disappear, like the Icely Brothers," Daisy added.

Claire stopped. Hesitated.

"Claire, we have to leave." Tom had one hand on the door.

"Sue's right," Vernon said. "Think about it. Our lives are already over. We'll never be free of them. Can't move on, can't make plans. We'll be their slaves for ever."

Held by an invisible forcefield, Claire stood on the spot, conflicted, the two sides of her brain almost certainly having a raging debate. Both not giving an inch.

Daisy broke the deadlock for her. "What if you want to do something with that lovely voice of yours, Claire? They'll never allow you to be anything other than what you are now. That's fine if you're happy selling their drugs and doing the odd children's party, but what if you want more for yourself? What if you want to be on stage? You've got the talent."

"I'd like to do that one day." Claire's words sounded brittle, as if they might shatter at any moment. "I love doing the kids' parties, but I dream about being on the West End. I don't think I'm good enough, but I'd like to give it a try."

"You could easily be on the West End," Daisy said.

"But only if you make a stand now," Partial Sue added.

"What about you, Tom?" Fiona asked. "Isn't there something more you want from life?"

Defeated, Tom's body slumped and his mouth turned down. "Claire's got her whole life ahead of her, and, if I were her age, I'd want to do the same thing. But at my stage in life, I'm just happy taking things easy. Mooching around, sitting in the sun, taking strolls along the river, spotting kingfishers. But I can never really enjoy it. I'm never relaxed. The ice-cream mafia's always lurking at the back of my mind somewhere."

"What do you need from us?" Claire asked.

"Do you know any other ice-cream sellers out there?" Vernon asked. "Illegitimate ones?"

Claire and Tom slowly nodded.

"We need you to persuade them to join us," Vernon said. "I'll talk to the ones I know. We need as many of them as we can get, and we need them to spread the word to any others they know. What we're planning only works if everyone's on side."

"Show them, Daisy," Partial Sue said.

Reluctantly, Tom and Claire shuffled back to the table.

"To help get the message across, I've come up with a nice visual matador." No one picked up on Daisy's metaphorical mix-up. She produced a single wooden lolly stick from her pocket and held it in front of her. "One lolly stick can easily be broken." She snapped it without any trouble, placing the two broken halves on the table. Then she reached into her pocket and brought out over a dozen lolly sticks, butting them together into a bunch. "But many are impossible to break." Holding them in her fists she tried and failed to snap them.

"This only works if all the ice-cream sellers act as one," Fiona said. "United."

"Okay, and once we've persuaded them to join this suicide mission, what then?" asked Tom.

Partial Sue grinned and held up her phone. "You get them to join our WhatsApp group. It's called Just Desserts."

Tom and Claire stared at her, dumbfounded, then at each other, clearly wondering what hairbrained scheme they were getting involved in.

CHAPTER 44

It happened the following Wednesday. An odd day for such a significant event. The middle of the week was always a subdued affair, normally reserved for such activities as dental check-ups, or waiting in for bulk deliveries of kitchen roll because it was cheaper that way. Certainly not a day when you'd expect the local mafia to show up at your door, especially as a drab and drizzly weather front had moved in, dousing Southbourne in fine, bothersome rain.

An intimidating little convoy of cars turned up outside the shop. Well, the first two were. A big black Range Rover, followed by a sleek black electric Jag, both with tinted windows and black alloy wheels. The third was a little less impressive — a sensible navy-blue Toyota Corolla. Although it was entirely possible that this belonged to a random member of the public who'd popped out to get some bits in Southbourne.

Fiona presumed it was the mafia, hoped it was them — a strange emotion to exhibit when a carload of mobsters had possibly turned up outside, demanding information. Debilitating fear would have been more appropriate, but she felt strangely relieved. That this might finally be over. The beginning of the end.

Unlike Daisy and Partial Sue, who seemed to have enjoyed staying in the protective enclave of the shop, treating it like an indoor camping adventure, minus the fact that their lives were at stake, Fiona couldn't wait for this to be over. Though she loved her friends dearly, she longed to hunker down in her own space, surrounded by her own things, and to be in her own bed again. The quality of sleep the shop's floor offered hadn't exactly helped matters, and she'd been operating in a sleep-deprived delirium. She almost wanted to tell the mafia outside to get a move on, as she had a lot of shut-eye to catch up on.

Fiona's tinnitus squealed, warning her that she needed to get a grip of herself. To stop thinking about sleep, to focus and take things seriously, or she wouldn't be going back home at all.

She called out to the other two. "This could be our mafia."

With the swiftness of a flicked rubber band, Partial Sue darted out of the storeroom. Daisy's head popped up from behind the counter, where she'd been cleaning the inside of the cupboards. She got to her feet and joined the other two, staring out at the assembled vehicles. Pulling her trusty spork from her pocket, she brandished it in front of her. "You two should get tooled up, as they say in the hood. Grab your weapons."

Partial Sue nodded towards the first car. "I don't think a spork is going to be much use against that lot."

The Range Rover's doors opened, dispensing four very large men onto the damp pavement. They could've been extras in a Viking saga, apart from their skinny black suits, which made them look like very large year tens who'd outgrown their school uniforms.

Partial Sue jittered on the spot. "Have you sent the WhatsApp message?"

"Not yet," Fiona replied.

"Why not?"

"We have to be sure before we send it. We won't get another chance at this, and I don't want to waste it on a false alarm."

Partial Sue scoffed. "False alarm? Who else could it be? Two big gangster-style cars with blacked-out windows parked outside. A bunch of henchmen has just got out of one and I expect the mob boss will get out of the other."

"What about the Toyota Corolla on the end?" Daisy asked. "It's letting the side down in the menacing-car stakes, and the Jag's electric. I've never heard of an environmentally friendly mob boss."

"Nothing wrong with a Toyota Corolla," Partial Sue said. "I used to have one. Very reliable and economic if you have to drive around collecting a lot of drug money. Same with the Jag. Electric's still more cost effective. Maybe these gangsters have to watch their pennies like the rest of us."

From out of the Toyota came a face they recognised — the man from the council who'd warned Bella that she needed to get a trader's licence. Smartly dressed in a business suit, he carried a plain black briefcase by his side.

"Oh my gosh!" Daisy exclaimed. "That's, that's . . . what's his face?" She clicked her fingers, attempting to recall his name.

Partial Sue filled in the gaps. "Craig Hill from the council's regulatory department."

"That's the one. Do you think he's behind this?"

"He could be here on council business," Fiona suggested. "Maybe he's checking up on Bella's licence."

"But she doesn't own an ice-cream van anymore," Partial Sue said. "And her licence application was all done online. Why would he need to check in person, and why has he got those four gorillas with him? Fiona, send the message."

She still wasn't convinced, until a second man emerged from the passenger side of the Toyota. Another face they recognised. The long form of the lay-by lackey unfurled himself from the car, finally leaving Fiona in no doubt. She pulled out her phone and sent everyone on the WhatsApp group a pre-written message.

Just desserts now being served.

"Message sent." Fiona fiddled with a few more buttons on her phone, then went over to the till and left it in the pot where they kept an assortment of pens and scissors.

"Do you think Craig Hill is the mob boss?" Daisy asked.

"Not driving a Toyota Corolla, he's not," Fiona replied. "It's whoever's in the back of that Jag."

"I think we're about to find out," Partial Sue said.

A screech of tinnitus hit Fiona's ears.

Another towering man in a black suit — far too small for his weight-trained body — got out of the Jag's driver's seat, circled around the car and held open the rear passenger door. A pair of smart-trousered legs swivelled out onto the pavement and a spike of adrenalin hit Fiona in the chest. They were about to get their first glimpse of the head of the elusive ice-cream mafia. However, they were denied it at the last second. The driver popped open an umbrella to shelter his passenger from the rain, unwittingly shielding his face from the ladies' view.

The whole entourage made its way to the shop's front door and trooped inside. Henchmen first, then the driver, still holding the umbrella over his master. Daisy gave a grunt, clearly not liking an open umbrella inside the shop. Craig Hill followed next, with the lackey bringing up the rear. He closed the door firmly behind him, locked it, then spun the shop's 'Open' sign around to 'Closed'.

Finally, the umbrella collapsed in a shaken shower of water, which went over some of the merchandise, immediately getting Fiona's back up, but only for a split second. Her attention was quickly diverted to the man who'd been sheltering beneath it.

She gasped.

"Hello, ladies." He smiled with all the charm of a hyena.

CHAPTER 45

"Wh-what?" Fiona stuttered. "You're the head of the ice-cream mafia?"

Jed Garret, the owner of Flowers For A Fiver, who'd first discovered Kevin Masterson's body, appeared very pleased with himself as he strutted through the shop. "Why, I don't know what you're talking about. I'm just here to browse."

He nodded to one of his henchmen, who attempted to intimidate the ladies by tipping over a nearby set of shelves full of children's books. However, being extremely safety conscious, especially where youngsters were concerned, Fiona had secured it to the wall, going overboard with the number of screws she'd employed. It refused to budge. Another henchman lent a hand, grabbing it from the other side. Despite their combined efforts, the thing barely moved, apart from a copy of *The Very Hungry Caterpillar* falling onto the floor. The first henchman abandoned the shelves and turned his attention to the hat stand, kicking it over, but instead of clattering to the floor it landed on a bean bag, which broke its fall and nullified the effect. Simon Le Bon, who normally reacted to aggressive behaviour, didn't think their clumsy actions merited so much as a warning growl or bark.

Jed rolled his eyes. "Sorry, this is the first time we've been officially out as a mafia. Still need to work on a few things."

Sitting himself down, he slung both feet up on the table, gesturing to his outfit. "How am I looking, by the way?" He'd forsaken his normal casual attire for black trousers and a black leather jacket over a black T-shirt. Straight out of the mafia playbook, he'd also slicked back his unkempt chestnut hair, darkening it in the process. He was clearly smug about ditching his geeky persona for something edgier.

Daisy's high standards of hygiene outweighed any fear. "Do you mind keeping your feet off the table, please?"

He ignored her. "You know, I thought you'd figure out it was me. But I think I credited you with too much intelligence."

"How so?" Fiona asked.

"Because it was so obvious," he replied.

"Why, because you were the one who found the body?" Fiona asked.

Jed scoffed. "No, no one ever suspects the person who finds the body, do they? The early-morning jogger, the dog walker, or, in my case, the divorced dad having his kids for the weekend. Plus, there was nothing to connect me with Kevin Masterson. No, I think I was pretty safe on that score."

"Why did you kill Kevin Masterson?" Partial Sue asked.

Jed wagged his finger. "Don't be jumping ahead now. I'll come to that in a minute. Let's focus on your failure to suspect me. Didn't put two and two together, did you? I thought it was so obvious, but then maybe I'm just smarter than you."

The ladies exchanged confused glances, then stared at Jed, confused.

Relishing their fear and frustration, he stretched out the conundrum a little longer. "It was hiding in plain sight all this time. They say that's the best place to hide something. There was a huge clue staring everyone in the face this whole time. A motivation. A big one. I thought you would have picked up on it, Sue, being an ex-accountant."

"Me?" a shocked Partial Sue asked. "How did you know I was an accountant?"

"I know everything about you three, especially when it comes to your families." He winked. "That's why it helps having

263

someone from the local council on the payroll." He waved at Craig Hill, who smirked devilishly. "Now, enough digression. Come on, I thought you were supposed to be detectives."

The ladies exchanged more infuriated glances. No response came forth, not even a guess.

Jed took his feet off the table. "The clue's in the name of my business — Flowers For A Fiver."

Daisy had a stab. "Oh, you came up with the name by accident, sort of."

"Not that," Jed replied.

"You told us how important it was to have a good name," Partial Sue said.

"Yes, you went into great detail about that," Fiona added. "You even drummed it into your kids."

"And Alan from Alan's Place," Partial Sue said. "It's the secret of your success."

Jed put his hands behind his head and tipped his chair back in that way teachers would tell you not to. "Yeah, that's right, and it was all a great big failure."

Fiona's eyebrows came together, forming a deep crease. "Wait, what?"

Jed righted his chair. "Okay, sure. Names are very important in business, especially online ones, and mine was a success, initially. An unbelievable success. I had a memorable, catchy name. Did what it said on the tin. A unique selling point. Send a bunch of flowers anywhere in the UK for a fiver. Overnight, I cornered the flower delivery market. Made a ton of money. I thought I was an online genius, but I was an idiot. I'd created a business with a built-in self-destruct system."

"Oh—" Partial Sue jerked as if she'd been electrocuted — "because of inflation, rising prices, but yours have to stay the same."

Jed snapped his fingers. "Exactly. The whole business concept is built around five pounds. While the cost of everything goes up — shipping, supplies, wages — the price of my product is static. Big mistake."

Fiona wanted to kick herself, several times, if that were physically possible. They had suspected Somerford Ice Creams for the same reason, but had abandoned the idea once the police had proved them wrong. However, the ladies had been right, apart from looking at the wrong company.

Jed continued. "It makes less and less each year. Which is why I had to turn to crime."

"So why do you keep it if it's running at a loss?" Partial Sue asked.

"It's very handy for cleaning my drug money. Through dozens of fake non-existent flower orders. Ghost laundering, which also makes it appear profitable."

"Why not just start another business?" Fiona asked. "Or put your prices up?"

"Because I'd lose all credibility. Flowers For Eleven Pounds Fifty doesn't have the same ring to it. Plus, do you know how hard it is to make a new venture work? Sixty per cent of all new businesses fail in the first three years. No thank you. I needed a new avenue. I was desperate, to tell the truth. I'd become accustomed to a rich lifestyle and so had my ex-wife. I needed something I knew would work. Something that would make money fast and was always in demand. Drugs was a dead cert. The guy who imports my flowers said he could supply me. I just had to pay off a few Border Force officials. All I needed was a distribution network. Ice-cream sellers are perfect. They're all sole traders so they're vulnerable, easy to intimidate. Craig vets them first, and tests the water with some licensing issue, just to get the measure of them."

"I'm connected with local councils across the country," Craig explained. "I can find anyone's family or friends. One of the guys here will snap pictures of them, and hey presto, we've got employees who will do whatever we tell them."

"And I never have to meet them," Jed grinned. "Well, apart from Kevin Masterson."

"What happened with Kevin Masterson?" Fiona asked.

"Come, sit down." He beckoned for the ladies to join him at the table. "You're making me nervous standing there."

"We're making *you* nervous?" Partial Sue snorted. "How do think we feel?"

Fiona suddenly felt the presence of the henchmen behind her, a solid wall of beef coercing her and the others towards the table. Simon Le Bon barked. Not wanting him to get hurt, Fiona shushed him reassuringly while her tinnitus cranked up a few notches. The ladies grudgingly took a seat.

Jed glanced at the man nearest. "Make us a cup of tea, Freddie. Ladies, would you like one?"

Tea was a drink best enjoyed with friends or when making new ones, not in the presence of someone who had killed and enslaved people, just because his precious business model didn't work. They all shook their heads.

"Er, where's the kettle?" Freddie didn't appear too pleased about being the designated tea-maker. He knew he would probably be mocked by the other henchmen later.

"Storeroom," Partial Sue said coldly.

Jed continued. "Now, where was I? Oh, yes. Kevin Masterson. We'd just recruited him. He hadn't started selling for us yet. We'd only just done the blackmail thing with pictures of his mum, but he turned the tables on us. Tried blackmailing me, can you believe it?"

"Oh, the irony," Partial Sue said.

"How did he blackmail you?" Fiona asked.

"Somehow, this little weasel knew where I lived. Knew I was behind it. To this day I don't know how he found out, but it could've been the end of me. However, he wasn't particularly bright. Turned up at my house really early on Sunday morning, trying to catch me off guard while my kids were asleep. I was furious. I didn't want him anywhere near them, so I suggested we speak in his van. He agreed and off we went."

"Weren't you worried someone would see you?" Daisy asked.

"I had no choice, but it was early. Just after seven. No one was around at that time, and you've seen the houses in my road, all hidden behind high gates and hedgerows. Plus, the windows of his ice-cream van are covered in stickers. It's hard to see what's going on behind them. Once inside, he showed me the pictures we'd used to blackmail him — pictures of his mum coming out of Asda. He said if I didn't cough up a quarter of a million pounds, he'd go to the police with them."

"What did you say?" Fiona asked.

"Of course, I denied it all. Said I'd never seen those pictures before in my life. I pointed out that there was nothing to connect me with them. It was clear he hadn't thought this through. He started getting angry, and said I had to pay. I saw red. How dare he turn up outside my house and threaten me with my kids at home? So I shoved him hard. He fell backwards and banged his head on the edge of the freezer, killing him."

Freddie placed a weak, pallid cup of tea in front of his boss. Fiona wondered if the henchman belonged to the school of thought that if you make bad tea then you'll never be asked to make it again.

It didn't work. Jed peered at the second-rate beverage. "Maybe more tea and less milk next time, eh?"

"So was it an accident?" Fiona asked.

Jed shook his head, then raised his cup and took a sip, wincing at the taste. "Nope, I wanted to kill him, but in my rage I'd created a big dilemma. I had to get rid of his body, and there was the risk that my DNA and fingerprints would be all over him and his van. I'd have to drive it somewhere, set it alight while my kids were still asleep, then jog back home. I couldn't drive it with a dead body rolling around in the back, so I stuffed it in the freezer. Nearly broke my back in the process, but I managed it. Was about to drive away when I realised I had my phone on me. The police could track any phone in the vicinity of a burnt-out van with a body in it, so I ran back into the house to drop it off. A second later my kids came thundering down the stairs, telling me they'd seen an ice-cream van outside and could they have one. I had to think fast, adapt my plan. I decided to follow through with their request. Play the innocent passer-by who finds the body. It might actually work out better, especially if the kids were with me, to give me an alibi to back up my story. It also gave me an excuse to go inside the van to look for lollies in the freezer. I'd pretend to discover the body and check for signs of life. That would explain why my DNA and prints were all over him and the van. I knew there wouldn't be any traces of drugs, because he hadn't started selling for us yet. Nothing would incriminate me. The only suspect items were the blackmail photos, so I grabbed them and stuffed them down the back of my track-suit bottoms. Then I went inside the house to call the police. Worked out nicely, I'd say."

A chill spread from Fiona's midriff, down her limbs to the end of her extremities. Jed had been so cold and calculating — impetuously killing someone and not thinking twice about involving his kids so he could strengthen his story.

Partial Sue wanted to delve deeper into his explanation. "Hold on a second. All the news reports said Kevin Masterson's body was frozen. How was it frozen if you'd only just dumped his body in there? Weren't you worried about the police discovering the time of death and pointing the finger at you?"

"Firstly, I never said the body was frozen. I said it was cold, which was true. You know what the media's like. A frozen dead body in an ice-cream van makes a better headline that just a dead one. But putting the body in the freezer did me a big favour. Even though Kevin had switched off his engine when he arrived — he probably didn't think our meeting would take very long — I knew the freezer would keep working for a bit, using the charge left in the batteries. By the time I'd called the police he'd been in the freezer for well over twenty minutes. They took another twenty minutes getting there. Then Forensics took another thirty minutes to arrive. By the time they did a proper examination, his body had been in the deep freeze for well over an hour. Cold enough to blur the time of death and put me in the clear."

Jed smiled, leaning back in his seat. "I've confessed my sins. Now it's your turn. Who tipped you off about the dead drop? And who else have you told? Tell me, or people will get hurt."

The chill that had spread from Fiona's core to every bone in her body quickly turned into the searing heat of fear and panic.

CHAPTER 46

Now it was Fiona's turn to think fast. This was the real reason he was here. To extract information one way or another. To find out how much they knew and who they'd shared that information with. All part of the plan, she reassured herself, all part of the plan. A plan that was taking a little longer than expected to come together, if she was brutally honest. Maybe the traffic was bad. Whatever the reason, she desperately needed to stall him, because once he got his answers, their lives would be worthless.

"How did you know Kevin Masterson hadn't told anyone else about you?" Fiona asked.

"Because I know people. He was a cheap little scammer. A money grabber. He would've kept it a secret so he could keep all the blackmail money for himself."

Partial Sue interjected. "His mum told us he was going to pay her back everything he owed her, and he cancelled his subscription to the *Ice-Cream Seller*. That would explain why. He thought he was about to come into a lot of money."

"But weren't you worried he might've told his mum about you?" Daisy asked.

Jed shook his head. "I called round with a big bunch of flowers, offered my condolences, mainly to see how she

270

reacted. See if she felt scared or intimidated by me. If she had been then Freddie and the boys would've dealt with her, possibly poisoning her with that awful tea of his."

He grinned at Freddie.

Freddie didn't react.

Jed continued. "When I met her, I got no sense that she'd heard of me or knew what her son had been up to. I felt pretty sure that I was in the clear. However, after he'd showed up at my door, I realised I'd been complacent." He nodded to his henchmen. "Now I have these guys watching my house twenty-four-seven."

"Were your men there when we called round?" Fiona asked.

"Some of them, yes. They've got quite good at staying out of sight, but ready to pounce if anyone threatening appears at the door. They didn't consider you a threat." He rounded off his sentence with a condescending smile.

"Coming back to Kevin's mum," Daisy said. "Why did you put us in contact with her in the first place?"

"I needed an excuse to pop in and see how your investigation was going. See if I was in any danger. Plus, it didn't hurt to give you a bit of misdirection and a nice big donation. Keep me off your list of suspects. But it seems I was worrying needlessly, as you hadn't a clue."

Fiona noted that he'd only taken one sip of his wishy-washy tea. She seized her chance to stall him a bit longer. She rose to her feet. "Actually, I think I will have that cup of tea now." She reached out to collect Jed's cup. "Do you want me to make you a proper one with a bit of colour in its cheeks?"

"Sit down," he said.

Fiona obeyed.

"Nice try." Jed smiled. "You're putting off answering my questions. Now, who tipped you off about the location of the dead drop? And who else have you told?"

All three ladies remained silent, gazing down at the table.

Jed sighed. "I see. It's like that is it? Well, maybe I can help you remember." He clicked his fingers. Craig approached the table and placed the briefcase flat on top. Popping both latches at once, he flipped it open and removed three large-format black-and-white photographs, then slid them across the table towards the ladies. Each one showed a covert shot of Vernon, his hoodie up. They'd been taken in quick succession as he warily ambled along a street, but were cropped too tightly to tell the location.

"This guy tipped you off, didn't he?" Jed asked.

Heat prickled around Fiona's neck as she silently stared at the images, pretending that she didn't recognise him. Daisy and Partial Sue did likewise.

"Here's something else that might jog your memory." Craig slid three more shots across to them, showing both Vernon and Bella carrying groceries, leaving a convenience store.

Daisy gasped.

Jed tapped his finger against one of the shots. "Bella may have slipped through our fingers, but we haven't forgotten about her."

"Leave her alone! She's done nothing!" Daisy cried.

Retrieving another set of photos from his briefcase, Craig slid them over to Fiona. She felt the air suddenly evacuate from her lungs, as if she'd been punched in the stomach. The shots captured her sister and her two grown-up children coming out of a restaurant in London. Fiona swore.

"And just so you don't feel left out." Craig pushed three more photos towards Partial Sue. "If I'm not mistaken, that's your cousin in Wales."

Ever the feisty one, Partial Sue gave him what for. "Don't you dare hurt him or you'll be sorry."

Jed threw his head back and laughed. "I like it! Bit of spirit. But may I ask, just how are you going to make us sorry?" His voice turned to ice. "Look around you. I've got all your lives in the palm of my hand. You step out of line, and you're the ones who'll be sorry, get it?"

Partial Sue cowered. "Please don't hurt my cousin."

Jed became jovial once more. "Oh, don't worry, I'm not here to kill you or anyone else. There's another reason I'm here. Recruitment."

"Recruitment?" Daisy asked.

Jed interlaced his fingers, happily playing the part of the villain. "You three are going to help with my expansion."

"Expansion?" Fiona had not been expecting this.

"Yes." His voice overflowed with glee. "Let me explain. You see, the problem with ice-cream vans, as you're probably aware, is there aren't that many of them. Dying breed, which makes them a finite resource. It's holding back the growth of my business. I've hit a plateau in sales. Can't sell more without more vans. That's where you three come in."

Fiona gripped the edge of her chair, horrified and a little confused at where this might be going.

"Do you want us to drive ice-cream vans?" Daisy asked.

Jed shook his head, amused at this idea. He rose to his feet, spreading his arms wide, preparing to announce his intentions. "I'm going to start selling my products in your charity shop. A smart, new strategy, and I wouldn't have thought of it if it wasn't for you three. I got the idea when I visited you the other day. Oh, don't worry, it will all be below the counter. On the QT, as it were. You can still raise money for homeless dogs and all that. But it's the perfect setup, the perfect cover. No one would ever suspect a charity shop of selling drugs, and you'll have the honour of being the first. My glorious guinea pigs."

All three ladies stared at him, incredulous.

Reading their expressions as confusion, Jed continued to explain his idea. Not that it needed any further explanation. They completely understood his diabolical plans. Their beloved shop, their safe haven of friendship, was about to become a front for illegal narcotics, and there was nothing they could do about it. Not when their families' lives were in danger.

Jed began pacing, circling the table as the ladies listened in horror. "I'll trial the idea. Iron out any problems, but I don't foresee any. Then once it's running smoothly, I'll set up the same operation in another charity shop and another, and so on and so on. It's the most insanely brilliant idea. Charity shops are everywhere. More springing up every day. Think of it as a franchise. Like Costa Coffee or KFC. I'll have locations all over the place. Go national. My own chain." He stared into space, his eyes glinting at the prospect.

"Aren't you taking a big risk?" Daisy pointed out.

Enamoured by his own idea, and shocked that anyone would question it, Jed glared at her.

"Daisy's right," Fiona said. "You've taken a big risk just coming here. You're out in the open. No longer anonymous. I'm sure a couple of CCTV cameras will have caught you coming into this shop."

"Yes, they probably did." Jed grinned devilishly. "Craig made sure all the ones we passed were council owned. He can make stuff like that go away, and if he can't, we'll just do what we normally do — threaten people to make them do what we want. But in any case, we haven't done anything wrong. Just visited a charity shop. No law against that."

"Word might get around," Partial Sue said. "People might hear about what you're really up to."

Jed approached her, getting in her personal space, inches from her face. "And who's going to tell them? You?" He swiped at the pictures in front of her, scrunching them up in his fist. "You seem to forget who holds your families' lives in their hands."

Not wishing to goad him any further, Partial Sue shrank in her seat, hunkering down under the force of his maniacal threats.

Satisfied with the effect of his outburst, Jed tossed aside the photos and quickly resumed his default setting of self-satisfied dictator, parading around the room continuing his victorious diatribe.

Concerned for Partial Sue's wellbeing, Fiona sent her what she hoped was a look of support and reassurance. However, instead of seeing fear in her eyes, she detected what appeared to be optimism. Fiona shot her another look, this time a questioning one. By way of an answer, Partial Sue slowly reached up to scratch her ear but, at the last second, she surreptitiously tapped it a couple of times, indicating she wanted her to listen.

Not easy when Fiona's tinnitus was playing a whining din in her ears. Concentrating hard, she filtered out her audible affliction. Nothing came through at first, except Jed's bragging, but gradually she began to tune into something far in the distance, above the traffic noise. A cheerful ditty vibrating its way through the air towards her. The chimes of 'Popeye the Sailor Man' heralded the approach of an ice-cream van.

CHAPTER 47

Daisy must have heard the chimes too. Their happy but distant lilt caused her defeated, lopsided body language to right itself. Perching upright in her chair, she cocked one ear to the side, as Simon Le Bon often did when he heard a food packet opening.

Fiona allowed her gaze to drift over to the assembled ice-cream mafia, to gauge if they'd noticed anything amiss. They were too wrapped up in their boss's speech to spot that the ladies' demeanours had changed, or to be bothered by the sound of an ice-cream van approaching.

Jed stood in the middle of the shop with his hands on his hips, enjoying the sound of his own voice. "Of course, I'll need to scale up my operation. Take on more people to cope with the expansion. This lot won't be enough, not with all the new charity shops that will be under my control." He playfully punched Freddie on the arm, although Freddie didn't look particularly pleased about it.

"So, is this your entire operation, right here?" Fiona asked.

"Yep, that's right."

"All in one place?"

276

Jed nodded.

"Oh." Fiona masked her excitement with surprise. This was perfectly convenient. The ice-cream mafia were nicely contained. All the bad eggs in one charity shop basket.

Jed assumed she had expected his operation to be bigger. Rather than seeing this as a drawback, Jed regarded this as an exemplar of his commercial prowess. "You have to run a lean operation in business. Keep costs down, and I intend to keep it that way."

He continued to witter on about how his expansion into the world of charity shops would be carefully controlled, erring on the side of caution and not growing too quickly, as this had been the downfall of many a promising enterprise.

The ladies listened intently, but really their ears were attuned to what was happening outside, further up the street. In the distance, a second set of chimes — 'Greensleeves' — joined 'Popeye the Sailor Man', playing at equal volume, as if the two tunes were having a battle with each other. This was quickly followed by a third ice-cream van, also playing 'Greensleeves', but a few bars behind the other, as if it were an echo.

Fiona glanced at Jed's men to gauge their reactions. Only the lay-by lackey, standing closest to the door, appeared to have heard the approaching cacophony. Fidgeting slightly, not knowing what to do with his gangly arms and legs, he kept quiet. Presumably, after allowing the dead drop to go up in flames, he wasn't in Jed's good books, which was probably why he was reluctant to speak up and alert them, or do anything that would land him in more trouble.

"Just one last thing," Jed announced. "Then we can conclude our business here today."

Fiona assumed he would continue to interrogate them, pressing them for answers about who they'd talked to. However, distracted by the importance of his new pet project, and perhaps his own invincibility, he had other matters on his mind.

Craig Hill reached into the open briefcase and pulled out a small, bulging cheese and onion crisp packet, sealed along the top with brown tape. He placed it on the table in front of Fiona.

"I don't like cheese and onion," she said.

Jed guffawed. His men quickly joined in until the shop was thick with belly laughter from all except the three ladies sitting at the table. Overdoing the theatrics, Jed wiped a tear from his eye. "This isn't for you to snack on, Fiona. This is your first delivery — your drugs to sell in the shop."

Fiona's face went numb. She regarded the package in front of her as if it were a bomb. She didn't want to touch it or have anything to do with it at all.

"It's just a small amount to get you going," Jed explained. "In there you'll find twenty bags of high-grade merchandise." He began outlining exactly how he wanted his drugs to be sold and how much product he expected them to shift per week, but Fiona's attention was drawn outside to the road beyond. A fourth and a fifth set of chimes had joined the others, and were heading their way. She just about recognised the theme to *The Third Man*, but the other tune was lost in the malaise.

By now a couple of the henchmen had heard the collective chimes too, and were exchanging puzzled looks. One of them pulled Freddie by the arm and whispered in his ear. He didn't appear worried, just confused. Staring out of the window, he checked in both directions for signs of the oncoming racket, which seemed to be increasing with every second. With a vacant expression, he shrugged to his colleagues, signalling that he couldn't see anything.

Jed was too preoccupied with his pontificating to notice that his men were distracted. He continued with the ladies' instructions. "We'll put the word out that our customers can now buy from Dogs Need Nice Homes. They'll use a special code so you know who they are. If someone comes in and says, 'I want to make a cash donation', that means they want to buy drugs."

"What if someone genuinely wants to make a cash donation?" Daisy asked.

"Does that happen?" Jed asked.

"Oh, yes," Daisy replied.

"Really? People just hand over cash to help homeless dogs?"

"Well, you did, remember?" Partial Sue reminded him.

"Yeah, but I thought that was a one-off."

"Lots of people make cash donations," Fiona said. "Admittedly, not as big as yours."

Jed thought for a moment. "Okay, fair enough, so we need a different code."

"Er, boss?" Freddie attempted to get Jed's attention.

The ever-increasing chimes of the approaching ice-cream vans could no longer be ignored, and resembled a giant clatter of saucepans and cymbals played on a loop. Fiona felt her confidence soaring with every crash and clang.

Craig Hill heard it too. "What is that racket?"

"Guys, be quiet." Jed was annoyed at being interrupted. "I'm trying to think. I know. We'll change the code to, 'I want to make a happy donation'. How does that sound?"

Fiona screwed up her nose. "Er, no. I don't think it's going to work."

Jed nodded. "Yeah, it's a bit of a weird thing to say, isn't it? Let's think of something else."

"No, I don't mean that." Fiona folded her arms assertively. "I mean no, as in no to the whole thing. The selling of drugs in this shop. I'm afraid it's not going to happen for you."

Jed stared at her, unblinking in disbelief as he absorbed her defiance. His face flushed with rage. "What did you just say?"

"You heard her perfectly," Partial Sue snapped. "Answer's no, sunshine." She flicked the crisp packet of narcotics back towards Craig Hill. "Take your drugs back, because it ain't going to happen."

"We're like the cast of *Grange Hill*," Daisy added. "We just say no."

"Boss?" Freddie asked, keeping watch out of the window. "There's something you should see."

"Not now!" Jed snarled, then turned his fury on the three ladies. "You listen here. I've been nice so far. I haven't mentioned the dead drop you sabotaged or the drugs that went up in flames, or that you owe me for what I lost. But you're going to do as you're told, or the people you care about will end up like Kevin Masterson." He paused his rant, suddenly distracted. "What is that awful noise?"

At that moment two ice-cream vans rumbled to a halt outside, one from either direction. Sergeant Bilcone arrived from the left, while Vernon arrived from the right, with Bella sitting beside him. Both vans bookended the parked mafia cars, boxing them in tightly. To make sure they had no means of escape, three more ice-cream vans, including the Ice Queen's, double parked alongside the mafia cars, hemming them in. All five vans had their chimes blaring at full volume, an incomprehensible and deafening mix. More ice-cream vans appeared, adding to the peculiar sight and the maddening noise — five more to be exact. They swung in at various angles, fanning out around the other ice-cream vans. More and more vans piled in behind them, gridlocking the road. Traffic bunched up behind them, horns beeping angrily, adding to the chaos.

Jed darted to the shop window, surveying the bizarre sight outside as his intimidating gangster vehicles — including the innocuous Toyota — became hopelessly ensnared by a fleet of bright and cheerful ice-cream vans pumping out an eclectic mix of their greatest hits.

Fiona didn't know what was worse for him. The terrifying spectacle of all the people he'd ever threatened showing up at once, or the deafening noise of their collective chimes, plus all the car horns.

Either way, Jed appeared to have lost control of the situation. Enraged, he growled some angry words in Fiona's direction.

"Pardon?" She couldn't hear him over the pandemonium.

He mouthed his words again, which she deciphered as, "Make them stop or else."

In response, Fiona shrugged, as if she had no idea what he was talking about.

Freddie spoke rapidly into his boss's ear while he urgently tugged him towards the door, indicating that they needed to leave, with or without their cars. But being prideful and stubborn, Jed snatched his arm away and marched over to Fiona, fists clenched. "Tell them to back off," he shouted, "or I swear they'll never see their families again and neither will you."

Slowly, Fiona rose to her feet and retrieved her phone from the pen pot on the counter. She sent a message to the WhatsApp group. A few moments later the noise ceased, apart from the odd car horn still bleating.

"That's better." Jed straightened his jacket in an attempt to portray calm. "Tell them, if they back off and leave now, no harm will come to their families."

"Tell them yourself," Partial Sue said.

Jed froze, terrified by the prospect. He turned to Freddie. "Get out there and tell them what I've just said."

Freddie didn't move, equally terrified at the idea of confronting a gaggle of angry ice-cream sellers. Jed shoved him, which was like watching a gnat push an ocean liner, but the henchman wouldn't obey, and neither would any of the others. None of them wanted to face the mob outside.

"This mafia lark's a lot harder when you're outnumbered and the whole world's watching, isn't it?" Daisy said.

Jed was about to blow his top when sirens interrupted him.

"Oh, hark at that," Fiona said. "Police are on their way. Will probably want to know what this roadblock's all about. I wonder what they'll do when they hear it's a protest against being blackmailed by the local mafia."

Jed scoffed. "We're just here doing a bit of shopping, aren't we, lads?"

Their response was less than enthusiastic. A few grunts at best.

Partial Sue pointed out a problem with Jed's tactic. "Er, you've shown up with a crisp packet full of drugs and a stack of threatening pictures."

Jed shrugged. "They're not mine. Never seen them before in my life. I'm the Teflon Don. Nothing sticks to me. Your little pantomime hasn't worked."

"Oh, I think it has," Fiona replied. "You were right about one thing. We had no idea you were behind this. Not a clue. However, we did know that you would come for us, eventually, to find out what we knew. And once you'd got that information, you'd want to shut us up for good, like you did with Kevin Masterson. Obviously, we didn't know about your plans to sell drugs in charity shops, which seemed to have eclipsed everything else on your mind. But coming back to my original point — we arranged for some protection. Safety in numbers, which was, admittedly, a bit late arriving, but it got here in the end."

"But it was really all a bit of a distraction," Partial Sue remarked. "Ironically, to extract information from you."

"A distraction extraction," Daisy smirked.

Fiona held up her phone. "This has been sitting in that pen pot over there. It's been silently livestreaming you. Our friends in the ice-cream vans have been listening in this whole time, as well as our IT expert. She's recorded it and made sure it's popped up on all the right desktops and phone screens — local reporters, crime bloggers, oh, and the two police detectives assigned to this case. So you see, those sirens aren't just uniformed police officers coming to sort out a traffic jam. There'll also be an unmarked police car, along with backup, on its way here to investigate everything you've conveniently confessed to."

"That's entrapment," Jed barked.

Partial Sue shook her head. "Entrapment is if we force you to commit a crime you wouldn't normally do. Seems like it's the other way around. You're the one forcing everyone else to commit crimes they'd never normally do."

"Which you've just admitted to," Fiona said. "It's all right there. Yes, I'd say the wide-angle lens has captured you rather nicely." She picked a bit at random to play and flipped her phone round. The screen showed Jed barking into Partial Sue's face, photos gripped in his fist as he threatened her.

The lay-by lackey had seen and heard enough. He made a run for it, fumbling with the latch on the door. After several clumsy attempts to unlock it, he finally got it open. A few henchmen decided to join him and make their escape, but they came face to face with the surreal sight of Tom standing in the doorway. The owner of Sergeant Bilcone, who for some inexplicable reason had donned his full Santa outfit, did not appear jolly in the slightest. And neither did the other ice-cream sellers, who had abandoned their vehicles and massed behind him. Slightly sweaty at being dressed in all his red garb on such a mild and drizzly day, Tom growled at the lackey and the assembled henchmen. "You're all going on my naughty list."

There was nothing more terrifying than a damp, angry Santa. The lackey backed up, as did the henchmen behind him.

The crowd of ice-cream sellers suddenly parted, and the reassuring sight of DI Fincher and DS Thomas threaded their way through them, followed by a dozen uniformed officers.

"Uh-oh." Fiona turned to Jed. "Looks like your assets are about to be frozen."

CHAPTER 48

A van pulled up outside Dogs Need Nice Homes. Not an ice-cream van but a regular one. Big, bland and spacious, the kind you hire when you want to lug a lot of belongings from one place to another.

Fiona watched Bella slide out of the passenger door and onto the pavement. She was the personification of joy and happiness, so much so that it appeared she might split at the seams she was so full of the stuff. From out of the driver's side, Vernon rounded the front of the van and met her on the pavement. Pulling her to his side, they kissed on the lips, their combined happiness radiating off them, bright as sunshine.

Daisy sniffed.

"Are you okay?" Fiona asked.

"I'll be fine. I'm happy for her, but, you know, sad at the same time."

"Of course," Partial Sue said. "You've got used to having your little girl around. But look on the bright side, she's got herself a decent fella who cares about her."

Fiona placed a reassuring hand on Daisy's shoulder. "Sue's right. Vernon would do anything for her. And vice versa. Those two are going to be unstoppable."

"Yeah, I know. It's just hard having her leave home for a second time."

The couple entered the shop, hand in hand, beaming from ear to ear.

"We're all packed and ready to go," Bella announced.

Daisy rushed to her daughter, clamping her arms around her. "I don't want you to leave."

"Mum, I'm only moving to Swanage. It's fifteen miles away, and I know how much you like Swanage."

"I know, but I've got used to having you here."

"Don't worry," Bella said. "I'll be back over this way all the time. We can go out for coffee and lunch."

Daisy cheered up at the prospect.

"And please come and visit us anytime you want," Vernon added. "Our door's always open. That goes for all of you."

"You can come over for Sunday lunch," Bella suggested. "Vernon makes a mean roast dinner."

"Followed by a hearty walk," Vernon said. "I know some cracking routes over the Purbecks."

"Now you're talking." Partial Sue rubbed her hands. "I am partial to a good walk on the Purbecks."

"That reminds me," Fiona said. "Good luck with your new job. When does it start?"

"Week on Monday," he replied.

"What is it you're doing again?" Partial Sue asked.

"I'm going to be a ranger. Looking after the Purbeck hills."

"Can't hills look after themselves?" Partial Sue asked.

"Well, they need a lot of management. Keeping the place open for all the visitors without spoiling it. I'm just looking forward to a change of scenery, in more ways than one."

"Completely understandable," Fiona said. "What about you, Bella? What have you got lined up?"

Daisy stood taller with pride. "Bella's got a job at the arts centre in Swanage. She's going to be running the place."

"Steady on, Mum. I'm just front of house. Looking after visitors and selling theatre tickets. But I want to work my way up."

"You'll be running the place before you know it," Partial Sue gushed.

"Oh!" Daisy made everyone jump with her outburst. "Talking of theatre, I nearly forgot. I got a text from Claire this morning. She's got an audition next week for the chorus line of *Hamilton*."

"That doesn't surprise me," Partial Sue said. "That girl's got talent."

Fiona nodded. "She's bound to get the part."

"We should all go and see her when she does," Daisy suggested.

"I think that's a great idea." Fiona picked up the teapot. "One that deserves a cup of tea."

After the tea had been poured, the conversation flowed around the table, interspersed with outbursts of laughter and infectious giggling. The atmosphere in the shop had never felt warmer or more positive. Friends and family sharing a special moment as they put the unpleasantness behind them, looking forward to a future tinged with gold and scented with rose.

Fiona already knew this would become a treasured memory. Like a favourite book on a shelf, she would return to it again and again, whenever she needed comfort, or to bring a smile to her face. She would enjoy revisiting the warm fuzzy glow that currently surrounded her, but knew there was a price to pay for such reminiscing. Each visitation would remind her of the fleeting and ethereal nature of these slivers of pure happiness. Part of her wished they could last for ever — a foolish notion, she realised. Their evanescence was what made them so rare and precious.

Fiona allowed herself a lingering smile. If this moment were fleeting then she would feast on it, gluttonously enjoying every second with every part of her being. There was only one way it could be improved, and that was with more tea. "Who's for another cuppa?"

Every hand shot in the air.

"Tea all round then." Fiona picked up the teapot and took herself off to the storeroom.

"I'll give you a hand." Vernon rose to his feet, collected up the cups, and followed her in.

Fiona filled the kettle and left it to boil while Vernon washed up. He looked uncomfortable as he wiped the sponge around the rim of Daisy's Paddington mug, his circular movements deliberately slow.

Fiona decided to make it easy for him. "Something on your mind, Vernon?"

He ceased his cleaning and let the mug drop beneath the suds, gazing at them as they popped and shifted. He took a deep nervous breath. "I owe you a massive debt."

Fiona felt decidedly uncomfortable.

He turned towards her, his eyes reddish and on the verge of tears. "If it weren't for you, Daisy and Sue, I'd still be trapped by the ice-cream mafia." He raised his arm to blot a tear with his sleeve.

"You're very welcome, Vernon," Fiona said. "All in a day's work."

He dried his hands with the tea towel and tossed it aside. "No, you don't understand. I'd lost all hope. I never thought I'd ever be happy again. I guess what I'm trying to say is you gave me my life back. More than that, you gave me a better life now I've met Bella. I don't know how I'll ever repay you."

Fiona held his hand to reassure him. "There's nothing to repay, honestly. It's what we do. And you make this all sound one-sided. Remember, you helped us bring them down too. You took a big risk, divulging the whereabouts of the dead drop. That couldn't have been easy."

Vernon shook his head dismissively. "I didn't really do that much."

"Don't underestimate your part in all this. Without you taking that risk, Jed and his merry men wouldn't be behind bars."

"Well, maybe. But I still feel I owe you."

Fiona smiled. "Well, I think the promise of a roast dinner over on the Purbecks will more than suffice. Plus, finish washing up those cups and we'll call it quits."

Vernon beamed. "I'll take that deal."

The tender moment was shattered by a commotion out in the shop. Fiona and Vernon popped their heads out of the storeroom to witness the appearance of Sophie, tears streaming from her eyes. She was followed into the shop by Gail, whose sole purpose appeared to be holding a box of tissues for her boss and to collect the spent ones she dropped.

"Sophie, whatever's the matter?" Fiona asked.

"Oh, it's simply dreadful!" She flung herself against a rack of shelves stacked with china, sending them wheeling everywhere. Thankfully, none of them broke.

The ladies were used to her melodrama, usually fuelled by insignificant first-world problems, which had previously included having to repack and send back a top she'd ordered online, because, in her words, the sizing was far too large for her slender and well-toned frame.

However, on this occasion the reason for Sophie's trauma didn't seem paper-thin and trivial. Fiona saw genuine panic in her eyes. "What's happened?"

Sophie sobbed. "He's cleaned me out!"

"Who's cleaned you out?" Partial Sue asked.

"Alan from Alan's Place." Sophie sniffed. "I hadn't heard from him in a while, so I popped down there to check how everything was going and the place was empty."

"Empty?"

"I couldn't get in, so I peered through one of the windows and everything had gone. No tables, chairs, nothing."

"Last time I was down there, I thought the place seemed a bit quiet," Bella said.

"Have you tried calling him?" Daisy asked.

"Of course I've tried calling him!" Sophie snapped. "What do you think I am, stupid? It said, 'The number you have called has not been recognised'." Sophie snapped her fingers. Gail jumped to it, replenishing her with more tissues. "Sorry." She blew her nose. "I didn't mean to be rude. It's just he's made off with all my savings."

"How much did you invest?" Partial Sue asked.

A second wave of tears bubbled from Sophie's eyes. Her whale-like moans filled the shop, forcing Simon Le Bon to whimper.

"Okay, don't answer that," Fiona said. "We'll find him and get your money back."

Sophie looked up through two red-raw eyes. "You will?"

Fiona knew she didn't deserve their help, not after the way she'd belittled them. That was nothing new. The ladies were used to it. For whatever reason, something inside that bloated, egotistical mind of hers had made it her mission to deride who they were and what they did every chance she got. But a new reoccurring pattern had begun to emerge. The second her perfect life went pear-shaped, she'd come running to the ladies, throwing herself at their feet. Probably because she knew they'd made a vow to always help anyone who needed it, no matter how vile they were. Perhaps it wasn't just Daisy who was too nice for her own good. They all were.

"Of course," Fiona said. "Leave it with us."

EPILOGUE

Alan liked Belinda Bebbington. Liked her a lot. For all the wrong reasons, of course. He didn't like her as a friend, nor for her scintillating conversation, although, to be fair, hers was better than most. All the people he'd conned so far had that awful combination of money and self-importance, which gave them the illusion that they were interesting. At least he didn't have to pretend to be riveted by the tales she had to tell. Her yarns of rubbing shoulders with the London elite were, on the whole, quite captivating. He might even procure a few of them for himself, passing them off as his own stories to charm his future victims. She was attractive, too. For a woman in her sixties, Belinda had a youthful twinkle in her eye, a mischievous air.

However, he was under no illusions. She wouldn't be attracted to him for anything other than his investment potential. Alan — though she knew him by a different fake name — had the look and attitude of an overfed cat. Not ideal for attracting partners, but perfect for luring people with more money than sense into non-existent investment deals with his haughty, highfalutin persona. And Belinda Bebbington was as perfect as they came.

She fulfilled his criteria for the ideal victim. His rich list, as he called it. First and foremost, she was dripping in disposable cash. She reeked of it, like the expensive perfume she wore — Tom Ford, if he wasn't mistaken. There was no checking the price on the label for her, whether she was buying bulgar wheat or a Bugatti. Secondly, and closely related to the last point, she wasn't a details person. With all that money she could afford to be careless and dizzy. She'd quite freely admitted that she had invested in properties all over London but couldn't for the life of her remember where some of them were. He knew she owned a hotel, which she lived in, and had decided to buy it so she always had someone on hand to do her laundry and make her food whenever it took her fancy — a highly expensive and convoluted way to ensure she had clean clothes and hot meals. It would have been cheaper to employ a full-time chef and a housekeeper. So, thirdly, she wasn't too bright either. But lastly, and most importantly, Belinda was extremely trusting, believing every word he said — almost like a child at Christmas. He'd dazzled her with his grandiose plans, although he had to admit, the empty venue in which they stood had done most of the heavy lifting.

This was why he always picked Grade II listed buildings in which to work his con. Not just any old listed buildings, but ones that would beguile even the most cynical punters. He had to admit he'd outdone himself this time. Yes, it had high ceilings. Didn't they all? But these were lofty and adorned with the most exquisite tiles inlaid with pretty, geometric patterns. Distinctly Eastern, its slender marble columns were smooth to the touch, and its pointed arch doorways were accentuated by finely carved stonework.

Belinda strained her neck as she took in the full majesty of the space. "I must say, this place is amazing. What did you say it used to be?"

"A Victorian bathhouse," Alan replied.

"Isn't it bizarre to think that this is where Victorians came to wash their bits and now it's where our exclusive clientele will sip champers."

This was Alan's new line of deceit. Same concept as his high-end tearoom scam but with champagne bars. However, he'd adjusted the concept slightly to make less work for himself. Instead of moving in tables, chairs and furniture, and one or two fake staff, he'd walked it back a step, to proposal stage, rather than mocking it up for real. Far cheaper and a lot less work. Of course, he still needed to throw a little glitter over the proceedings, so he'd contacted a struggling interior designer online, who'd produced a computer-generated image of what the finished champagne bar would look like. The designer was never reimbursed for their work, but Alan did splash out on enlarging the visual to almost life-size proportions and mounting it on a stand.

He led Belinda over to the image which he'd covered with a red silk sheet for the big reveal. "Now for the *ta-dah* moment."

Whipping off the sheet in one slick flick of his hand, the fictitious champagne bar was unveiled in all its fake glory.

Belinda cooed with wonder, and took an involuntary step back, the visual impact nearly knocking her off her feet. "Oh, my. This is quite spectacular. I adore it. I absolutely adore it!"

"It's marvellous, isn't it?"

"I'll say." She dared to edge forward, overwhelmed by the design. "I simply love this balcony thingy. What do they call these?"

"A mezzanine." Alan chuckled inside. English Heritage would be frothing at the mouth if they knew someone was proposing to hack into the existing columns to insert a steel beam and create a second upstairs bar.

"And this spiral staircase looks incredible. Are those steps made out of real glass?"

"That's right."

"Are you sure they won't break?"

"They'll be toughened glass."

She was definitely not the brightest match in the box.

"Well, I'm blown away by it all." Belinda gazed at the proposed logo in the top right-hand corner. "And I love the name. Saint Swithin's."

This pleased Alan no end. He thought he'd done a pretty good job with the branding, following the logic that any name with 'saint' popped in front of it sounded posh and premium. Yves Saint Laurent, Saint Tropez, St Remy. Okay, they were French, but there was St James's Park. You couldn't buy a poky one-bedroom flat in its well-heeled streets for less than a million. Truth be told, he'd taken the advice of that dot-com know-it-all Jed Garret about the importance of names. Alan felt more than a bit smug that Jed had been arrested for running an ice-cream mafia of all things. What an idiot. That would never happen to him. Alan knew the secret to not getting caught was to keep moving like a shark. Never stay in the same place for too long. Once he'd fleeced this attractive rich singleton of all her money, that would be it. He'd be off to another city to swindle someone else, using a different fake name and identity. He only wished they were all as easy to dupe as her.

Belinda shivered with excitement. "This is going to be London's next It place. I can feel it. And I should know — I used to be an It girl."

"Really?"

"Oh, yes. Back in the eighties I hung out with all the New Romantic bands. Not that I can remember much of it." She snorted and slapped him playfully on the arm.

Alan produced an iPad he'd had slotted under his arm the whole time. "Well, that's an excellent omen. So now there's just the formality of the investment, and then it's full steam ahead. Saint Swithin's will be the capital's number-one champagne bar."

"Oh yes, sign me up!" Belinda giggled. "Get in at the ground floor, or the mezzanine, as it were." More snorts.

"Yes, you're making one hell of a smart investment, Belinda."

"Oh, please. Call me Bitsy. Everyone else does."

"Very well, Bitsy." He held the iPad up so she could examine the screen. "I've arranged everything. All you have to do is transfer the money into this account."

"Right you are, partner." Bitsy's phone rang. "Oh, wait. Let me just get this." She answered the call. "Oh, hiya. Yeah, yeah. Now would be a good time, deffo. I'm just about to do the transfer. That would be great. See you in a tick." She hung up.

"Who was that?" Alan asked.

"My accountant."

"Your accountant?"

"Well, she's an ex-accountant. More of a friend, really. She's just popping in with another two friends. Said they wouldn't mind having a little peek at things."

Alan didn't like the sound of this. "What, right now?"

"Yes. If that's okay? Said she'd like to have a nose."

"Well, I'm not sure that would be a good idea."

Bitsy pushed out her bottom lip childishly. "Oh, please. I'm investing in the place with you."

"Good point." Alan tapped the screen. "Let's do the transfer now to make it official."

"Yes, but they want to look at the finer details before I do that."

"They do?"

"Surely that's okay, isn't it? Unless there's somewhere else you need to be."

"No, no. I've got nothing to hide." The alarm bells thundered in Alan's small ears, dazing him slightly. He didn't like people who looked at the fine details. The so-called fact-checkers of this world. Facts were not his friend. They were uncomfortable, a pain in the behind for someone who operated with the aid of smoke and mirrors.

The heavy flagstones beneath his feet began to feel as soft as sponge, as if he might sink beneath them at any moment. He would just have to hold his nerve for a little longer. Grin and answer their stupid questions, keeping them distracted by pointing out how beautiful the place was. That usually worked.

Behind him, the rumble of the two big wooden entrance doors made his heart jump. Keep calm, he told himself, keep calm. Big smiles, big smiles. The cheesier the better. He prepared himself and spun around ready to receive Bitsy's friends, only to encounter a sight that sent his fake grin packing.

He knew these three faces well. Those meddling cows from that dreary charity shop in Southbourne bundled through the entrance and made their way towards him.

"This is Fiona, Daisy and Sue," Bitsy announced. "But I think you already know one another."

"Hello," they all said in unison as they stood in front of him.

"Fancy seeing you here, Alan." Fiona spoke as if this were all a great big coincidence. "Oh, by the way, Sophie sends her regards. Said you disappeared with all her savings she invested in that tearoom that never existed. She'd like them back, if you don't mind."

"H-h-how?" Tongue tied, it was all Alan could manage, the shock having starved his brain of oxygen.

"Well, it wasn't difficult," Fiona explained. "We figured your social media posts showing you living in Ringwood weren't real, but the last time we tried phoning you at Alan's Place—"

"Alan's Place." Bitsy giggled. "That's a terrible name. Nearly as bad as Saint Swithin's."

"Saint Swithin's?" Partial Sue nearly choked on the name. "Is that what you were going to call this place?"

"Sounds like a bit of a wet weekend," Daisy said.

A searing, humiliating heat swirled around Alan's head, adding to his debilitating fear.

"Sorry, Fiona," Bitsy said. "We've gone off-topic. Please continue."

"That's okay. Yes, when we phoned your fake tearoom in Wick, you weren't in. However, the waitress let it slip that you were in London, scouting out new venues. So we knew your next venture would be somewhere in the capital."

Alan felt his brain stall and misfire. "B-but . . . London is huge. How did you find me?"

"We knew you always work your con in Grade II listed buildings. You told us so yourself. Still, there are over a thousand Grade II listed buildings in London, so we narrowed it down to the ones you could rent. It was a pretty long list. However, we figured that someone working a short-term con is only going to want a short-term rental, like these pop-up shops you get. I mean, why incur all those extra costs upfront if you don't need to? That's when we made a breakthrough. There are only a handful of Grade II listed buildings offering short-term contracts. This was the third one we looked at. Of course, you weren't using the same name, so we sent in Bitsy to make contact and make sure it was you, up to your old tricks again."

"Me and Sophie go way back," Bitsy said. "And I became dear friends with these lovely ladies when I had a beach hut on Mudeford Spit. I really miss that beach hut. You know what, I fancy buying another one."

"Oh, that would be wonderful," Daisy gushed.

Partial Sue beamed. "We'd get to see more of you."

"Anyway, we're digressing," Fiona said.

"Yes, sorry," Bitsy apologised. "So, when Fiona asked me if I could do a bit of undercover improv to catch someone who'd ripped off my bestie, I had to say a hard yes."

Alan swayed a little, caught in an invisible forcefield of confusion. His face was blank with befuddlement, and he was surely wondering how this had happened, how he'd been played, when usually it was him doing the playing. Or perhaps he'd already accepted he'd been caught and was now weighing up his options. He wasn't going to wriggle out of this one, that was for sure.

Truthfully, there was only one option left. Abandoning all dignity, he made a run for it, dashing towards the door.

Not built for speed, it was uncomfortable to witness his awkward dash for freedom, although it was more of a hasty waddle, not helped by the iPad under his arm. He made it to the front doors, flung them open and darted outside, only to be confronted by a Maginot Line of police officers.

Undeterred and probably high on fight-or-flight adrenalin, he attempted to break through them. The ladies were treated to a brief, fleeting image of the officers quickly swarming around him before the wooden doors closed with a funereal thud.

Bitsy clapped her hands. "What fun! Taking down a perp. Sophie's going to be so pleased."

They swamped her with hugs and praise for her flawless performance.

"Thanks for all your help," Fiona said.

Bitsy waved it away as if it were nothing. "Oh, please. Don't mention it. I was just being myself, truth be told."

"Well, he bought it, hook, line and sinker."

"I think this calls for a celebration," Daisy suggested.

"Anyone know any good champagne bars around here?" Partial Sue joked.

Normally Bitsy, who never needed an excuse for a celebration, would be quickest out of the door and first to the bar, regardless of what time it was. However, she appeared momentarily distracted, gazing up at her surroundings, not aware that anyone had cracked a joke.

To completely quash any hope the joke had of being funny, Daisy decided to explain it to her. "Sue said, 'Do you know any good champagne bars around here?' You know, because this was supposed to be a champagne bar."

"I think she gets it," Partial Sue said.

"Oh, yes," Bitsy muttered. "Sorry, get what?"

"You okay, Bitsy?" Fiona asked.

Her eyes drifted over to the ladies. "Sorry, I was miles away."

"What's on your mind?" Partial Sue asked.

"Well, I was just thinking. Though he was a conniving, thieving little toad, he did have an eye for venues. This would make a thoroughly charming champagne bar. I mean, look at that mock-up. Don't you agree?"

They stared at the giant visual with its sophisticated clientele ensconced in luxury, sipping all manner of expensive bubbly. A hedonistic heaven if ever there was one.

"Er, I'd definitely agree." Partial Sue was hesitant, possibly considering the fact that one small glass of champers would cost more than a large round of drinks and several packets of pork scratchings in The George back home.

"I'd go." Daisy beamed.

"Me too," Fiona said.

"That settles it!" Bitsy announced. "If it's good enough for my three friends, then it's good enough for London. I'm going to see if it's for sale."

Daisy pulled her phone out and started snapping shots of the grand interior. "How exciting!"

"But what would you call it?" Partial Sue asked. "Not Saint Swithin's, I hope."

Bitsy grinned and shook her head. "Oh gosh, no. I have a far superior name in mind. Bitsy's Place."

There was a pause. One of polite disbelief, until the penny dropped and it became clear by the impish look on Bitsy's face that she was gently tugging their collective legs. Belly laughs echoed around the Victorian interior so loudly that Fiona was sure it drowned out the officers outside, currently reading Alan his rights.

THE END

ACKNOWLEDGEMENTS

I still get a thrill whenever I hear the chimes of an ice-cream van. These little portable purveyors of frozen joy send me straight back to my childhood. The clunky music would often break the monotonously long and hot school summer holidays. I'd dart into the kitchen faster than a sprinter out of the blocks to beg my mum for a few pennies (I'm showing my age now, but back in the seventies, ice creams really did cost pennies). Clutching them in my sweaty little fist, I'd run across the road (looking both ways first, of course), and swap my cash for a strawberry split, sometimes called a Mivvi in other parts of the country. Then I'd dawdle back, revelling in the delicate process of stripping off the outer icy layer to get to the soft vanilla bit. But there was also a sense of achievement buying from an ice-cream van, that you simply don't get from a shop. That you managed to catch it before it drove off. I think that's what makes them so wonderful. Like mythical creatures, their appearance is fleeting and therefore special.

With such affectionate childhood memories, it was a bit of a no-brainer to write a story around an ice-cream van. An indulgence, you could say. But I do hope I haven't spoiled anyone else's memories by dumping a dead body in one of them. Apologies if I have.

I was lucky enough to have not one, but two very talented publishers helping me bring this story to life. Steph Carey immediately green lit the idea and helped me immensely, finessing the plan and giving me various nudges in all the right directions. Halfway through the project, Steph was lured away to new pastures. However, I was left in the very capable hands of the brilliant Laura Coulman-Rich, who seamlessly picked up where Steph left off and has been amazing. So massive, heartfelt thanks to you both.

Along the way, various people have pruned, prodded and polished this story to make it so much better than it was before. They are all lovely to work with and brilliant, and include Cat Phipps structural editor, Faith Marsland copy editor and proofreader Julie Hoyle. Nick Castle has once again blown me away with yet another fabulous cover design and, as ever, I am indebted to the wonderful team at Joffe Books who work tirelessly to get my novels out in the world.

When I first plotted this idea, numerous questions popped into my head. Mostly stuff about how the police would handle a dead body in the back of an ice-cream van. Like all my books, I never leave it to chance and fire off email after email to the amazing Sammy H.K. Smith. She's a superb, real-life police detective and a bloody good writer in her own right. So thank you, Sammy, for answering all my silly questions.

Every time I finish a book, another raft of weird and wonderful new characters joins the world of the Charity Shop Detective Agency. I always look forward to hearing how Zara Ramm, the narrator of my audio books, is going to bring them to life. I don't know how she does it, but they are always exactly how I imagined them. Big thanks must also go to Lorella Belli, the hardest working agent in the business who is constantly securing me new opportunities in far-flung places.

I am so lucky to have a wonderful family around me, so biggest thanks go to them for all their support, patience and love. To my wife Sha, Billie my daughter and my son Dan, my sister Jane and my mum — I really can't do this without you.

And lastly, while we're on the subject of support, remember to buy from your local ice-cream van, because if you don't, these national treasures will disappear forever.

THE JOFFE BOOKS STORY

We began in 2014 when Jasper agreed to publish his mum's much-rejected romance novel and it became a bestseller.

Since then we've grown into the largest independent publisher in the UK. We're extremely proud to publish some of the very best writers in the world, including Joy Ellis, Faith Martin, Caro Ramsay, Helen Forrester, Simon Brett and Robert Goddard. Everyone at Joffe Books loves reading and we never forget that it all begins with the magic of an author telling a story.

We are proud to publish talented first-time authors, as well as established writers whose books we love introducing to a new generation of readers.

We won Trade Publisher of the Year at the Independent Publishing Awards in 2023 and Best Publisher Award in 2024 at the People's Book Prize. We have been shortlisted for Independent Publisher of the Year at the British Book Awards for the last five years, and were shortlisted for the Diversity and Inclusivity Award at the 2022 Independent Publishing Awards. In 2023 we were shortlisted for Publisher of the Year at the RNA Industry Awards, and in 2024 we were shortlisted at the CWA Daggers for the Best Crime and Mystery Publisher.

We built this company with your help, and we love to hear from you, so please email us about absolutely anything bookish at feedback@joffebooks.com.

If you want to receive free books every Friday and hear about all our new releases, join our mailing list here: www.joffebooks.com/freebooks.

And when you tell your friends about us, just remember: it's pronounced Joffe as in coffee or toffee!